# NICKEL'S LUCK

## A NOVEL

### S. L. MATTHEWS

© 2019 S. L. Matthews

*Nickel's Luck*
First edition, November 2019

Cinch Ranch Publishing
Walling, TN
slmatthewsauthor.com

Editing: Shayla Raquel, ShaylaRaquel.com
Cover Design: Stuart Bache of Books Covered, BooksCovered.co.uk
Interior Formatting: Melinda Martin, MelindaMartin.me

"Lorena" song lyrics transcribed from purchased copy of sheet music dated 1856; original lyrics by Rev. Henry De Lafayette Webster.

ISBN 978-1-7341162-0-5 (paperback)

*In loving memory of Pops,*
*the man who gave me my first Zane Grey novel.*
*You taught me to follow my nose,*
*never to take wooden nickels,*
*and to be wary of those ornery "hillside gougers."*
*Love you, Pancake Cowboy. I'll never forget.*

*And*

*In loving memory of Bev,*
*who always believed.*
*My Guardian Angel.*
*My heart bleeds, yet I know you're there.*

# CONTENTS

**PART 3: ON THE TRAIL**

# PART ONE

## *GOLDEN BOY OF INDIANOLA*

# CHAPTER 1

# THE WAVE-HOPPER

*Indianola, Texas, September 1870*

The first time young Ryder drowned, it became the beginning of something new—an idea he perceived as infinite immunity to the perils of daily life. Ryder was ten and eager as usual to try new things. Things no one else said could be done. His brothers' favorite pastime, aside from eating, was helping him achieve an impressive list of can't-be-dones just to see him try.

Scampering to the end of the pier with two of his brothers, Ryder stopped short and turned into the stiff, salty wind with a huff. It was a good run. The three of them had leaped and bounded throughout town, dodging citizens and wagons, and even raced through the netmaker's tangled web of real estate.

Trouble was brewing though, for the workday ended and they were ready for more fun before heading home to face dinner with the brats and, even worse, the dreaded chores.

"Whatcha wanna do now?" Ryder asked, receiving a swift punch to the shoulder in reply.

"Do that, Ry, I dare you!" Zelus jumped up and down as he pointed, yelling something about wave-hoppers.

"Do what?" he asked. He saw nothing except a group of dolphins breaking through the waves in graceful leaps.

"Oh-ho, ride 'em, Ry," Alastor, the elder brother, said. "You always say you can ride anything."

"So?"

"So, bet you can't ride a dolphin. They ain't easy like Uncle Sly's old milk cow."

Ryder clinched his jaw. "I guess I could ride one if I wanted to," he declared, frowning at the slick-skinned beasts playing in the horizon.

Alastor stuck his hands on his hips and laughed in Ryder's face.

"Not even one!" he argued. "I guess you're just like Daddy says: a braggart and a liar."

"I ain't a liar!" Ryder's cheeks grew red.

"Shore you are. You're lyin' now, 'cause you can't do it." Alastor leaned in close. "You're too scared to try."

Ryder wasn't scared. He had ridden all manners of critters around town—sheep, cows, goats, even a camel or two. Most anything that walked, hobbled, flew, or hopped off one of the big trade ships was fair game to him.

Without regard to the waves crashing below the pier, Ryder tugged at his shoes. A finger pierced through the thin, worn hide, but he was too angry to care about another hole his daddy would have to patch. He was not a liar, or a braggart, either. It was true—he could ride anything he set his mind to. He'd show them!

Barefoot, the boy dove off the pier and surfaced below. The waves were stronger than usual, and his shirt and britches clutched his skin as though they were in a desperate plea to turn around. The race through town had tired him, yet Ryder knew little fear. He was a fisherman's son, after all; swimming was as instinctive as breathing. He took a few deep breaths, focused on the band of wave-hoppers, and swam at an angle to intercept their path.

At least, he tried. The waves near the beach weren't this bad, and he remembered too late his mother's advice not to dive off the pier. He swam against the breaking current, sputtering as big waves broke over him, washing him backward.

*Liar. Can't. Braggart.* Didn't they know better? He was born of luck and skill, everyone said so. What were a few strong waves between him and his goal to ride a wave-hopper?

Tiring, Ryder tread water, lining up his progress, only to discover his plight too late. The dolphins were not any closer. In fact, they were gone. Even worse, waterlogged britches sagged around his scrawny waist. He feared the weight would yank them right off his ass.

Had he paid attention before diving in, Ryder might have noticed the storm clouds offshore driving heavy waves that rolled him without mercy.

He turned back to the pier, now out of reach, and screamed the names of the ancients.

☙

Alastor and Zelus watched, amused at the joke their brother was playing on them. Ryder was a good swimmer, so it was funny, his pretense of trouble.

"I told him he couldn't catch a dolphin," Al said, snickering.

"He's just funnin' us, ain't he?" Zelus, only eight, still didn't understand the difference between pranks and sincerity.

"He won't say he's wrong, so he's playin' to scare us into forgettin' he couldn't catch a hopper. You know Ry—he's always funnin'."

Brows furrowed into a tight line, Zelus clung to Al's hand and watched his favorite brother bobbing up and down in the water. He wasn't flapping or hollering. If anything, it looked like he wasn't able to hold his arms over his head.

"He don't look much like he's funnin' to me," Zelus said, looking up at his brother. "Al?"

Alastor didn't answer. Ryder, it seemed, had given up on swimming and was being carried farther out to sea. His head bobbed along the surface, then vanished.

"Al!" Zelus screamed. "I don't see him! I don't see him!"

Realization sank like an anchor into the pit of Alastor's stomach. Ryder wasn't playing a game at all. He was drowning.

Alastor stood rooted to the dock, mouth agape. Fleeting thoughts knotted up in his brain but never reached his legs.

Zelus, failing to coerce his older brother into action, spotted a fishing boat. They were veering toward shore, coming in with their catch. Obeying their momma's rule that a whistle be hung around the neck of the oldest sibling when near the water, Zelus reached up, found the chain tucked under Al's shirt, and yanked.

Alastor bent in an attempt to recoil from the earsplitting blasts of his brother, yet his eyes remained fixated on the place where Ryder battled for life.

Zelus blew and blew on the whistle, jerking Al one way, then the other to attract the fishermen.

"My brother!" he yelled as one stood upright in the boat, already searching for the disaster. "There!" he pointed, where, for a moment, Ryder's body was spotted in the surf. He looked like a strange boy-fish, surfacing for a moment, only to disappear again. It was enough. Zelus watched the boat turn into the wind, the men aboard yelling and gesticulating. Now he was crying.

Zelus wailed every time he saw a man dive below the surface and come up empty-handed. They would not find him. The sea had claimed Ryder, just like in all the tales told by fishermen and sailors alike. Two, three, four times they dove before he lost count. He hoped they'd find his body so he could be buried in the ground instead of lost to the sea forever.

Dropping to his knees on the dock, he hugged his legs and glared through his tears at his remaining brother. This was all Alastor's fault, but he stood there, still as the stone statues Momma said they were named for, and he let Ryder die. Zelus swore a silent retribution.

A chorus of shouts from the boat drew the grieving boy's attention. Rocking to his heels, he saw a man swimming toward the boat with something in the crook of his arm. The boy stood on tiptoe, stretching tall for a better look. His heart hammered in his throat. They found Ryder.

☙

Drownings happened from time to time; it was a part of living by the Big Water. No one understood that better than the sailors and fishermen, and they did their part to spread the word with hushed tones when tragedy struck. Some shied away from using the unfortunate's name altogether, believing an already angry sea would rise up and retaliate, swallowing them whole.

For a time, citizens and sailors alike would gather to pay their respects and ponder over the brevity of life, so fragile compared to the monsters of the deep. This was different. When they dropped Ryder on the dock, there was no breath. No heartbeat. Dead was dead, the fishermen said. The boy swallowed enough seawater to flood all of Indianola.

He looked like some sort of half-boy half-sea creature dragged from the depths, drenched to the bone, cold and pale. Zelus sat by his head and cried his name. Over and over he cried, his hatred toward Alastor exuded in a glare, who looked on with his shoulders slumped.

Ryder's body seized and jerked. A sailor with more ink than a newspaper print noticed a sign of life, grabbed his body, and rolled him over, pounding his back. His chest heaved, and he began expelling alarming amounts of water.

Zelus and the fishermen jumped back, regarding the marvel warily. It might be some sort of trick or curse. The Mistress, she was full of tricks meant to lure men to a watery grave. One could not be too careful.

Only Old Joly the sailor continued to work on the boy, pounding on his back until he coughed, again and again. Ryder wheezed, hacked, and spit, his cold wet cheek smooshed against the planks of the dock, expelling water back to the sea.

*No one ever comes back,* they said. Word spread through the streets of Indianola, a mere boy of ten years faced Davy Jones and walked away to tell the tale.

୪

"Keep up, you sodden little imp." Following the shifty amble of his father through the streets of town, an aching Ryder lengthened his stride. His father never moved fast, but Ryder's legs still wobbled. Once in a while, his knees would take a fit and buckle, but he brushed himself off and carried on. It had only been two days since the drowning, and Momma would pitch a fit at his father for dragging him from his bed and out into the town without her say-so.

He longed to close his eyes and feel his mother's hand smooth back the ruffles of his gingerbread-baked brown hair. His limbs and feet were heavy, his eyelids sagged, and every time he stifled a yawn, his stomach seized up and he tasted salt. Something stung him while in the water, for he had a painful welt on his shoulder blade and another splotch on his left leg. Plus, it felt like fish were swimming around in his gut.

Miserable as he was, Ryder grinned at the surrounding town. So what if he still coughed up seaweed? He was alive to enjoy the warmth of the sun on his face and the dry ground under his feet. No matter his drowning occurred within sight of shore—he had battled the ocean and won.

Yet, it was not the drowning bolstering the young imp's grip on life, but a lifeless object, used well and without value in a port town.

A spur.

During their stroll, the town favored Ryder with kindness. Men rumpled his hair and patted him on the back, grinning.

"You're a luck child, boy," they'd say. "It was lucky for you that fisherman got to you before the Mistress did."

Ryder knew who the Mistress was and glared dolefully toward the edge of their world. Seagulls dove through salt-laden air, calling noisily to their friends. He sniffed and choked back a cough. The smell of the saltwater town never bothered him before, but then, his lungs had never been baptized in it before, either. Women they passed stopped to pet, hug, and kiss Indianola's golden child, marveling at his bravado in overcoming his drowning so quickly. Ryder glowed under their praise, especially the pretty ones, but his father never let him enjoy their attentions for very long. The boy groaned when Oren led him to the tobacco shop. Daddy's vices—and his pleasures—always came first.

Inside, Ryder slouched on a crate by the counter and hacked great racking coughs. His lungs still hurt, and the smell of exotic tobacco, dips, and cigars were overpowering. The proprietor looked at him and shook his head.

"Your wild boy still looks blue around the gills today, Oren."

"He's fine," came the reply.

"Wicked cough, though. If I'd swallowed that much water, I'd be—"

"I said the boy's fine!" Oren Wheeler's bark silenced further discussion, but the man behind the counter tousled Ryder's brown hair and patted his shoulder.

"You're a brave boy, and a lucky one at that," he whispered.

"Thank you, sir," Ryder said with a raspy squeak. He wanted to get into the fresh air where the smoke wasn't scraping his lungs and searing his eyes. He waited, hacking and clearing his throat, while his father perused cases of cigars. The man selected the best a meager paycheck afforded—a pair of smokes that smelled to Ryder like the fart end of a bloated fish lit afire. Momma would be mad over that too. The money dropped for tobacco would have put food on their table, but he dared not mention it aloud. His daddy was touchy about money because he never had it. With over a dozen kids to feed, Oren was always grumpy.

Outside, he steered Ryder to the smoking bench outside the cigar shop. It was time to face his father. Judging by the set jaw and narrowed slits of his eyes, it would not be a pleasant conversation.

"You gonna tell me about it, boy?" Oren lowered his chin and curled his fingers. They looked more like stout claws to Ryder, but he ran his mouth anyway.

"Al and Zelus should've done that already," he said.

"Alastor didn't have much to say. Zelus says you jumped in to catch a damn dolphin 'cause Al said you couldn't ride one. Is that true?"

Ryder slid to the other side of the bench and picked at his fingernails. They were a sight more interesting to look at than Oren's pinched face.

"Yessir," he replied, hoping a simple answer was enough to satisfy Oren. It wasn't.

"So you wanted to ride a dolphin."

"I would've done it easy enough—if I caught one."

Oren seized Ryder's arm and thrust his snarled lip in the boy's face. "You didn't pay much attention to the water, did you? Didn't notice the wind drivin' in from a storm? You didn't pay mind to the tide either, did ya? Goin' out, wasn't it . . . and carried you with it!" Veins pulsed in Oren's neck. They seemed to be propelling the loud, angry tone—lightning to match his father's thunder.

"No. Al made me mad, and—" Ryder coughed again.

"You're a damn fool, boy," his daddy interrupted. "These townsfolk'll say how brave you are, but you and me, we know better. You're weak between the ears. They all say you're lucky, but eventually your empty head's gonna catch up to your sound luck. Zelus said your brother just stood there watching you drown. You would've died if not for your little brother. What if someone drowned trying to save you? Do you think their lives were worth yours?"

Ryder shrugged. "Nobody died."

"The sea, she's marked you, boy. You escaped this time, but she'll come at you again. The Mistress always feeds on dumb-headed little boys like you."

"If that's true," Ryder mused, "she'd have claimed you years ago, Daddy."

Oren struck out so fast, Ryder didn't have time to jump out of the way. His father's arm clamped around his waist like iron shackles, and he found himself balanced over Oren's knees, staring down at the sand-strewn planks below. To his horror, his father yanked his baggy, hand-me-down britches down in the middle of Indianola and, having no belt, wailed on his backside with a piece of wood from a fish crate. Ryder's blood raged as the plank sang through the air and bit hard against his bare skin. The boy bit his lower lip, refusing to cry out. That's what he wanted—wails and tears. His means of discipline always demanded tears.

*Too damn bad, I ain't gonna cry!*

It wasn't a whooping—it was a beating. He didn't think to count the blows, for they came with a force fed from rage, designed to hurt and humiliate. To maim.

Splinters from the broken board penetrated his hindquarters, and his vision blurred. They were getting stronger too. Ryder swallowed a howl and coughed against the lump in his throat. He bit down on his lip but refused to scream.

As Oren wailed on him, cursing his fool head and impertinent mouth, a strange little melody jingled in Ryder's ear. It was accompanied by the sound of heeled boots on boardwalk. Tilting his head sideways, he tried to focus on the boots that appeared under his face. One boot was bare, but the other was adorned with a spur decorated in tarnished silver. Tiny jangles hung from a rowel, dusty but ornate in design.

Hearing the wind whistle through a hole in the board, he cringed in anticipation, but the next blow never came. Instead, a stranger's voice cut the air.

"That's enough! You've drawn blood on him. That's enough for a man, too damn far for a boy. Strike him again, and I'll do the same to you."

Ryder felt, rather than saw, his father's slow burn at the insolent remark.

"Mind your own damn business, stranger," he growled. "I'll do what I please with my boy."

He lifted the broken board again, but the stranger caught his arm, ripped the splintered weapon from his grip, and dealt him a smart blow across the face.

Ryder rolled free, coughing and snatching at his britches to cover himself before anyone saw. If one of his friends—or worse yet, a pretty girl—saw his ass-blistering in the middle of town, he was done for, drowning or no.

Swiping red-rimmed eyes against tears not quite held in check, Ryder turned in time to see his father lunge at the one-spurred man. The man stepped aside with an air of boredom, and Oren's momentum propelled him off the boardwalk and facedown in the street. Despite his rump burning like hellfire, he laughed out loud.

"You done?" the man drawled.

Oren waved him off and stayed down, keeping his head and hands in the dirt. Ryder gaped, slack-jawed. Why wasn't Oren showing more fight? He swayed side to side, slurring a few of the devil's words, but he did not retaliate. Oren Wheeler never gave up a fight unless he was drunk—then he usually passed out.

The boy's attention turned to something sticky snaking down his legs. Blood. It hurt to stand, yet sitting wasn't an option, either.

A firm grip on his arm startled him, and he looked up. The stranger knelt low, and as he locked eyes with the one-spurred man, Ryder took an involuntary step back. He was a cowboy from the dark, broad-brimmed crown atop his head down to the worn leather boots at his feet. His face was impassive, masked behind a stern jaw and the most intense eyes Ryder had ever seen. They were a dark brown, yet flecked with gold and green, like the sand when illuminated by a brilliant sunset.

"You all right, boy?"

Ryder shook his head, then thought better of it and nodded.

"Yessir."

The cowboy hesitated, as though he didn't believe him. Ryder didn't blame him—he didn't believe it himself. Not really. If only he'd hold back his tears! He didn't want to blubber like a baby, not in front of a real cowboy.

"That your Pa?"

"That's what Momma says."

"Guess she'd know."

"Yessir, I guess," Ryder said with a sniff and wiped his runny nose on his sleeve.

"You got somewhere safe to go?" the cowboy asked.

"Home. He took me away from my bed. Momma said I was to stay in it."

"You sick, boy?"

"I drowned."

The man reared back on his haunches, a quizzical gaze sweeping Ryder from head to toe. Ryder noticed he kept one hand on his arm. It was strong and he leaned into it, grateful for the support. He waited for the cowboy to ask about the drowning. Anyone else would have, so why didn't he? The man's lack of curiosity nettled him. Didn't the stranger want to hear his story?

*Maybe I should tell him anyhow,* he thought. Before he opened his mouth to explain, his father's voice cut through him. He was getting up, and he was angry.

"You wait till I get you home, you little whelp!"

The boy retreated, but the cowboy didn't. Planting himself between Ryder and Oren, the man rose to full height, which was considerably shorter than his opponent. The staredown made Ryder twitch, but he decided he'd stake his best bet on the stranger, should it come to a battle.

"The boy's bled enough," he said.

"He ain't your business!" Oren plagued their ears with the worst of the fishermen's language and stomped a few false steps forward. For all his bluster, he did not sway the small, brown-eyed man. When he ran out of breath with which to curse, Oren threw his hands in the air.

"You wanna stick your nose where it don't belong? Fine. *You* take him then!"

Ryder sagged when his father ambled off to crawl under a porch somewhere with his bloated-fish-stench cigars to nurse his anger.

"You sure you're all right, kid?"

"Yessir, thanks."

The cowboy dipped his head.

"Boy," he said, "I'll be in town a few days, waitin' on a telegram. If your Pa takes his grudge out on your hide again, look me up and I'll take care of it. I'm stayin' at the inn on the corner. Hayworths' place."

Ryder watched the man stride off down the street, one spur jingling. Something akin to grief settled in the pit of his stomach.

"Wait!" he cried, trying his best to catch up. The cowboy paused, kneeling again to face Ryder square in the eye.

"Why didn't my daddy hit you? I thought he was gonna."

"Kid," the cowboy replied, "some men are all blow and no rain."

"Rain? But my daddy ain't wet."

"Ain't what I meant, son." Rising, the cowboy crossed the street without another word. Ryder watched him duck inside the telegraph office, only to reappear a moment later empty-handed and tired. Was it just his imagination, or did the man look a little older coming out? What changed in such a brief moment?

# CHAPTER 2

# REVELATIONS AND REBIRTH

Afraid to go home for fear his father would be waiting on him, Ryder limped over to Les Harold's house. Les was his best friend. They shared everything from birthdays to ass-whoopings. That Ryder got into so much trouble without him irked Les, and he said so.

"Why didn't you wait for me?" he asked, pointing toward the docks. "I would've gone with you!"

"You can't swim as good as I can," Ryder reasoned. "Besides, you wasn't around anyway."

Les threw his hands in the air and muttered something unintelligible under his breath.

"I swear," Ryder said, lifting a hand to his ear, "I can hear better'n most, but you mumble so soft only road lizards can hear you, seein' as how they're so low to the ground."

Les rolled his eyes. "I *said*, guess you didn't swim too good anyhow, seein' as how you drowned."

"Ain't my fault a storm blew in," Ryder said, leaning against the post that held up the Harold family's front porch.

"Did you really drown? People are saying you died and came back to life! I didn't think anyone got better after dyin'."

"I'm here, ain't I?"

Les pondered the possibility, but the truth was obvious. "You sure are lucky. Luckier than a penny."

"I know, I know. You say it all the time. Five times' worth the luck," Ryder finished for his friend.

"Yeah, well. Speaking of luck, Magdalena Hayworth asked about you," he added with a sly grin.

Ryder's face brightened. "She did?"

"She's too scared to go up to your place, what with all your brothers and sisters around, but she's asked me if you're okay three times."

"What'd you tell her?"

"Told her you was makin' up to Lucy Parker." It was an age-old joke, the number of girls who ran after Ryder. Even at ten, he had a natural charisma made for charming the Indianola girls, and he used it. Well.

Magdalena Virginia Hayworth and Lucy Parker were his favorites. Les was content to play one girl over the other in Ryder's name. As expected, Ryder punched his friend in the arm, but his heart wasn't in the usual skirmish.

"You okay, Nickel?"

Ryder didn't even grin at the use of his nickname. Les Harold was the only one who called him Nickel, a nod toward his sound luck.

"I don't feel much like a nickel anymore," he admitted. "My daddy beat me with a board." Upon hearing his friend's confession, Les quit grinning. "It had splinters in it. He cut me up. Did it where everybody could see, right in front of that awful cigar shop." Ryder shifted from one foot to another, still hugging the post.

"But . . . but . . . you drowned!"

"He don't care."

The boys were quiet for a while. Les understood the trouble Ryder and his siblings had with their daddy. Most everyone did. The Harold family took Ryder in often, feeding him and letting him sleep over.

"I can tell Momma," Les offered, but Ryder shook his head. "But what if he's waitin' on you when you go home?"

"She can't stop him."

Then, Ryder told his friend about the cowboy and his part in his father's humiliation. Les was incredulous.

"Who was he? Does he have a name? What'd he look like?"

"Ain't never seen nobody like him," Ryder said. "He hit Oren across the jaw with the same board he was beatin' me with. I thought they was gonna fight. I think he'll beat him up if he hurts me again."

"How do you know? Did he say that?"

"Yeah, and he . . . he called me 'son,'" Ryder whispered. "Oren ain't never called me that."

"Too bad that cowboy ain't your Pa."

"He's young, not like my old man, but I wish he was my brother instead of Al."

"Heard about that too," Les offered. "Zelus told me he didn't help you."

Ryder shrugged. He didn't know what to say about his brother's failure to rescue him. Even if he didn't jump in the water after him, why didn't he run for help instead of just standing on the pier, watching him die?

"Come on!" Les shouted. "Let's go walk around. You can't sit down anyhow, and I wanna look for the cowboy."

Ryder didn't feel much like walking around, but Les was right about one thing: he sure didn't want to sit.

"Let's take the long way home," Ryder said. "I'm awful tired, and Momma'll tend to my hurts and send me off to bed."

CB

"Is that him?"

"No! Stop askin' me."

Every stranger they saw brought the same question to Les's lips.

"Let's quit lookin', okay? He's got a horse. He might be in Matagorda by now."

"Boy, you really don't feel good, do you?" Les complained. He started to say something else, then checked his own speech with a rapid tug on Ryder's arm.

"Look! There by the sheriff's office. Ain't that your Pa?"

Ryder didn't need to confirm the tall, brawny form of his father. He was chewing on the remains of his fish-butt cigar and approaching a blue roan. The owner wasn't far, for the animal wasn't even hitched. It just stood twitching an ear at them, reins dangling in the street.

"What's he doing?" Les asked. Oren appeared to be talking to the horse for reasons Ryder didn't want to guess. What did he need with a horse? He didn't even like horses—they were too big and smelly, he said, and they ate too much. The first time Ryder asked if he could have a horse, his father laughed in his face.

"Anything shits bigger than me don't need to be eatin' my food." That was the end of that discussion, yet there he was, Oren Wheeler, trying to befriend a horse. He moved quickly, also unusual for his father, and dug around in the saddlebags. He came up with a flat leather envelope, tucked it into his shirt, and ran around a building, disappearing from sight.

Shame was a heavy weight—Ryder wore it like a hooded cape. Les tried to think of something to say, but his stutters and apologies fell flat in the face of Ryder's revelation—his father was a lowdown, fiddleheaded thief.

Les Harold had the perfect family: parents who loved their children. They were poor too, but it never bothered them. Mr. Harold worked hard to keep bellies full around his table, even if their clothes were a little frayed. Often, Ryder's family scraped by on whatever the boys wrestled in from the sea. Oren worked odd jobs, sometimes on boats, other times delivering to the markets, but the brood rarely benefited from the money brought home—at least, not without a grand fight from Momma.

Sometimes, Oren would forget their names, and as the offspring grew, he assigned numbers.

Much as he hated to be called by a number, Ryder preferred that to his given name. In that moment, he saw empathy in his best friend's eyes. Pity! He had never been pitied before, not by anyone, and the cloak of shame grew heavier still.

Then, Ryder thought of the brown-eyed cowboy with the single spur. He was the most exciting, wonderful, and terrifying person he had ever met.

*I bet that cowboy would care for me if I was his son.*

"Your daddy's awful good at taking what isn't his to take," Les said. The comment was unnecessary. Ryder knew that. Shoot, most all of Indianola knew that.

"It's hard enough holdin' my head up when somebody uses my name," he complained. "People don't like us. I don't need you pointin' it out."

"Just because you're a Wheeler don't mean you have to turn out like him. You never stole nothing from anybody." Then he called Ryder by name. Had Les chosen different words, or, better yet, kept his mouth shut, Ryder might not have slammed so viciously into a world of make-believe. But Les did speak, and called him by name. Not his nickname, Nickel, nor Ryder, the name he had given himself. No, Les chose that moment to call him by his given name, first and last, and Ryder rejected it immediately.

"Maybe I ain't no good," Ryder said. "I'm just born of a no-'count thief who'd rather whip me and give me away than call me his son. I ain't as smart as you, Les, but I guess I've got a right to be who I wanna be. And I ain't never gonna hear that name again. You can call me anything else, though," he added, to soften the bite in his words.

Les furrowed his brow, scratching his head. "But what about your last name?"

Ryder hesitated. If he had known the cowboy's last name, he would have blurted it aloud.

"I don't have one no more."

"So you're just . . . Ryder?"

"Nickel, to you, if you want."

"I didn't know you can just quit a name," Les mused.

"Plenty of people do it," Ryder said. In truth, he didn't know anybody who had ever done it. Of course, most people weren't called after some story-book Greek god, wherever that was. Most people weren't branded by the last name of a thieving, worthless father, either.

"Ryder Nickel, then," Les said. "What about your dad? What do you thinks in that envelope he stole?"

"Money, I guess. He took it from the cowboy." Ryder closed his hands into fists, punching at his thighs.

Retreating a few steps, Les slapped his hand across his mouth. "What? *Your* cowboy?" His voice came out garbled, and Ryder yanked his hand free.

"Quit talkin' through your hand like that. You'll call up those road lizards." He gestured to the saddle horse hitched to the post. "That's his horse, shore."

"Well, maybe it's just paper or something," Les offered.

"If he comes home drunk tonight, we'll know where the money came from," Ryder said, scowling at the spot where his father disappeared. *I wish that cowboy would'a killed him outright.*

"You're not gonna do anything?" Les asked.

"I'd steal it back, but I can't keep up with him. It hurts, what he done to me." Ryder's admittance was low; he wasn't accustomed to a defeat of any nature. "He usually comes home to make another number with Momma after he gets shitfaced. I'll try to swipe it back then."

"What if you get caught?"

"Then it won't make no difference what my name is." Ryder screwed his lips into a mocking smile.

"Maybe we should tell the cowboy."

"He'll just hide what he stole. Then the sheriff'll lock him up, or the cowboy'll kill him. I wouldn't care so much, but for Momma."

The boys stood awhile, watching for the cowboy, but Ryder was spent. He even allowed Les to help him home. It felt good to limp in the door, supported by his best friend, to be greeted by the open arms of his mother.

❧

"Momma!" Ryder bellowed at the prick of her needle.

"I'm sorry, I'm so sorry!" she cried. Indeed she was, for tears slipped down her cheeks to dampen her battered son. She had to dig out the splinters, some of them long and jagged, from his red, tender hide. Blood blisters oozed, and one cut looked as though it needed a few stitches, though she had used the last of her thread to patch Oren's shirt. Les, loyal as a pup hoping for a ham bone, was sitting by Ryder's head. She had put him in her bed, hers and Oren's, for it was the only private room they had.

"Les Harold," Momma said, "go and fetch a touch of salve and a bit of thread from the new doctor, will you? I'm fresh out."

"Yes ma'am."

"Mind you bring the salve, and not the doctor!" After he left, she buried her face against the thin hollow of her son's back. "I almost lost you," she whispered, stroking his hair. "You were blue when they brought you home, limp in some fisherman's arms. I . . . I thought—"

"That was days ago, Momma. I ain't dead."

"No, but if they hadn't found you . . ." Her voice trailed off. She couldn't think about it, didn't want to picture Ryder, the boy who always had a smile on his lips and laughter on his tongue, swallowed up by the monsters in the sea. The ocean always scared her with its murky depths and wicked storms, but deep down, she realized the real danger for her family lie not in the waves, but in the monster she was married to. How far would he have gone, beating her golden child if someone hadn't interfered?

"He ain't never gonna do it again, Momma. Not to me."

"No, he won't," she agreed. "I promise." Molly was still worrying about what it would take to fulfill that promise when Les returned with the doctor in tow.

Molly's heart sank.

"I told you not to bring the doc, Les," she scolded.

"I'm not in the habit of lending treatment without having a look at my patients first, Mrs. Wheeler." Molly glared at the physician. He was what most women might call handsome, with a smooth face belying his age, a thick head of hair, and intense gray eyes. It was the latter she didn't trust, for they were constantly moving, as though searching for trouble.

"I can't pay for your visit today," she declared a little too loudly.

"It's true," the doctor retorted, "your boy here is racking up a sizable bill, ma'am, but I won't turn away just because you don't have the money to spare."

"I don't do charity, Doc." She spoke to the back of his head, for he was already bending down to examine Ryder.

"Let's see what we've got here, boy." The doctor worked with swift fingers, stitching up the deep cut on Ryder's left cheek. He left the salve on the night-stand and patted Ryder's shoulder. "After the excitement you've had these past few days, I will not ask what happened today, but I will say this: you're to stay in bed, young man. I'm leaving a special tea with your momma. I want you to drink it, every drop, to soothe that cough in your throat. Bed rest will heal everything else, but if I were you, boy, I'd stay away from water and splintered boards for a while."

Molly followed the doctor out of the room, shut the door, and wrung her hands.

"Thank you, sir, for tending to my boy. I didn't need you to come today, but I'm thanking you all the same." She cleared her throat and waved her hand, hoping he'd get the message: *go away.*

"He's a good kid, your Ryder, ma'am. A madcap, though, isn't he?" He shook his head and chuckled.

"He don't like to be told he can't do something. His brothers know that. I wish they'd stop taunting him." Wringing her hands, Molly took a few steps toward the door, hoping the doctor would follow. He didn't.

"Hopefully they've all learned a lesson this time."

"I hope so." Molly rested her palms against her cheek, watching the doctor survey her dingy one-room kitchen with a scowl. She knew what he saw: rows of bedrolls stacked against each other to be dragged out at night. Her children slept on the floor and under the table. A few chipped dishes paired with bare boxes where foodstuffs should be stored told the story of the Wheeler clan: Oren was driving them to poverty. Molly squeezed her hands together and shuddered deep in her throat. Why didn't he just leave?

"Mrs. Wheeler, about the bill . . ."

Molly twisted her fists inside her petticoat, glaring at the filth growing on the windowsill from Oren's tobacco. "He's always emptying his pipes on my windowsill," she complained aloud, unconsciously changing the subject. "I tell him to quit, but he won't never listen to me."

"Where is he, ma'am?"

"He's . . . working, I suspect."

"He's the one who did that to your boy, isn't he?"

"I'm not sure when I'll get the money to pay for your visits," she said, ignoring his question, "but I told you before, we won't be beholden."

"Mrs. Wheeler, I'm not much good at dropping hints. I say what I'm thinking, and it gets me into trouble more times than I care to admit. So I'll say it now, and you can judge me as you will. You'll never get the money to pay me, not with the brood you've got to feed and clothe. You still owe me for the last visit, and I hear you owe the other doctor for the last three babies he delivered. Now, with Ryder—well, ma'am, your luck child is expensive."

Molly hung her head. "We're doing the best we can," she mumbled.

"I'm sure you are, but you're at a disadvantage with that husband of yours. What I propose is this: let me bed you, ma'am, just till we're square on that bill. Then, if you'll consider seeing me regular, I'll pay you for your trouble."

Molly curled her fingers into fists. She wanted to hit him, to give him cause for a physician of his own, but fear kept her hands at her sides and her mouth shut. Fear . . . that unadulterated terror that kept her enslaved to Oren's every whim. If he lashed out again, if he hurt her, or worse, one of the children, where would they be? She dared not alienate the town's newest doctor, and they both knew it.

"Mrs. Wheeler, you can think it over and get back to me."

"There are other doctors in this town, Dr. Flatt!"

"Yes, and they understand your inability to pay bills more than I do, otherwise you would not have called for the *new* doctor's services."

"I didn't call for you!" Molly Wheeler protested.

"Your husband has a rather stained reputation for delinquency. Others have families to feed too, ma'am."

"You're saying they won't help us if we need them?"

"Oh, I'm sure they would if you needed their services. Do you really want to owe money to more people in this town? I heard them tell your husband he won't extend any more credit over at the general store, and I doubt he was the only one." The doctor plunked a spool of thread on the rough-planked family table. It rocked under the weight of his hand, and he bent to gaze at the offending table leg. "Not much of a carpenter, your husband, is he, ma'am? Too bad, seems a man who knows how to fix things ought to be the one polishing your table."

Before Molly summoned a reply, the door slammed open and Posse, the eldest, strode in with a trio of youngsters running circles around his heels. They all stopped short to gawk at the doctor. Molly wrapped her arms around Posse, letting her eldest shield her from the doctor and his filthy propositions.

"We won't need your services any longer," she informed their unwanted guest. The doctor grinned and tipped his hat.

"Then I'll see myself out, Mrs. Wheeler. I'll drop by later to see how young Ryder's getting along. I just might fix that table of yours too."

"My table don't need fixin'!" she yelled, but the man was already gone.

"Ry all right, Momma?" Posse asked.

"Yes, but we've had a bad day today," she said, wiping the sweat from her brow.

"Fishing weren't much better, Momma," he replied.

Molly looked down into the empty hands of her fifteen-year-old son and collapsed onto a kitchen chair. They were down to two, one for each adult, so the children either stood at the table or took turns sitting on the laps of the older kids on the floor. One of the girls climbed into Molly's lap and purred like a kitten, while six-year-old Hera tugged at her skirts with grubby little fingers.

"Momma, I'm hungry," she whined. The complaint swept through the children like ripples from a rock tossed into calm waters—except Molly Wheeler had little in common with calm waters.

Feigning bravado, Molly scrounged through their meager pantry and put together a thin stew mixed from the last few tins of canned meat, watery broth, and a handful of carrots. While her family slurped their soup, Molly brought a bowl to Ryder, who was lying on his stomach, sound asleep. Les Harold still sat by his friend, and Molly said a silent prayer of gratitude for the loyal boy.

"Have you eaten, Les?" she asked.

"Yes ma'am, my momma fed me 'fore I came over," Les lied. She overlooked his falsehood with a nod and left the room before he noticed welling tears. She had to get out—even for a few minutes—so young eyes would not see her failing strength. The stew would run out, and she would have to send her eldest boys back out in the morning, and pray the Mistress would not try to take them as she had done Ryder.

Leaving Posse to watch over the others, Molly wrapped a threadbare shawl across her shoulders and ducked out into the early-evening air. She no longer noticed the fishy aroma of the town. The scent, sometimes mingling with cattle destined for the shipyards, seeped into the pores of Indianola's community until their nostrils learned immunity to the clash of odor. Molly detoured around Dr. Flatt's dwelling so as not to meet him by chance. The physician's crude proposal lodged in her head, his words, the gleaming of truth in his eyes made her shiver.

They both knew he had her cornered. Graham Flatt wasn't in town long enough for anyone to know him, not really. Still, Molly supposed he was a decent man. He was always polite in public to her and her children. He was a growing beacon within the community. From what she saw, he treated his patients with dignity, tending to their health and well-being regardless of payment. He often traded foodstuffs and goods for his care, but this . . .

Was she the only woman he approached? Or did the doctor have dark secrets with other struggling women within town? Did she even have a choice? Her children were always hungry, and she was growing thinner from giving her portions to the little ones. She would never keep up with the mending, patches were wearing thin on britches and skirts, and most of them ran barefoot. She would never raise enough money to pay the doctor, not with Oren's dreadful spending habits.

Molly veered through the streets without memory of those who called to her in greeting, and stood on the watery edge of her crumbling world, her insides trembling and sloshing like the turbulent sea that had nearly claimed her boy. Water lapped at her shoes, leaking in through a hole to dampen her stocking.

Lifting her foot, Molly scowled into the depths of her adversary and shuddered. She despised unpredictability, feared it, and yet she surrounded her life in the most fickle forces of nature—the ocean, vile in its instability—and Oren Wheeler.

They were made of the same matter, her Oren and the Mistress he loved. He spoke of her as he would a lover, calling her name with a starry grin, his tone soft and sensual. Molly had not heard that tone directed at her since they were wed. That Oren loved the sea far more than her, Molly understood. He spent hours, sometimes days, drifting in the Mistress's embrace, floating on the waves, stirred by the salty air and the lapping of water against the boat.

For Oren, fishing trips were a necessary evil. He went, for the Mistress called him to her again. And again. He listened to the ocean's call not to provide for his large family—sometimes he went out for days only to return without enough fish to last them through the week—but to be near her. Upon his return, he would pull Molly into bed and attempt to slake his carnal thirst. She tried her best to satisfy him, but nothing Molly ever did was enough. Oren would grow agitated, and when Oren Wheeler was miserable, everyone else was too. She loved him once. Deep down, she still did.

"We can't both have him," she told the sea. "You stole him from me long ago, you bitch! You want him that bad, take him, but you ain't getting my kids!" Molly picked up a pebble and flung it into the waves with a ragged scream. "They're mine—you hear me? Ryder and the children are mine!"

# CHAPTER 3

# SACRIFICE

A bove the snores and deep breathing of his siblings, Ryder lay facedown in his corner pallet bed, listening for the footfalls of his father. If they were staggering, the cowboy's billfold would be a lot lighter. He had to swipe it back, but how?

"He catches me," Ryder told himself, "ain't no time to run. Oren'll break my legs."

*Maybe I'd better not,* he thought, but as soon as the idea entered his mind, he shoved it aside with a shake of his head. The cowboy didn't have to go out of his way just to save his rump from a savage thrashing. He didn't have to. Yet, he did.

Ryder did not have long to wait. He heard Oren coming long before he tottered into the door, bellowing for Molly. The children stirred, but experience taught them to snuggle deep into their beds and ignore the sounds made by their parents when Oren came home on a tear.

This time, Ryder paid little heed to the rule. He owed yesterday's cowboy a debt and meant to repay it the only way he knew how. Beating or no, he was getting that billfold back.

His rear end protested movement, but he slipped from his pallet and crawled across the floor, careful not to bump into one of his siblings.

Momma and Oren had the only separate room in the house. Separate, but not private. The walls were thin, so everyone knew what happened behind that door.

*I shore hope they don't hear Daddy catch me!*

His parents were arguing. Ryder folded his ten-year-old body as flat and small as possible, positioning himself just outside the doorway. Oren left it open, so he peeked around the corner to see inside the room. It was lit by one small oil lamp.

He saw nothing to speak of on the bed, but the table near the doorway hosted a pistol. Ryder wondered at that. A pistol? He never saw his daddy carry a gun before. Even in the dim light, it looked scary. Lots of folks had them, even sailors. But a good pistol cost money, and Oren Wheeler preferred smokes, women, and boats to firearms. Why did he need one now? Ryder suspected he had lifted it, just like the billfold.

He didn't see the cowboy's rucksack, but it was there. Somewhere. It had to be. Something inside told him to wait, so he turned his attention back to his parents and their argument.

"Are you gonna tell me what happened to your face?" Momma asked. Her voice was angry but hushed.

Oren Wheeler did not take her lead. His slurs resonated off the walls to pollute the ears within. Momma, Ryder saw, was fighting tears. Again.

Ryder shifted his gaze once more, scanning the room for the leather billfold. It bothered him—Oren had it somewhere! Where was it? His father was too careless to keep it hidden away for long.

"Whatever happened," she said, "you deserved it for what you did to Ryder!"

"Damn that weak-minded kid!" Oren yelled. "He tried to ride a dolphin! Those fishermen stirred up the Mistress, draggin' him out like they did. Everybody knows it's bad luck to steal a sacrifice from the sea!"

"He's our child, not a sacrifice!"

"He oughta be. Why'd anyone want him anyhow? Even the sshhea wouldn't want him." He leaned on the last word, drawing it out as he uncorked a bottle and took a hefty swig. "Don't matter nohow. Goin' out again."

"Out? Fishing?"

"Bought a boat. Bigger boat."

*Oh, shit, no!* He really did steal the cowboy's money!

"Where did you get the money to buy a bigger boat?" Molly asked with a screech.

"Might head for warmer waters," Oren said, ignoring her alarm. He tugged at his britches.

"You can't do that!" Molly cried. "What are we supposed to do with you out to sea? The boys, they're already workin', but I can't afford to raise this family alone. What'll we do for money?"

"Shhend 'em away—you can't afford 'em. Ain't seen none of their money nohow," Oren grumbled. "What the hell's wrong with this button? If you sewed it shut, Molly . . ."

Ryder scowled and shifted his knees against the floor. That was a lie. Posse and Alastor worked hard, but the money they brought home rarely made it into Molly's hands. Oren smoked and drank it all away, or purchased something to "warm his belly."

Ryder didn't understand what that meant, but he often overheard his father talk to his friends about the belly-warmers he bought on days when the boys brought home money.

"I will *not* send them away, and you ain't gonna leave us penniless while you go off fishing!" Momma broke her whisper, and Oren backhanded her across the jaw. She fell into the broken old armoire, and Ryder bit his tongue and winced. *Bastard!*

Oren seemed to forget what he had smacked her for and struggled instead with the stubborn button on his britches.

"Help me, Molly," he pleaded.

Molly Wheeler pulled herself up, holding her hand to her face, and obeyed with a twist of her fingers. Oren kicked off his britches and tossed them aside. A large, worn leather envelope thumped to the floor, and Ryder, still crouched by the doorway, wet his lips. The cowboy's double billfold! Was there any money left inside? He hoped so, for he did not cotton to the idea of Oren's retribution if he caught him stealing it back.

Ryder figured Oren seemed more interested in pestering Momma than the billfold. He meant to wait for his chance but didn't bank on Oren's violence. His father, now bare-assed, shoved Molly to the bed and climbed on top of her without bothering to take off his smelly old shirt. It was the only one he had, and it reeked of seawater and fish guts. To Ryder's astonishment, Molly Wheeler fought back. She yelled things—words no one dared say other than Oren, of course. Since when did his mother have it in her to say such words aloud? She struck at her husband, swearing and spitting, for what he did to her and her children. For what he did to Ryder.

Oren reared back, and the sound of his fists striking flesh soured Ryder's stomach. Molly Wheeler fell back with a cry, toppling over the bed where Oren grabbed at her dress, trying to rip it free of her body. He hit her, again and again, the way one might slap a dusty old rug against the wall. Molly cried out.

No one dared move, though he knew his brothers and sisters behind him heard every word. The fear was too great. No one, not even Posse, was a match for Oren Wheeler.

As Ryder crouched, watching blood stain his mother's mouth, listening to the sickening thunks of balled-up fists against her cowering body, he didn't care. He was only a kid; he couldn't beat his father the way the cowboy did, but it didn't matter. His eyes drifted back to the revolver. It was still there, gleaming in the yellow lamplight. No longer would Oren beat on his momma . . . or anyone else. He'd kill him, if he had to.

Ryder crawled, flat-bellied, wriggling like a worm across the threshold of the door. He glanced at the billfold, lying inches away from his grasp, and at the hulking figure of his father, his hairy ass swaying with each strike.

Bouncing to his feet, he snatched up the gun and cocked the trigger. It made a satisfying little clicking sound, but Oren did not hear it.

"Get off my momma!" he screamed.

His parents scrambled, her to cover herself and he to find his feet. Oren swayed like a ship caught in a squall. The interruption angered him, but the sight of his ten-year-old brat holding his brand-new gun infuriated him.

"Go back to bed, Ryder!" Molly cried, falling over her feet to reach him. She was blocked in by the wall, the bed, and, far worse, Oren. "I'm all right. Put the gun down, Ryder! Go back to bed, please!" Her words were frantic, and her motions jumpy. Oren shoved her against the wall and ordered her silence.

Ryder thought of the beating he suffered only yesterday, and the one Oren was giving his momma now. The beatings would never stop. Not unless someone did something about it.

"No, Momma. I won't." Instead, he aimed, glaring down the short barrel at his father's sweat-stained face.

"You don't put that gun down right now, you little shit, and I'll whip you bloody and throw you to the sharks!" The slur was gone. Oren stood frozen in front of the barrel of his own gun. His face was red from exertion, and his rumpled fish-gut shirt didn't cover the part of him he loved most. Even that pathetic tool looked surprised and agitated. Ryder would have laughed, had his rage left enough room for hilarity.

"You ain't no good," Ryder said. "We're hungry, 'cause you take Momma's food money. I saw you steal from that cowboy too. I don't guess I'm gonna let you do it no more."

The boy did not brandish the weapon. His fingers stopped trembling under the weight of the gun. A calmness fell over him. He held steady, knowing he had committed himself to shoot. If he didn't, Oren Wheeler would make good his threat.

"You don't really think I put bullets in that gun, do you, boy?" Oren asked with a sneer.

Ryder's eyes widened. He hadn't thought of that. What if it wasn't loaded? If he pulled the trigger on an empty gun, Oren would kill him. Taking his eyes off his target, Ryder glanced at the revolver. It was only for a second, but a second was all his father needed.

Oren lunged forward, fists ready. The first blow struck Ryder's temple, sending an explosion of tiny lights behind his right eye. The other smashed into his stomach, folding him in half. As he crumpled to the floor, Ryder prayed for a little more of his sound luck and mashed down on the trigger. The bark of the gun mingled with his mother's screams, and Oren Wheeler's world grew dark.

☙

Indianola was still sleepy, the streets empty save for fishermen preparing for the day. A few cannery laborers trudged past him, heading to work early, he suspected. The boy felt a twinge of jealousy. They didn't care about the upheaval his family had just endured. Their lives rambled on as usual—without beatings and bloodshed.

Raw, bleeding, and unsteady on his feet, Ryder trailed through the streets, searching for yesterday's cowboy. He wasn't at the Hayworths'. It didn't occur to him that the man might have already received his message and left town. He would be looking for his billfold, so Ryder would find him. The boy stopped a small group of fishermen to inquire the whereabouts of one out-of-place cowboy, and his heart slammed against the pit of his stomach when they pointed toward the beach.

"He's outta place, all right," one told him. "You'd think the man never saw water, the way he's out there lookin' at it. Pretty mornin' though."

He was right. The last shadows of night slipped away. In its stead rose the gilded light of the sun glittering off the water. Ryder admired the sky, painted in rosy pastels, dipping low to the ocean's edge.

The sunrise cast two dark forms into silhouettes, one a man in a broad-brimmed hat, the other a prancing horse. He admired the animal from a distance, watching as it pawed the lapping water. A wave rushed in at its feet, and the horse threw its head in the air and spun in a tight circle. The man laid his hand on the horse's neck. He looked to be speaking to it.

Gradually, the horse settled, though it didn't seem to like the rush of water under its feet. Ryder was glad of that. A horse who loved the ocean was apt to be a kelpie.

*Sure don't wanna test my luck near one of those watery beasts!* he thought.

As he neared the beach and the lone figures, Ryder's throat itched. He coughed to clear it, but it was closing in—panic. The vivid memory of salt water rushing into his mouth as he tried to scream—of waves battering his body and driving him under—surfaced in his mind. He would go no farther. Not one step. Bile rose in his throat, and he limped back to the safety of the boardwalk where the water was out of sight. There, he could still keep his good eye peeled for the return of the cowboy.

"Nickel!"

Ryder looked to his left. Les was running so fast he feared his friend might run right over him if he didn't slow down. Ryder retreated a few steps, just to be sure. His friend, tripping over his own feet to stop, grasped him by the arms, panting.

"Your . . . brother . . . told us," he wheezed. "My Pa . . . ran to help . . . your Ma." Les wiped his nose on a grungy sleeve and gaped, his breath still escaping in puffs. "You look awful, and your eye's bleeding!"

Ryder grunted. Whatever he looked like, he felt much worse.

"Did you really shoot your Pa?" Les asked.

"Guess I did," Ryder said. His voice sounded flat, even to his own ears. He didn't care; he was glad he shot him.

Only thing was, his aim hadn't been too good, and now he had to learn to watch over his shoulder.

"Why are you just sitting here, then?" Les asked. He bounced on the balls of his feet and waved his arms.

*Jumpy as a jackrabbit in a coyote den,* Ryder thought. "I'm waiting for that cowboy," he told his friend aloud. "He's on the beach, just now." He started to point but ended with a loose, half-hearted wave. Les knew where the beach was, why bother pointing it out? He let his hand drop to his lap and stifled a yawn.

"Cowboy?" Les cried, still flailing about. "Who cares about him? You shot him, Nickel! You shot your daddy!" He grabbed Ryder by the shoulders, shaking him as if to rattle some sense into his brain.

Ryder pushed him off—he'd had enough manhandling for one day. "Please, Les," he pleaded. "I got it back—the billfold Oren stole from his saddlebags."

Les threw his arms in the air. "Don't you even care what happened? Who cares about a billfold? Use it, whatever's there."

It seemed a reasonable suggestion, but Ryder shook his head. "Yeah, but it ain't mine," he said. "It ain't right. That man helped me yesterday. He stopped Oren from whoopin' me. He didn't have to do that." Ryder tightened his arms across his tender midsection. The leather was still there, tucked safely inside his shirt. "He hit me hard," he said. "I don't feel too good."

He leaned into the awkward arms of his friend. Les Harold didn't understand Ryder's decision to shoot his father, he knew that. Les realized the troubles between the Wheeler family, but he didn't comprehend what it was like to have a no-account for a father. One who yelled, beat, and abused. One who instilled fear, starvation, and shame within his family. Violence? Well, it just wasn't in Les's nature.

"What are you gonna do when you talk to the cowboy?" Les asked.

"Give him his billfold." What else could he do?

Once Les got a worry in his head, he didn't like to let it go. The boy spun in a slow circle, scanning the town around them, just in case the cowboy meant to ambush them. "What if he shoots you?" he asked, satisfied they weren't in immediate danger.

Ryder laughed out loud at the notion and winked at his worrisome friend. "What for? Bein' busted up?"

"He'll think you stole his money."

"You worry too much," Ryder grumbled, still chuckling.

"You're not afraid?" Les shifted from one foot to another, still scanning the town for an angry cowboy.

Ryder jabbed himself in the breastbone. "Me, scared? Of what? I guess if I can survive Oren Wheeler, I can talk to a cowboy."

But Les Harold *was* afraid, he could tell. Afraid of getting in trouble, afraid of Oren, and afraid of the cowboy.

"You have the billfold now, Nickel?"

"Yeah."

"What's in it?"

"Never looked."

"What if there's money in it? You should give it to your momma—it might be enough to buy food. Maybe you could even get a pair of shoes or something."

Ryder rubbed his stomach and closed his good eye.

"Don't talk about food. I can forget about being hungry, most times, if we don't talk about it."

"Just look in it, Nickel. If there's money there, that cowboy don't need it—not like your family does."

Ryder's fingers sought the worn leather of the billfold tucked into his arm. He thought of entertaining Les's suggestion, just to see what was inside. Money? Or did his father already spend it? What sort of treasures did a cowboy carry on him, anyway?

He picked at the thong, which was wrapped and tied tight around the leather with bloodstained fingers, but his vision slurred through a red haze. In fact, thanks to Oren Wheeler, he couldn't even see out of his right eye.

Ryder tucked the leather envelope inside his shirt, pressed against his skin by the fold of his arms, and shook his head.

"No, Les, I ain't gonna be like him. I ain't gonna steal, no matter how bad we need it. Just tell me when you see the cowboy, okay?"

# CHAPTER 4

# YESTERDAY'S COWBOY

Perhaps Ryder dozed, or maybe he blacked out. Whichever it was, his consciousness shook him awake before Les did.

"Nickel! Hey, Nickel, wake up. He's comin'!"

"What? Who?" Ryder tried blinking back the fog to sit up, but his temple pounded like a drum. Through the persistent little black spots floating around in his vision, Ryder spotted his quarry.

Les poked him in the arm. "Uh-uh, he'll shoot us, Nickel! He's gonna think we stole it."

"Go home, Les. I'll be fine." He rubbed his temple. "He ain't gonna hurt me, or he would've let Oren do it."

"I'm not leavin' you here."

"Go find your Pa and make sure my momma's okay. Help Posse take care of the babies for me till I come back. Please?"

Les, spurred by the approach of the fearsome man on horseback, ducked and ran for the Wheeler home, leaving Ryder to square off against the stranger on his own. Ryder struggled to his knees, then his feet. His temporary blind spot unnerved him as he had to twist his head to gain a better view of the man in the saddle.

"Hey, Mister!" he called. The cowboy halted his horse at the boy's call and leaned down, surveying him.

"I know you. You're that kid from the cigar shop."

"You said . . . to look you up if . . ." Ryder lifted his head, and the cowboy swore.

Dropping from the saddle, the man knelt and grabbed his chin, lifting it to provide a better view of Oren Wheeler's work.

The boy flinched at the touch of the man's rough, calloused fingers.

"Your Pa?" the cowboy asked.

"Yessir," Ryder said with a sniff.

"Where is he?"

"I don't know, sir. He ran off after I shot him."

"After you *what*?"

"I'd've killed him, shore, if there'd been more bullets in the gun." At that, the man rocked back on his heels and appraised Ryder from the top of his scraggly, tousled hair down to his grime-caked bare feet. He mumbled something unintelligible.

"I came to find you, sir. I saw you at the water's edge, but I can't go down there no more."

He grimaced. "You don't like water?"

"No sir, not no more. I drowned in it the other day."

"You drowned."

"Yessir, the Mistress, she's gonna claim me now."

The cowboy scratched the scruff on his face. "Kid, you tellin' me that just this week, you drowned in the ocean and you shot your Pa?"

Ryder shrugged. "Guess it's been a slow week, sir," he said with a smirk.

The man took off his hat and ran his hand through his hair. It was coffee-colored and flattened from the crown of his hat. His eyes weren't just dark; they were black in their intensity. The boy shivered and lowered his gaze.

"A slow week," the cowboy repeated. "Ah-huh. Your Pa—he hit you anywhere else?"

"Yessir, in the gut. Hard."

"Lift your shirt."

Ryder hedged, then worked the worn leather pouch out of his shirt and offered it to the cowboy, who grabbed it up with another curse.

"What the hell?" The sharpness of his voice and the sinister tone sent another chill down his spine, but Ryder held his ground.

"My Pa stole it off your horse. Me and my friend Les, we saw him do it yesterday. I-I got it back." Ryder glanced down at the parcel. "I don't know what's in it, Mister—or what he took out of it, neither."

The boy expected a barrage of questions and accusations, not the stony silence he was receiving now. He watched the man untie the leather thong, loosen the strap, and search the contents.

Ryder said a little prayer that Oren Wheeler hadn't blown through all the money, whatever might have been there. The billfold held an assortment of papers, but he couldn't tell if there was money inside.

Watching the stranger's eyes, he saw them narrow. His heart sank.

"What's your name, kid?"

"Ryder, sir."

"Ryder?"

"It ain't my real name, but it's what everyone calls me. Ain't got no last name no more, and I won't *never* use my first." He stood with his feet planted and held his chin high, ready for the torrent of questions.

Again, the expected queries did not surface. The man cut him a look—one the boy couldn't decipher—and nodded.

*That's it?* The boy raised an eyebrow. "You mean you ain't gonna ask me why?"

"Nope." The cowboy paged through his billfold again and put it away.

"Don't you wanna ask?" Ryder wanted to know. Drawing his head back, he crossed his arms and blinked with wide, green eyes.

"No." The cowboy met his gaze, his features steady, unflinching. "A man ought to go by the name he chooses for himself, no questions asked. No reason it shouldn't work the same for a boy."

"Nobody's said that to me before," Ryder told him. "Everyone always wants to know why, and some of 'em try and use my real name, anyway."

"I understand," the cowboy replied.

Ryder wondered how he understood. Did he have a bad name too? What was his name, anyway? It was on the tip of his tongue to ask, but he held back.

The cowboy's attitude didn't lend much room for broaching a subject as intimate as a name. Maybe he would just offer it to him, like a handshake.

"Mister? I didn't take your billfold, I swear. You believe me, don't you?"

"Look, kid. Ryder. I've got something in my bag back in my room. It's an ointment we mix up at the ranch for bruises. Works for cuts and scrapes too. You damn sure need it on that eye. Come on back to the Rooming House. You can explain what the hell's going on along the way."

He didn't offer up a ride on his horse, but he didn't mount it, either. The two walked down the street, the boy at a slow, pained shuffle and the cowboy shortening his stride to match, leading his horse.

Ryder began his story at the dock, where Alastor and Zelus dared him to catch a dolphin. He described his drowning, and the fear crept into his throat as he spoke of his recovery and the events leading up to Oren's brutal attack on his backside with the plank. Then, Ryder told the cowboy about his father's theft and how he got it back.

"He was beatin' my momma, threw her into the wall and kept punchin' her. The rucksack he stole—it fell out of his britches when he took 'em off, and I meant to grab it and run. But he wouldn't stop beatin' on her. He was tryin' to rip her dress, and I saw the gun lyin' there by the door. We ain't never had one before last night—don't know where he got it—but I picked it up and he got mad and threatened to beat me bloody and throw me to the sharks. He started punchin' me, so I shot him."

Ryder held his hand over his eye, feeling the pulse behind the bruise.

"I can't figure what happened after that, sir. I guess there was a lot of screamin' and yellin', and I picked up your billfold and ran off before Oren got up and killed me."

As he finished his story, he waited, expecting a barrage of questions. Again, the cowboy's silence mystified the boy. What was wrong with the man? Adults always had questions. Lots of them, and usually fired them off one right after another. This one was different. He was silent when they entered the Indianola Rooming House and remained quiet during the short walk to his room. He closed the door behind them and broke the strained silence with a one-word order.

"Sit."

Ryder sat, shifting from one cheek and then to the other. Unable to tolerate the pain, he groaned and sprawled out, flat on his side. Oren Wheeler was really good at leaving a lasting mark. The cowboy set to work gathering the tools needed to clean Ryder's eye and settled into a chair by the bed. The water he used for the compress wasn't cold, but it was wet, and after the initial flinch of pressure against his head, Ryder thought it was almost soothing.

"Are you a doctor?" he asked.

"Most men in my line of work learn doctoring by necessity, kid."

"Cowboying?"

"You can't run to a sawbones every time you get stomped on or flattened by a mean cayuse—or a drunk with a cagey fist."

"What's a . . . cayuse?"

"A feral horse. Wild, loco."

"Do you ride cayuses, sir?"

"Bannack."

"Huh?"

"My name's Bannack."

Ryder grinned. The stoic cowboy had offered his name after all, and he didn't even have to ask. He wondered if the name was his first or last, but judging from the stern expression on his face, it was the only one he would get.

"So do you, Bannack? Do you ride cayuses?"

He smiled. "What do you think?"

"I think you gotta be the toughest man I ever met. I bet you've ridden hundreds of 'em, and broke 'em too. Me, I'd sure like to ride one, someday. I can ride anything I set my mind to."

Bannack raised a quizzical eyebrow. "Is that so?"

"Yessir, that's why I named myself Ryder."

Bannack snorted. "Didn't do too well with that big sea-fish, did you?"

"The dolphin? Oh, I would've rode it, sir—only it never gave me chance enough to catch it."

Bannack dropped his hand from Ryder's temple, closed his eyes, and drew a ragged breath.

"Some things ain't meant to be caught, kid."

"If I had some rope—"

"Rope don't do nothin' but prolong the inevitable." Bannack rummaged through his saddlebag and came up with a tin container, which, when opened, nearly gave Ryder the running fits.

"You ain't gonna put that on me, are you? It smells like a damned octopus belch!"

Bannack, ignoring the ten-year-old's choice of language, dipped two fingers into the greenish sludge.

"What the hell's an octopus?" the cowboy asked, smearing the slop over Ryder's eye.

"What?" The boy gaped at him. "You mean you don't know?"

He shook his head. "Nope. Sure don't."

"Well, it's a big round fish with eight big ole legs. Squirts ink out of its ass."

"Boy, back where I come from, they'd call you a damn fine liar."

"I ain't lyin'! It's true, I seen 'em. Poked one with a stick, and it up and shot black inky clouds at me."

He stifled a laugh. "Out of its ass?"

"Yessir! Well, close enough, I guess. I ain't real sure it has one. Its butt is more like its mouth. Ain't really got a nose, but it has big old eyes. How come you never heard of one?"

Bannack shook his head a few times, glancing from Ryder to the sludge in the tin.

"Where I come from, we have a lot of things. Eight-legged fish with big eyes and no face, squirtin' shit out of its mouthy ass ain't one."

Ryder giggled. "You got a funny way of talkin'," he said. "Where are you *from?*"

"A long way from here," Bannack said, drawing nearer with the ointment.

Ryder clapped his hands over his nose and gagged.

"Hold still unless you want it in your eye."

Ryder did his best to obey, but idleness never suited him on a good day, and Bannack's fingers were coarse against his raw temple. Besides, the offending smell of the gloppy green goo made his eyes water.

He coughed and pinched his nose shut between two fingers and nearly refused when Bannack bade him lift his shirt, but the man's abrasive attitude did not lend much room for argument. Snot was running like a waterfall from Ryder's nose. He wiped it off on his shirt sleeve, then raised a knuckle to rub his eye. Bannack grabbed his wrist and flung it down.

"Grind that salve into your eye, and you'll wish your old man had finished you off."

Ryder was still gagging when Bannack stepped back, his doctoring complete. The cowboy scrubbed green goop off his hands with a bar of lye soap and dried them off on the seat of his britches.

"How long do I gotta keep this stuff on my face?" he asked, plucking and twisting his fingers. He shifted and fidgeted, wishing he could scratch until every trace of the offending ointment was gone.

"Till it cracks and falls off."

Ryder groaned.

"Tell me, kid, and I mean the truth. Why did you bring my billfold back?"

Ryder paused, observing the man out of one red, watery eye. Bannack folded his arms across his chest and frowned. Again. Does the man ever smile?

"I don't know," he admitted. "My friend told me not to—he thought for sure you'd think I stole it. He said I should just keep whatever I found in it and give it to my momma so's we won't starve."

"But you didn't."

"No sir, Mr. Bannack. Lots of people don't like us much, on account of my Pa. I overheard a man tell my momma once that us boys didn't have a chance, that we was gonna grow up just like him, and we'd be good-for-nothin' bastards. No! I don't wanna be like him, sir—don't wanna be a good-for-nothin' bastard."

"Son," Bannack said, squatting low to look Ryder in the eye, "you're what—eleven or twelve?"

"Ten, but I got a birthday tomorrow."

"That so? Eleven then, fine. Ryder, I want you to picture a forked road. You're standin' in the middle. Road to the left's worn smooth, a boy your age could travel it without tiring. The other cuts right, and it's full of rocks and brush leadin' up to a mountain."

"What's on the other side of the mountain?"

"Don't know without climbin' it, do we?"

"That one sounds scary."

"Might be. Which road do you pick?"

Ryder scratched his head as he thought about his options. "I can pick whatever road I want?"

"No one's stopping you, kid."

"What if I don't want neither one? The first one, that's too easy. I guess if it's that smooth, too many people already been there, and that ain't much fun. I don't mind not knowin' what's ahead or nothin', but what if I want to go straight on instead of turnin' one way or the other?"

"You mean make your own road?" Bannack asked.

"Yessir. Can I do that instead?" Ryder watched the corner of Bannack's lip curl into a fleeting grin. It was gone as fast as it appeared, but he saw it just the same.

"Ryder," he said, clapping the boy on the shoulder, "you're gonna turn out just fine."

"You really think so?"

A soft knock at the door interrupted the cowboy's reply.

"Mr. Bannack, sir? My mother says food is on the table if you're hungry."

At the sound of her voice, Ryder wobbled into the center of the room.

"Magdalena," he whispered.

Bannack cocked an eyebrow at the boy as he rose. Young Magdalena Virginia Hayworth stood poised in the doorway, her hair long and flowing over her shoulders in onyx waves, and Ryder's throat constricted.

"Ryder!" she cried, espying him hovering near her family's boarder. Without thought, the girl ran and threw her arms around his neck. "Ryder! What happened to you? And why— oh, what's that awful smell?"

"Bannack says it's medicine. My Pa hit me, and Bannack fixed me up."

"Oh, no! Not again!" Magdalena, sniffing back tears, pressed her lips against Ryder's face and kissed him square on the corner of his mouth. Her rosy skin flushed a deeper shade of pink, and she whirled and fled in a flurry of petticoats. Magdalena had never ventured close enough to kiss him before, Ryder mused, rubbing his jaw.

Not that he hadn't tried, either. But if a beating was what it took to gain kisses from girls as pretty as Magdalena Hayworth, then that was okay with him.

Bannack was leaning against the doorjamb, arms folded across his chest, appraising him with a keen eye.

"Ahuh, you're one of those."

"Sir?"

"A lady-killer."

"I ain't never killed anybody!" Ryder protested. Except Oren Wheeler—if he was even dead.

Bannack rolled his eyes. "Come on, Romeo."

"Where to?"

"Breakfast, then to see about your family."

"But I don't have any money."

Ryder's protest fell by the wayside as he followed Bannack out to the kitchen. The aroma of fresh-baked breads and assorted meats and fruits made his stomach clench. He couldn't remember the last time he saw so much food at one table. No fish-scrap soup! Bacon, sausage, and fried ham steak with eggs. Plus, canned peaches and dried apples. Several loaves of bread decorated the center of the table with slabs of butter.

"Ryder!" Mrs. Hayworth, the wife of the Rooming House owner, gave him a hug and stroked his hair. "Magdalena told me you were visiting our guest this morning. Just look at your face!"

Ryder murmured a reply but could not keep his eyes, or his mind, off the spread awaiting them at the table.

"I said that man of Molly's was no good! I saw it and told her so. Now look what he's done to you!" She clucked. "Poor thing. You're very lucky, it could have been much worse."

It *had* been worse, but he didn't bother telling Mrs. Hayworth that. She, and the rest of the town, would discover what he had done to his Pa soon enough.

As it was, a veritable feast was staring him in the face, and Oren Wheeler wasn't worth the pound of bacon sitting inches from his nose. Mrs. Hayworth guided Ryder to a chair and sat him down. He grinned up at her, his reward for her generosity. It was plain enough to see where Magdalena got her long flyaway mane and her chiseled, doll-like features. Mother and daughter both resembled the beautiful mermaids he saw painted on the signs around town, and he told her so.

Mrs. Hayworth beamed. "Eat your fill, Ryder dear. Lord knows how much you need a good meal. I wish your mother would bring you here once in a while. You tell her not to be such a stranger now."

"Yes ma'am."

"Is there anything I can get for you, Mr. Bannack?"

"No ma'am, this'll be fine."

"If you need anything, either of you, call on me or my daughter."

The woman edged a little closer to Bannack, grasped his arm, and lowered her voice.

"Ryder's a dear boy, but his family's always been troubled. That father doesn't take care of his brood, and they go hungry. There's over a dozen children, last I recall. Ryder's the gem of the bunch, if you ask me. He's full of life and laughter, and we all do what we can for him. You're a stranger to us, Mr. Bannack, so I just hope he's found a real friend in you. That boy doesn't need more hurt in his life."

"I don't friend many people, ma'am, but I defend the ones I got."

Mrs. Hayworth studied his unwavering gaze and patted his arm before releasing it. She excused herself, and Ryder sat in a comfortable family kitchen, alone with good food and a quiet cowboy no one knew anything about. He watched Bannack sit with his back against the wall, his eyes roving as though looking for someone, or something, to jump out at him.

Magdalena came to fill his plate when he emptied it and poured Bannack another cup of coffee. The girl glowed in Ryder's presence, smiling and brushing against his arm. Ryder kept her coming by shoveling in three platefuls before slowing down, and cleaned his last plate by sopping up the remnants of his meal with a thick slice of bread. Bannack leaned back in his chair, fisting his coffee cup, and hooked the heel of his boots under the rung of the table. The little jingle of his spurs drew Ryder's attention.

"You're wearin' your spurs today," he commented around a wad of bread.

Bannack regarded his own feet and shrugged. "I wear spurs every day."

"But you only had one yesterday."

"I lost one—had to dig out my spare set."

"Oh. I like the way they clink like bells. Do all cowboys wear 'em?"

"Most of them." Bannack took a swig of coffee and sighed. "I'll be leavin' tomorrow mornin', Ryder."

"No!" Ryder blurted. The outburst drew Mrs. Hayworth's attention, for she poked her head in the door.

"Everything okay here, gentlemen?"

Ryder nodded, and after she left, he amended his protest.

"I wish you didn't have to go. I was hopin' you'd be my friend."

"I'm not friend material, kid."

Ryder rubbed his fingers over his temple. The green sludge began flaking off from his skin, revealing his now swollen eye. Moisture welled behind his lids and, fearing he couldn't control them, he cradled his face in his arm. Bannack continued.

"Now that I've got my things back, I've gotta go, kid. The ranch I ride for—it's a little over three hundred fifty miles north of here. If I push it, I can be home in less than two weeks."

"Two weeks?" Ryder asked, his voice muffled by a dirty shirt sleeve. "You live that far away?"

"The ranch land lies in the middle of hill and prairie country, kid. Some call it the Blacklands. There's a helluva lot of country between here and there."

"Then I won't never see you again." Shoulders slumped, Ryder kicked at the table leg.

"Never know, maybe you will." Bannack leaned forward across the table. Ryder felt the man's hand, tough, wrap around his wrist. "Look at me. You asked if I was sure you'd be all right. There ain't no certainty about anything in life, kid. No promises. Hell, asshole like that for a father, I'd be worried too. It's tough, but I think you already appreciate who you are."

"But what do I do?" Ryder whimpered.

"Boy, you live. An eleven-year-old took a beating for a stranger and fought for his mother. You've proven yourself today. Falling into your father's vices, that'd be easy. Standing up for your beliefs, that's what makes a man."

"Even if you're scared?"

"Were you scared when you faced your father?"

"Yeah, but I shot him anyway."

"And why did you do it?"

"'Cause he was hurting Momma!"

"Any other reason?"

"'Cause he'd try to kill me if I didn't."

"Would he really have killed you?"

"Yessir. I didn't want him hurting my brothers and sisters like he done me."

"Would you shoot anyone again?"

"No! Not if I don't gotta. It was awful. I didn't wanna do it, but he made me."

"Then you did what you had to do, even though you were scared."

Ryder chewed over the information, then bounced back for another onslaught. "Bannack?"

"Yeah?"

"How old are you?"

The cowboy measured him with another odd look. "Why?"

"No reason, just curious."

"Twenty-six."

"How'd you get to be so smart? Did you go to school?"

"I learned my lessons the hard way."

"Like me?"

"Like you, only I never tried to ride a damned dolphin."

Ryder threw his new friend a lopsided grin. "Bet you just never had the chance. Me, I would've rode it, only the water got in the way."

# CHAPTER 5

# COWBOY DENTISTRY

Indianola's lucky Nickel perched atop a real-life cow horse and waved goodbye to Magdalena Hayworth and her mother. Bannack had fashioned a bandage from his neck rag to cover Ryder's injured eye. He already noticed a difference, for he wasn't trying to squint or peer through it like before.

"Mr. Bannack? Everything looks smaller from up here! Is it really smaller, or are we more important now?"

"It's us, kid. We're more important." Bannack swung up behind him and tapped him on the shoulder.

"Which way?"

"Do you gotta take me home?"

"I expect your momma's worried."

"But what if Oren's still there? He was awful mad when I left. Howlin' and yellin' somethin' awful."

"If he's there, I'll take care of it."

Ryder wasn't convinced. "I dropped the gun—what if he shoots me?"

"He won't get a shot."

"How do you know?"

Bannack answered with a cold, steely gaze bearing the weight of deep-rooted promise. "No one's going to hurt you, Ryder. Not today."

With a sigh and a shrug, he replied, "Okay. I live just down thataway." The boy pointed, and Bannack turned his mount with an unseen command.

Ryder found the rhythm of the horse painful to his tender rump roast, though he dared not complain. The squeaks and creaks of saddle leather blended with the soft jingle of the cowboy's spurs, but it was the wide-eyed stares, the smiles, waves, and whispers from the girls they passed that made Ryder realize new truths: women loved a man on horseback, and someday, he intended to be one. *If* his father let him live.

CB

Molly Wheeler attacked the bloodstains on her bedroom floor, blubbering all the while. Oren's blood tainted everything it touched yet wouldn't wash off. Ryder was her sweetest child, always grinning, so full of life and adventure. Everything was trying to take him away from her. Now, life turned him into a killer . . . or, if Oren still lived, a would-be murderer of his own father. That was the hell of it, Molly mused. He lived long enough to run off, but would he succumb to his wound?

As she blew her nose and dried her eyes, she prayed he would.

The latter didn't help. Like most floods, hers would never be contained from within. Molly had become adept at curbing her tears so as not to alarm her brood, but no one was here to see her now.

After Ryder ran away, Les Harold's father came by to whisk the rest of the children off to his home, where his wife would tend to them until they deemed it safe for their return. He had promised to look for Ryder, but only after he secured Oren Wheeler with the law.

Molly scrubbed harder, wishing she could block out the sounds of Oren's fists striking her son, and the report of the revolver in Ryder's hand followed by the agonizing screams of her husband. The horrible things he spewed from his mouth—threats upon Ryder's head—set Molly to contemplate killing Oren herself. She had even picked up the gun, but despite Oren's claim that the chamber was empty, it bore just one bullet. Ryder was fortunate—but he left her with nothing to finish the job.

A brisk pounding at the door sent Molly skittering across the floor, heart pounding in her throat. Ryder would not knock, but if it was news of her boy . . . Molly thrust the thought from her mind as she answered the persistent knock.

"You!"

Dr. Flatt tipped his hat. He was clutching his medical bag.

"I did not send for you!" she shouted.

A faint smile flitted across his rounded lips, partially hidden by a salt-and-pepper mustache. "No, but I ran into Mr. Harold a moment ago. He was looking for your boy and told me about your latest misfortune. I thought someone might need my services."

"We don't," Molly assured him and tried to slam the door. The good doctor jammed his foot inside to block the door and held it open.

"Mrs. Wheeler, if your son or your husband needs medical treatment—"

"They aren't here just now. Go away."

"You have blood all over your clothes."

Little black bag in hand, Graham Flatt shouldered past Molly and through the door, stopping to peer around the room.

"Get out!" she yelled, but he paid no heed.

"Harold said he had your kids safe at his place, and to tell you his wife is tending to them. Mrs. Wheeler, you do realize there are some who'd seek to take those kids away from you?"

"What?" Molly reared back, pressing her hands to her stomach. "Who would try such a thing?" she asked through trembling lips.

"Lots of folks. They'd do better in an orphanage than with a mother who can't care for them. They're starving, beaten, and left to wander around the docks to fall into the ocean and drown."

"That's not fair! It's Oren. He usually only beats me, but I bucked him after he hurt my Ryder yesterday—"

"And from what I hear, he forced violence on a ten-year-old, obliging your little boy to shoot him."

"They can't take my children!" Molly's voice rose in pitch until her voice cracked. "I won't let anyone take my children!"

Dr. Flatt ran his hand through his mustache and chuckled. He took a few steps closer, driving Molly into the middle of the room. "What will you do now, Mrs. Wheeler?" he asked, his voice hard, yet mixed with an air of amusement. He was enjoying this. "They're all saying your husband ran off but won't survive his wounds. That leaves you alone with a passel of young'uns. You can't even feed and clothe all those kids *with* a man. How will you do it now, on your own? I may be new here, but it's still my duty to see to the welfare of the people in this town. No judge will see the condition of your kids and let you keep them, not when I'm offering them a better life."

*"You?"* Molly wheezed. She pulled at the neckline of her dress, for it was suddenly strangling. "You would try to take them from me?"

"I wouldn't try, Mrs. Wheeler. I would succeed." Molly wished she could clobber the doc's smugness from his mouth. Maybe it was a façade. Maybe it wasn't. Either way, she could not take that chance. She stood a little taller, feigning a bravado Oren had beaten out of her long ago.

"You can't do that. I . . . I love my kids. They're all I've got."

"That may be so, but you can't take care of them." Flatt's posture was perfect. His chest jutted out as though it was the source of his superiority, but otherwise he stood straight and tall, unyielding in body and mind. She could not fight him.

"I'll manage," she mumbled. "I'll find a way. And . . . and I'll fight you!"

"You would lose, ma'am, and I think you know it." Dr. Flatt reached for her hand, grinning.

Molly staggered backward, nearly falling over the only chair they had left—the only one Oren hadn't broken. She sank into it, clutching the arm-rests with the white-knuckled grip of desperation.

"What do you want, Graham?"

"Look at me, Mrs. Wheeler."

Molly gazed straight ahead, seeing nothing. She could not obey, nor bear to see the little smile on his lips. She didn't need to; it was in his voice—triumph.

"There's the matter of settling your bill," he told her. "I've spoken to several merchants who can no longer extend credit to you or yours. Once word gets out that your husband's gone, others will follow."

Molly closed her eyes. The boys needed to find more work right away. They would never appreciate childhood, only the inside of a factory or the perils of the sea.

"I'll be abrupt, Mrs. Wheeler, since you have a lot on your mind. I don't believe in forcing a woman into bed, so I'm giving you a choice." His smile turned sinister. "Work off your debt to me, let me bed you when I choose, and I'll leave your children with you."

"And if I don't?"

Dr. Flatt shrugged. "You still must pay my bill, but I'll do what I think is best for your brood."

"I'm a decent woman, and yet you'd turn me into a whore to keep my children? That isn't a choice!"

"Mrs. Wheeler, your husband talked long and loud of his accomplishments in your marital bed. To hear him boast of your . . . ahh, talents . . . you already are." The doctor closed the distance between them, lifted Molly's chin, and clucked at her tear-stained face. "It won't be that bad, Molly," he said. "It's just the natural balance of humankind—to fornicate." He pulled her to her feet.

His hand slipped from her chin, large fingers trailing down her throat to her chest, and rested upon her breasts. He kneaded, as though working a lump of dough.

"Why else are women like you made so plump and pretty but to offer pleasure to men?" He trailed his mouth down the side of her neck, and she shuddered. He reeked of fancy aftershave. It clogged her nose, and she tried to shift her body away from his busy hands.

She closed her eyes, tilting her head away from him. "Please don't make me do this," she pleaded. It was the only protest she had left, for the fatigue of life weighed her down, dragging upon her shoulders like an anchor.

"It'll be good, Molly. You should be so lucky to have me. Lots of women in this town have shared your fortune."

"What?" she asked, for she had nearly entered a far-off place in her mind. A place where her children were safe.

"You're not the only family who can't pay their debt," Dr. Flatt said in her ear. "Women come around, one way or another. Just last night, Mrs. Butler dropped by my office."

"But she's married!"

Flatt laughed a great, bellowing laugh and snatched at her petticoats with his right hand. "The best kind of woman to have, my dear."

"But why?"

"Because." A stern voice rang out from the doorway. It was as stiff as winter wind blowing over the water, and just as frigid. "Because a man like him can bury himself between the legs of another man's wife and throw her away without obligation."

Dr. Flatt snatched his hands away from Molly and spun to face the intruder.

"Who the hell are you?"

"I might be your reckoning."

Molly peeked around Doc's back to study the stranger standing in her doorway, and shuddered. Slipping from her chair, she backed against the wall, wishing she was within reach of Oren's gun. Not that she knew how to use it.

"Momma!"

When Ryder pushed past the cowboy in a run, she screamed his name and dropped to her knees, flinging her arms around him.

"You're squishin' my air, Momma," he complained. She loosened her grip, but only a little. "You don't need to cry no more, Momma. I brought my friend. He helped me."

Molly rubbed her blurry eyes on the hem of her patched, threadbare dress so she might see the welcome intrusion better. "The cowboy?" she asked.

"Yes ma'am." Ryder beamed, showing every tooth, even the snaggled one tucked in his left jaw. Oh, how she loved that grin! The boy's nearness calmed her nerves, so she held him close, confident they were safe enough with his friend . . . for the moment.

"I didn't realize you had a cowboy friend, Ryder," Molly pressed, ignoring the dark glare smeared across Dr. Flatt's face.

"His name's Bannack," Ryder said.

The doctor, who had been trying to decide the best method of chasing out the intruder, paled.

"What d'you say, kid?"

"You heard the boy," the cowboy said. He took one menacing step forward, then stopped. He had not been invited inside.

"Bannack?" Flatt cried. It was his turn to retreat, tripping over the same chair he had backed Molly into. "*You're* Bannack?"

Bannack dipped his chin, the only sign of acknowledgment. Flatt beat a hasty retreat through the house, hoping to make it to the back door.

"It's just a misunderstanding, Mister," he cried over his shoulder. "A mistake!"

Bannack snorted. His eyes didn't fall from his target, not even when he addressed Molly.

"Ma'am, do I have permission to enter your house?"

"Don't let him, Molly! Don't give it to him!" Flatt was still retreating. Molly Wheeler raised to her full height, still hugging Ryder to her.

"I don't know you, Mr. Bannack, but my son calls you his friend. Is that true?"

"Close enough." Bannack's eyes were locked on his prey, who was fumbling with the lock on the back door.

"He stopped Oren from beatin' me, Momma!" Ryder piped in.

Molly struggled to her feet, using her son as a crutch to lean on. If the cowboy helped Ryder, well, that was good enough for her. "Then, yes, if you're a friend of my son, come in."

"I step over this threshold, ma'am, and there'll be bloodshed." Molly watched the cowboy's fist clench and unclench at his sides, his dark eyes keen on the frantic doctor. Stranger he may be, but at least he was man enough to show respect: He could easily have burst through her doorway without thought to her or her home. Molly's lips slipped into a tiny smile. Dr. Flatt didn't know the latch on the back door had been stuck for so long, the Wheeler clan forgot about using it. There was only one way out, and Molly would see revenge done to the immoral filth who called himself a physician.

"That's fine with me, so long as you don't hurt my family. I did *not* invite that man into my house," she announced, hands on her hips.

"Molly!" Dr. Flatt screeched. He was yanking at the latch, swearing. Sweat beaded on his forehead, and his eyes darted from side to side.

"What's wrong with this door?" he cried as the delightful sound of Bannack's spurs jingled with the clomp of his boots across the floor. Ryder smirked into his mother's petticoat.

"Think of the woman and the kid, Bannack!" Flatt pleaded. "Her husband was shot here. Blood has already been spilled!"

He grinned. "Then I guess she won't mind the mess."

Molly grabbed Ryder, herded him outside, and closed the door. She glanced at the cowboy's horse waiting by the steps and sidled to the far side of the porch.

"Momma, what are we doing?"

"Waiting."

"Bannack's real tough, ain't he?"

"He frightens me, Ryder."

"Aww, he won't never hurt us, though. I'm glad he's gonna whip old Dr. Flatt."

"Me too, my little Nickel," she whispered. "Me too."

෨

Graham Flatt's screams proved too much for the tiny house to contain. The fight sounded one-sided, and there was no doubt which man held the winning hand. Molly bent her head at the sound of the cowboy's voice.

"Where is she, you ——? Where did she go?" Molly did not discern a reply, but whatever he said, Bannack didn't like it. Obscenities flew like spray from the Mistress's mouth, but Molly was too weary to move Ryder out of earshot. Instead, she closed her eyes. Apparently, a cowboy's grudge ran as deep as a woman's.

"Is Bannack askin' about you, Momma?"

"No, Ryder."

"Who then?"

"I don't know, and you're not gonna ask him, you understand me?"

"Yes, Momma."

Something crashed inside, and Molly winced. It sounded like a body falling into something. It sounded like the old table that housed the big candle lantern.

Dr. Flatt yelled again. "You knocked my teeth loose, you crazy son of a ——!" A few more thwacks cut him off mid-sentence.

As Molly pulled Ryder into her lap, the door banged open so hard it flew back and bounced off the wall. Bannack stormed off the porch, straight to his horse, and unwound a length of rope from his saddle. Molly rose, meaning to intercept the cowboy, but he waved her off.

"Ain't done yet," he growled, slamming the door shut behind him.

"What's he gonna do with that rope, Momma?"

Molly shook her head. "I'm afraid we're gonna find out," she whispered and clapped her hands over Ryder's ears to drown out the screams.

"What are you doing? Get out of my bag!" Flatt hollered upon Bannack's return. The sound of glass shattering and metal thumping to the floor attested to Molly's guess: Bannack must have dumped Flatt's medical bag. The doctor's yells escalated into wild, garbled screeches.

When he emitted the first of several ear-splitting screams, Molly squeezed her hands tighter around Ryder's ears. The boy, however, appeared unruffled and far more at ease than she was. Bannack's voice was barely discernable through the verbal slaughter, his speech emanating the low growl of a feral dog rather than a man. Flatt's screams were growing ragged, and then . . . silence.

It was eerie, the sudden quiet. No voices, no screams, no garbled yells or pleads for mercy.

*He's done it,* she thought. *He's killed a man in my house. And I gave him permission!*

The door opened, and Bannack emerged, dragging Flatt by the foot. Young Ryder's eyes bulged, and Molly gasped.

He had trussed the town doctor like a steer, one leg and two arms bound in some odd-looking knot. With one hand, Bannack dragged him face-first across the porch, trailing little smears of blood across the planks. Flatt's head bounced down the three steps, and the cowboy continued the march out to the street where he dropped him and yanked his rope free with one quick tug. The man glared down at the prone figure that lay crumpled in a pile of blood, sand, and horse dung. He coiled the rope around his left arm and returned it to his saddle.

For the breath of a few moments, Bannack just stood with one hand on his horse. The other was clenched in a white-knuckled fist. He opened that fist, peered down into something in his palm, and winged it at Flatt. Passersby eased up to the scene, wide-eyed and curious. They exchanged whispers behind hands, and the crowd grew. Bannack ignored them all and returned to the porch. Molly stood to face him, clutching Ryder tight.

"I'll pay the damages," he told her.

"My belongings aren't worth that much," she replied. "Um, is he—did you—?"

"No. He's still breathin'. Sorry 'bout the blood on your floor."

She nodded, casting another glance toward what remained of Dr. Flatt, but she barely saw him through the throng of milling people.

"It's all women," she said.

The cowhand shot her a questioning look, and she gestured to the gathering crowd.

"Women."

"It ain't a crowd. It's a mob," he replied.

Molly saw it was true. The women weren't asking questions, and the looks they threw in Bannack's direction were not expressions of accusation, fear, or horror, but rather of respect, gratitude, and even cheer.

One woman spit on the back of Flatt's head, and others joined in, kicking and spitting. One woman broke free of her pack and made straight for Bannack. She threw her arms around his neck, knocking his hat off, and kissed him square on the mouth.

Instead of returning the affection, Bannack untangled her arms and pushed her away. She dove in for one more peck on his jaw and fluttered away, nose in the air. She cut through the herd of milling women and walked across the good doctor's back, grinding her clunky little heel into his spine.

"He won't be bothering nobody's woman anymore," Bannack said, resolute.

"That's why you're here, in Indianola. To retrieve your woman." It was not quite a question, but Molly waited for the reply. It was the only thing that made sense. Why else would the cowboy be here, chasing the likes of Graham Flatt?

When he did not reply, she pressed deeper.

"There's blood on my floor, and a broken man in front of my house. I guess I'd like an answer."

He looked at her then, and Molly flinched. Those eyes were bronzed, deeper than any shade she'd ever seen. Yet, for the purity of those eyes, Molly saw the storm clouds behind them. Bannack was harboring pain worthy of a man much older than he was.

The cowboy was dangerous; of that, there was no question. The wrecked body of Graham Flatt would never heal to its former glory. Yet, Molly was not afraid of the vengeful cowboy.

"Well?" she asked.

"She ran back home. I reckon she'll be waitin' on me when I get back."

"The way you say that makes me think she's done this before."

"I ain't no stranger to cleanin' up her messes."

Molly shook her head. Oren had a few women on the side from time to time, most likely professionals. What woman would tolerate Oren Wheeler if she wasn't paid for her aggravation?

But this man . . . this strong, virile cowboy brutal to his enemies and kind to women and children . . . what sort of she-beast would ever run out on him? For Graham Flatt? Doctor or not, it was not a worthy exchange. Molly said as much, and Bannack snorted.

"He ain't no damn doctor."

"Of course he is." Molly glanced at the broken mass whimpering in the road. "Well, was. He moved into town recently and saw those of us who can't pay as much for doctorin'."

"And that didn't strike you funny?"

"Well, no. Not until today."

"He ain't no sawbones. Probably killed the poor bastard who owned that medical bag. His name ain't Flatt, either. I reckon nobody knows what his real name is, he's used so many. Jumps from town to town, takin' up occupations just to sidle up to women, one way or another. Steals the bed of married women if he can and lines his pockets with the money of the innocent. He played a preacher up north, when he ran off with my wife. 'Fore that, he was a dentist. Ain't no tellin' how many other jobs he's had. Ran into a fellow bent on killin' him outright. Said he claimed to be a miner. He mined his way into his woman's bed and ran off with his plunder."

"No! You mean all this time . . . ?" Molly's voice cracked, and she let her words die away. "He *seemed* like a real doctor!" She shook her head back and forth, trying to make sense of this new truth.

"No one takes time to question the details," Bannack replied. He folded his arms across his chest and leaned against the post, fixing her with eyes capable of slaying a woman.

His voice took on a tone of weary tolerance, as though a teacher patiently instructing a student.

"People see a man with ink stains on his hands, they reckon he's a printer. A man smells like horseshit, they think he works in a livery. And if he carries a black bag, they assume he's a doctor. Nobody questions nothin'." He glanced at Ryder, still sitting owl-eyed against his mother's lap. "That'd be a good lesson for you, son. Don't take nothin' a man says at face value. Learn to question, observe. You take that medical bag. Did anybody notice the initials carved into the handle? They don't match Graham Flatt, as he calls himself. Did anybody think to ask why?"

Molly huffed, rubbing at her temple. "That's true enough—but I don't understand how so many fall for that."

Bannack shrugged. "He don't take no for an answer. I reckon you saw that."

"He—he threatened to take my kids."

"That'll do it, won't it?"

Molly scowled. "Did—did he force your wife?"

"She'll *say* he did."

"Do you believe her?"

"Hell no."

Molly considered the immediate reply and touched the cowboy's arm.

"Mr. Bannack? It seems you've married below what you deserve."

"You did too, ma'am."

"I couldn't get out of mine—not until last night when Ryder . . ." Molly's voice trailed off, and she sniffed in her hand. "You can leave yours," she pointed out, changing the subject.

"I reckon not." Glancing down at an owl-eyed young Ryder, the cowboy tapped his fingers against the dark bruise on his temple with a scowl.

"At least my wife don't hurt nobody but me," Bannack said.

## CHAPTER 6

# GAL LEG

"Stop staring at him."

Ryder ignored his mother. He couldn't help it; he had never seen a real live hero before, and yet there was one right on their front porch, soaking his hands in their ugly old basin with the cracked enamel.

"Do your hands hurt?" Ryder asked. Bannack glanced at him but said nothing. "The water's pink."

"Blood," came the reply.

"His?"

"Mostly."

"What did you throw at Dr. Flatt?"

"What?"

"After you drug him out, you had somethin' in your hand and threw it at him."

"Teeth, kid."

"Teeth? You knocked out his teeth? Boy, your hands gotta hurt!"

"Yanked 'em."

Ryder's eyes widened, and Molly muttered something under her breath.

"You pulled his teeth out?" she cried. "With what?"

"Does it matter?"

"Well, no," Molly mused. "I can't imagine how a man would yank out another's teeth."

"Used his pliers."

Ryder sidled up to his champion and grinned his infamous lopsided grin.

"Dentistry don't make me a hero," Bannack growled. "Boy, don't look at me that way."

"But you're one to me, and Momma too. I never met a real hero before, or a cowboy, neither. And you're both!"

A sigh escaped the man's lips. He took his hands out of the basin and dried them off on an old rag Molly handed him.

"Don't put me on a damn pedestal, kid. I ain't the kind to sprout wings."

"But—"

"I've killed men, boy. There's no glory in it."

"But you didn't kill Flatt."

"He's only breathin' 'cause I can't spare the time to get my neck stretched right now."

Ryder looked over at the doctor. Strange, guttural sounds escaped from blood-frothed lips. Crimson stain gushed from his forehead, nose, and mouth to paint the sandy gravel below. He pushed himself up with his elbows and knees, clutching his hands against his chest. His fingers were bent at odd angles. A few dangled as though they had a mind to jump clean off his hand.

With a shiver, the boy clenched his fingers inside his palms. What would it feel like to have your fingers snapped in two and smashed in? He turned back to the brutal man who had done the snapping, mulling judgment.

"I don't care what you did, or how scary you are," he declared after a few moments of indecision. "Nothin' you say'll change my mind, Mr. Bannack. I wanna be just like you when I grow up."

"The hell you do," Bannack muttered, rolling his eyes skyward. "Hell you do."

☙

Momma was taking a long time to talk to Bannack. Ryder paced, still miffed at her for sending him indoors where he couldn't listen in to their conversation.

Someone had cleared the broken doctor—or whatever he was—off the street. Bannack's comment about neck-stretching worried him. What if men took him away? What if they hanged him from the courthouse? Or maybe they'd lock him up in a pit. Oren Wheeler liked to tell stories about bad men being chained up and thrown in dark pits where they survived on rats and lost their minds, wasting away to dust and bone. Bannack had said he had killed men before; what if they threw him in a rat pit?

Ryder pressed his nose against the cloudy window, trying to peer through layers of grime and dust with one eye. The patch Bannack made for him was itching, but he ignored it as he snubbed the pain and swelling behind it.

Momma quit trying to clean the glass a long time ago—Oren covered it most of the time anyway, so their one little window was growing dim. Badged deputies were outside, two or three of them, and they were talking with Bannack and Molly. She was crying—again.

Ryder's heart lurched. No! They *were* gonna throw him in a pit! He yanked open the door, but his mother blocked his path and sent him back inside with a stern word.

Ryder sidestepped the gruesome remains of Bannack's one-sided battle and collapsed on his corner of Wheeler family real estate: a pallet with a few old blankets wadded up on the floor.

Much as he tried, Ryder couldn't lie still. Images of his new hero dangling lifeless from the town square, or rotting away in a dark cell, gnawed at his brain. He rolled one way, then another, lifting his head to listen. Would he go willingly when they arrested him? Or would he fight the lawmen as he had Graham Flatt?

"Fight," he whispered to himself. "He'd fight."

Hearing the door, Ryder pushed himself up and picked his way through the shattered remains of Momma's lantern to meet Bannack and Momma. Her eyes were puffy, but she'd quit crying, at least.

Ryder's gaze traveled past his mother to the man behind her. Stoic, stern, and devoid of cheer, Bannack stood like a ship's mast. Ryder threw his arms around the cowboy's legs and clung tight.

"I ain't gonna let 'em take you," he cried.

Bannack tried to retreat, his arms held in the air, but the boy wouldn't budge.

"Let him go, Ryder," Molly said. "You're making our guest uncomfortable."

"No! I don't want no rats gnawin' on his bones!"

"Has your father been fillin' your head with nonsense again?"

"He said they throw bad men in a dark pit, and after their mind's gone, the rats eat 'em and sharpen their teeth on their bones."

"Lived through worse than that," Bannack said, trying to shake Ryder off his legs. "No one's takin' me anywhere." Succeeding in disentangling himself, he rumpled the boy's mop of hair.

"Ryder, there aren't any pits in Indianola, sweetheart," Molly added. "The sheriff was here with his deputies, and they spoke to us. Asked a lot of questions, but they won't arrest Mr. Bannack."

"They won't?"

"He just has to tell the sheriff when he leaves town in the morning."

"That's it?"

"That's it. It seems the sheriff wasn't too fond of Graham Flatt, either."

"Did Dr. Flatt bed the sheriff's wife like all the others?"

"Ryder! Watch your tongue!"

Ryder shrugged and let his mother tug him away from his hero. She turned him around to face her.

"Honey? Do you understand what you've done to your Pa?" she asked.

Mention of his father brought battle to the boy. He tensed, clenching his jaw, and those green eyes snapped. Molly took an involuntary step back.

"He ain't my Pa!" Ryder shouted. His lips curled back, revealing a snarl, as he dared his mother to argue.

Molly sighed, bending so she could look him in the eye. "Yes, he is. But he's gone now, and I have to feed you. All of you. Alone."

Ryder's tone relaxed, and his youthful face softened again. "It's okay. Oren Wheeler ain't gonna hit you no more, Momma. He ain't gonna steal food money, neither."

"I suppose not, but that doesn't help us, does it?" She twisted her dress into wrinkled knots, blinking at the filth caked on her son's legs and feet. Just like her own.

Ryder stayed her hands, and she dropped her wrinkled skirt, only to rub her fingers across her mouth. Why was it so hard to explain? Ryder was smart, he knew she had more to say, yet she stalled. Once it was said, it would come true. Which meant . . . Molly looked up at Bannack. He nodded at her, and she sighed. She was going to lose her golden boy.

"Ryder," she began, closing her eyes so she could concentrate on the words. "Mr. Bannack wants to give us the money we need for food, clothes, and shoes. He's going to wire us money when he can so we don't go hungry." She paused, stifling an inward sob. "If he helps us, we must return the favor. Do something for him, Ryder."

"Really? What?" he asked, looking from one adult to the other. Something important was about to happen; he could tell from the way Momma kept looking at Bannack and rubbing at her nose.

She looked like she was about to cry again, so Ryder turned his attention to the stern face of the cowboy, waiting for an answer. It was not long in coming.

"Ryder, I'd like to make you into a cowboy," he explained. "You start learnin' now, and in five years, you'll be old enough to come north and ride for me on the ranch. If your momma swears to send you and a few of your brothers, I'll see to it your family doesn't starve."

"You mean you'll stay here? With us?" Ryder's eyes bulged, and he couldn't wipe the grin spreading across his face. His new hero did it for him.

"No," Bannack replied. "I'm leavin' tomorrow. Told you that. I'll come back in five years to get you."

"Five years?" Ryder exclaimed, clasping his hands to his head. "*Five years?* But I'll be *old* by then."

"You'll only be fifteen, dear, almost sixteen," Molly reminded him.

"Old!" he cried, and kicked at a broken anchor Oren had discarded on the porch weeks ago. No one ever bothered to pick it up. No one dared.

"Five years, that's my offer." Bannack removed his hat, studied it, and frowned. He shook out his hat, and his scowl deepened. He pawed at splotches of sand and dust on the brim, rubbed his thumb over a yellow-and-red quilled band, and placed it back on his head. Ryder wondered if the man really cared either way what he decided.

"And I'd work with you?" he asked Bannack.

"Nope. You'd work *for* me."

"You'd teach me? Everything?"

Bannack nodded once.

Ryder cocked his head to one side, chewing on his fingernail. Bannack sure didn't say much. "Why can't I just go with you tomorrow?" he asked.

"Five years—that's my offer." He stuck out a rough, calloused hand.

Ryder grabbed it and pumped his arm up and down, beaming.

"Yessir! Don't see how I'll wait that long, but I'll do it! I'll be a cowboy as good as you!"

"Hell, kid, you'd better learn quick." Bannack turned to Molly. "Wages I send depends on how many of your boys join him. I'll be looking to invest in strong hands by then, and I'll pay—if they're willin' to learn hard work for me."

"I'll send my three oldest to start," she mumbled. "Posse, Al, and Ryder."

"Fine." Bannack paused, then gestured toward the glowing boy ogling him. "I'd like to take him for a ride before I go."

Molly hesitated. With Oren out of the way, and her other children staying at the Harold house, she would be alone. Lonesome as she was with Oren around, she was no earthly good at solitude. With a herd of kids underfoot all the time, she had forgotten how. Ryder was such a comfort to her. She peered down into his beautiful face and rubbed the bruise over his eye.

"Momma, please?" he begged.

"I'm not ready to give you up to him yet, Ryder," she whispered.

The boy tugged at her skirt. "Please let me go with him, Momma. I'll come back before dark, I swear."

Molly Wheeler chewed on her lower lip. It was the most nourishment she had all week.

"Ma'am, the boy needs proper boots. I'd like to take him."

"Boots?"

"No more bare feet. A man needs to depend on his feet like he does his horse."

"I done the best I could," she began. Weary of feeble excuses, she relented with a whimper. "Just . . . bring him back to me, cowboy."

☙

Ryder sauntered down the boardwalk, gaping down at his feet. He wiggled his toes and laughed. For the first time in years, he couldn't see his own feet.

"Boots," Bannack said. "From now on, wear them. Keep your feet clean and tended."

"The leather squeaks!" Ryder announced.

"It'll soften to the shape of your foot."

"What if I outgrow them?"

"You will. I'll have them replaced when you do."

Ryder looked at Bannack. "Why?"

"A cowhand ain't worth much if he's got bad feet."

"No sir, why are you doin' this for us?"

"It ain't for you." Bannack's tone was gruff. "You're an investment, like your mother said."

Ryder stared down at his boots again. "You send my momma money so's we can live, and we come work for you in five years?"

"Yes."

"But I don't know nothin'. Why don't you just hire other cowboys—ones who know what to do?"

"Hands," Bannack corrected. "We call them hands."

"Okay. Why you want me instead of a real hand?" Apparently, Bannack was growing weary of questions, for he did not answer Ryder. Instead, he boosted the boy to the back of his horse and swung up after him.

Bannack did not believe in wasting time. He had one afternoon with his future ranch hand and seemed bent on making the most of it. Ryder's first lesson began with Bannack showing him how to hold the reins between his fingers.

"When you use a fork, hold it like you're holding the reins now," he instructed, placing Ryder's fingers in position. "By the time you get to me, it'll be second nature."

Ryder practiced his handhold and studied it, hoping he'd remember how to hold his fork from now on. Under the young wrangler's guidance, Ryder learned to steer the animal, but a toss of his head yanked the boy across his neck. Bannack caught him and kept his forearm trained across Ryder's midsection.

"Ease up, boy. He's tellin' you to give him rein."

"He nearly yanked me off him!"

"You weren't paying attention—else he wouldn't have surprised you."

"He's too strong for me," Ryder said.

"You're weak 'cause you've been starving, Ryder. That changes today."

Bannack tapped his right arm, and the boy turned the animal to the right. They rode up to the beach, and Ryder pulled the animal to a stop.

"I don't wanna go that way," he said.

"Do it anyway," Bannack said.

"No! I can't!"

The cowboy grabbed the reins and urged his horse into a rapid walk, not quite a trot, straight into the lapping tide. Ryder clutched at Bannack's arm and squirmed.

"Please, no!" he gasped, but the man ignored him and turned the horse into the water's edge. Ryder inhaled the heady scent of salt and fish scales. Bile rose from his gut in the form of a hot, bitter lump. He could not swallow.

Waves rolled under the horse's belly and then retreated, teasing little crabs and fish toward the sea, only to roll them shore bound again. The waves were beckoning; every crash seemed to call his name.

"Ryder!" Bannack yelled. "Calm down. Breathe!" He stuffed the reins in Ryder's trembling hands.

The boy tried to protest but only made a noise halfway between a gurgle and a scream.

"You're not gonna drown, Ryder. Take a breath. You can't go through life feeding your fear. Never retreat from it, son. Walk right up to it and kick that sonofabitch in the balls."

"No!" Ryder screamed. "Please, I can't . . . I can't . . . the Mistress!"

"Face her, boy. You can't live your life till you do."

"You don't know!" Ryder sobbed. "You don't understand what it's like. I can't move!" He screamed again, and Bannack clutched him about the middle. The horse, patient to a fault, had enough of the waves and the frantic boy on his back and spun in the water, fighting for his head.

"I know," Bannack retorted. "Ain't no stranger to fear, and I know rage. Men like me, we've suffered both, kid. It's the worst kind of hell, and I live it every damn day."

Nothing had ever scared Ryder before, not since his drowning. Even shooting Oren Wheeler hadn't bothered him . . . much. Everything had potential to be fun—or have fun poked at it if one looked hard enough. This was different. He couldn't control the violent quaking within his own limbs. His teeth chattered, and he had to fight to tear each ragged breath from his lungs.

"Easy, boy. One breath at a time."

"She's gonna take me," Ryder wheezed.

"I ain't gonna let you drown. If you're gonna work for me, you'd better learn to trust me."

"I'm gonna fall!"

"Look, you're holding the reins. Tarantula'll stop spinning when you calm down." Ryder shook his head and squeezed his eye shut tight. A mistake, for without sight, his mind took over, recalling his last conscious seconds before drowning.

"Breathe," Bannack instructed, over and over. "You're a good kid. You saved your kin from the devil this morning. This is just another damned demon to shoot."

Gradually, Ryder listened to the low, sharp tone of Bannack's voice in his ear. Under the cowboy's command, there was no room for failure. He demanded with finality.

Despite the swirling animal, Bannack stuck like a thorn to Tarantula's back, and Ryder managed a deep breath. He wasn't falling, even though he had the reins. He gave them a tug, and the animal crow-hopped in the waves.

"Horses smell fear," Bannack told him. He gripped Ryder's hands but did not take over the reins. "Calm him. Use your legs to tell him where to go."

Again and again, Ryder succumbed to fear, fighting both the man and the thousand pounds of horseflesh under them. Why didn't Bannack just take the reins and control the animal for him? *Just let me go ashore!* his mind screamed, but words wouldn't form. The cowboy was crazier than Oren, and just as relentless. He was only ten; he couldn't control a raging animal!

Ryder found his voice and swore. He called the cowboy every name he could think of. Every bad word dropped from Oren's mouth, every slur his mother forbade him ever to say, he yelled it aloud. Ryder was so intent upon raining verbal vomit upon Bannack's head, it never dawned on him that his teeth quit chattering. When he used up every foul word he remembered, he invented his own, mixing sludge with Oren's colorful vernacular. By the time he ran out of breath, he had forgotten about his fear. The horse stopped trying to buck the waves and stood quietly, still knee-deep in the sea. He tossed his head and arched his neck to look back at Ryder.

"What are you lookin' at?" the boy snarled. Then, as consciousness took over, and he realized the weight of his words, a new fear crept in. He had just called the most terrifying man he'd ever met words a grown man wouldn't dare say. Ryder turned his head in slow motion, daring a peek back at Bannack's face.

"Oh, shit," he mumbled.

"You 'bout done?" Bannack asked.

"Yessir," came the meek reply.

"Then ride."

Bannack made Ryder keep to the water; his horse Tarantula splashed along the shoreline. Gulls, the beggars of land and sea, hovered over their heads, squawking. A few pipers ran back and forth ahead of them, dining on tiny morsels. Ryder thought those sandy little birds were braver than he. Again and again, they darted in, racing the tide for their dinner.

Once, Bannack made Ryder dismount at the water's edge. He rested, grateful for the land under his feet, but only for a moment before Bannack called him to climb back up and do it again. Sometimes Bannack made him turn the animal into the waves and let it break over them. The first time another dose of panic seized him, the cowboy pulled him through it. They did it again and again until Ryder faced the depths with little more than an inner flinch. It was still there, fear, but now it was a gnawing sensation of dread. Something in the pit of Ryder's gut told him it wasn't over—the Mistress wasn't through with him.

CB

"Do you really gotta go?" Ryder asked. They were sitting cross-legged in the sand, watching shades of pink and purple paint the horizon. Bannack rarely tore his gaze from the water, but he looked over at him.

"You know the answer to that," he said.

"But I'm scared. What if something happens? Oren might come back. What if he does?" Ryder bit his lip, touching the sore spot in his belly where his father's fist had folded him in half. "I don't guess he'd want to, though," he added, answering his own question.

"Probably not," Bannack agreed. "Seems the type of man who'd run from responsibility."

"We ain't nothin' but burdens to him, anyhow. Don't know why he had to go and make so many of us kids, seein' as how he don't like us." Ryder dug in the sand, sifting the tiny grains through his fingers. "Shoot, maybe he died from his wound. I hope he did." He palmed more sand, drawing little patterns in his palm, and squinted into the fading light. "No, I don't expect he'll come back now."

Bannack cut him a long, level stare. "You pulled that trigger, son. Just remember that. No act goes without result."

"I guess nobody told that to Oren," Ryder said.

"I guess not."

The cowboy stared at the sea, watching the waves lap the beach for so long Ryder thought he had fallen asleep. Maybe he was one of those fellows who slept with their eyes open. Les said some people did that from time to time. Just to be sure, Ryder gave the man's shoulder a little shake and received a "hmmph" in reply.

"What if you forget to come back for me?" Ryder asked, clapping the sand off his hands.

"Kid, your mind changes with the wind down here," Bannack said with a snort. "I won't forget."

"Five years is a long time," Ryder said, worried. "You might."

"I don't forget anything," Bannack told him. His faraway gaze and tightlipped grimace made Ryder believe he wished he could. He propped his foot over his knee and unbuckled his left spur. "Give me your foot, Ryder."

The boy obliged and watched, wide-eyed, as the cowboy strapped the spur around his brand-new boot and bore down on the buckle, cinching it down as tight as he could.

"Spurs come in pairs," Bannack said. "This one's yours—your reminder that I'll come back."

"Really? It's mine? To keep?" Ryder grinned so hard his cheeks began to ache.

"Take care of it. Wear it. In five years, I'll give you the mate to it." Bannack wiggled the heel of the boy's boot, and the jinglebobs sang their pleasant melody.

"Are you gonna wear the other one so you remember to come get me?" Nickel asked, ogling his new hardware.

"If you want."

"You swear?"

"I swear, kid."

Ryder pulled his brand-new spurred boot close to his face to study the roweled contraption, and grinned.

"It's a lady's leg!"

Something akin to the ghost of a smile tugged at Bannack's lips.

"From heel to thigh," he said. "It's called a gal leg, and you'd do well not to let your momma get a real good look at it."

"Wow, it sure is fancy."

The shank of the spur was indeed cut just like a lady's leg, shapely from the toes all the way up to the buttock at the top of the heel band. The leg bent at the knee, and Ryder tried to picture what a real girl might look like with her legs bent that way. Tickling the little metal drops to listen to their jangle, he grinned at Bannack.

"I like the spur music."

"Jinglebobs," Bannack explained. "Most Texans don't wear 'em much, but I like the music. Always take 'em off on the trail, though."

"Why?"

"They're free advertisin' for outlaws and thieves."

"Oh. Well, do girls like the jinglebobs?"

Bannack rolled his eyes but chuckled. "The smart ones do," he said.

"Momma won't never let me keep it," Ryder complained, tracing a finger up the leg to the ample cheek at the top.

"Not if you keep stroking that gal, she won't." Bannack rose and offered his hand. "Come on. We promised your mother I'd have you back by dark."

As he strode to clamber up on Tarantula's back, Ryder stomped his left foot. Pride swelled within his chest at the sound of his brand-new jinglebobs. Maybe Bannack really wouldn't forget him, after all.

CHAPTER 7

# OLD JOLY

*Wheeler household*
*A few weeks later*

For reasons Ryder didn't understand, his mother forbade him from telling his brothers about the five-year arrangement with the cowboy.

"I'll tell them in my own way," she said.

That "way" took two weeks of stalling, and then she blurted out the news over the breakfast table one morning. As the tale unfolded, Alastor's face grew pallid. His gaze, dark and accusing, pinned Ryder to his seat.

"Momma! You're giving us away?" he asked, never taking his eyes from Ryder's face.

"But you'll be together, Alastor, and Mr. Bannack will teach you things I can't. Don't you see? It'll be a better chance at a good life . . . more than your father would've given you."

"Don't talk about Pa like he's dead. He ain't dead! That spoiled little shit shot him, and he ran off. Ryder ought to be in prison."

"Ryder is eleven years old! He was only trying to protect us."

"He wasn't thinking about nobody but himself," Al shot back. "Just 'cause Pa beat him. Well, I'm glad he nailed Ry! Wish he would've blinded him in both eyes!"

"I ain't blind, you mush-brained oyster's ass!"

"Go to hell, Ryder!"

"Stop it!" Molly grasped her second eldest by the shoulders. "It's a gift, Al," she pleaded. "You must look at it that way. That man came into our lives and blessed us with the help we needed. He's paying us up front for your work. You'll have room and board, wages and honest work. You'll—"

"Talk to them," Al interrupted with a gesture toward his brothers. "I ain't going."

"But I promised I'd send you and Posse with Ryder."

"When a woman makes a man pay to bed her, she's called a whore. What the hell's that make you, Momma? What's it called when a woman sells her sons to a man?"

Molly Wheeler's hand flew up in the air, palm upward, ready to strike. Al jerked his head and flinched, waiting for the slap. It never came. She gaped at her hand, then at the all-too-expectant expression on her son's face. She had nearly resorted to Oren's preferred habits—and without thought. Molly lowered her hand.

"Alastor! Don't you *ever* talk to me like that again."

"Yes, Momma," Alastor mumbled. He kept his head low, but his eyes never left Ryder's face. The older brother ground his teeth until Ryder winced at the sound and held his hands over his ears. Al's grinding was more aggravating than a stubborn mule with the chilblains, and he said so.

Alastor smirked at him, stuffed a bite of bread in his mouth, and chewed open-mouthed. Every so often, he glanced at their mother. As soon as she left the room to chase down one of the young'uns, Alastor whirled to Ryder. Lowering his voice to a whisper, lest he be heard, he grasped Ryder by the back of the neck and stomped on his new cowboy footwear.

"Next time you take those precious boots off your feet, I'm gonna give 'em to Davy Jones," he said with a sneer.

"Alastor!" Molly yelled from the doorway. "Leave him alone!"

Al released his grip on Ryder's neck and shrugged. Snatching another piece of bread, he slunk through the door, whistling a tune as he stalked off, slamming the door behind him.

Ryder watched their mother turn her last hope for understanding on Posse, the eldest. He sat at the table, propping his chin in his fists as though afraid his face might slide off. Silent, as usual.

"Posse?" she whispered. Her firstborn sat with his feet tangled in the chair under him.

He sighed and rubbed on his temple. "If that's what you want, Momma, I'll go."

"What else am I to do?" she cried.

"It's okay, Momma. I'll go with Ryder when the time comes. Someone's gotta watch over him. We'll just keep it between us."

Posse was the head of the household now, but that didn't change much. That thin, stony-jawed youth was a young man in his own right, old enough to make it on his own, yet he stayed on. Womenfolk said his gray eyes could write love letters without his hand penning a word. They said he'd be a looker, if he'd ever eat enough to gain weight, but Posse surrendered most of his meals to the younger children. The Wheeler clan called him a peacemaker, but Ryder thought of him as a fixer. When Oren drank or smoked their last cent, Posse went out to make more. Sometimes he'd leave before dawn only to work straight through midnight, trying to fix the things Oren busted. None of it seemed to rattle him. He never yelled, fussed, or complained.

Sometimes Ryder wondered what he thought about. Nothing excited him, not even the prospect of leaving to work for Bannack. Posse, Ryder decided, was *dull*. Maybe Posse read his mind, he didn't know, but his brother's eyes swung to meet him, his face bland of expression.

"Besides, Momma," Posse said, still studying Ryder, "a lot can happen in five years. Something might change between now and then."

"Not for me, it ain't," Ryder retorted. "I'm gonna be a cowboy just like Bannack."

"Do they have one-eyed cowboys up north, Ry?"

Ryder glared at his big brother. "I can see just fine," he growled. It was only partly a lie. Of course he could still see, but Oren Wheeler's knuckles did more damage than they thought. The swelling had gone down, but his vision was no longer sharp on that side. He refused to admit it, but he had to turn his head instead of using the corner of his eye to see beside him.

Ryder excused himself, but before he left, Posse caught his arm.

"I'll go with you, little brother, but as far as Alastor goes, I'd learn to sleep with those boots on if I was you."

⊗

After Alastor's outburst, no one in the Wheeler family spoke of cowboys, ranches, or even mentioned Ryder's new boots, even though he wore the jinglebobs on his spur faithfully. The fragile bond of brotherhood had shifted; Alastor was a tight-lipped ghost who filtered in and out without comment. He spoke little to Molly and regarded Ryder as he would a roach under his shoe. His resentment did not mean he ignored the golden brother, however.

One morning, as Ryder and Les Harold walked to the docks, Les glanced at the stealthy shadow lingering behind them and swore.

"Don't he ever leave you alone?"

Ryder didn't even have to turn to see who his friend was referring to.

"Nope. Still thinks he can pinch my boots, I guess."

"What do you do at night? I'd be awful scared he'd steal them."

"Sleep with my boots on, and the spur too."

"You sleep with your spur?"

"Sure. It ain't easy to do. First night it got tangled and shredded the blanket. Momma was some mad, but she didn't make me take 'em off."

"My momma would have made me throw it out if I'd have done that," Les complained. Ryder didn't doubt that. Mrs. Harold was nice enough but ferocious in cleanliness. The Harolds certainly weren't rich, but they were comfortable.

Thanks to Les's momma, what little the family *did* have was spotless, and always in just the right place.

She hadn't come over to visit with Molly Wheeler more than once—Les said she couldn't stomach the conditions.

"Posse says she can't say much about it 'cause she's obliged to Bannack now," Ryder explained. "Still, now I gotta sleep with a hunk of smelly old leather under my feet so's I don't shred the blanket. Al, he snuck over one time when he thought I was sleepin' and tried to take 'em off me. I kicked him with my heel and the rowel caught his arm and sliced a big ole gash in it."

"What'd he do?"

Ryder shrugged. "Yelled."

"Weren't you scared?"

"Nah, Alastor don't fling nothin' but words. He won't never try to take 'em off me again, neither."

"I wish you never met that cowboy," Les admitted.

Ryder stopped walking to face his friend.

"Why not?"

"Because! In a few years, he'll take you far away and I'll be here by myself. We never had a day apart, Nickel." Hugging his elbows, Les scowled, dragging his heels on the ground. He unearthed a pebble and kicked it with a toe, watching it skitter. Life without his best friend would be colorless.

"Then come with me," Ryder said, rushing to catch up. "You can be a cowboy too, same as me."

"But I don't know how to be a cowboy," Les said. He picked up the pebble and gave it a hard fling. It bounced off the wall of a house, a little too close to the window. Throwing one pebble didn't do much to satisfy the knots in his gut, so he searched for another.

For Ryder, the idea of running away, bound for a new life with his best friend by his side, had already taken root.

"I don't know how, either," he said, "but that don't matter. I expect all you gotta do is stay on a horse. You can balance standin' in a boat, can't you?"

"Sure, but—" Les started to say. As usual, Ryder cut him off.

"Besides, Bannack'll teach us."

"That cowboy?" Les shuddered. "He looked awful mean. Real scary."

Ryder waved his hand, not quite stifling a lopsided grin. "Aww, he's just quiet."

"He broke Dr. Flatt's fingers—all of them—and yanked out his teeth! They say folks had to take him out of town." Les glanced around, as though expecting to see the remains of the unfortunate man still scattered in the road.

"So? He deserved it."

"What if he does that to us?"

It was Ryder's turn to roll his eyes. "Bannack ain't gonna snatch our teeth."

"How do you know?" Les asked, punching his friend in the shoulder. "You only just met him."

"Ugh!" Ryder grabbed his arm, feigning a stagger. "You worry too much. Listen. Alastor don't wanna go. Al might leave me alone if we tell him you'll go instead. You do wanna go, don't you?"

"Well, yeah, if you're going, I do. But my momma won't ever let me."

Ryder groaned. *Why do mommas gotta get in the way of everything fun?* It was like something made them block out joy, sucking every ounce of thrill out of a boy's life. *Are all women like that?* he wondered, *or is it only after they turn into mothers?*

Les wore a pinched-in face, his eyes narrowed into slits. He was miserable. It was a wonder that Mrs. Harold let Les run free with him every day.

"Then we've got five years to change her mind," he said, clasping his friend on the shoulder.

Les shrugged and kicked at a shell lying by his feet. Clearly, he did not hold much hope for success. "Come on," he said. "Let's go watch the boats."

Slipping from vessel to vessel and dodging fishermen, nets, and traps always put a smile on Les Harold's face. He glorified in the sights and sounds of the sea, and of the men who sought their livelihoods from her depths. Growing up in a developing seaport had not altered Les's reverence of the lifestyle. He still loved it, Ryder mused. Les could afford the luxury of his saltwater admiration—he never had to fish with Oren Wheeler.

Where Les got to spend an enjoyable day fishing with his father, Ryder and his brothers were dragged to the boats by a staggering Oren, who fell into a drunken stupor halfway through the trip. And that was on the good days.

With Oren's temper out of the way, the boys were able to help bring in a haul—enough to share with the other fishermen on board. It was the sober trips Ryder hated most. Manhandled for every blunder, they were given the worst jobs to undertake.

One time, while alone in a small two-man craft, Oren gutted his catch right in the boat. Once ashore, he left the boat to bake in the sun with buckets of fish guts overturned inside and forgot about it. A week later, Oren remembered the boat and solicited the nearest son he found. Memories of scrubbing the remains of week-old fish guts and gull shit off the Wheeler family boat still made Ryder's stomach churn and his eyes water. It was the main difference between the two boys; while Ryder begrudgingly humored his friend's seafaring obsession, he would never bring himself to share it. Not anymore.

He followed Les toward *Picaroon*, a vessel bound for open sea. As the fishermen prepared for their trip, one spotted the boys and waved. Encouraged, Les yanked on Ryder's arm, pulling him over to say hello.

"It's Old Joly! He's the one who pulled you from the sea."

"You already told me."

"Maybe he'll let us climb aboard and look around," Les whispered.

Ryder shrugged. He didn't much care for climbing around boats—they were too close to the Mistress. What if she reached up and snatched him into her depths? She might turn over the whole boat just to get to him.

Still, the fisherman had saved his life. He owed him his thanks.

Joly was a tall man, thick with scruff. Years of wind and sun carved his face with cavernous wrinkles, but he had a pleasant smile and friendly eyes that crinkled around the corners. He greeted the boys, but when his eyes fell upon Ryder, his demeanor changed. His eyes sparked and hopped a little, gripping Ryder by the shoulders. Heavy yet heartfelt claps on his arms attested to the sailor's greeting.

"There you are, boy! Ryder, isn't it?"

"Yessir. Thank you for pullin' me out of the water! I ain't seen you 'round to thank you."

"It wasn't an easy task! Davy Jones himself had hold of your leg, boy, and was pulling you under with all his might. Thought sure I was too late, and you was fish fodder."

"*Davy Jones?*" Ryder whispered.

Les sucked in a lungful of sea air. One didn't just say that name aloud, not so close to sea!

"You must bear good luck!" the fisherman said. He bent his head in as though telling a dark secret. "Mind you, most of these seafaring boys can't swim a stroke and would've watched you drown rather than wet their feet. You would've been a sacrifice to the Beast."

"A sacrifice?" Les asked, his mouth gaping open like a codfish.

Ryder knew the story well.

"My . . . uh, Oren told me that story," he said. "If a man falls to the Mistress, a crew might leave him to drown."

"Why?" Les asked, bewildered.

"'Cause if they give him to the sea, she might leave the rest of them alone. Supposed to be like his fate or something."

The fisherman nodded. "That's right. The sacrifice of one might satisfy the sea, keep her from taking a whole crew."

"But that's not right!" Les cried. "He might have died!"

"True, but he didn't—because I was there. I don't tempt fate, but neither do I believe in sacrificing a mere boy to the Mistress, or Davy Jones—either one."

"It was the Mistress," Ryder exclaimed. "She wanted me. My . . . someone told me she was gonna come for me again 'cause I cheated her."

"Well, now there's no proof of that. The sea, she's the only one who knows what she'll do for sure." The fisherman winked.

"She won't get you, Nickel," Les declared. "You're too lucky."

"Nickel?" the fisherman asked, scratching his chin. "What sort of name is that?"

"His real name is Ryder," Les explained. "But I call him Nickel 'cause he's five times luckier than finding a handful of pennies. Always has been."

"That be so?" The lines on Old Joly's forehead crinkled. "A nickel's worth?" the man asked Ryder. A broad grin started at one end of his face and slowly spread to the other.

The boy nodded. "That's what people say."

"Mm, might explain a few things."

"Sir?"

The fisherman patted Ryder's shoulder. "Luck's not been with me, young Nickel. My nets have been emptier than a beggar's belly—traps too. Went back out after pulling you in, and boy, I'm telling you, the fish have returned! Paid off my debts and bought 'er a new sail," he said, gesturing toward the boat. "Sound luck it is, I say! Maybe it's yours?"

"My luck ain't never let me down before," Ryder said, beaming with pride.

The fisherman rolled up his sleeves, squinting from Ryder to his boat, then back again. Ryder grinned, and Les nearly toppled over by the sight of the massive tattoos running from wrist to shoulder on each bulging arm. Tattoos were a common sight around Indianola, but Les's mother hated them. At every opportunity, Mrs. Harold warned the boys of the evils tattoos brought. Ryder loved to listen to her rants—they were always funny. Once, she warned them of how "bad" women were attracted to them. Ryder wanted one ever since.

"You shore got lots of tattoos," he said, studying the pictures on the man's arms.

"Like those, do you, boys?" Joly flexed his muscles so the boys could get a better look.

Ryder did indeed. They were better than the pictures in storybooks, and he said so.

"Likely they're not any stories your momma read you," the man said with a laugh. He flexed his muscle to show off a bare-breasted mermaid spearing a monstrous black-headed sea serpent.

"The Beisht Kione," he said. "Now if that beast had you, Nickel, you'd have been a goner, luck or no."

Terrifying as the inked sea monster was, Ryder was more impressed by the ample breasts of the mermaid.

"How do I get one of those?" he asked.

The fisherman's laughter rang like a raucous bell. "The mermaid, or the ink?" he asked, after half-heartedly subduing his mirth.

"Either one," Ryder replied with a smirk.

"The ink, I can do that. The fine-breasted siren, you'd do well to steer clear of those, boy." He pointed to the coast. "They lure a sailor into the shallows with song and dash his ship against the rocks, they do." Joly's smile vanished. "Many a sailor's skull has been batted about by the tail of a siren. Vengeful she-fish, they are! You'd be lost, boy, if one sank her nails into you. Razor sharp, not like human hands." Joly curled his fingers until they resembled claws and held them over the boys' heads. Les ducked, retreating a few steps.

Ryder just grinned. "I'm not gonna be a sailor, or a fisherman, neither," he declared. "I'm gonna be a cowboy."

"A cowboy, you say?" Joly rocked back on his heels, regarding this new information.

"Yessir!"

"And just where do you mean to cowboy around here? I hope you don't mean to herd seahorses. I won't always be around to pull you from the clutches of the Mistress."

"My friend Bannack's a cowboy. He's gonna hire me to work up north on his ranch. He says I gotta wait five years, though. Look, he bought me boots!" Ryder wiggled his proper leathered toes and jingled the bobs on his gal-leg spur.

"Well, that explains where you got those boots, now don't it? You don't need a boat if you're going to be a horseman, so I guess you needn't worry about the sirens."

"I'd still like one on my arm, like yours." Ryder couldn't tear his eyes away from the unclad woman on Joly's arm. She was beautiful, with dark flowing hair just like Magdalena Hayworth's.

"How old are you, boy?" Joly asked.

"I just turned eleven," Ryder said, holding his head high.

"Ahuh." Joly scratched his stomach and spat a wad of something dark and sticky on the ground. "Got a momma?" he asked.

"Yessir."

The old sailor shook his head and waved his hands in the air. "Now I'll tell you, boy, that Beisht Kione, she's the worst killer of the seas, but I'd rather face her than a fire-breathin' momma bent on skinning my scales for drawing a naked woman—permanent-like—on the arm of her young'un." He chuckled, almost to himself. "No sir, not at eleven."

Ryder's face fell. Didn't he deserve the mark of the sea? He had drowned in the siren's sea and lived to tell the tale. "I earned it, Mister," he said, boldly eyeing Joly with his hands at his waist.

"I expect you did, son. Find me in a few years, before you go to cowboy-ing. I'll do it then if you still want one."

"You'd do that?"

"Sure I would. Your friend want one too?"

They turned to Les, who shook his head so hard his hair slapped him in the face. "No sir! Momma says tattoos are evil!"

Old Joly snorted. "They keep evil away. They protect us, son. Didn't any-body ever explain that to you?"

"No sir! Only my momma, and she—"

"I see. Mommas know best for most everything, but somebody misinformed yours, young man." Joly took off his shirt, revealing more ink than skin on his chest and belly. "I done lived a long life, escaped many a storm. The ink I wear, they're my life stories. They keep me." He pointed to a large star on his chest. "Compass Rose. Leads a sailor home."

"Is that a chicken?" Ryder asked, pointing to a bird on his forearm. "What does that mean?"

"In case of shipwreck," he replied, pushing back a lock of long, stringy hair, "the heavens above will peer down upon a hapless animal flapping in the water and will take the bird into His hand and lead the sailor to safety."

Les shook his head, refusing to believe his mother was wrong all these years. "Momma says proper women cover from neck to ankle—they don't clad about flaunting their skin for men to ogle. Only sinning men cover themselves with pictures like that." He stared at Joly's arms. "But you have ladies all over you for people to see!" he cried. "They don't have dresses on or nothin'!"

Joly's loud guffaws tickled Ryder, who giggled at his friend.

"You listen to your momma too much, Les," he said, grinning.

"But they don't have clothes on!" Les protested with a stamp of his foot. Arguing was one thing, but he didn't like to be laughed at.

Ryder wrapped an arm around his friend's neck until Les chuckled in spite of himself. "Every sailor in Indianola has naked girls tattooed on his arms," he pointed out. "Don't you want to be a sailor someday?"

"Maybe. I don't want one of those, though." He gestured to the siren tattoo on Joly's forearm.

"Do you believe in luck, boy?" Joly asked.

"Yessir. I believe in my friend Nickel."

Joly's eyes twinkled. The old sailor's smile was contagious. "Well, the bosom of a woman calms the sea, lad," he said.

Ryder nodded in mute agreement. Fishermen loved to talk about big-breasted women. It didn't take much time near the ships to learn everything a boy needed to know. Those ample ladies carved into figureheads on the big ships—they shamed the Mistress into suppressing her rage. It was good Les was finally listening to someone who actually knew the sea. Perhaps now he would learn to follow his own mind, not his mother's sharp tongue.

"Don't it hurt?" Les asked, now curious.

"Only where you pierce the skin. It heals up fast enough." The painted fisherman turned back to Ryder with a good-natured grin. "Like I said, come see me in a few years' time and I'll do your ink, boy, if you'll do me a turn now."

"What can I do?"

"Let me buy a nickel's worth of your luck, son."

"You wanna *buy* my luck?" Ryder exchanged glances with Les, who was trying not to giggle. Whoever heard of buying luck? Maybe the ink from all the picture tattoos was seeping into the man's brain somehow.

"I'm about to head out for the day," Old Joly explained. "With a little of your good fortune, you'll bless my boat and she'll bring in another haul."

"I don't know how to bless a boat, sir, but I can try—so long as I don't gotta go in the water." Ryder glared at the offending Mistress and cleared his throat with a raspy cough.

"Don't want to set sail, eh?"

"No," he wheezed. The mere thought of water made his throat close up and his stomach churn.

"Can't say as I blame you there. Cowboys generally don't like boats anyway."

Did cowboys like boats? He supposed they never had much use for one, wherever they came from. He had never heard of a horseman toting a boat around the prairie, anyhow. They certainly weren't in the dime novels Les read to him all the time.

Refusing to admit his limited knowledge on the cowboy's preference of travel, he ducked his head and clambered into Joly's boat. He felt a little silly walking from port to starboard, from stern to bow, running his hands over nets, wheel, and everything in between. Even the meager crew stepped forward, grinning and ribbing, to shake his hand, tousle his hair, or pat his head with brown and blistered hands.

Joly reached inside a dingy old vest pocket and pulled out a handful of coins. He sifted through them with a finger and pulled out two nickels.

"A coin for each."

Lifting his hand, Ryder watched him plant a flat, dull nickel firmly into his palm. He felt sure Les Harold's wide-eyed, slack-jawed expression mirrored his own. Joly clasped his shoulder and smiled. A few of his teeth held a bluish-black hue, a little like the depths of the sea, but his smirk was genuine.

"Come and see me again, boys. If my boat's here, so am I. Thanks for the luck, young Nickel."

Promising to visit again, the boys retreated before Joly could come to his senses and change his mind about spending two whole nickels on an idea as silly as providence. It was a gamble. Everyone knows you never gamble on the sea and still come out ahead.

"Whoever heard of buying luck?" Ryder asked on the run.

Les threw his head back and laughed. "A whole nickel's worth, at that!" he said. The boys tore through the streets, headed straight for the Haller bakery to digest their earnings.

# CHAPTER 8

# THREAT OF THE DEVIL FRUIT

*1873*

Indianola was at her finest. Brilliant pink-and-white flowers still blossomed, even though it was nearing fall. The prolific colors contrasted with the white-shelled streets. Nickel cast a warm gaze over the houses, painted blue, yellow, green, and white, and heaved a sigh. It was a picturesque town—the kind artists flocked to, canvases in hand. He hadn't noticed its charm when he was younger, for it was all he knew.

Three years ago, when Bannack came and offered him the deal, it was all he wanted. To cowboy. To grow up just like his storybook heroes. They were cowboys too, but only one came close to Bannack in his eyes. Mustang Grey, the hero of his favorite dime novel. To have a life like theirs? He would have traded anything. Hell, he *did* trade everything to live a life like theirs. Only thing was, at ten years old, he didn't comprehend what he had.

In the old days, there was no seeing past the loathing of Oren Wheeler and the hunger pains that plagued them. Now that Oren was gone, the brothers held jobs, bringing home money without Oren pilfering it away. When his feet began to outgrow his boots, Bannack made him send a tracing of his feet so he could send him a brand-new pair—handmade on the Middle C, just for him. They had food and, combined with the money Bannack sent from time to time, they fixed up their house and painted it bright blue, his mother's favorite color. With the painted house, peace settled over his family, save for one.

Alastor Wheeler still hadn't forgiven his part in the deal with the cowboy and claimed Nickel had signed their souls away to the devil. It was a ridiculous notion. Bannack was a good man, but now, Nickel wondered if his wayward brother was right—at least in part. Perhaps he had acted rashly. Three years ago, he understood nothing of what he had to leave behind him.

Now, Indianola was his universe. The town loved him as much as he loved them. Old Joly said no matter where he set his sail, his ship would always turn course for home—Indianola, the gem of Texas. He likened it to a tropical paradise, something Nickel knew nothing about, but he believed the old sailor.

He turned his head toward the breeze and inhaled. Ocean. Sweet, salty air and the heady fragrance of oleander. He watched the gulls cry and dive, fluttering over the edge of town where the fishermen were off-loading their catches. Two more years, and he'd have to leave.

For a moment, something akin to panic seized him. He couldn't go! How would he ever say goodbye to his hometown? To the people he loved? And for what—a place he'd never seen? Maybe he could tell Bannack he changed his mind; he could always try to pay him back. But as the notion entered his mind, he shook his head, dismissing it at once.

*No. I ain't Oren Wheeler. I ain't my brother, neither. I won't go back on a promise, no matter what.*

"Damn," he muttered under his breath. "I hope the next two years go by slow."

Thoughts of saying goodbye to his beloved Indianola turned Nickel's route down the familiar street to call on Magdalena Hayworth. He rounded the street corner, heading to her family's hotel, and ran smack into Alastor with a group of his friends. The brothers sneered at one another.

"Watch it, you little sellout." He spit the words.

"Oh, come on, can't you do better'n that? Figured by now you'd come up with somethin' new to call me." Nickel stifled a mock yawn.

Alastor responded with a slew of his father's words and boxed Nickel in the ear. He retaliated with a quick jab of the elbow into his brother's chest but was grabbed by Alastor's oafish buddies and yanked into an alley. One wrenched his arms behind his back, pinning the thirteen-year-old in place. His brother grabbed Nickel by the jaw, thrusting his face in his own.

"I been thinkin' 'bout what you done, signin' us away to that damned cowboy devil. If I was you, I'd write that sonofabitch and tell him you done changed your mind."

"Hah!" Nickel sneered. "Nothin' doin'!"

"You don't, and I'll bring hell to that hero of yours."

Ryder scoffed. "Like you could ever hurt him!"

Alastor grinned. "There's things you don't know, little brother. Lots of things. Call him off."

"Go to hell," Nickel said.

"I'm not leavin' this town, baby brother."

"Les'll go in your place."

"You ain't changed his momma's mind in three years! What makes you think she'll change in two more?"

"She will. She's gotta."

Alastor spit in his face.

Nickel jerked, but his brother's friends were stronger and held him in check. A wad of saliva trickled down his cheek, and he twitched, wanting to free his hands if only to wipe it off.

"You think you're so great," Alastor said, a twisted snarl painted across his lips. "Golden boy of Indianola. Everybody loves you. They say you're so damn lucky, but might be your luck's gonna run out, you ever think about that?"

Nickel screwed his lips back, a sneer plastered on his face. "Can't happen. It protects me."

"Oh, I'm bettin' it can. Tell me, little brother, just how far can that golden luck of yours reach?"

"What do you mean?"

"I mean, can your providence, fortune, whatever Momma calls it—can it protect that cowboy friend of yours?"

Nickel lunged against the older boys holding him, sensing a threat.

"What if he don't never show?"

"He'll show," Nickel said through clenched teeth.

"What if somethin' was to happen to him?" Alastor asked. "He could get kicked by a horse or scalped by an Indian. Hell, somebody might just up and shoot him in the back. Two years is a long time to worry whether your hero's just been kilt. I guess you oughta call him off, L Bee."

"Damn you to hell, Alastor!" Nickel yelled. L Bee. Little Brother. He ignored the baby name his brothers used when they wanted to rile him. What he refused to do was ignore the threat to Bannack's life—even if it came from Alastor.

"Watch your mouth," Alastor chided, drawing back a fist and connecting with a right hook to Nickel's jaw. He fell backward into the pair of fools holding him. "Hold him down! I'm takin' those damned boots."

Nickel laughed aloud. "You're just as Momma says—jealous! You can't stand it. I've got things better'n you. *I am* better'n you. Go ahead and try it. Take 'em." He glowered, his eyes fevered in their intensity.

Alastor froze, slowly lifting his head as Nickel offered his foot.

"Take 'em off," he growled, low in his throat. "I dare you."

"Why?" Alastor snapped the word in the air, but it held a ring of uncertainty.

"You been tryin' to swipe 'em off me for years. Do it." His muscles tensed, body rigid, as though a fearsome beast ready to spring. It was impossible, for Alastor's friends held him down, and yet . . .

Alastor rolled his eyes from side to side, expecting one of Nickel's signature tricks. He held onto the heel of his boot but quit tugging. Nickel grinned at his brother's discomfort.

"And you're just gonna let me?" he asked.

"Do I look like I'm fightin'?" Nickel offered his other foot, but Al just stared at the boot. Furrows creased his brow, and Nickel laughed at him.

"I don't need to fight," he said. "I done told you. My luck protects me. Protects my friends too. If anybody ever tried to hurt Bannack or my friends, they'd be dodgin' a curse as black as Davy Jones's heart."

Alastor dropped his foot. "You sayin' you'll curse me?"

"I guess you listen after all."

"Hah! You don't scare me, L Bee."

"Then how come my boots are still on my feet?" Nickel asked. Alastor shifted, clenching and unclenching his fists. While he considered the situation, Nickel untangled himself from his brother's moronic friends and stood up. His jaw throbbed from where Al punched him, but it didn't matter. He held the winning hand.

"I curse your fool head, Alastor Wheeler," he said, circling his wary brother. "You've had the last of sound luck. So have they," he said, pointing at both of the older boys. Wide-eyed, they fell over one another in their haste to retreat to a safer distance lest Nickel act upon his threat to bestow bad luck.

"Aww get back here, he's only bluffin'!" Alastor shouted after his buddies.

Nickel snorted. "You lose friends fast," he said.

"So will you if you don't listen to me."

*That's it!* Nickel lunged forward, tossing caution aside, and threw his weight into his fist. He cracked Alastor in the jaw, yelling as he doubled his fists for his brother's attack.

"Ain't nobody shootin' Bannack in the back, you hear me? Nobody!"

"You little shit!" His brother came at him with both fists. Nickel held his ground, taking punches and returning them twofold. The fight would have been fair, had Alastor not called for his friends to jump in. Deeming three against one a fair deal, they obliged, driving Nickel to the ground.

Yanking him up by his neck, Alastor propelled him forward.

"I'm gonna drown that luck right outta you," he said with a snarl.

Nickel perceived the truth—it was no idle threat. Like Oren, he was capable of anything so long as it didn't require a lot of brainpower. They hauled him, kicking and fighting, to the beach and dumped him deep in the surf. He tried to rise, but Al held him down by the neck, jamming his knees into his back. Waves rushed over Nickel's head, and he struggled against the hands pinning him down.

"Call him off!" Alastor yelled.

"No!"

Three sets of hands shoved his face under water, but only one pair held him there. She reached watery hands into his mouth, gushing down his throat, and he clamped his lips together. He knew better than to yell. If he opened his mouth again, the Mistress would climb inside.

*Breathe through your nose. Don't panic. Breathe through your nose. He'll let me up—he's just tryin' to scare me.*

Only . . . he didn't.

Wave after wave crashed over his head. Kicking out with his legs, Nickel jerked his head from side to side but could not shake the death grip of his brother's hands. They were harsh and strong, harnessing the hatred burning within his dark soul.

*He's killing me!*

Realization hit hard. His own brother meant murder, using the one force that struck terror in Nickel's heart. The Mistress had him once. This time, she might not be denied.

He flailed, his memory conjuring up memories of his first drowning. The burning, the pain, then the weightlessness as his body solidified.

No breath. Rational thought ceased. He didn't feel his brother's hands jerking him about in the water, trying to finish the job. Death nibbled at the corners of his mind, and he quit kicking.

Then, strong hands grasped his arms and pulled him from the waves.

"Breathe, boy! Breathe!" A fist beat upon his back, but Nickel was already coughing up seawater, wheezing and sucking in air. "Easy, Nickel. Cough 'er out."

Joly.

He grabbed a tattooed arm and pulled himself up. The waves rushed at his shaking legs, but the water was not deep enough to knock him off his feet. Bending at the waist, he spat into the water and closed his eyes until the panic settled. Joly had him by the shoulders. He was talking, but Nickel listened to the tone, not the words.

With the old sailor's instruction in his ear, Nickel wobbled in the water, heading for the beach.

His brother tried to kill him. The thought pounded in the back of his throat like a mantra. *Murderer. My brother's a murderer!* Flesh and blood meant little when you hated enough to drown your own sibling.

Alastor was in the sand, fighting two large fishermen who held him between them as they would a child with a tantrum.

"I'll finish you!" he screamed over and over. "Gonna finish that cowboy too!"

Gasping like a beached flounder, Nickel tilted his head and took a small step forward. The tide shoved against him, nearly knocking him off his feet. He stumbled sideways, and something washed up against his skin. Thinking fish were swimming around him, he looked down at his feet and stifled a yell.

Bananas. Bunches of them were washing up around his legs. Panic threatened to bubble up within his breast, but he remembered Bannack's lesson. His hero wouldn't be afraid of a bunch of bananas, no matter how bad an omen they were.

When he pointed down, Joly grabbed at him to run, but he stood his ground, pushing his old friend toward shore.

"I'm okay," he rasped.

Driven by the old knowledge that bananas caused sailor's deaths and shipwrecks, Joly bounded out of the water to the safety of the beach. Nickel's mind was returning. Here was his retaliation.

He scooped up a bunch of spotted brown fruit, staggered to shore, and walked straight up to his brother. The fishermen yelled at him to toss out the devil fruit, but he held them in front of Alastor's face, grinning his infamous grin.

"Look what you done," Nickel said. "By tryin' to kill me, you sealed your fate. The Mistress, she's thrown bad luck at you. You're marked now." The rasp was back in his voice. He coughed and spit a wad of seawater at his murderous brother.

"Why won't you just *die?*" Alastor screamed. Rage and its eternal brother, hatred, carved every line and every curve of his face. Spit flew from his mouth when he yelled, but Nickel would not be cowed.

"Ain't nobody gonna stop me from livin' my life," he declared. Nickel's voice was waterlogged, but the rasp only made him sound tougher. "Not you. Not her, neither," he said, gesturing to the ocean.

"Another damn minute, and I would've," Alastor said.

"Touch me again, and the Sea . . . she'll kill you. Then *you'll* see how it feels to drown." Nickel spoke with the authority of experience.

"The sea ain't gonna kill me," Alastor said. His nostrils flared, and sweat dripped from his chin.

"If she don't, I will," Nickel warned, twisting his mouth into a smile. His big brother's eyes bulged—Alastor was afraid.

"It's you she wants, L Bee."

"Is it? I'm bettin' it's you." He dropped the bananas at his brother's feet. The fishermen released Alastor and ran, yelling something about demon fruit. His brother backed up a few steps, eyeing the spotted brown produce sent from the sea.

"You shot Pa," Alastor said. "You made Momma sign us over to the devil. I hate you, Ryder Wheeler."

"I hate you too," rasped the reply.

"Guess I'll see you at home." Nickel took the odd reply for what it was—a veiled threat, and a thin one, at that.

"You'll see me, but you ain't gonna touch me."

"This ain't over, L Bee."

"Look at the water." Nickel pointed again to the bay and the ocean beyond. He looked, and Nickel followed his gaze. Splintered bits of what appeared to be wooden crates were washing on shore with masses of bananas in various forms of decay. Shifting from side to side, he glowered at the little brother who refused to die. One more glance at the fruit-laden beach, and Alastor Wheeler walked away.

As Nickel looked on, a frightened girl with tresses the color of Indian ink ran down the beach toward them. She stopped in front of Alastor. The exchange was brief. Before he said a word, she reared back and slugged him in the mouth with her fist, spit in his face, and left him in the lurch.

*That'a girl, Mags!* He grinned with pride when she called his name and ran into his arms.

"I guess I love you for that, Magdalena Hayworth."

# CHAPTER 9

# THE BEAST THAT GROWS

J oly's shack sat by itself, built on the shifting sands of his own little corner of the Texas coast. Nickel often stayed there when Joly was at sea, eager to escape the chaos of his siblings and their constant din. He liked to sit on the front porch and watch the Mistress ebb and flow. Much as he distrusted her and refused to voyage out to sea, he loved the crash of the waves, the call of the gulls. They filled him with a longing he could not grasp. Why was he restless for the open water? To go meant his death. He did not want to leave beautiful Indianola, yet neither was he meant for this seafarer's life.

Even now, damp and shaking from his latest drowning, he felt the pull of the ocean and what lay beyond. He turned from the glimmering water, and his gaze found Magdalena's eyes brimming with tears.

"Aww, hey, Mags, what's wrong?"

"I'm afraid for you, Ryder," she whispered. "Your brother nearly killed you!"

*Beautiful Mags, still refusing to use anything but my old nickname.*

"Almost," Nickel said aloud. "He threatened Bannack too. And I been sittin' here thinkin' how maybe I need to send him a wire. I don't know what Al could do, but I oughta warn him."

"You sound more worried about that cowboy than yourself."

He studied the contours of her face while he formed a suitable reply. Magdalena was always beautiful, but these three years had transformed her. Her cheekbones were now more defined, her eyes brighter, hair longer, and her curves . . . He ran a finger across his lip and smiled. The lovely girl who stole his heart long ago had blossomed into a young woman before his eyes. And she was his.

"Ryder," she called, snapping him out of his reverie. "Are you listening to me?"

"You wanna know if it worries me," he said. She nodded, and he brushed a lock of her dark, unruly hair from her face.

Of course it worried him. He was living under the same roof as a brother who would rather kill him than leave Indianola. Nickel had been mistaken in thinking Al didn't have murder in his heart. He recognized him for what he was now: a shadow version of Oren Wheeler.

Would he try again? Possibly—but Nickel also considered Alastor's yellow streak. He was brave—when he thought he had the upper hand. That, and a lot of backup. But, Alastor was also a coward. Fear of life or limb almost always sent him on the dodge.

Perhaps Nickel's threat of eternal bad luck would keep him at bay. Maybe. Before he voiced his concerns, Old Joly intervened.

"Your girl's right, Nickel," he said. The sailor appeared from his shack, carrying a small box in both hands. As he spoke, he sat down on a small, three-legged stool and flipped open the lid. "You can't give that brother of yours another chance," Joly said, rummaging through the contents inside his box. "He'll take it, and I won't always be around to pull you out of the sea." He paused, scratching at his dark, wiry beard, and frowned at the mashed crates still washing up on the beach.

"Evil's been declared today, boy. It's an ill wind blowing that devil's fruit at us. Might be a warning to you."

"Warnin'? For what? Alastor?" Nickel asked.

"Maybe so, boy." Joly, finding his pipe, slammed the lid shut on the little box and dumped it by his side.

"Mr. Joly?" Magdalena asked. "I thought bananas washing up on the beach meant we lost a ship?"

"And that's not bad luck to you, young lady?" He huffed as he pulled the makings of his pipe out of a grungy little leather pouch worn around his neck, and lit it. "You're right enough," he said. "A ship was lost out there, somewhere. What did they expect, carrying black luck in the hold? Bananas mean death to a sailor, girl. No crew ought to face transporting deadly cargo! Cursed fruit!"

Joly drew a long, rattled breath, puffed on his pipe, and closed his eyes as if to steel his nerve.

"The bananas could have washed up anywhere," Magdalena said. She bit her lip as she usually did when something bothered her. Nickel watched her, wishing Joly would walk away so he could lean in and try to bite it for her. "Do you really think it was because of Ryder?" Magdalena asked the sailor.

He met her question with silence. Joly took his time smoking his pipe and knocked the ash out on his foot. Only then did he look at Nickel. "There's something about you. Might be a blessing, but might be a curse too. I see the good in you, son. Always have. But there's something else too. You share Oren's blood. Alastor's too."

Nickel's face darkened, and his lip curled into a cruel snarl.

"And there it is," Joly said, poking a bony finger against his breastbone. "Deep down. You've got the makings of a monster inside you, boy, and I guess the Beisht herself would be some scared if you was to let it out."

"A monster? *Me?*" Nickel blinked, furrowing his brow. "I guess I don't figure what you mean."

"Yes you do, boy. It was there when you threatened to kill your brother. Rage. How many times did you feel that rage before?"

"He meant to drown me!" Nickel protested, ignoring the old man's question.

Joly nodded. "Got something I want you to have, boy." He stepped inside the back door and opened some trunks, tossing his gear and grumbling.

His interest piqued, Nickel watched his old friend search for the object from the security of the porch where flying articles weren't likely to hit him in the head. Joly groused like an old bear with a passel of cubs clambering over his back. Looking for lost items was not his strong suit, but after nearly destroying the inside of his shack, Joly let out a boorish yell.

"Hah!" he exclaimed. "There it is! Nickel, take off your boots."

Nickel puffed his chest and shook his head. "No sir! I ain't takin' off my boots!"

"I won't be hurting them, boy." Joly handed him a six-inch double-edged dagger, handle first. Nickel's eyes widened as he grasped the smooth wooden handle. It fit his palm well, and he lifted his hand to study the blade.

"Balanced," Joly said. "The maker knew his fire when he forged that blade. It'll serve you well, should you need protection."

"You just called me a monster!" Nickel cried. "Now you're givin' me a dagger?" He glanced at Mags, but the girl just shrugged. She didn't understand it, either.

"The beast that grows is the one you feed," Joly said, patting Nickel's hand that still clutched the handle.

The boy shook his head. "I don't . . . are you sayin' I'm s'posed to kill Alastor with it?"

"That's up to you. Either way, you better carry that blade on you. If your luck ever fails, she'll be there. I'll show you how to use it. Now take off your boots, and I'll sew a sheath inside. No one needs to know you're armed, not unless they force your hand."

Returning the blade, Nickel bit his lip as he tugged off his boots. "I ain't supposed to take 'em off," he said, jingling the little bells on his single spur.

"That Bannack fellow won't know the difference," Joly said. "Won't take me but a few minutes, anyway. You go on, boy. You aren't a cowboy yet, so you put some good ole Indianola sand between your toes. Take your girl to the bakery, or buy her an ice cream at the saloon. Court on her a little. Let 'er calm your nerves. I'll have your boots done when you come back."

Nickel hesitated. Alastor was always after his boots—he hated to leave them behind, even with Joly.

Still, strolling through Indianola with Magdalena was a temptation too great to resist. She smiled at him, shyly offering her hand. He accepted, grasping her fingers in his own, and grinned. He felt a little better already.

They walked hand in hand until they reached the heart of the town, where the wrong pair of eyes might report Magdalena's hand-holding back to her father.

It was strange, traipsing in bare feet again after so many years of leather soles. His feet found every pebble and he curled his toes, hoping Mags wouldn't notice his awkward gait.

On the way to the new ice-cream saloon, people greeted them with friendly smiles and kind words. Nickel walked a little taller for the praise bestowed upon his head. Several fishermen stopped them to press a coin in his hand, asking for a blessing for their catch.

"You're famous, Ryder," Magdalena exclaimed. "Everyone loves you."

"What's not to love?" he asked with a wink. She laughed, soft, and Nickel's pulse accelerated. With luck money in his hand, he escorted her into the soda parlor and bought her the biggest ice cream his luck money afforded. Raspberry.

They sat at a little table away from the big picture window, choosing seats in the back so Nickel could keep his back to the wall. His freedom was over—and caution was never his strong suit. Now he needed to be always looking over his shoulder, listening, watching. Waiting. Alastor would not quit, but he was underhanded; he would wait for when Nickel's back was turned.

He nibbled on his ice cream, his eyes searching the crowd of people for his murderous brother, when Magdalena spoke.

"What do you suppose Joly meant?" she asked.

"About what?"

"Comparing you to a monster."

Nickel waved his hand in the air. He couldn't begin to understand what Joly meant half the time he spoke, but this? It was strange talk. The way the old man looked him in the eye sent shivers down his spine. Bananas washed ashore, Joly reminding him about sharing his father's—and his brother's— wicked blood . . . it knotted an already queasy stomach, and he coughed. *Was* he capable of becoming just like them?

Magdalena pulled her chair closer and changed the subject.

"You coughed like that the first time you drowned. I remember."

"I ain't sure I'll ever get the seawater out. Hurts to breathe, sometimes."

"You won't ever be a sailor, will you?" she asked.

"You know I won't."

She covered his hand with her own and squeezed it. A few drops of raspberry ice cream decorated her skin, and he wiped it off with his thumb and licked it from his finger.

"Mmm, good!" he said, letting the taste of the sweet berries melt over his tongue. "Maybe I should've gotten raspberry too." He glanced down at the delectable chocolate in his glass.

"Do you think I'd be a good sailor?" she asked.

He abandoned his ice cream to stare at her, puzzled by the question.

"What do you mean? You're too pretty to be like one of those crusty old men."

"What's it like out there, Ryder? Out there on the sea? Just you, the crew, the wind, and the horizon?"

He shook his head. "The Mistress, she's out there too. Always. It's beautiful though," he admitted. "Ain't nothin' like a sunset over the water."

"I wish I could see it. Sailing the sea, I think you must become part of it."

"You see it from the beach every night."

"It's not the same," Mags said with a frown. "That would be like you watching a herd of horses, knowing you were never allowed to ride one."

"I know you love the water," he said, "but I shore didn't realize you wanted to sail so bad."

She nodded. "I do. Sometimes I dream about stealing a boy's clothes, cutting my hair, and sneaking onto one of the big ships."

Nickel jerked so fast he nearly spilled his dish, and his spoon clattered to the floor.

"You can't do that, Mags! It's bad luck!" he exclaimed, wide-eyed.

"Shh! People are looking!" she whispered, a bit too loudly. "And why not? Because I'm a girl?" She stuffed her hands on her hips and glared at him, daring him to argue.

The thought of her posing as a boy, sneaking aboard a ship and setting sail—his insides grew hot, and he wiped his brow. If she did that, he would lose her!

"Yes! Because you're a girl!" He picked up his spoon, glanced at it, and rubbed it on his shirt. Magdalena wrinkled her nose when he replaced the utensil in his ice cream.

"I understand everyone thinks women are bad luck aboard," she admitted, "but I can't fathom why! Sometimes I wish I were a boy. Like you—free to go wherever I wanted. I'd sail around the world, just like Joly. I want to see those places he talks about. How do people live on the other side of the water, Ryder? Don't you want to know?"

"I guess same as us, mostly, only their beach is probably facing the other way. They talk funny too, so I hear."

"And they say you are the adventurous one!" Magdalena tried to sound scolding, but she sympathized with Nickel's panic, for she tugged at his sleeve and gifted him with a teasing smile.

Nickel chuckled. "I'd sail with you, Mags, if I had a mind to go," he said. "Don't make no difference to me, you bein' a girl, but I'm not goin' out there. The Mistress, she'd kill me. I feel it in my chest every time I get too close to her."

"Then you shouldn't go. I would never forgive myself if she took you. It's too bad, though. You and I sailing around the world together? It's my dream, Ryder. Nearly every night. I wish I had a place to stash them away."

"Your dreams? You mean like a box?"

"Yes. Some place safe, where I can just lift the lid and pull them out any time I please."

"Mm. And . . . you dream about me?" he asked, waggling his eyebrows.

She smiled a forlorn little smile and ate a big bite of her ice cream. "Don't you?"

She needn't ask. He touched a lock of her hair and wound it around his fingers. Magdalena Hayworth was no cowering heart with stolen touches. Her beam told him everything he wanted to know. Of course he dreamed about her! Every waking moment of the day. Every night too, and he told her so.

There was no flushed face with the knowledge, only that bright, encouraging smile.

"One day soon, Magdalena, I'm gonna show you what it's like to sail in *my* world."

"When?"

"Soon, I swear."

She tilted her head and nibbled on her lower lip.

Emboldened by the touch of her hand on his arm, he ducked across the table and kissed her cheek. Onlookers be damned.

"I'm gonna marry you one day, Mags."

"You're spilling your ice cream," she told him.

"I mean it, beautiful."

"It would be a sad waste of chocolate."

"Mags . . ."

She pulled his glass out of harm's way and took a bite of his dessert. Her eyes closed slowly, and she exhaled with a faint smile painted across her lips. When the bite was gone, she frowned and offered him her glass.

"Switch?"

He laughed, reaching for the raspberry.

"I swear, Mags, I knew you wanted what I got."

She stuck out a chocolate-coated tongue at him.

"I mean it, what I said," he told her. It was the only thing he was certain of: Magdalena would always be his. He needed her to understand the depths of his admiration.

"Yes, Ryder. I heard you. Are . . . are you going to kill your brother?" She faltered over the words, and her fingers trembled. Nickel guessed it wasn't the sweet, cold cream making her shiver.

"What's that gotta do with you and me?"

"He scares me. I don't want anything to happen to you. It almost did, twice now. My daddy says you're too dangerous. He also says you're too young for me."

"That's an excuse 'cause he don't like me. You're only a year or two older'n me," Nickel said.

"True. I don't suppose he'd care, either, except that he doesn't like you. My mother is the one who allows me to be with you."

"It's my family, ain't it? Why your daddy hates me?"

She confirmed his suspicion with a nod.

Nickel frowned. He supposed he shouldn't blame Mr. Hayworth for not liking the Wheeler clan. The two men had words once. That night, Oren broke into Hayworth's warehouse, robbing him of a few hundred dollars' worth of goods and setting fire to everything he couldn't carry off. The job was quick and undetected—since no one saw Oren do it, he went unpunished.

Nickel knew the truth, and so did the Hayworth family. To her credit, Magdalena never once blamed him for his father's crime, even though the financial strain put her father at odds with the local bankers. If they hadn't opened their home to feed guests and grant them lodging—

"It's not my fault," Nickel said with a sniff. The girl linked her fingers through his, sidling against him as they finished their ice creams.

"You're right," she said. "It isn't your fault. I don't care what my father says, or Joly or anybody else. You are no monster, and it's not fair that people blame you for your family's sins!"

"Now who's gettin' loud?" he asked, nodding at the folks who appraised them from the soda counter.

"But it's not fair! First it was your own father, now Alastor," she said with a growl. "Why don't they leave you alone?"

"It's okay, Mags."

"No! I just . . . well, if you will promise yourself to me, I guess you should stay alive to see it through. How will you do that living with a brother who wants you dead? I'm scared, Ryder."

"You're like a swan," he told her. "Beautiful. Swans, they always reminded me of you. Graceful birds, my momma says, but strong enough to break a man when they're mad. I like it, how you always got me under your wing, you realize that?"

He shot her his best grin, but she looked away.

"Come on, Mags, smile. When've I not been okay? My luck holds me—"

"And you've been selling it away for three years!"

"It won't run out, darlin'. I swear."

"I'll feel better when you learn to use Joly's knife."

"I got the dagger on my side, and I got you too. Don't I?"

She smiled again, at last. "Yes, Ryder. Always."

"Good. Just don't spread those big white wings and fly away on me, okay?"

# CHAPTER 10
# CINNABAR DREAMS

The shadow hovered overhead, alerting him to the reality of his mistake—he hadn't been paying attention to the doorway of the ice-cream saloon.

Nickel clenched a fist under the table and turned his head. The shadow belonged to a bearded man taller than a church steeple. It was necessary to tilt his jaw upward to peer into the shadow's face.

*Aww, shit.* Hayworth. Magdalena's father hovered over their table, his arms folded across a barreled chest, glaring at Nickel with enough frost to freeze Matagorda Bay.

"Hi, Daddy," Magdalena purred.

"What've I told you about that boy?" he asked, refusing to take his eyes off Nickel.

"Howdy, Mr. Hayworth," Nickel said, offering his hand.

He ignored it. "I don't like you, boy. You aren't near good enough for my daughter."

"Well, shore, I'd agree with you, sir, but only 'cause I figure ain't nobody good enough for Mags."

"Magdalena, you're done here." Hayworth's voice rose as he grabbed his daughter's arm, inviting the other patrons and the shop owner to look up and watch.

She started to protest, but Nickel shook his head. If she put up a fight now, Hayworth would never let him see her again.

"Don't mean no disrespect, sir," he said. "We was just havin' ice creams."

"I see. And who paid for them?"

"I did, sir."

"With your own money?"

"Yessir."

Hayworth's scowl deepened. Disbelief was etched in every line of his hard-edged face.

"Get up, Magdalena."

She rose, and Nickel winced at the anger in his eyes.

*Don't do it, Mags. Don't buck your daddy. Not now!* He stood slowly, wishing he were at least tall enough to look Hayworth in the eye like a man, instead of staring at his angry, purple throat.

"Where did you get the money, boy? Steal it?"

Nickel's jaw clenched, but he held fast to his temper, lest it flare out of control.

"No sir. I ain't no thief."

"Of course you are. You're a Wheeler." Taking his daughter by the shoulder, he turned her toward the door.

"Sir?" Nickel called after them. They turned, and he rose to his full height, holding his chin high. "I know you think I ain't much, but I ain't like Oren Wheeler. He wasn't no good, and I'm glad he's gone. Mags, I reckon she's the best part of my life, and I'd shore like to come callin' on her." He held to Hayworth's gaze, even when the older man's eyes narrowed.

"Not in my house, you're not! Besides, aren't you supposed to be leaving soon?" He waggled his fingers, as if to shoo Nickel away.

"That ain't for another two years."

"And what happens when you have to leave and break my girl's heart?"

Nickel was getting tired of people sneering at him. He'd had enough ugliness poked in his face, what with Alastor and the Mistress. He wanted to show Hayworth what he was made of, but a glance at the angry tears welling in Mags's eyes checked him.

"I don't plan on breakin' it," he replied, keeping his voice low and even. "I figure me and her, we'll—"

"No! Hell no!" Hayworth wrapped his arm around Magdalena but pointed his finger at Nickel. "I won't have that Wheeler boy in my house, girl. You hear me?" Hayworth was nearly shouting. For a minute, he looked as though he might strike. If he did, so be it. Nickel waited. He held no fear of being punched or hit; he would stand any beating to win Mags to his side.

Hayworth relaxed a little, though his shoulders were still rigid. "Come, girl."

Magdalena looked mad enough to pin back the gills of a shark and swallow it whole, but Nickel grinned and winked at her. It was all right. He was still grinning when they walked out, Hayworth leading a fuming daughter by the arm like a child. They passed Les Harold coming in, and he turned to watch them as he entered.

"What was all that about?" he asked, craning his neck to watch them disappear down the street.

Nickel stared down the gawking patrons until they remembered a modicum of shame and resumed their own business. Then he answered. "Hayworth don't like me much. I asked him to call on Mags, anyhow."

"You *what?*" Les stared at him, his mouth slack-jawed. "You been touched in the head? What's wrong with you? That old bastard hates you!" He rubbed his head, a nonverbal reminder that Nickel's antics often gave him a headache.

Nickel paid him no mind. "Shore does." He leaned on the table with his and Magdalena's glasses, gazing out the window, and laughed. "He shore was mad," he said.

"Then why are you smiling? He didn't say yes, did he?"

"Nope. Swore at me."

"But you're happy." Les sounded tired.

"Yep. He forbid Mags from havin' me in his house. He didn't say nothin' 'bout the rest of the town."

Les groaned. "Dammit, Nickel," he said. "It's shore hard work bein' friends with you."

He turned to face his friend, and Nickel stepped back and swore. Les was sporting a brand-new bruise over his eye. It was darkening. Nickel looked again and realized Les's jaw was puffy and swelling, someone split his lip, and he held his arm at an awkward angle, cradling it in his other hand.

"What got a hold of you?" he asked, placing a hand on his friend's back. Nickel tilted Les's jaw, turning his head back and forth to better see the damage. How could Les get into a fight without *him?*

"Ran into Alastor. He crowed over what he did, so I hit him." Les showed his fist, which was far too soft to be tangling with the likes of a Wheeler. Nickel figured even his little sister Hera could beat Les in a fight, if she really wanted to.

"Aww, Les! Dammit, you ain't no good at fightin'! You can't take him on by yourself!"

Les hung his head with a wince. "I was mad!" he exclaimed. "I wanted to beat his brains in."

"He don't got none to beat." Nickel fingered Les's jaw and clicked his tongue, wishing Bannack were here with his foul-smelling, healing sludge.

"Yeah, well, maybe not, but he throws an awful punch. Told me he'd let me go, so I'd give you his warning. He says he'll wait until your back's turned, and do what you done to Oren."

Nickel downed the last bite of raspberry ice cream, set the glass down, and strode through the door to the street, pulling Les after him.

"Come on," he said. "We're goin' to go see Joly. He's gonna teach me how to kill my brother. Besides, I gotta get my boots back 'fore Alastor learns they're off my feet."

03

Old Joly was true to his word. When he returned, the sailor had sewn a leather sheath inside his boot, securing the blade against his foot. It made the boot fit tighter, but Joly promised it would soften with wear. A little discomfort, he reasoned, was better than dying at the hands of Alastor Wheeler. Of course he was right, and the blade did offer a bit of comfort. Better yet when he learned to use it.

With his enemy living under the same roof, Joly deemed it imperative to give Nickel his first lesson at once. He showed him how to hold and sharpen the dagger, how to pull from the boot with unerring speed, and even where to sink the blade, should he need it.

Les stood by and watched the lesson with infallible interest. Joly even gave him a few turns with it. It intrigued Les, but he was out of sorts from his fight with Alastor and soon went home.

"Might be wise to get Les a weapon too," Joly told Nickel. "He's a loyal friend to back you like he done."

"He ain't much of a fighter," Nickel replied.

"I saw that. Now pull the dagger again."

After his first lesson handling his brand-new dagger, Nickel pressed his luck. He had a weapon, but there was something else he needed. Something no self-respecting seafarer went without. He voiced his demand, and the old sailor studied him with a twinkle in his eye and chuckled.

"You remind me of somebody I knew once," he said.

"You?" Nickel asked.

"My son."

"You got a son?" Nickel tilted his head. "I didn't know that. Where is he?"

"Oh, he's out there somewhere," Joly said, waving his hand across the bay and the ocean beyond. "Took after me, bless his poor momma's soul. Turns up every few years. Captain of a new ship."

It was all he said, and Nickel didn't push. When not at sea, Old Joly was happiest when he was reliving his life through tall tales. He spun wonderful lies and truths, all at once, enthralling his listeners. But of all those stories he told Nickel, none of them mentioned his son. There was something bitter about the pragmatic way he mentioned his own flesh, something that stopped Nickel from asking more. Bad blood, maybe?

He studied the old sailor but forgot the subject when he procured an ornate box carved with intricacies the likes of which Nickel had never seen.

"This came from Asia," he said, opening the box. Inside was a little tray full of needles. They were lined up by size, and Joly selected several and bound them together so the multiple points were at a slant. Nickel leaned in to examine the sharp metal points, and a shiver snaked through his spine. They looked like crude blades used for torture, not tattoos. Joly glanced at him and chuckled.

"Last chance to change your mind. I won't ask again."

"I ain't changin' my mind," Nickel said. He hoped he meant it.

"Well, then, what do you want?"

"The siren riding the Beisht, like yours."

Joly snorted. "Too much time for your first ink. What if you change your mind partway through? I've seen grown men blubber when I stab skin."

"Aww, Joly, I ain't gonna cry." He rolled his eyes, waving him off.

"I'll do the serpent and the siren if you make it through the first one. Pick something smaller."

Nickel thought it over, but nothing special came to mind.

"I dunno," he said.

With a shrug, Joly poured inks of black and red into little bowls and mixed them with a healthy dose of gunpowder. Nickel's eyes widened, and he watched, fascinated, as Joly blended the gunpowder into the ink with a bit of water.

"Take off your shirt. Best to hide your ink from your momma if you can," Joly advised. Nickel obeyed, though he didn't know what his mother could do after the job was done.

"It ain't like she can make me wash it off," he argued, poking at the red ink with a deft finger. "What's that? I only ever saw black ink."

"Vermillion," Joly said. "It's from the best Chinese cinnabar I could find. Paid a steep price, but it's worth it. I can charge more for my work." He lifted the side of his shirt to reveal a chaotic flesh-colored canvas of black-and-vermillion pictures tattooed all over his body. Nickel whistled.

"You got any skin that ain't inked over?" he asked.

Joly winked at him. "Might as well give a woman something to look at while you're prodding her, boy." The old man grinned. Nickel could almost see a secret memory flutter through his friend's brain, and he thought of Magdalena. *That's it! Mags!*

"I know what I want first," Nickel told his friend.

☙

The sheath of the dagger rubbed his skin in the stillness of night. Stifling a yawn, Nickel moved his hand, intent on snaking a finger inside the cuff of his boot to scratch the irritation. A floorboard groaned, and Nickel saw a crouched silhouette not three feet away. He grabbed for his new blade.

"Nickel Ryder?"

He froze mid-pull. That was not Alastor! It was Hera, rising from the quilts she shared with the youngest of the Wheeler flock.

"Go to bed, Hera!" he ordered in a fierce whisper.

"But I slept about monsters," the little girl cried. "They came up from the ocean! Can I sleep in your bed?" Hugging her doll made of corn husks against her chest, she rubbed her eye with a grubby knuckle and whimpered.

"Please?"

"Come on," Nickel said, flapping the blanket aside. Hera bounded into his lap and burrowed under the covers. She reminded Nickel of a baby rabbit he found curled up in a patch of grass once, on the ranch outside of town. It was so innocent, so trusting. Helpless. Like Hera.

Nickel's eyes snapped, and he clenched his jaw as he traced his fingers through her messy ringlets. He nearly pulled a knife on his favorite little sister. All because of Alastor. Damn him!

He scanned his enemy's bedroll, only to discover it was empty. He gave a little jerk, whipping his head around to search the slumbering children.

*Where are you, you bastard?* Nickel thought and wrapped his arms around a wriggling Hera.

"Honey, where's Al?" he whispered in the little girl's ear. She pointed to Nickel's left, where a lone shadow sat cross-legged in a dark corner. The hair on Nickel's skin raised, but he copied his opponent's position. Sitting up with his back to the wall, he crossed his legs and pulled his sister into his lap.

"Do you think Al slept about monsters too?" she asked.

"Monsters won't get you, Hera," Nickel said.

"What if they do? They got you!"

"I'm still here, ain't I?"

"But I slept about them. Sea monsters—they was bringing the Mistress to you in big ships. They threw them out on the prairie, lookin' for Nickel Ryder."

"Threw what on the prairie?"

"The ships!"

"Ships on the prairie?"

"They turned the whole world to water!"

"Why'd they do that?"

"You won't go in the ocean. You won't go, will you? Don't go in the water, Nickel Ryder."

"Shh! Whisper, little girl, you don't wanna wake up Momma and the others." The shadow against the wall moved slightly, and Nickel's head snapped up. Alastor eased into a more comfortable position, yet still sat upright. It looked like he meant to sit there all night, waiting on Nickel to fall asleep. He'd have a long wait.

Hera buried her head against Nickel's chest, and he winced as she leaned against his aching skin. Scooting her sideways so her head fell against his opposite shoulder, he kept his eyes trained on the dark figure in the room's corner.

"I'm not goin' nowhere, Hera love. Nobody's gonna get me." He heard a snort from his left but ignored it in favor of consoling his little sister.

"I slept it," she cried, over and over, and hugged him tighter. "I slept it."

Nickel rocked the little girl in his arms, humming a tune under his breath.

"It's just a bad dream, pretty little Hera. Nobody can turn the whole world into a sea, or throw ships out on the prairie, neither."

"Are you sure?"

Nickel kissed her forehead. "There," he said. "A kiss for luck. You know how lucky I am, don't you?"

Hera nodded. Of course she did.

"Well, I just gave some of it to you. Now you'll have good dreams, and nothin'll ever hurt you, Hera Wheeler." He ran his thumb over her tears and wiped them away. The little girl pressed her tiny hand into his large one and stretched up to his face. She pressed a wet, sloppy kiss on his cheek.

He grinned at her. "What was that for?"

"I'm givin' the luck back to you so's the Mistress don't get you when she comes."

"Save some for yourself, darlin'."

She snuggled against him, closed her eyes, and before he could say another word, she was sound asleep in his arms, dreaming—he hoped—of good things. Flowers and candy, dolls and ponies, all the things Hera loved.

*All the things she loved.* Placing a hand over his chest, he slipped his fingers inside his shirt and felt of the throbbing, swollen skin taut against his heart. The tattoo. He could almost feel the outline of the swan standing over the boy in the boat, its wings spread wide to shield against harm. He now had the protection of his Magdalena and India ink to pair with his natural luck and Joly's blade. What did Alastor have? A fool's brain and the curse of the devil's fruit. He clamped his mouth shut to avoid laughing out loud.

Hera wriggled in her sleep. Nickel leaned against the wall where he could stare back at Alastor in the darkness and rested his chin on his sister's head. He would not make the mistake of falling asleep again.

# CHAPTER 11

# SAND CRABS

*1874*

When one is knowingly stalked, habits change. Slumber lightens, where the merest breath awakens the victim. New habits form out of necessity: new routes to travel, avoiding alleys and doorways where one is susceptible to ambush. The senses heighten, reflexes quicken. Nickel fell into these behaviors without conscious thought. They rose from an obligation to life, though the boy held little fear of his murderous brother.

Nickel was growing taller and stronger. He built boats with Indianola builders eager to pay the boy who sold good fortune. Sometimes he cut or stacked timbers, but always, he found time to ride and work on the ranch outside of town. He learned to break horses, and did it well. His straight, boyish form was turning to solid muscle. Soon, he would catch up with Alastor's strapping build and be able to match him in a fistfight.

With Joly's teachings, Nickel fell into a life of constant awareness. He moved with purpose, yet without thought. Lithe and quick, he could pull his dagger from his boot and sink it into the throat of Joly's crude mannequin target in one fluid motion. Nickel met his learnings with a hunger never quite satisfied, and always with twinkling green eyes and a broad, toothy grin. Convinced his luck grew, fed by Alastor's curse, he was a force loved by all and hated by one.

Merchants stopped him in the street, inviting him to enter their establishments, thereby blessing their growing trades and businesses.

Among other businesses, a photographer moved into town and built a studio. A man of smarts, he was quick to learn of the prominent locals. Nickel's name surfaced again and again, so it came as no surprise when the photographer, donned in a sharp suit, tracked down Nickel and offered him a free portrait if he would sit for his likeness. Nickel obliged and even polished his boots. The photographer positioned him in a rigid, unsmiling pose, but Nickel scoffed at him. Rolling his sleeves up to his elbows, he revealed his greatest source of pride—his tattoos—and then shoved his hat back on his head.

"Better let me show off my handsome mug if you want customers comin'," he told the man. He gripped his beloved dagger, both to showcase his weapon and his latest tattoos—the letters H O L D on the knuckles of his left hand, F A S T on his right.

"People say you're not a sailor, but you have the tattoos of one," the man said as he checked his equipment. Nickel didn't know what any of it was, outside of the big wooden camera box itself.

*Magic,* he thought. The cameraman was still talking.

"Hold Fast," he asked, "isn't that believed to help sailors hold to the ropes?"

Nickel cocked an eyebrow, appraising the man with the magic box.

"I don't know where you're from, Mister," he said, "but it's called riggin', and it does help 'em hold fast. More'n that, though. It brings us strength to carry on, even through tough times."

"To persevere."

"Yessir."

The photographer peered at him over the magic box.

"Folks were right about you, boy. You're a wonder."

Nickel propped a booted foot on a chair and stood with his thumb hooked into the band of his britches.

"I got friends, you know," he said. "I'd shore like to bring 'em with me. I'd like to send a likeness of us to my boss up in the Blacklands."

"Bring them," the man said. "Long as you don't mind me advertising your picture all over town, I'll make a portrait of your friends too. Now stand perfectly still. Don't breathe or blink until I tell you."

◌ଓ

The sea was behind him; a stiff breeze ruffling his hair like a large, affectionate hand. Light was waning, but the setting sun painted a magnificent sky against the horizon at his back. To his left, Joly's brand-new clipper cast a fine silhouette against the docks. It was a perfect night for a beachside gathering.

The beautiful, dark-haired Magdalena was there, appraising him with looks that sent little fires streaking through his veins.

Les was there, and Lucy Parker with a small group of friends. Even a few of the younger cowboys from the nearest ranch Nickel apprenticed for rode in, eager to hear new tales from their seafaring neighbors. Old Joly even scuttled off his ship long enough to share in the storytelling by their little fire on the beach. He began the evening regaling in tales of the sea, stories of sea monsters and storms, and of faraway places none of them could imagine.

Old Joly had seen everything, having sailed clear around the world. He even wore the pierced earlobe to announce his greatest achievement. For, as he put it, only sailors tough enough to sail around the horn wore gold loops in his ears. Nickel wondered about that, for he knew plenty of sailors who wore the earrings for another reason—paying for their funeral should they die at sea. Still, he never dared question Joly's word as gospel truth.

Nickel loved those stories, but he loved watching Magdalena love those stories even more. Her eyes lit up, sparkling like tiny jewels. Her lips formed a perfect "O" as she listened; he could see her envisioning the streets of all those faraway cities Joly described. She was roaming the streets of China, of India and the Caribbean, taking in the sights, the sounds, the colors and tastes. Those places, they lit a fire within the girl, one which would never be extinguished.

He knew, for he had the same smoldering fire burning within himself. Only, it was not the places that stirred him to such depths. It was her. She looked like what he imagined the sirens to look like—if she had a mermaid's tail. Long dark hair billowed free in the Indianola breeze, though she wore the sides twisted behind her ears and braided down her back. Her skin seemed to glow with the sunshine, her mouth always smiling, unless she was looking seaward. He recognized the pout. She still longed for the life she couldn't have—the life of a sailor—an explorer, an adventurer. It was that which he loved and feared most, for he knew he would marry her before he left Indianola.

His life was slated for a different kind of adventure—one on land. How would Mags react to prairie grass and horses instead of the ocean and dolphins? Was it fair to steal her away from the world she loved so well?

Again, he thought of staying, but he followed her gaze to the watery horizon and a tremor shook his body. No. He loved Indianola more than ever, but the Mistress; she was no friend of his. He trusted her as he trusted Alastor Wheeler. Both of them tried to kill him. Both would come at him again, sooner or later.

Old Joly wrapped up his storytelling with the offer for Nickel to take his place. At thirteen, he was already known throughout the town as one of the best storytellers in Indianola. He loved to work an audience and thrived on the attention he received.

As he stepped up to the center of the group, Nickel grinned. He had their attention. Hopping up to the lid of a large blue-painted trunk, he stomped his foot, knowing the single spur would play a melody with his voice. His tattoos, numerous as they now were, only added to the intrigue of his natural ability to charm his audience. They were worth the initial squawking of his mother—she had tired of the fight soon enough, for she knew her son was destined for a life on land. Glancing around the faces of his circle of friends, he crouched low on his platform, curling his fingers into claws.

By default, he faced the loveliest girl in Indianola: Magdalena Hayworth.

"The Beisht," he said in his best drawl, "she wanted me. She could taste me! I heard her comin', slicin' through the water below me. Her scales, they was as big as dinner plates and as black as the depths she came from. I was shore tuckered out from swimmin' against the riptide, but I heard the rush of water. She was comin' in fast, her mouth open and ready to strike!"

"Did it have teeth?" Lucy Parker asked.

Nickel turned his head, fixing the blonde-haired girl with a half-crazed stare.

"Did she have teeth?" he repeated. "Did she have teeth?" Opening his mouth wide, he snapped it shut. "Fangs they were," he said, "longer'n my arm and sharper than the blade of a cutlass. She could bite clear through a man with enough fang left to spear two more. I was just a boy then. What chance did I have? I knew my time was comin'."

Amid the cries of the girls, Les Harold rolled his eyes and grunted. "You're so full of shit," he whispered, just loud enough for Nickel to hear.

Without losing momentum, he winked at his best friend.

"The Mistress, she reached inside my mouth, up my nose, and in my eyes. She burned and choked with salt, rolling me under. Waves broke over me, and I couldn't feel my limbs. Her scales wrapped 'round my legs."

"Oh no!" the girls cried in unison.

"It was the Beisht! She tightened her grip, snakin' across my waist and 'round my arm. I thought shore she was gonna break every bone in my body 'fore she drug me down, down into her watery lair."

Nickel paused for breath, studying the broad shimmering eyes of Magdalena, wide with delight. He knew she was afraid of no Beisht, real or imaginary, yet she hung on every word he said.

"What did you do, Ryder?" she prodded.

Jumping off the big blue trunk, he landed in front of Mags and took her arm. Reeling her in against him, he helped her up on the box and climbed back up after her. He knew Magdalena defied her father's wishes every time she saw him, but he didn't care. Mrs. Hayworth loved him, and that was good enough for him.

"I shore didn't know what to do," he said, wrapping his arms around her waist like a serpent's coils. "She had me bound so tight I couldn't move nothin' but my fingers. She rolled me 'round and 'round, fillin' my lungs with seawater. Wasn't no way I'd ever squirm free—she was too strong. I started wigglin' my fingers against her scales, and guess what? That black-headed beast has a soft underbelly!"

Eager to demonstrate, Nickel tickled Magdalena and was rewarded with a low, melodic giggle.

"I heard a great roar in my ears, and she recoiled. I poked my fingers deeper into that spot, and she laughed!"

He doubled his effort, and the girl of his dreams laughed in his arms. Nearly everyone laughed at the ridiculous notion of tickling the deadliest beast in the seas, except for two. Lucy Parker's face flushed red, and her eyes hardened at the sight of Nickel and Magdalena's obvious attachment. The other was Les Harold, who slapped his hand over his forehead and shook his head.

"You mean to tell me you tickled yourself free of the Beisht?" he asked, dragging his fingers down his face and over his mouth.

"I expect everyone's got a ticklish spot. My luck was shore with me that day, 'cause I found hers. I tickled that scaly belly until that serpent body of flesh shuddered and released me. She dove under me, and that's when Joly and his crew jumped in and drug me from the sea."

"Seems to me something changed from the last telling of that story," Les said, suppressing a grin.

"It's true as I'm standin' here," Nickel declared. He looked around the circle and caught Lucy Parker glaring at Magdalena. Her visage changed when she caught him watching her, and she flashed a smile designed for slaying a boy's heart.

Nickel didn't notice.

"Well, I think you're the bravest boy in the world," Lucy purred. "The smartest too! How did you know to tickle the belly of that awful monster?"

"It's like you said, Luce. I'm awful smart."

Mags ducked out of his grasp and sat down on the trunk. He plopped down beside her and regaled his friends in story after story, fed by Les, whose apparent irritation for stretching the truth was, of course, nothing more than an excuse to bicker. It's what the boys did best: honing their craft with sharp wit and loose tongues.

In honor of his cowboy ranch-hand friends, Nickel retold the tale of his favorite dime-novel hero, Mustang Grey, the Pony Express rider.

With the telling, he relinquished his title as storyteller for the night and slipped Magdalena away from the hard glare of Lucy Parker. He angled for a few stolen kisses, but when she hesitated, he unbuttoned the placket of his shirt, revealing part of the swan inked over his left breast. She glanced at the graceful bird and cast her eyes away, though not before he noticed his favorite smile playing at her lips.

The evening air was delicious on his skin, cool and damp with the caress of saltwater spray. He wished he could remove his shirt but dared not do so in front of Mags.

*One more year,* he thought. *I ain't so shore I'll ever be able to say goodbye to Indianola.* Rolling up his sleeves, he led her to his friends' horses.

"I'm borrowin' your horse," he called to one of the cowboys. The owner waved his hand and sipped from a jug Joly passed to him. Nickel laughed. He knew what was in Joly's pottery jug and what it did to the unsuspecting.

The young cowboy hacked and spewed until Les Harold swatted him on the back. Everyone laughed at the red, watery face of the cowpoke as he passed over a second round.

"Show 'em how it's done, Nickel," Joly called. Hesitating only a moment, he bade Magdalena wait and marched up to Joly and the jug. Upending it, he took a long swallow, letting the burning liquid sear his gullet, and handed it back without a flinch.

"You call yourself a cowpuncher," he said. The cowboy, coughing and sputtering, managed to curse at him. Nickel just laughed—one sip had taken the wind out of his sails.

He sauntered back to Mags and led her over to the horses. Selecting the reins of a dark chestnut, he started to help her up.

"Wait, what are you doing?" she cried.

"I told you one day I'd show you what it's like to sail in my world, didn't I? Today's the day."

"But I don't know how to ride."

Nickel winked at her and patted the saddle. "You don't know how to sail, neither. Does that stop you from wantin' to try? Put your foot in the stirrup, and I'll boost you up."

"Ryder . . ."

Nickel leaned in and placed a well-aimed peck on her lips.

"You wanna sail, don't you?"

"Yes, but—"

"Trust me, darlin'."

She surrendered with a sigh and did as he suggested. He boosted her into the saddle and swung up behind her, wrapping his arm around her waist. She clung to his bare arm and tilted her head to peer at the permanent pictures on his skin in the dark.

"How many tattoos do you have now?" she asked.

"Seven, so far. He says he's gonna start the serpent on my right arm, soon as he's done my left."

"Some girls wouldn't like all that ink decorating your skin. You don't need it, the decoration." She was nervous. Magdalena always chattered when she was nervous.

"Don't you like 'em?"

"I love them!" she cried. "But you don't need them to look good."

"Oh, I know," he said, and they both laughed. Hers was tinged in fear. "It's okay, darlin'. I ain't never gonna let you fall."

The horse took a few steps forward, and she gasped.

"Welcome to my world," he told her. He urged the horse into a lope up the beach, toward the setting sun.

She was stiff in the saddle, tense and afraid of the beast under her, but it wasn't long before he felt her relax. She leaned back, snuggling into his arms, and succumbed to the thrill of the ride.

He splashed them through the surf, always pointing them to the last rays of light, and when it disappeared into darkness, he stopped the horse, letting a gentle tide break under the animal's belly. She twisted in his grasp. Slipping her arms around his neck, she gifted him a kiss he would never forget. It was not a kiss between a girl and a boy, but of woman and man. He returned her caress with fervor, playing at her lips with his tongue. She opened her mouth, daring an invitation he refused to resist. Red, pulsing heat pounded in his brain and down through his body.

"You should take me back," she purred when they came up for air.

"Aww, Mags!" His protest was low, breathy in her ear, and he tightened his grip around her waist. "Don't make me."

She heaved a ragged sigh. "If you don't, I'll forget myself," she murmured.

"That's what I'm hopin'." He adjusted himself in the saddle, struggling to alleviate the urge for release without drawing attention to his britches. She had to notice, to feel the difference. He felt no shame, only hope.

She kissed him again and turned her neck. Lifting her tresses, he kissed her skin all the way to her jaw. She heaved a sigh—of contentment, he hoped—then turned her face toward the sea.

Again.

Always, she faced the horizon.

"Ryder."

"I know." He turned the horse, and they plodded back to the beachside campsite, where both cowboys were stretched out on the sand, snoring.

"What'd you do to them, Joly?" he asked, kicking one in the ribs with the toe of his boot. The young man didn't move.

"I might ask you the same about her," Joly fired back, eyeing the bright-eyed Magdalena. The girl smiled, but Nickel didn't say a word. His britches were still a little too tight for comfort.

Les had been drinking, for he was unusually bright-eyed and tottery. Nickel hoped he didn't get off his chair, else he'd tumble face-first into a sand crab again. Joly's bonfires were always adventurous.

"They thought they'd outdrink you," Les said, waving his arm at the two beached lumps. "I told 'em nobody'll never do better'n Nickel." He rose to reach for the jug, toppled over the big trunk, and lay over it, his rump roast sticking up in the air as though it was trying to catch the stars.

"Hey, you all right?" Les asked, unaware he was the one who had fallen. Nickel grabbed him under the arms and hauled him off the trunk and away from the heat of the crackling fire.

"I swear, Les, you fell on a sand crab again," Nickel told his friend. "Hey, Joly, look at Les's earring!"

Les swung his head and yowled when he realized a little crab had attached itself to his earlobe. He pawed at it but missed his ear completely, hitting nothing but air.

"Ain't a proper gatherin' without sand crabs," he told Magdalena. He ripped the crab off Les's ear.

"Aah!" he yelled.

"Pour some rum on it. It'll be fine," Joly and Nickel said in unison. Joly grabbed Nickel by the shoulder and pulled him a short distance from the fire.

"That pretty little blonde girl sulked off after you took off with your Mags."

"Luce?"

"I'd watch her if was I you, son. I don't care how old they are. Women be like the Mistress—they be the devil when scorned."

Nickel chuckled. He hadn't noticed Lucy Parker had slipped away and thought nothing of her leaving without saying goodbye.

It was getting late; soon Mags would go home too. The fact that she was allowed to roam free attested only to her mother's insistence the girl have her time to run before she became saddled with a man and family. Left up to her father . . . Nickel cringed, thinking of Mr. Hayworth. The man hated him more than ever.

*Let him hate me,* he thought. Lucy Parker pushed from his mind, he turned back to Mags, who was sitting on the big blue trunk examining the painted pictures on the lid and sides. He winked at her.

"That's yours," he told her.

"What?" she asked, looking around. "Les? He's nice, but I don't want him. He draws in too many crabs."

"Aww, only when he's drunk." Nickel rested his foot on the edge of the trunk and tapped it with the heel of his boot.

"You told me once you wanted somethin' to keep all your dreams in," he said. "So I done traded for this big ole blue box."

"You did that? For me?"

"Shore! You can hold an awful lot of dreams in a box that big," he said with a grin.

"Did you paint the pictures on it too?"

"Joly gave me the paint. Those swallows on the lid? I painted them like my tattoos—so if you ever do sail, you'll find your way home."

"And the compass rose?"

"To guide your dreams, you know that. For luck."

"Of course, and I love it, but . . ."

Nickel tilted his head. "But?"

"Why did you paint the compass wrong?"

Nickel studied the indigo-and-red compass. It took him hours to paint, painstakingly lining the alternating colors in straight lines. The letters proved the most difficult, since he only knew how to scribble an "R" for the first letter of his name.

Joly had given him a map to look off, and he duplicated the letters as best he could. He figured she would be proud of his progress.

"What do you mean, wrong?" he asked.

"Well, north. It's supposed to be on the top of the compass, but you have it pointed where west should be."

"What?" Nickel's grin slipped. Scratching his head, he stared at the compass he was so proud of, and shrugged.

"Well, that's where north was when I painted it! It moves around, you know."

Mags looked at him, and laughter bubbled from her throat. Giggling, she threw her arms around his neck and clung tight.

"Ryder Wheeler, I love you!" she cried.

# CHAPTER 12

# INK AND WISDOM

*April 1875*

Grinning through the pain, Nickel watched his old friend work. He was quick yet meticulous, dipping the sharpened blades into ink and gunpowder, pricking his skin and rubbing the combination into his raw wound. The head of the Beisht was beginning to take shape, and the beautiful siren wielding a sword with it.

Joly worked until his fingers seized up. Stretching and cracking his knuckles, he cleansed his tools and put the inks away.

"More tomorrow, Nickel," he said.

"Will you finish in time?"

"I don't see why not."

Nickel sat down on the bunk next to his discarded shirt to examine his newest art.

"I shore wish I drew as good as you do," he lamented.

"You have the knowledge—you just need to practice your shading, boy." The sailor shook his head and chuckled. "It doesn't feel right anymore, calling you 'boy.' It doesn't suit you. Look at you! Working with those Matagorda horses like you been doing these past few years, you've earned stripes. Tall and strong. You be growing into your own skin and muscle more every day. I've taught you just about everything I know to teach, without getting you out on that water to sail with me. You'd make a damn fine sailor."

Nickel glowed under the praise. "I'll make a damn fine cowboy too," he retorted.

"Aye, that you will. Guess I hoped you'd change your mind by now. Luck like yours, we'd own the seas!"

Nickel chuckled but shook his head. "The Mistress won't never let me own her."

"No man ever does, no matter how much we might want to."

"I'll come back to Indianola, Joly," he said. "I ain't leavin' for good. It's my home."

"Don't make promises you can't keep, son. We pave good intentions with regret. Best you move forward—no room for moving back."

Nickel wasn't sure he understood Joly's meaning, but he nodded anyway.

"I shore appreciate you lettin' me stay here all this time," he said. Joly turned his back and waved him off with a brusque grunt.

Ever since he nearly pulled his dagger on little Hera, Nickel refused to sleep under his mother's roof. He couldn't close his eyes around Alastor for fear of being knifed in the back. His brother's war was growing desperate, and he did not want an innocent sibling caught up in the crosshairs of Alastor's hatred.

Sometimes he stayed with the Harolds, but mostly he stayed with Joly. The old sailor was often out at sea, so it bore no ill will for Nickel to care for his shack while he was away.

Whenever he returned, he offered to house him in exchange for small chores. Aged beyond his years, Joly was borne of a life of rum, wind, and weather. It was catching up to him; Nickel saw it in the way he curled his fingers when he thought no one was looking. Nickel said nothing. To bring it up would be to damage the old man's pride—an unforgivable offense. Still, Nickel wanted to see the old man cared for, so he hatched a plan.

"Joly?"

"Mmm," came the reply.

"I was thinkin', my brother Zelus, he's a few years younger'n me, but if I'm gonna be away cowboyin', I won't be here to see he don't fall into the Wheeler Curse. Maybe when you ain't sailin', you could look after him like you done me."

Joly froze, mulling the notion around the corners of his mind. A slow grin tugged at the corner of his mouth, but he huffed and swore. "I don't know," he said slowly. "You Wheeler boys are an awful lot of work. What if he ain't as lucky as you?"

"Someone's gotta pick up where I left off. Ain't nobody else gonna defend my high steam."

"Esteem," Joly corrected, and laughed. "I guess I could teach the boy a few things if I can find the time."

"I'd shore be obliged," Nickel said, pretending not to notice the lift in Joly's spirits. He was growing older, and his son was far away. Who else would he have to mentor once Nickel was gone? Much as the old man refused to admit it, he was lonely. Zelus was a good answer, and Nickel patted himself on the back for the idea. Now he needn't worry about either.

Pulling a box from under his bunk, he lifted the lid and pulled out a small stack of letters. Inside the top was the tintype Bannack had sent in reply to the likeness made on the streets of Indianola—Mags and Les on each side of him, and Old Joly too.

Bannack had pulled a photographer out onto the ranch, though, instead of going into town. He stood, stoic and unsmiling, staring into the lens with the same unnerving gaze Nickel remembered. He held a saddle over his shoulder and leaned on a fine rifle. Other cowboys posed around him. Bannack wrote out their names but had not labeled who was whom. They looked like a tough lot, most of them lean and hard, their faces weathered by the same elements that lined Joly. Even so, some of them bore traces of a smile. It was enough to convince Nickel they were good men, and he would be okay working among them.

"I hope you find what you're looking for, Nickel." Joly took the tintype and studied it before handing it back. "Those men live different lives. I hope you don't find out too late—you already passed the life you want."

"My hero's a cowboy. Least he was. I wanted to be like him since I was a kid."

"Bannack?"

"Him too, but Mustang Grey."

"The dime-novel hero Les is always reading about."

"Shore! I don't know what happened to him, but I bet he's out there somewhere, livin' a grand life."

Joly dug into his pack and brought out a cigar. He took his time lighting it and looked outside, where the sea beckoned.

"I understand the call, wanting to live the life of another. But it's folly, Nickel. Quicksand. You're destined for your own life—not somebody else's.

The more you try to find what ain't yours, the deeper you sink. Don't bury yourself in heroics, son. People in books ain't often what they're made to be."

Nickel wanted to argue, but Joly seemed so . . . sad. Putting the tintype away, he clapped his friend on the back. "You're gettin' weepy in your old age, Joly."

"Hell I am!" he shot back. "Somebody's gotta tell you these things!" He puffed on his smoke, and pointed. "Your tribe's here for the monthly gathering."

Nickel poked his head outside and laughed. The Fireside Gathering was about to begin. As he grabbed his shirt and headed for the door, he heard Joly's voice behind him whisper:

"Sometimes, a man can't see the hero he already is for the shadow of an impostor."

# PART TWO

## *EDGE OF THE MAP*

# CHAPTER 13

# BAWL OF THE PEACOCK

*September 14, 1875*
*Mustang Grey*

"*Eighteen hours in the saddle, and the last station burned to the ground, the horses stolen! Unable to switch mounts, Mustang Grey raced straight through his painted foe, depending on the swiftness of his tired mount to carry him another fifteen miles westward. Oh, pray the next station stands for our bedraggled rider, Mustang Grey! And so he rode through blistering sun and on into the gloom of night, chased by the howling devils closing in. Blood oozed from the hole in his shoulder; feathers protruding from the shaft sunk deep in his flesh. Still he rode, the rhythm of his horse's hooves the beat of life or death for our hero. His pursuers followed, screaming like ethereal haunts in the night, thirsty for the blood of a young man called Mustang Grey. A second arrow pierced his taut skin, but exhaustion dulled his senses. Impervious to pain, the rider clung to saddle and to life even as the speeding world around him blurred before his eyes. His horse stumbled, throwing injured rider on the neck of his horse, but the pair did not fall. The mail must go through!*"

Les Harold licked his finger to turn the page, when the book was snatched from his grasp.

"Finish your dime novel later. It's time to eat." Molly Wheeler held the book over her head amid a chorus of sharp complaints and groans.

"Momma!" Nickel cried over the protests of his siblings. "He was almost done!"

"You'd all be complaining too if your supper got cold. You've made poor Les read that book so many times the cover's falling apart. We all know what happens to Mustang Grey."

Molly plunked plates on the table where her children gathered. Thanks to the financial help of Bannack and the lack of their father and his luxurious spending habits, they had a suitable table and benches long enough to hold the whole clan—and Les when he came over.

Nickel still spent most of his time living in Joly's shack. Molly didn't even argue . . . much. She demanded Nickel place his boots under her table once a day, when he wasn't working with horses or building boats to earn money. Like every other night, Molly said grace, including Bannack in her prayers.

"I bet that book's nothin' but a pack of lies."

"What the hell would you know about it?" Nickel shot back. "You couldn't ride a sheep, let alone a horse."

"Shit shoveler!" Alastor yelled.

"Fish fu—"

"Ryder! Don't you dare finish that sentence! Both of you, just stop it. You'll be apart soon enough since Alastor won't be honoring our obligation to Mr. Bannack anymore."

"Can't leave soon enough," Al muttered under his breath, scowling at his younger brother. Out loud he aired his complaint, heard a thousand times before. "I never promised that cow-chaser nothing! Why would I wanna go off to shovel horseshit and stare at the back end of a bunch of dirty animals all day?"

"Be an improvement over the way you smell now," Les said.

"Go to hell, Harold."

"Can't. You already took the last spot." The giggles around the table at Alastor's expense subsided when Molly Wheeler set out the last bowl and plopped down.

Les, too polite to fuss like the Wheeler crew, paled. No one took their eyes off the horror sitting in the middle of the table. Les leaned over to whisper in Nickel's ear.

"Is that . . . ?"

"Bear grease," Nickel said with an exaggerated groan. "On biscuits."

Ever since some old sailor paid Molly for a meal with a jar of bear grease he had picked up somewhere from some place called New England, mealtime became something to suspect, like crawling through an empty battlefield. You never knew when the enemy might raise his ugly head and ambush you.

No one dared complain . . . well, not too much, anyway, for they understood what it meant to be hungry. Molly not only cooked her dough in the stuff but slathered it overtop each biscuit like butter.

"Stop staring at those biscuits and eat them," Molly ordered. "They're good for you."

Nickel watched his mother spear a biscuit and reach for his plate. Grease dripped off it and pooled on his plate when she dropped it.

"Ack! How?"

"That sailor said bear grease is good for growing children—keeps illnesses from sticking to your innards."

"Keeps your ass from sticking to the shitter too," Nickel replied. "Slid right off it last time you made those greasy bear biscuits, Momma. Got a splinter in my butt and everything."

The table erupted in hoots of laughter; even Alastor bit back an oily grin.

"I bet Mustang Grey would eat my bear grease biscuits, and probably ask for seconds," Molly said after the laughter died down.

"Bet he'd jump on his horse and ride off like the devil was after him. Wonder what happened to him, anyway?" Nickel mused.

"You heard the end of the book. He made it through the ride," Les said. He reached for the novel, but Molly gently smacked his hand with a wooden spoon.

"Yeah, but the book said he disappeared after the Pony Express scattered. I guess no one knows where he went."

"I know where he went," Nickel said. "He went north, to the Middle C Ranch."

Les gaped at him, tilting his head as though trying to decide whether he even wanted to ask. Curiosity got the better of him. "How'd you figure that?"

"I think Mustang Grey is really Bannack." Nickel's announcement brought groans from his family.

"Have you lost your senses?" Posse asked. His face confirmed his statement; he thought his little brother's brains had rattled loose.

"How else do you explain it?" Nickel retorted. "Nobody knows where he comes from. He's the best horseman in the whole world!"

"You barely saw him ride," Molly reminded him, but he ignored her negativity.

"It's Bannack! Gotta be. Ain't nobody tougher than him."

Les picked up the novel and examined the cover. "No," he said, shaking his head. "Mustang Grey don't look much like Bannack."

Nickel didn't care what anyone said. He only wondered why he hadn't thought of it before. What started out as nothing more than a statement to spur a sporting argument with his brothers began to gain ground in his mind. He was right: Bannack *was* Mustang Grey; Les just didn't want to admit it. Nickel jumped up, bent on picking up the argument, but succeeded in overturning the biscuit bowl. Grease puddled into the table, creating an oil slick.

"He is Mustang. I'd swear on it!"

"Will you two quit harpin' on Mustang Grey?" Alastor sneered. "It's just a stupid story made up for little kids. You think a man could ride that long overnight with two arrows shot through him and a passel of Indians chasing him? He'd have bled to death, or the horse would've collapsed. He ain't even real."

Nickel choked down a mouthful of greasy biscuit, bolted his food, and chased it down with a glass of water. He only had a short time left in Indianola. Mustang Grey or not, when Bannack did come, Nickel would have to face leaving his best friend behind.

"Come on, Les, let's go. I ain't wasting our time listening to him." Nickel kissed his mother's cheek, guzzled another glass to get the taste of grease off his tongue, and started for the door.

Molly caught his arm and pulled him back. "I knew you wouldn't eat if I gave it to you before dinner," she explained, pulling a crumbled envelope from a pocket sewn into her apron. "A letter," she whispered in his ear. "One came for you today. Take it with you. Les can read it to you."

His heart lurched as he grabbed the envelope, stuffed it in his pants, and ran out the door, Les following on his heels.

They rounded the corner of the street, away from the Wheeler household and Molly's greasy bear biscuits.

"Your brother sure is an ass," Les said.

"Alastor can think whatever he wants to, but I know better. Maybe Bannack ain't Mustang Grey, but he's as real as me and you." As the boys walked to the wharf, a sadness fell over them. Les even looked like he might cry.

"Wish I was going too," he said.

"I can't believe you ain't goin' with me! Can't we change your momma's mind?"

"She hasn't changed her mind in five years. She won't do it now."

"Won't your dad talk to her?"

"He's tried, but she won't hear of letting me go. She never lets me roam the way your momma does." Les shuffled his feet, staring at the ground, and kicked a pebble out of his path. "Been thinking, though. In a year or two, if I keep saving my money, I might strike out on my own and head up to the Middle C Ranch. Think you could get me a job with your friend Bannack, then?"

"Yeah, Les, I'll make sure you get one." Nickel's voice was low, and he focused on the ground rather than his friend. Time was passing, and it was becoming clear to them both: Mrs. Harold would not relent. Soon enough, Nickel would have to face saying goodbye to his best friend.

"Thanks, Nickel." Les opened his mouth to say something else, then changed his mind. The boys reached the wharf, each dwelling in uncomfortable silence. To break it, Nickel retrieved the letter, meaning to ask his friend to read it, but Les turned away.

"I think I'm gonna go home," he said.

"What? Why?"

"Bear grease isn't setting in my stomach too good."

"Want me to go with you?" Nickel asked.

"Maybe you'd better not. Thank your momma for dinner again for me, okay?"

"Yeah, sure."

"See you tomorrow, Nickel."

Nickel watched his best friend walk off alone, and for the first time, he felt truly lonely.

*It all seems to be ending,* he mused, squinting into the stiff sea wind. Usually, he loved a good breeze. Cleared the mind of dust, leaving more room for ideas, and he was infamous for his ideas. They often led him into trouble, but so what? Life was meant to be lived, and he meant to live it without trepidation.

For the first time, his thoughts betrayed him. They were heavy, as though someone had chained him to a great ship's anchor. Soon, he would leave the only home he knew. To go where? What would he face, who would he meet when he reached the Middle C Ranch with Bannack? Once again, he marveled at his haste to leave. Indianola was his universe now.

As he walked the beach, threading through clusters of fishermen and children, he smiled but only on the outside. Men clapped him on the back and shook his hand, offering him kind words of greeting. Young boys rallied around him, chanting the oft-spoken phrase heard along the docks.

"Nickel's luck! Nickel's luck! Nickel's luck!" The steadfast rise to popularity among the fishing community seemed surreal, looking back. How was he to guess the turn of events spurred from one small coin, and the selling of his luck?

Old Joly returned that fateful day, as he told the story, "fuller than a whale's belly." His catch brought grown men scrambling to offer a mere five cents to the boy of luck. Trouble was, not everyone shared the fishermen's enthusiasm for Nickel's newfound status. Other children, his siblings included, grew jealous. After a short time, Nickel had reasoned to a few big-mouthed fishermen he could not, in fact, be everywhere at once. Banking on his own reasoning that Les Harold was paid that first time, too, wouldn't it be just as lucky to hand out nickels to other boys *and* him?

In five years' time, he had built a new tradition, a bond between waif and fisherman. Whenever a man felt his luck slip, the coins went far to help a young boy's spirit and fill his stomach.

*Just as they helped me.*

Men of the sea never tangled with tradition. They didn't even question it. He was confident that, just like so many odd superstitions carried on for hundreds of years, Indianola would carry on Nickel's luck. Only, he wouldn't be there to see it.

ℭ

*September 15*
*Midmorning*

It was a fickle wind blowing in off the water. Nickel clutched yesterday's letter, still unread, and tucked it inside his shirt for safekeeping. Squalls of rain were intermittent, and the town dodged clear patches to watch the wind carve white caps into the waves, battering the coast.

He took a deep breath of salty sea air and sighed. There was nothing more refreshing than the sea air just before a storm. He loved it. Indianola was overflowing with strangers who seemed bent on watching the weather too. Most of the ones he spoke to were from Victoria and surrounding counties.

Wherever they came from, they were all there for the same thing: to see the trial of a pair of men who had murdered someone in a feud. Nickel didn't care much for trials, and feuds? Hell, he and Alastor were living one.

Stuffy men in suits talked too long, and they were always declaring one thing or another. Trials were boring, and he hated sitting still that long for a bunch of rambling accusations.

His oldest brother Posse took a different view. He argued up and down that the men were guilty of murder and needed a good hanging. He frequented the courthouse, hoping to spy the murderers, and spoke of little else ever since the accused were brought into Indianola for trial.

Nickel yawned just thinking of those hard-backed benches and red-faced men arguing. He appreciated a sporting argument, but where were the stories? If there weren't tales of horses and cowboys, loose women, or of sailors and monsters, was it really entertainment? An awful lot of people must have thought so. He barely recognized anyone scattered across the beach, watching the wind-fed waves. They scurried as though they were made of sugar whenever a squall hit, watching with childish excitement. He heard a woman nearby exclaim to another, "I don't know which is more exciting, the trial or the Indianolan weather! My family will not believe me when I tell them of this wind, and the height of those waves!"

He chuckled a little and met the woman's eye with his female-slaying grin. The women blushed. Nickel rolled the sleeves of his shirt up to his elbows, revealing some of Joly's fine workmanship on his arms. The women stared at his bare skin, and when they remembered themselves, he winked at them and blew a kiss. The pair broke eye contact and spun on each other so fast they collided, smacking their foreheads together. Nickel cackled at their hasty retreat.

He was still laughing when a shift in the wind blew Magdalena's scent toward his nose. She always smelled of lemons and honeysuckle, mixed with the wild spray of the sea.

If any one girl had the power to alter a man's universe, it was Magdalena Virginia Hayworth. She met him near the beach, sheltered by a bank of land so the wind did not hit them directly in the face.

"Are you embarrassing ladies with your artwork again?" she asked. She plied the question with her hands upon her hips, but a bright smile graced her lips. Mags understood his impish nature and loved him for it. There was no fault for his harmless flirtation, for she knew his heart. Still, she liked to rag him.

"It's fun!" Nickel replied with a wink. "I don't know why they get so worked up. I guess I'm too handsome, and they don't wanna fall in love with me."

"It's easy to do, Nickel," she informed him. When she reached for his hand, he gave her his envelope.

"Another one." Magdalena accepted it with a frown and extracted the letter within. "I suppose you want me to read it?"

"Please," Nickel urged. Only one person ever wrote to him—everyone else he knew was already in Indianola. He watched her scan the page to herself, waiting for the telltale pout to form on her lips. He was not disappointed.

"It's from *him*," she said.

"Always is. What's it say?"

Magdalena read aloud:

> *Ryder,*
>
> *Five years, as promised. I'm on the way. Might be you see me before*

*this letter if the weather holds. I expect you and your brothers will be packed and ready to go by the time I get there. Hope you learned to ride something besides dolphins.*

*—Bannack*

Magdalena balled up the letter and threw it at him with a cry.

"You're smiling!" she yelled, stamping her foot on the ground. "That man writes nothing nice, only demands, and you want to leave home to work for him!" When he reached for her, she gave him a little shove and ran off, her hair flying behind her. She wasn't moving fast enough for him to worry . . . too much.

Carefully cloaking his excitement, Nickel chased after Magdalena and caught her within a few long strides. She had a mad-on the size of the sea itself, judging by the tilt of her chin and the slope of her shoulders.

"Aww don't be mad, Mags," he urged, spinning her around to face him. "Bannack ain't one for talk, I guess."

"He's crude," she sniffed, grasping frantically at her skirts. The rain had stopped, but the wind seemed to be intensifying rather than slowing down.

"Don't talk like that about Bannack!" Nickel's voice was streaked with a hint of anger, but he softened his tone immediately. He couldn't yell. Not at her. Instead, he grasped her shoulders in his hands. "He sent my momma money enough to keep us fed since the day Oren . . . well, left. He *saved* my brothers and sisters, and me."

"And now you're leaving too." Magdalena kept her face turned away, refusing to meet his gaze. A few overly loud sniffs hinted at the truth. She was trying not to cry.

"You knew five years ago I'd be leavin', but I don't wanna leave you behind, Mags."

Finally, she turned to meet his gaze. The moment she did, her hopeful, tragic eyes slayed him. "Then stay, Ryder," she murmured, clutching at his chest. She gathered the folds of his shirt in white-knuckled fingers. "Stay, for me?"

Nickel shifted his weight and heaved a sigh. *The one thing I can't do!* he thought. He couldn't stay, not even for her. "I promised," he said. "You know I gave my word."

"Yes, you did," she replied, her voice soft again. "I'm reminded of your promise every time you walk." She kicked at the single spur on his boot. "I guess you'll get the other one soon enough now."

"Guess so." Nickel bent in to steal a kiss, but she blocked him with her hand.

"My father says I'm not to encourage you." Magdalena's ploy was weak, and they both knew it. He sidled in closer.

"I thought you loved me."

"I do. Everyone does—except Daddy. That's the problem."

"What's wrong with that?" he asked, pressing his luck. "Never bothered you before. I told you I wanted to marry you, Mags. We could do it right now, before Bannack comes. You'll marry me, and we can go north together!"

Magdalena's long, dark hair whipped out behind her as though trying to flee the top of her head. She turned her head to protect her eyes from gritty sand.

Brushing her windblown tresses aside, he entwined his fingers between hers and leaned in, still angling for a kiss.

"Ryder," she breathed, "what would all your other girls say?"

"Aww, stop that. I don't want no one but you, Magaleene, and you know it."

Magdalena tried to stifle a giggle but failed. "All these years, and you still can't say my name right."

"I just said it," Nickel teased. He loved the girlish giggle and the blush of her cheeks every time he mispronounced her name.

"You said it wrong."

"Well, how do you say it?" he demanded, mimicking her stance by slamming his hands against his hips.

"Mag-da-lee-nah."

"I don't hear the difference, darlin'."

"Stop it." She playfully smacked his chest. "You're making me laugh, and I'm still mad at you."

He cocked his head to one side and grinned. "I don't want anyone else," he repeated.

"Yes," she lamented, "but Lucy Parker says she means to have you for herself."

"Who cares what Lucy Parker says?"

"It's not even that I care so much about all the other girls wanting you," she said. "It's just that . . ."

"What?"

Magdalena clutched his hand and leaned against him with a sigh. "You make me soft-headed," she whispered. "I can't think straight."

"I don't think about nobody but you, either," he confided. "It's 'cause I love you, Mags."

"But you'll be leaving!" she cried, pulling the conversation full circle. "You heard what he wrote—he'll be here any day now."

"I don't understand why you're makin' this so hard. I done told you—come with me! We could find one of those preacher fellas to say words over us, then you'd have to go where I go. I love you more'n my own life, darlin'."

Magdalena's eyes, jade-green like the sea on a glimmering day, widened, and as her lips parted, Nickel darted in to taste them. It wasn't the first time he had kissed her, but it was the first time he kissed the girl he was on the verge of marrying. The sweetness of her lips, moist from the promise of her tongue, bubbled straight to his blood. At fifteen, a day or two shy of his sixteenth birthday, Nickel meant to claim her, to make her his. She had to realize she already was, just as he was hers. A hundred girls like Lucy Parker didn't equal one Magdalena Hayworth.

She sighed into his mouth, and he deepened his kiss, searching for the core of her breath.

A ragged shriek behind him jerked the young couple out of their reverie. Nickel whirled, his hands still entangled with Magdalena's. His immediate focus fixed on a giant bird coming in at eye level. Whistle, Indianola's crazed birdman, ambled up to them, his pet peacock squawking its displeasure on his arm.

The boy stepped in front of Mags. No one ever knew what Old Man Whistle would do when he emerged from his hut—or what he'd have perched on his arms and shoulders. This was the first time Nickel saw the peacock. Usually, it was some brightly plumed parrot fresh off a ship; once in a while, a gull or a crow.

Once, he carried a full-grown gobbler around like a baby, scaring the children in town. One November day, the turkey disappeared from Old Man Whistle's hut. Nickel had to stifle a chuckle at the memory—stuffing that big ole flapping gobbler in a sack hadn't been easy; nor had running through the city at night undetected, but boy oh boy, was it ever worth it. Old Man Whistle searched for the bird for a month, gobbling and flapping his arms every time some poor soul ventured too close. Now here he was, standing too close again and blinking like he had sand in his eyes. Whistle didn't know the meaning of proper distance.

Magdalena pressed against Nickel's back, her fingers digging into the flesh under his shirt. The peacock bobbed its head and emitted long, obnoxious screams. Its wings smacked Nickel in the face, and he wondered whether peacock tasted anything like turkey.

"When the peacock loudly bawls, soon we'll have both rain and squalls," Whistle announced, jabbing a bony finger into Nickel's breastbone.

"Tell it to somebody else!" Nickel had to shout to be heard over the wind and the infernal bird.

"If the cock goes crowing to bed, he will rise with a watery head."

"Look, Whistle, you're scaring my girl!"

"Should be scared, she's a'comin'!"

"Who?"

The old man pointed toward the gray, choppy sea.

"The Mistress?" Nickel asked.

"She be lonely. Wants you back, Nickel boy."

He rolled his eyes. "Then you go tell her she can't have me."

The old man shook his head and waved four bony fingers in his face. Four, because his thumb was missing; probably bitten off by the turkey.

"Bye-bye, boy. Bye-bye."

Nickel grabbed Magdalena's arm and led her up the beach toward the shelter of town, away from the crazed old man and his screaming peacock. As they retreated, Whistle's call followed them.

"Bye-bye, boy. Bye-bye!"

# CHAPTER 14

# THE SQUALL

*September 15*
*Midmorning continued*

Nickel and Magdalena ran until they could no longer hear the rants of man and bird.

"That bird's as cracked as he is," he told her. "Bet it'd make us a better meal than that tough old turkey."

Magdalena didn't laugh. Her gaze, fraught with worry, was riveted to the end of their world.

"It's okay, Mags. Everybody knows he's not right in the head. His bird's got more brains than he does. He just wanted to scare us."

"You aren't afraid?"

"Of course not."

"But look at the waves! There's a storm coming—even I can feel it. It's so gray. Something's blowing in on the wind!"

"Just another norther, Mags. We've seen 'em all. They don't exactly sneak up on us." The threat had been hanging heavy in the air for some time. The wind was so heavy, Mags had a hard time adjusting her skirts. Every grizzled old fisherman they met on the street complained about a throbbing ache or pain, a sure sign of bad weather.

"But what if he's right? What if the sea takes you again? She nearly did once."

"Once? Ha! I've slipped from her grasp many times." Nickel wrapped his arms around his girl for all the world to see and kissed her face. "Nothing can kill me, Mags. You know I was born with luck."

"And you've been selling it away all these years," she reminded him. "What happens when you run out?"

Nickel hedged, risking another glance at the ocean. He hadn't thought much of his luck running out, not since the last time she brought it up. Was it possible?

"I guess I ain't run out of luck yet," he declared. "Come with me, Mags. Me and you both—we can start a new life together. If you don't like it, we'll come back to Indianola."

Nickel squeezed her hands as he spoke, painting his word pictures of what their life would be like on the ranch, somewhere a few hundred miles north of home. He knew her folks would never let her go, but she was old enough to have her own free will—if she wanted to run off and marry him, he didn't see how Mr. and Mrs. Hayworth would ever stop them.

"And you don't think it's a bad idea?" Mags was wavering. The notion, however rushed, had merit. If only she wouldn't let fear stop her.

"There ain't no such thing as a bad idea—only poor execution," he told her. "Joly said that, and I believe it."

Magdalena was a girl of ease and confidence, but now Nickel saw little to support the traits he loved so well. Her hands became her central focus, and she studied them as though she had never seen them before. They moved to her skirts, where she rubbed her palms over the fabric, twisting the pretty material in her hands. Round and round she twisted, scrunched, and then released. She cast her eyes downward and did not drag her gaze to meet his, not even when he called her name.

"Mags? What's wrong?" he asked, though he was not certain he wanted to know.

She cast a sideways glance before retreating to the inspection of her busy hands. He grasped them both in his own and held them still.

"Mags," he repeated. "You're makin' me nervous. If it's the storm brewin'—"

"It's not the storm, Ryder!" she cried. "It's that letter." *The letter again. Damn.* Nickel raked a hand through his hair, watching her anger build with the wind.

"The one you threw away? From Bannack?" he asked, even though he knew the answer.

"Ugh, Bannack!" Mags wrinkled her nose. "I know he saved you, but I still don't like him."

*"What?* Why not?"

"Because he's coming to take you away from me!" Magdalena screamed, her voice choking with emotion. She curled her arms over her head and rocked back and forth, unable to stand still. "Don't you understand? We'll never see each other!"

He clutched her waist and pulled her close, desperate to touch her, yet fearful he would lose her if he didn't.

"He ain't takin' me away from you, darlin'!" Nickel replied, catching her hands within his own. "You're comin' with us. You'll be my wife. Didn't you hear me? I want to marry you!"

"I heard." She fidgeted, biting her lower lip. Tears welled in her eyes, and Nickel's stomach clenched.

"Mags!"

"I don't want to go, Ryder!" she cried, pulling her hands free and shielding her face.

"*What?*"

"I mean it! I . . . I can't do it. Leave Indianola? You know how much I love it here! I want to be close to the sea. There's no ocean where you're going, is there?"

Nickel just stared at her, slack-jawed.

"Don't look at me like that," she pleaded. "I *want* to marry you. I love you, but . . . I can't go with you. If . . . if you would stay here, I'd marry you today. We can live here, just like we always have, and you can work for that ranch outside of Indianola. We'd share a perfect life together."

She looked at him then and took his hands again. Her eyes were brimming, but so were his.

"Mags. I can't do that, you know I can't! I have to work for Bannack," Nickel reminded her. "He's paid out five years worth of wages so my family wouldn't starve. I've gotta go!"

"And I want to stay, Ryder. I love you more than anything, I swear, but I don't want to leave Indianola."

He stared at her, mouth agape. "All these years, you heard me talk about the Middle C! You read Bannack's letters to me, you dreamed with me, but you never said you wouldn't go with me."

"You never asked."

"I did too!"

"No. You said you would, but you never asked."

"I didn't think I had to!"

"Please, can't you just send someone else in your place? One of your brothers, or Les Harold?"

"I promised Bannack, and I ain't gonna be like Oren Wheeler. I mean to keep my word."

She huffed at him and tried to pull away. He softened his tone.

"I don't know what else to say," he said. "It *would* be a perfect life here, you and me, except I'd be goin' back on my promise. I owe him, Mags."

"You keep saying that, but you owe yourself more!" she cried. "Doesn't your happiness mean anything? Your future? Me?"

"I figured my future was ridin' off to be a cowboy, married to you! Why didn't you tell me this before? You had five years, Mags, and you wait till now? Bannack's done left!"

The wind was ripping the words from his tongue. He had to shout to be heard. Oh, how he hated the ocean and her storms! That frigid bitch was keeping him away from Mags. Was she really going to choose a bunch of smelly old salt water over him?

"I started to, but I thought maybe something might happen," she said.

"Something?" Nickel wanted to know. "What kind of 'something'?"

"I don't know what exactly. A lot can happen in five years," she said, prattling fast, tumbling over her words. "I thought perhaps Bannack wouldn't come. He might change his mind. Who comes this far to hire a hand? He could have just sent for you. I never wished him ill will, but, well," she said with a shrug, "cowboys live dangerous lives."

"So do sailors!" Nickel shouted. Pain radiated like heat through his chest, and it felt like he had a dry old cotton field in his mouth.

"I know," Mags agreed. "It's just . . . there's so many things that might keep him from coming, or you from leaving. I hoped you might change your mind by now." Despair leaked from her eyes.

"But I ain't changed my mind. I can't! He's on his way, Mags. He might be here now, for all I know. You should've told me."

She ducked her head. "I'm sorry I didn't, but . . . would it have changed anything? You want to go, and I want to stay."

Nickel chewed on his lip and turned his head, afraid she might see the pain leaking from his own eyes. "Dammit, Mags," he cried. "Maybe you're a swan, but you're a siren too. You done lured me in, and now you're leavin' me bashed on the rocks."

"Except *you're* the one who's leaving."

"Don't do this, darlin'. It's like I said, let's give it a year up north. If you don't like it, we'll come back to Indianola and try it your way."

"I love you, my brave Ryder. You'll always be my shiny nickel."

Nickel gasped. Always? It sounded like a "farewell."

Magdalena threw her arms around his neck and squeezed so tight she took his breath. He wrapped his own arms, now full of India ink, around her slender waist. He held her against the lashing wind, and of the sea whose love she preferred over his own.

Nickel clung, burying his face in dark, flying hair, inhaling her scent. With every shudder, every heartbeat, every twitch of muscle, he silently begged her to reconsider. She held him for a long time, and he tightened his grip, sliding his fingers across her waist to the small of her back.

Nickel knew by the tremble of her body, the tears slipping from her eyes, the desperation in her embrace . . . Magdalena's decision was already made.

He did not try to change her mind. If she thought she would be happier living by the sea without him than living anywhere else *with* him . . . He shuddered, shutting down the thought before he could finish it. A sob escaped his lips, and he covered it up by kissing her.

He tasted tears on her mouth but didn't know if they were hers or his own. She ran her hands through his hair, down his neck, and across his arms, covering his open mouth with the soft, heady flavor of her lips. It was a kiss of desperation, each pleading with the other to give in, each knowing they could not do so.

He tried to melt against her, shielding her from the foul weather, but Magdalena pulled away as sharply as she had fallen into him. He reached for her, afraid to let her go, but she stepped out of reach and shook her head, fat tears rolling down her cheeks.

"I love you," she said, over and over, but retreated with each step.

"Mags, no!" he called.

"I-I'm sorry," she cried. The words, so soft on the wind, were barely discernable. "I love you." Magdalena turned and ran. She darted barefoot through the surf, then turned and made a beeline for Indianola. Heading home.

Home, where she would stay. Indianola was grand, but still, how dare she choose Indianola over him? She didn't even try!

Nickel stared after her until she disappeared from sight, then staggered against the wind. His hollow chest heaved as he watched throngs of people scurrying back and forth in the streets and along the port. They carried on as though the world was just and right, excited by the storm blowing in, not realizing they were witnessing a young man break in two.

A raindrop plunked on his nose and slid down his cheek.

Long after she was out of sight, Nickel turned an unseeing gaze back to the gray, choppy sea. Waves crashed at his legs, but he did not feel them.

Another raindrop splattered in his ear while a few of its friends began to follow suit. A tear tracked down his face, then another, but he let them fall, blending into the salt water smashing over his feet.

First Les Harold, now Magdalena. Old Whistle and his fan-tailed bird were right, after all. Something more than a squall was brewing.

Rubbing his arm, Nickel ventured back to the little shack he declared home. It was time for another pain-filled visit to see Joly. If the Beisht Kione raised its ugly head and swallowed him whole before he got there, so be it.

# CHAPTER 15

# RETURN OF THE MISTRESS

*September 15*
*Late Afternoon*

The waning light from the storm was too dim to inspect Joly's workmanship, so Nickel rolled down his sleeve, wincing as the fabric scraped over the Beisht wrapped around his raw arm. The pain would subside, and he would have a lifetime to enjoy the fruits of his discomfort.

If only facing Magdalena's decision would be so easy. At least for an hour or two, the bite of the needle swept aside a little of the turmoil within his heart. Her betrayal was far worse than any skin prick. He had supposed she would be with him forever, just like the art on his skin.

Hoisting an oilskin tarp over his head, Nickel stepped out into the foul weather, having declined Joly's offer to stay and wait out the storm. Joly lived too close to the edge of the world, and his little shelter had a habit of washing away during squalls.

Today, the wind had a tearing quality, screaming through cracks in the planks and shaking the walls. Even with luck in his favor, Nickel didn't feel much like tempting the Mistress by proximity. Best to retreat into the downpour now and reach the sanctuary of home than to fight off a raging, watery beast later.

Only, Nickel did not go home. Magdalena Hayworth heavy on his mind, he trudged through the downpour to see if, possibly, she had reconsidered. If only he could get her to see him one more time, to share in one more kiss—it might make a difference. Mags loved him. She said so! Why would she consider staying in Indianola without him? It might be the edge of their little world, but it wasn't the end of it, either. She would realize that—if she'd only go with him.

Bannack—he might not like it, but he'd have no choice in Magdalena's coming along if she was already his bride.

Convinced she would listen to reason this time, he marched toward the Hayworth home. When it was within sight, he stopped short.

She was there, standing under the porch, wrapped in the arms of another man. Her chin was tucked downward, buried into his chest, her arms encircling his neck. The young man lifted his head and, spotting a soaking wet Nickel standing in the middle of the street, began to smile.

Alastor Wheeler waved a few fingers at him, curled his hand to Magdalena's chin, and gently tilt it upward. The kiss his brother bestowed upon Magdalena's lips sent a silent scream ripping through Nickel's lungs. The wind tore at his breath, but he didn't care.

Dropping the oilcloth to the ground, he turned away, staggering into the onslaught. Reeling from Magdalena's betrayal, the young man went not home, or even to see Les, but to the house of Lucy Parker.

It was the only thing his scrambled brain could think to do. Any other day, Nickel would have attacked, fought for what was his. Seeing Magdalena—his Magdalena!—with Alastor Wheeler took the fight out of him. His mind shut down.

Maybe Lucy Parker would know what to do. If nothing else, *she* would be glad to see him, no matter what.

Lucy had been sweet on him ever since they were kids and suggested he visit her some time when her Pa was out of town. Mr. Parker's job carried him off a lot, often a few days or weeks at a time. Lucy never said what her Pa did, and Nickel never asked. She didn't have a Ma, at least not that he knew, so she fended for herself when her Pa was away. He had never gone to her house, not while she was alone, but she often dined with other families who took pity on her.

Even Molly Wheeler had Lucy over for dinner some nights, until Alastor tried turning her head. Not that Al wanted Lucy—or even liked her that much—he just didn't want Nickel to have her. Fights often ensued between brothers, so Lucy Parker's invitations slackened.

Now, here he was, standing in her house, unchaperoned and shattered.

"Nickel?" Lucy creased her delicate face with worry. She touched his left arm, and he yanked it away, rubbing the raw spot her fingers had grazed. "Nickel? Are you all right? You're soaked to the skin."

He was unable to string two words together, not even to lie. Alastor, that slimy bastard of a brother . . . and his beautiful Magdalena? Bile rose in his throat, and he shut his eyes against the memory. They were still there, burned in his mind. Holding one another. The bend of Alastor's head, the smarmy look of triumph in his grin, his lips on hers . . .

"Aaahhh!" Nickel sank into the nearest chair, holding his head, wishing he could squeeze them both from his mind for good.

"Nickel, what is it? What's happened?" Lucy sank to her knees, trying to peer into his face. Her hand rested on his arm again, only this time he let it stay.

"She let him kiss her," he said. Even to his own ears, his voice sounded flat. Lifeless. "She didn't wanna go north with me, didn't wanna marry me, but she let him maul her!"

"Magdalena," Lucy said with a sigh, tightening her grip. "You always wanted her."

"I guess she don't want me," he replied, "else she wouldn't be out there kissing on that bastard Alastor right now."

"Alastor?" Lucy staggered a step backward, covering her mouth with her hand. "Your *brother*?"

"Is there anybody else in the world named Alastor?"

"Magdalena Hayworth is a little fool, Nickel!"

"No, she's not!"

"She let you go, didn't she?"

*I shouldn't have come,* Nickel thought. *She ain't nothing like Mags—I shouldn't have come. Too late to turn back now. Too late for a lot of things,* he mused.

"It was a mistake coming here," he admitted aloud. "I gotta go." Nickel headed for the door.

"No!" she cried, grabbing his arm. "Wait, the storm!"

He winced, for she was digging her fingers into freshly tattooed skin.

"I'm already soaked—guess it don't matter much."

"But . . . I'm alone here, Nickel, and I'm scared of storms! Always have been. It'll blow over soon, and you can go then if you want."

Nickel hesitated, eyeing his escape.

"Please stay, Nickel," she pleaded. "I'm sorry for what I said about her. It's just . . ." Lucy paused, inhaling deeply.

"Just *what?*"

"Well," she said, "I hate to be the one to tell you, but I already know about Magdalena and your brother. He's been courting her for a few weeks now. Might be longer."

Nickel paled. "That . . . can't be . . . true. Mags wouldn't do that to me."

"She liked you, of course, but you're leaving and Alastor made it clear he's staying. I guess that made her like him more." Lucy sidled in, wiping the water from his face. "I'm sorry. I realize you love her, but it's the truth, I swear. I saw them together before." She pressed herself against him, whispering apologies. Slowly, the young woman began to unfasten the bodice of her dress. Nickel froze, and his weary, war-torn mind spun. He watched, blinking, uncomprehending. She shrugged the dress off her shoulders, shimmying her body until it dropped to the floor, revealing a pink-and-white-striped corset over yards of underlying petticoat.

"Magdalena's a fool," Lucy repeated, her purr low in his ear. "I'm glad you came to me."

Ↄ

Soft hands against his skin jolted him awake. He blinked into the yellow lamplight and sat up, stretching the knots from his back and shoulders.

"How long have I been asleep?" he asked, trying to peer out the window. Night had settled some hours before, cloaking the water-clogged little city.

"A few hours," Lucy said with a sniff. "You drifted after . . . after . . . well."

"Mmm."

"The storm's getting much worse, Nickel. I thought it would let up by now." Her voice sounded strained, and he realized she was crying. Not just a few wayward drops, either, but a torrent of shoulder-shaking, red-faced, snot-nosed blubbering.

Nickel wrapped his arms around the girl and yanked her close. Boy, she *was* afraid of storms. He had supposed he could be home before dark—usually they passed through quick enough. This one meant to linger. Rain continued to assault the town, and the wind picked up in velocity, sending waves hurtling over the beach.

"I don't guess the docks will hold by morning if it don't stop soon," he told her.

"You're not helping!"

No, he wasn't. Fact was, even though Lucy made him a man, it was Magdalena he pictured in his mind. What was she doing now? Was she sitting warm and dry with her parents, listening to the deluge outside? Was she thinking of him? Or was she letting Alastor Wheeler comfort her the way he was with Lucy? The thought sent a pang burning through his chest.

Crumpling his hands into fists, he rolled out of bed to pace like a lobo wolf trapped in a cage. He didn't want to be here, comforting Lucy Parker and her rumpled dress. He wanted to be with Mags, holding her hand. Kissing on her, and planning their future. Together.

Nickel figured the storm was bad, but he'd been out in them before. The Harold house was closer than home, so why not duck and run, and see that Les was okay? He would weather the remainder of the storm with the Harolds and go home from there.

Decision made, Nickel ventured so far as to open the door and peer out into the dark. Wind howled around him, nearly ripping the door from his grasp, and the driving rain smashed into his face when he stepped out to gauge the situation. A few men were out in the thick of the weather, slogging through the street donned in oilskin slickers and big, broad floppy hats tied around their chins with rope. They, too, appeared to be worried. Nickel hailed them down.

"She's blowing in east-northeast," one yelled. "Wind's picking up fierce, and the water, she's a'rising. Ain't seen her like that since back in sixty-seven."

"What about the docks?" Nickel asked.

"Docks and bridges are taking a beating. We're losing the bridges. You alone, Nickel?"

"Lucius Parker ain't home, and Lucy's real scared of storms," he told them.

"So you be giving that girl a little of your luck, eh?" The men laughed.

"Yessir! What if the water breaks?"

"Son, we've seen many a storm. This be a bad one, but the water, she'll recede by morning."

"You think so?" Nickel shouted.

"She always does. Best thing for you is to snuggle in real tight with that girl and wait it out. The water, even if she breaks, won't reach this far inland. You're sitting near the back of the town, Nickel, and this house is strong as any other. People along the waterfront are filling the courthouse now. The waves, they're coming in strong and the docks probably won't hold."

"You sure? Me and Luce could bundle up, go with you to the courthouse. I've got my family to see to."

"Stay put, Nickel! No need to be out in this!" The man shouted to be heard over the raging wind. "The waterfront's dangerous!"

"But my *home's* along the waterfront!" Nickel yelled.

"They're probably at the courthouse."

"But they don't know where I am!"

"I'll get word to them, boy. Don't you worry none. You just keep that girl warm and come morning, you'll see the storm will have passed by and the water retreated. She's gotta blow over some time."

Nickel watched the men pass on down the street into the darkness, yanking on their hats to shield their faces from blowing water.

*Grim,* he thought, and retreated, bolting the door. Magdalena, of course, was with her family, and Lucy Parker shouldn't be left alone to face the storm. She was trembling, her tear-streaked face glistening in the lamplight.

"Do we have to go out there?" she asked.

"It'll be all right, Luce," he said. "Those men said we were just to stay put and wait it out here, where we're warm and dry."

She threw her arms around him. "What would I do if you weren't here?" she asked, mumbling into his neck. "Thank you."

Nickel nodded, his gaze still on the door.

"You're thinking about her, aren't you? Magdalena."

"Yes," he admitted.

"I guess you feel for her what I do for you."

Nickel didn't know what to say. There was no denying the truth, so he said nothing.

"Well, I don't care, Nickel. Love her if you want—just stay here with me tonight and I won't care." She reached for him, at once both a frightened girl and an innate woman, both needful of the physical comfort within the hands of the only boy she loved.

Lucy undressed fully this time and slipped out of her petticoats with a nervous resolution. She brought his hands to her hips, wrapped her arms around his neck, and pulled him lengthwise against her.

She was sacrificing more than Nickel cared to understand. By all rights, he should stay away. But he never saw a woman unclad before—not all at once, anyway—and certainly not straining to receive him.

The first time they had coupled, it was awkward to navigate through yards of rumpled petticoats. He had nearly failed to find her center until she helped guide him in. Now he knew what it felt like to surge into the innocence of those beguiling feminine charms.

Undressing, Nickel needed no guidance this time. He sank deep into rosy flesh and soon found his rhythm, welcoming the respite from shattered nerves and heartbreak. The storm was stripping their strength, just as it was washing away the edges of Indianola, one wayward soul at a time. Those fishermen were right: this storm would cease and the water recede, just as it always did.

The howl of the gale outside, the memory of Magdalena's words whispered into the wind, he heard none of it, save the rising pitch of Lucille's moans and cries. Soothed by Lucy's hands, the constant droning in his ears faded away.

&#8478;

*September 16*
*Dawn*

Nickel rose with the dawn, an incessant roar of wind and waves hounding his ears. Waves? But that wasn't possible—Lucy's little window overlooked not the sea, but the far-reaching prairie stretching behind town. That is what he expected to see—prairie. After all, he'd never known a window to lie before.

Climbing into his britches and boots, he ran outside shirtless to gape slack-jawed at the new world around him. The prairie was gone, replaced by a fury of rushing water fueled by hurricane winds. Roads and cross alleys were now torrential rivers. Whitecaps grasped at his feet like foamy fingers, and his blood ran cold. The Mistress had escaped the confines of the bay!

To Nickel, her desire was clear. Since he would not go to her, she was searching for him, ripping through the hapless town of Indianola and everyone between them.

"No!" he screamed. "You can't have me, you greedy bitch!"

As if in reply, a splintered and torn wooden plank slammed against and lodged into the porch rails in front of him. The porch shook under the strain as screaming wind and water pounded against the debris. They were wrong. All of them. All of them—except little Hera. In a flash, he remembered her nightmare the night of Alastor's attack.

*I slept it, Nickel Ryder! They turned the whole world to water!*

Nickel backed up to the door in a rapid, side-to-side motion, his eyes wide, his mouth gaping. Grasping the handle, he wrenched it open and fell inside.

"Lucy! Dress, now! We gotta go!" He flipped the startled girl off the bed and threw her dress at her. There was no time for undergarments, frills, or fluffs. Soon as she yanked it over her head, he had her by the arm, wrenching her toward the water.

The foundation was shaking under their feet. He moved without thought, for there was no recourse. He had Lucy's life in his hands, and probably his own. The house was not strong enough to bear the Mistress's rage. If the house fell with them in it, they'd die.

Where did one go, when the world was water? Lucy's first sight of the screaming prairie sent the girl into ear-shattering shrieks.

Grabbing her by the waist, he yanked her forward and out to the porch, searching for a way through the violent water.

"Stop it, Luce!" he shouted. "You can't cry now! You panic, we're both done for, you hear me? I'm gonna get you to the courthouse!"

It was the only place he could think of. After all, the men last night said people were filling the courthouse. Swift waters rolled, driven by harsh winds that nearly blinded him. Holding to Lucy with one arm, he turned his face into the wind, squinting as he scrambled for a means of escape. A piece of twisted metal the size of a small building slammed into the side of the house, shattering a window near their heads.

Ducking low, he held her head down, shielding it with his bare chest the best he could.

"Can you swim?" he asked her, but she didn't hear him over the gale. He swore, though it didn't matter whether she was a swimmer. No one could plunge into the floodwaters safely.

Nickel closed his eyes and slid his right hand over his first, and favorite, tattoo. It was the swan on his chest, standing over the boat with a boy inside. The tattoo was his shield, a symbol of grace and protection. The swan was Mags.

*Magdalena, protect me. Send me a boat. I'm comin' for you.* He opened his eyes and spotted people across the torrential street lashing cotton bales together to form a makeshift raft. Another was fighting wind and water to secure ropes from house to house. Guidelines.

Nickel yelled at them and waved, gaining attention. The man pointed, and another tied a rope around his middle and floundered the makeshift raft into the current toward them. The man was knocked about like a child's doll. Twice the cotton bale raft nearly succumbed to the current, but the man maneuvered with a long pole, pushing and bumping off debris to steer.

When their rescuer was close enough, Nickel jumped off the porch, yanking Lucy with him. The current tore at their legs, knocking them off-kilter. The girl grasped at him as he struggled to swim. He hadn't realized it was so deep! Where was the street? He couldn't find solid ground. Nickel saw the man reach for him and thrust Lucy into his grasp instead.

"Take her!" Nickel yelled.

"Courthouse!" the man yelled back. He gave Nickel the end of the rope and pointed to Lucy's house.

*Secure the end,* Nickel thought, and turned back to the Parker house, where he tied a square knot around the main post of the overhang. It need only hold long enough for them to get across. He doubled his efforts and grabbed hold of the rope, now taut yet swinging across the flooded street.

Nickel floundered back to the raft and climbed halfway on. The man pulled him up and he lay down on top of Lucy, pinning her to the bale so she couldn't fall off unless he did.

Fist after fist, the man pulled them out into the raging torrent, clinging to the guideline. He tried not to think of what it felt like to drown.

*Breathe, dammit!* he told himself. No time for fear. He had to get to the courthouse, had to find Magdalena, Les, and his family.

Waves broke over them, drenching their skin and skidding the cotton bales in violent circles. They dodged timbers, twisted metal, and flotsam swirling out into the prairie sea. Nickel saw other boats, rafts, and makeshift floats along a web of guidelines, all of them headed in the same direction. One boy he thought he recognized rode in a large wooden tub. The boy waved at them as though taking a stroll down the street.

Finally, the courthouse was in sight! The lead man turned to shout something, an order perhaps, when it happened. A section of bridge as large as Joly's shack eddied around a corner and slammed into the house to their immediate right, knocking it off its pilings. With rapid precision, Nickel pulled Lucy back and let go of the rope just as the massive debris fell into the water. The guideline snapped, and it knocked their rescuer into the raging floodwaters. Nickel searched for the man, hoping to grab hold of an arm or a hand. There was no time, for they were now floating freely down into the debris field.

Keeping one hand on Lucy, he tried to steer them to the opposite side of the road. It was the dolphin hunt all over again. He could see his quarry but could not attain it.

Faintly, he heard Lucy scream and turned his head in time to see the section of bridge demolish a small boat filled with people. Nickel saw heads go under, but none rose. Something bumped his back, and he grabbed hold of it. A lost rake. He used it as a prodding stick, pushing them away from shredded boards much like the man had. As the storm pelted them, Nickel felt the ache of the Beisht Kione, that black-headed serpent tattooed on his arm, and wondered if it had the power to swim off his skin and swallow him whole.

The depth of the water, he could not determine, but the force was so strong he could not push against it. Rather, he steered in a diagonal line until he found another guideline running to the courthouse. He pulled them along until his arms throbbed, but at last they made it to the building where people rushed to help them.

Hands grabbed hold of him, pulling him inside. He kept hold of Lucy's hand, afraid he would lose her in the chaos if he let her go.

Inside, hundreds of refugees were flocking from the storm, most of them searching for loved ones. Shirtless and soaked to the skin, Nickel called for his family, asking for Molly, Zelus, Hera, and the youngsters. Where were Les, Magdalena, and Joly?

With every shake of the head, Nickel's panic heightened. They couldn't all be out in the weather! He checked every floor, but with the certainty that his loved ones weren't there rose the realization that he was going back into the storm. The Mistress was not through with him yet.

Well, that was fine. She was now between him, Les and his family, and Magdalena. Nickel wasn't through with her, either.

CHAPTER 16

# WORLD'S END

*September 19*
*Three Days Later*

66 "The world's done ended." The horseman's voice rang hollow. His companion just sat his horse and stared. The men drew rein and looked up, unable to comprehend the sight sprawled before them. It was several minutes before either spoke.

"B-B-Bannack?" Marbles stammered.

"Yeah, Marbles?"

"How . . . ? How f-far to the t-town?"

"'Bout five miles. Maybe six."

"F-Five miles," Marbles repeated. "That's a sh-ship."

"Shore looks like one," Bannack agreed.

"B-But . . . we're on a p-p-prairie."

Still miles away from the city that stretched along the bay, surrounded by a forest of debris, leaned a three-masted clipper ship, no less than two hundred feet long. It was the largest boat either man had ever seen.

Bannack's gaze drifted to the base of the grounded clipper. Broken boards and debris had washed against the side of the massive boat and collected in a heap of rubble. He spotted a shingle perched squarely atop the mess, advertising soda-fountain ice creams. It looked like it was carefully placed there.

But it was not that which caught the cowboy's attention. A spot of ashen gray showed from under the broken sign, and Bannack's poise weakened.

Dismounting for a closer look, he discovered the patch of gray was an arm. It was bent at an unnatural angle, and blue-splotched fingers seemed to claw at the earth even in death. Unspeakable dread filled the pit of the cowboy's stomach.

*Please, God, don't let it be that boy.* Bannack yanked at the boards, pulling and shoving debris out of the way. Reaching the unfortunate soul twisted among the rubble, Bannack dragged his hat off his head and into his hands. The deceased had, somehow, washed miles inland, just like the clipper. There was no identifying the mangled body, though the remains suggested a woman.

On his knees in the sodden, sandy soil, Bannack looked to the direction of Indianola, over five miles distant. While they could not yet see the town, the storm lay a wide swath of destruction before them—a swath as vast as the sea herself. Something told him this was merely the first of many bodies they would find.

"We ain't on a prairie anymore, Marbles," Bannack said.

"Wh-What is it?"

"A graveyard."

Leading their horses burdened with the woman's remains, the two men picked their way through fragments of buildings and timber, uprooted trees, and all manner of busted furniture and household goods. Drowned livestock lay tangled among the wreckage. Planks, boards, and siding, trunks, barrels, and cisterns littered the prairie. Just as expected, they encountered three more lost souls before reaching their destination. Dutifully, they retrieved each one so they could be accounted for and be afforded proper burials.

Bannack thought of the last time he heard from Ryder; the letter, he suspected, was not written in his hand, though the words themselves were undoubtedly his. The boy spoke of his eagerness to begin his new life, to learn to "cowboy" under Bannack's guidance. He would be ready, he said, and still wore his spur and jinglebobs faithfully.

*"I'll be the best hand you ever seen,"* he had said. That letter came with a picture—Ryder's friends stood with him for a photographer, just so Bannack could see that he had grown into a young man. The Ryder in the picture was much taller and stronger than the little boy he remembered, though his confidence smeared with mischief had not changed. What would he find when they reached town? Would Ryder be there, waiting on him? Or was he buried somewhere, ashen and lifeless, tangled among the wreckage of what had been a thriving seaport?

A shriek to their right brought Bannack and Marbles to an abrupt halt.

It was a scream-like sound, though one neither could identify. Veering off course, they found a sallow old man with long, stringy hair perched atop a three-legged chair in the midst of the debris field. His clothes were ragged and sodden, mud and filth caked on his skin so that, as they approached, no one could not determine the real color of his skin. A large sapphire bird hung limp over the man's shoulder; its long tail crossed his back to hang, bedraggled, to the ground. To the cowboys' surprise, they discovered the bird, clearly dead, was lashed to the man's shoulder.

"You hurt, Mister?" Bannack asked.

The man turned his head, stroking the bird's feathers.

"When the peacock loudly bawls, soon we'll have both rain and squalls," he said, and emitted another loud shriek.

Marbles jumped at the odd sound, took a few steps backward, tripped, and nearly fell over a cow carcass.

Bannack held his ground.

"Told 'em, we did," the old man said.

"Told who?"

"Nickel, Nickel lost his luck, couldn't grow wings, and now he's stuck. Hahaha!" The crazed man cackled over his own wit.

Bannack exchanged a look with Marbles, who shook his head.

"Wh-What's he t-talkin' 'bout n-nickels for?" Marbles asked. Bannack didn't reply. They would get nowhere questioning a man with a dead bird lashed to his arm.

"We told him! Told 'em all! They didn't listen to ole Whistle now, did they, beautiful?" The man lifted the bird's head and kissed it on the beak. "She took 'em all, just like we said. Bye-bye, Nickel! Bye-bye!"

The man was out of his mind, clearly an unfit source of information, so they trudged onward, eager to leave the birdman behind. He called to them to regain their attention and chanted amid a chorus of his own eerie whistles and bird chirps.

"Nickel, Nickel lost his luck, couldn't grow wings, and now he's stuck! Hahahaha!"

"Think that f-feller was always c-c-crazy?" Marbles wondered aloud. "Wh-What's he mean by stuck n-nickels?"

"Don't know, Marbles. Nothin' makes much sense today."

&#8729;

As they neared Indianola, more people cropped up, rummaging through the wreckage, many of them calling the names of those lost or missing. Bannack and Marbles both knew the atrocities of war; it was an unspoken bond between them, and one which needed no discussion. There was no need; it burned those years of slaughter into the haunt of their eyes and the grim set of their jaw. But this was not a war. At least, not one borne of human nature. There had been no battle between brothers here—no weapons fired, no artillery, no prisoners marched off to exist in squalid camps, and yet, the carnage was complete. The sea had come—the very one Ryder had feared as a child.

Indianola was gone.

Like the ship they found swept inland, entire buildings had been culled from their foundations and scattered to hell. Railroad tracks were erased from sight, and new tributaries had formed, carved helter-skelter through the land, their flow still full and swift. Nothing remained standing. Nothing.

How many citizens lost to the floodwaters and swallowed by the sea? In all directions, small groups of weary, ragged people armed with broken shovels, oars, and picks hopped across gullies and washes, digging through mounds of debris. Some had nothing but a busted board or their bare hands with which to dig. Burial details.

Bannack and Marbles approached the nearest group, who regarded them with the red-rimmed vacant stares only a soldier, having experienced combat, could understand. Bannack knew the gaze well. *This ain't a war,* he mused, *but shore as hell, it's a battlefield just the same.*

The Indianolans appropriated the bodies from the cowboys' saddles and laid them out. Each man knelt to examine the faces of the deceased, only to discover the remains were beyond identification.

"They're too ripped up," one man cried. "We can't even tell who they are!" Dropping his shovel, he palmed his mouth. "That could be my Sally. What if I bury my Sally and don't even know her?"

No one answered him. They didn't need to; the survivors all shared the same fears. Marbles, without speaking, retrieved his canteen and passed it among the exhausted men. Bannack noted that, thirsty as they looked, each of the four men only took a swallow or two before handing it back.

"Save the rest for women and children," the last man said. He was leaning on his shovel, probably the only thing holding him upright. Bannack grabbed the man's arm to steady him and took the shovel.

"Sit. I'll dig," he said. Marbles followed suit, and the Indianola men sank to their knees to rest, watching two strangers widen the hole for their fallen citizens. Just as the last shovelful of sand and earth was tamped down over the mass grave, they heard a rasping voice call out a name.

"Niii . . . ckeeel! Niii . . . ckeeel!" The name was repeated, drawn out in long syllables, creating a lingering echo as he wandered through the debris. The searcher was young, trapped in the awkward age somewhere between a boy and a man. Ryder's age. Hope sparked in Bannack's chest. Was Ryder alive?

He called out to the youth, kicking a plank out of his way as he approached. The young man turned, and the spark fizzled, burning a hole in the pit of his stomach as it died. No. Not Ryder. Definitely not Ryder.

The boy, however, seemed to know him. In an instant, Ryder's tintype surfaced in his memory, and he knew who it was. Something about the knowing didn't ease Bannack's mind.

Running forward, Ryder's best friend caught Bannack's hand and wrung it.

"My God, Mr. Bannack! Are you real?" he asked. His voice was jagged and worn from overuse.

"Les Harold?"

"Yessir," Les croaked. "For God's sake, help us, please!"

"Where is he, Les?"

The boy's lips quivered, and his eyes filled. "We've been searching since yesterday morning when the water receded. I . . ." Les looked around him and swiped at his bloodshot eyes. "I don't know where to look anymore. There's just so much . . . gone. It's all gone. My momma's gone too," he sniffed, rubbing at his throat. Judging by the rasp in his voice, it hurt him to talk. Bannack sat him down on a timber and handed him his canteen.

"Drink what you need," he ordered, "then tell us about it."

Marbles sat down next to Bannack, removed his hat, and wiped his brow on his sleeve. He, too, was ready to listen.

Les drank slow, savoring the fresh water. He closed his eyes for so long, Bannack considered nudging him awake.

"It was the wind," Les said, his eyes still shut tight. "She drove the sea in on us. Two, three days the wind and water were right on top of us. I don't know how long it's been anymore. Wh-What day is it?"

"Sunday. Nineteenth."

"Last I remember, it was Wednesday." Les shrugged, knuckling at his eyes. "Some of us made it to the courthouse, some of us didn't," he said.

"Ryder didn't make it to the courthouse, did he?" Bannack asked, his face deadpan save for a grim twist to his mouth.

"Oh, he made it. They say he wasn't wearin' a shirt, and he came in ridin' on a cotton bale. He fell in through the front door with a girl, Lucy Parker. She says he saved her life. But he got there before I did. His momma and the kids weren't there, and neither was his girl, Mags. People say he got mad at the Mistress, swearin' and frothin' at her. He done told her she wasn't takin' his family from him, and he went back out to find us."

*Aww, dammit, Ryder!* Bannack ran his hands over his face, dragging his fingers downward as he stared at the volumes of destruction before them. Was Ryder still out there, searching for his family? It didn't seem likely. If he were capable of movement, he would have come to the courthouse by now.

He gripped Les's shoulder. "I'm sorry, son," he said.

"No sir!" Les snapped. Rising, he faced the cowboys still crouched on the timber. "He's not dead, so don't you be sorry! He's not. I don't care how long I gotta look, I'm gonna find him alive! He went out there lookin' for me, and I ain't givin' up on him!"

"I'm not givin' up on him, either," Bannack said, his expression serious. "We'll look together."

Les looked from him to Marbles, and then his gaze glittered toward the littered bay and the sea beyond.

"A few men saw him comin' in," he said. "Somehow he had found his brothers and sisters and was bringin' them in on boats." Les paused, biting back tears. "He was in the lead boat with a few of the young'uns. They told me a timber eddied around a corner and struck the boats. They capsized. One man told me he thought he saw him clingin' to the timber, which caught in the side of a house. Nobody could get to him. He said debris struck him in the back, and Nickel . . . he went under." Les shook his head at the water, now receded. Fat tears rolled down his cheeks.

Bannack shut his eyes, picturing the ten-year-old boy he met years ago. Ryder was fierce in determination even then, adept at bouncing back from the hard lot dealt him with little more than a shrug. He knew nothing other than the sea. Hell, he probably never even ventured out of Indianola, and yet the boy was eager to drop his whole life and pick up a new one.

Damn. Damn! He didn't want to think about that sunny, bright-eyed boy lying out there somewhere alone, torn beyond recognition.

Marbles, who had been quiet until now, turned and stared at Les.

"N-Nickel? Who's N-Nickel?"

"My best friend!" Les cried out. "He's my best friend. Nobody ever calls him Ryder anymore except you, Mr. Bannack, his momma, and his girl. I'm real tired, sir. I don't know where to look anymore." Les swept his hand across the tangled remains of his city. "Where? How far does it go?" he asked.

"You can't cover the ground yourself, Les," Bannack said. "Combined, we couldn't cover it. Buildings and debris washed a good eight miles inland, son. We found a ship grounded almost six miles in."

Les gaped at him. "You mean . . . there might be . . . people washed that far?"

Bannack thought again of the bodies he and Marbles found, torn apart from raging water smashing them into debris. Those poor souls would never be identified.

"Yes," he admitted, "there are."

"No. No! No!" He vehemently shook his head.

"Les." Bannack stood, placing an awkward hand on the young man's shoulder. "He's out there somewhere. I don't know where, but we're gonna find your friend. I won't leave till we do."

"Alive? We'll find him alive?"

"I can't promise that, and you know it. But I'll stay till we recover him, one way or another."

"You saw 'em out there, didn't you? The dead?" Les asked.

"Me and Marbles here, we buried a few."

"My daddy said we'll never find most of 'em," Les muttered. "When the water turned and rushed back to sea, it took most everything with it."

"I expect he's right," Bannack said.

Wiping at blood-red eyes, Les sniffed a few times. "Well, that didn't happen to him! He's out there someplace. He can't drown again! Besides, Nickel wouldn't never give up on me if I was lost."

Bannack didn't answer. Words did not offer shelter, sustenance, or relief from worry over a town lost to the sea, or a boy mourning the loss of his best friend.

Marbles rose with a grunt, rubbing at a leather gauntlet wrapped around his wrist.

"Guess w-we know w-where to start l-lookin'," he said.

Bannack swung around. "Do we?"

"That old m-man with the dead bird on his sh-sh-shoulder kept t-talkin' about a n-nickel. Maybe it wasn't m-money he meant."

Bannack jumped as though Marbles had poked a hot iron into his neck.

"Nickel, Nickel," he whispered. "Nickel, Nickel lost his luck, couldn't grow wings, and now he's stuck."

Marbles nodded.

Les perked up at the mention of the birdman. "You saw a man with a bird?"

"Lashed to him. Spoke to it like a child."

"Crazy old man with long, gray hair?"

"That's him."

Les scowled. "*He* made it through? My family's gone, and he made it through?"

"Who's he?"

"Old Whistle. He's gone in the head, thinks he's a bird most of the time. Keeps birds all around him. Carried a big old gobbler around town scaring kids with it. Last November, Nickel decided his family was having a turkey dinner, so he tossed the bird in a sack and ran off with it. Whistle didn't much like him after that."

Bannack could picture that brown-headed boy crowing over a turkey feast.

"Let's go find that old birdbrain, Marbles."

"I'm coming with you, sir." Bannack hedged, undecided, then nodded.

Les knew the locoed sonofabitch—maybe he'd also know how to talk to him.

∝

Travel was slow, hindered by mounds of rubble and relentless gullies to cross, but the trio made their way back to Old Whistle's perch. The chair they found him on earlier was now empty, but they heard cackling, and with Bannack in the lead followed the racket around to a house swept off its foundation, now tottering to the left. The roof was gone, but there on an uncovered beam was Whistle.

Bannack and Marbles gaped, more than a little spooked over the sight before them.

"He's t-tailed himself!" Marbles muttered.

Sure enough, the bony old man had yanked the tail feathers out of his dead pet and poked the tips through the loose weave of his britches. They hung from his rear end, not quite the magnificent plumage of a regal beast. Whistle plucked feathers from the wings next, sticking them through the sleeves of his shirt.

"How the hell does a man talk to *that*?" Bannack grumbled.

Les stumbled forward, his eyes peeled on Whistle, until Marbles caught the youth by the shirt.

"N-No c-closer," he said. "That h-house could f-f-fall."

Les placed two fingers between his teeth and blew a piercing signal, gaining the old man's attention.

"Whistle!" Les shouted. "We're looking for Nickel! Have you seen him?"

"Hahahaha!" the old man cackled. "Nickel's sold his luck to the sea!" The man hopped on the beam, flapping his arms. Groans of complaint rumbled through the ramshackle pile under his feet, and the cowboys retreated a short distance, pulling Les with them.

Whistle shrieked at them, much in the same manner his peafowl used to do whenever anyone came near.

"Where is he, Whistle?" Les yelled. "Where's Nickel?"

"Nickel, Nickel lost his luck, couldn't grow wings, and now he's stuck! Bye-bye!"

"Dammit, man, have you seen the boy or not?" Bannack demanded.

"Seen him, seen him, seen him or not," Whistle parroted, and rearranged his wing feathers.

"I'll tear those wings off if you don't answer straight!" Bannack yelled.

His reply was a hiss and a series of hops, squawks, and singsong chirps.

Ryder—Nickel to his friends—was gone, and this shithead thought he was a damned bird.

Les picked up a nearby brick and lunged, screaming as he threw it. The boy missed his target by a few inches but insulted the birdman nonetheless. Old Whistle pitched a squawking fit and raised up with his arms stretched out. Blue, green, and purple feathers stuck out of him in all directions. He looked more like a human pincushion than a bird.

"Th-That idiot's gonna try to f-fly off that b-beam!"!" Marbles exclaimed. They watched Whistle test his newfound wings as he shrieked, yelling garbled man-bird language in their direction. The man hopped, his arms spread wide, and ran across the length of the beam.

The men called out to him, but Old Whistle, convinced he could fly, leaped from the tottering house and disappeared from sight. A distinctive clang announced his landing, and Les Harold yelped, clapping his hands over his ears to soften the bell-like after-tones.

"Locoed bastard," Bannack growled. "Guess crazy don't make you fly."

They rounded the corner and approached the feathered old man. Bannack nudged his side with his toe.

"He dead?" Marbles asked.

"Yep."

"You s-sure?" The stuttering cowhand leaned a little heavy on superstitious nonsense, in Bannack's opinion. He didn't cotton much toward close contact with people who grazed on locoweed.

"Dumb shit fell headfirst into an iron cook stove. Guess he won't be caterwauling anymore—not unless he's witched or something."

"That ain't funny, B-B-Bannack!"

"Do I look like I'm laughing?" Bannack retorted.

"Are we gonna bury him?" Les asked the cowboy.

"He ain't worth the time," Bannack said. "We've wasted enough."

Les followed Bannack's retreat but glanced over his shoulder for one last look at Old Whistle, Indianola's birdman. It didn't seem right to leave him there, even if he was crazy.

Marbles laid a firm hand on the boy's shoulder.

"Lots of p-p-people need h-help right now, b-boy," he said. "B-Bannack ain't one to . . . to waste time on a f-f-fool, alive or dead."

# CHAPTER 17

# MAN OF MUSIC

A group of survivors huddled, quivering, in front of the courthouse, where the steps used to be. Some tended to their wounded, others sat near their deceased, too exhausted to dig their graves.

Little was said among them, but as Bannack approached leading his mount, he felt their eyes scanning him. They were hoping to find recognition in his face, but as he neared, flickers of hope deserted their stone-cast faces. A few women began to cry, for he was not their lost husband, father, or brother, alive and returning for them.

He noticed survivors were eyeing up their horses and mentioned the fact to Marbles. The animals would have to stay with them. To leave them behind was to induce theft in even the noblest of these lost, desperate people.

Les Harold sank to the top step beside a woman who lay with her head in a man's lap. The man's troubled gaze centered on Bannack, but he said nothing.

"Mrs. Wheeler, ma'am?" Les spoke. The woman moved but did not uncover her eyes.

"Mr. Bannack's here—come to see you."

Great big tears rolled down her cheeks, but Molly Wheeler did not whimper. She sat up with great difficulty and clutched Bannack's hands, drawing him against her.

"You're too late," she cried. "Too late to save my boy." Her voice wavered, undertones of hysteria creeping in at the edges. "Most of my kids are gone. The young ones, and Ryder, my beautiful Ryder . . . they were . . . swept away. I knew it, Bannack, I knew something like this would happen all along! People got no business building their homes so close to the water. The Mistress, she needs her space. How many times have I said it over the years?"

Bannack removed his hat and crouched near the grieving mother. "I don't know, ma'am."

"People got no business building a town against the sea," she repeated. "No business!"

"No ma'am, I can see they don't." He cast his gaze seaward, not that a body could tell between land and water. It was all the same—a debris field littered with bodies.

"Some of these fools, they want to rebuild the town," Molly told him. Her pitch rose. "Right here, where it was!"

"Some men are bred from foolish stock," Bannack agreed.

"But my Ryder's still out there." Molly's voice trembled. "No one believes me that he's alive, but he is. My boy was born of luck—everyone knows it—and he can't be taken by the sea. He's not like the others." She gestured toward the great watery destruction, now nestled back along the shoreline, contrite and caressing. "She took my beautiful babies, my children. I know we cannot bring them back; I *saw* the Mistress take them, but I could not reach them." She paused, clutching her hand to her chest, and closed her eyes. She shuddered, but Bannack thought she fought valiantly against the madness threatening to overtake her. "My Ryder," she continued, "nobody saw him die, and that means he's still out there. That murderess won't never take my Ryder."

"I'll look for him."

"Yes. Search for him, Bannack," she pleaded. "Find him! Posse and Alastor haven't been able to."

Edmund Harold spoke up, his tone patient yet firm. "Now, you know we won't find him, Molly. Just let me take you to Victoria. We can rest and collect ourselves."

"Go to hell, Harold," she growled.

Les's father shook his head. "You're hurt, Molly, and the kids you have left—"

"My Ryder's alive!" Molly yelled, sitting up despite a sharp grimace of pain. "I'm not leaving this spot! He'll come." She repeated the last two words over and over, her haunted eyes darting back and forth as though she could bring him back just by saying so.

Edmund Harold groaned. "She might have a few broken ribs," he told Bannack.

"Bruises, maybe. I expect if her ribs were busted, she wouldn't feel much like sittin' up that way."

"He'll find us, so I ain't leavin'! As long as I sit in one place, he'll come."

Bannack thought the woman was on the verge of losing her mind, not that he could blame her.

"I want you to take the boys I got left," Molly told him with a sniff.

"Molly!" Edmund broke in to protest, but she waved his objection aside with a harsh tongue.

"Squelch your tongue, Harold."

"You can't be giving away your family, not now."

"I lost my children!" Molly shrieked. "I want my remaining boys to stay the hell away from this godforsaken place! You'll send Les with Bannack if you've any sense left," Molly scolded.

Les's father opened his mouth to argue, but there didn't look to be much fight left in the man.

"I'll take them if that's what you want," Bannack told her, "but we'll get you and your kin taken care of first."

"I want my boys with you when you leave. I *won't* lose any more of my boys to the sea."

☙

Hours, much like the list of missing or dead, piled up. Bannack and Marbles worked alongside the Indianolans, clearing unstable debris for searchers and burying the unfortunate. The men watched Molly Wheeler cling to hope of finding her son alive, whereas their own diminished to a mere wish of recovering Nickel's body for proper burial.

Bannack realized the chances of finding one sixteen-year-old boy were slim, but Molly Wheeler would not quit.

Bannack did not believe in luck. Fortune, good or bad, was what you made of it—and of yourself. A mere boy was not capable of surviving a storm of this magnitude, based merely on sound luck. He did not voice his opinion aloud to the grieving mother. Instead, he formed the remaining Wheelers into an organized party, with their young friend Lucy Parker watching over the few remaining children while Molly and her eldest remaining sons—Posse, Alastor, and Zelus—split up to cover more ground.

Les Harold and his father proved valuable in searching for clues as to the identities of the deceased and keeping record to report to the town officials—if indeed any remained. It hit particularly hard when they could not discern an identity. Even the clothing was gone; the storm had rendered the deceased nude, most with missing skin. Les reassured them none of them could be Ryder, for he was marked with tattoos across his arms, chest, and shoulders.

Throughout the washed-out town, multitudes of similar searches were taking place. Straggling survivors begged everyone they met for news on their loved ones, still missing in the wreckage. The death toll was climbing higher, hope growing slimmer as the day drew to a close.

It had been two days since the water receded, and still no shiny Nickel. Bannack worked in broad, ever-widening arcs, searching the splinters of homes torn from their foundations. Debris piles turned up bodies, many of them like before: beyond identification.

Bannack shut down; he worked methodically, without tears, and seemingly without empathy. Wounded were led to help, the dead buried where they lay.

With every stroke of the shovel, every overturned clump of sandy soil, Bannack feared that somewhere in the miles of destruction laid out before them, a stranger was burying Ryder. They wouldn't know of the luck he lost. The temporary undertakers wouldn't know his name. They would lay him out in a shallow grave in the middle of a dead city. The burial over, the shovel-wielding stranger would move on, and Ryder's grave forgotten. Just like what they were doing to these poor nameless souls.

Maybe it would be better if it swept him out to sea. Except Ryder hated the sea. He feared it, loathed it, and yet, Bannack recalled the ten-year-old boy being drawn to the very thing he feared. Bannack tamped earth over a grave, said a silent prayer, and moved on, searching through the shifting rubble of Indianola.

Cʒ

"Aahh!"

The anguished yell turned Bannack, who saw Marbles about fifty yards distant, fling the digging spade from his hands. Almost in slow motion, he watched Marbles sink to his knees, palming his eyes as if to erase the anguish from his memory. The cowboy, a veteran at thirty, broke down and sobbed.

Bannack approached his friend and, upon reaching him, wished he hadn't. He saw the petticoats first and followed his eyes to the sight of a grown man's undoing.

They were tangled together under a web of debris. The young mother had sought sanctuary in the attic of her home. He figured she tried holding her little ones over her head to escape the raging floodwaters until the house collapsed down around them.

Unable to look into those pale cherub faces, Bannack lowered his gaze to their feet. One tiny shoe still remained intact, the other probably bobbing in the swollen tidewaters. His stomach heaved, but he had eaten nothing to bring back up.

"I c-c-can't d-do this," Marbles said. His teeth were chattering, which made his stutter far worse. "This ain't no b-battlefield," he cried. "It's w-women and ch-children!"

Though they hadn't spoken of it, he heard Marbles had served in the war just as he had. On the field, and in camp, they learned to cope with hunger, suffering, and death from necessity.

But this was different; Marbles was right about that. This was no senseless battle between men; this was the structure of man against nature. And Nature doesn't choose among cradle, petticoat, and uniform.

Bannack laid a firm hand on Marbles's shoulder, but there was nothing left to say. Words fell cheap; they did nothing to slay a grieving soul. Instead, he reached back to the only remedy he knew: the medicine of his youth.

Bannack began to sing, softly at first. He sang not of war, but of love lost. It was the song, some said, that lost the war, for upon hearing it, men fled the soldier's life, desperate to return to their sweethearts. As he sang the first lines, Marbles let out a strangled yell and clapped his hands over his ears.

Bannack sang anyway. His words built, caressing the slow, mournful melody, which mere spoken words could not express.

> *We loved each other then, Lorena*
> *Far more than we ever dared to tell*
> *And what we might have been, Lorena*
> *Had but our loving prospered well*
> *But then, 'tis past, the years are gone*
> *I'll not call up their shadowy forms*
> *I'll say to them, "Lost years, sleep on! Sleep on!*
> *Nor heed life's pelting storms."*

Bannack continued the verses as he lifted the children from where they lay and cloaked them carefully in their own petticoats. Both men gave the same care to the young mother.

Marbles was not blessed with Bannack's grace in song, but as he picked up on the slow, somber melody, the man's constant stutter disappeared and he sang with the sweetened drawl of a man freed from his verbal prison. He searched for each lyric, letting Bannack's low, graveled tone carry the burdens cast upon them. When Bannack reached the final verse, Marbles regained his feet, rubbing away the tears as he sang along:

> *It matters little now, Lorena*
> *The past is in the eternal past*
> *Our heads will soon lie low, Lorena*
> *Life's tide is ebbing out so fast*
> *There is a future, oh, thank God*
> *Of life this is so small a part*
> *'Tis dust to dust beneath the sod*
> *But there, up there, 'tis heart to heart*

As the last note drifted away, silence fell upon the mutilated town; the only sound was the sea at their backs.

Bannack recalled young Ryder, and how he had thought of the ocean as a woman. The Mistress, he called her. It made little sense to him then, but he understood it now.

"She almost seems contrite," he said aloud.

Marbles gave him a quizzical look and sniffed.

"The ocean. Ain't it just like a woman to wreck hell, then say she's sorry."

"W-Wouldn't know 'b-b-bout that." And just like that, Marbles's stutter returned, enforcing what Bannack already knew in his battered soul: music alone heals what man never will.

The men locked eyes; Bannack's cold and penetrating, the other's bleary and red-rimmed. Bannack grasped his companion's forearm.

"I don't take well to others. Don't trust 'em."

Marbles nodded. "I know. The b-boss said as m-much."

"I guess Cashman told you more'n that."

"S-Said you never c-came home from the war."

"No one ever does."

"Didn't m-mean to b-b-break," Marbles mumbled.

"Cashman don't know near as much about me as he thinks," Bannack said. "He's right on one thing, though. I didn't come back. Don't intend to try. I trust in myself and my horse. To hell with everyone else." Bannack tightened his grip on the man's arm. "But after this," he said, sweeping his free hand across the remnants of Indianola, "I reckon you'll do to ride the river with. You'll sure as hell do."

Coming from Bannack, it was the highest compliment a man was likely to receive. Marbles knew it but didn't seem to know how to meet it. His face contorted with emotion, he wrung his friend's hand.

"Ob-bliged, B-Bannack."

"Let's lay these folks to rest," Bannack replied.

ॐ

The harsh, ugly mound looked too desolate for the innocents lying inside. Marbles broke off a slab, withdrew his knife, and began to carve a makeshift marker.

Bannack bent to fashion an upright for the mass grave, but he never stopped scanning for a sign of Ryder. Instead, an older man approached with a heavy limp.

"Mister, you the one I heard singin' so purty?" Bannack straightened, cracking his back as he did so, and studied the sludge-laden man standing before him. He had a broad gash in his forehead, and another in his leg, but what intrigued Bannack was what he cradled in his arms.

"I am."

"You're a man of music, ain't you?"

"Yes."

"Heard it in your voice. My boy was the same way." The man held out his precious bundle: a fiddle.

"Can you play this?" he asked.

"I can," he said, gaping at the instrument. It didn't even appear to be damp. The man must have gone through hell trying to keep it safe.

"Would you play it for my boy?"

Bannack glanced at Marbles.

"G-Go on," he said. "I'll f-finish here."

"Lead the way," Bannack said, following the wounded man as he stumbled through the ruins to the water's edge, and stopped.

"He's out there," the man said. "They all are." He pressed the instrument into Bannack's hands. "Play something for them, Mister. Please?"

Bannack ran his fingers along the smooth edge, noting the wear of the instrument. It was old but well cared for. Bannack clambered up on a piling deposited on the beach from the storm, tested the strings, and began to play. This time, he did not utter a sound but allowed the strings to sing for him. He played the songs of the hills—calling for the innocence of a childhood lost. He was back in his woods, running barefoot through mountain streams, moss and rich, damp soil squishing between his toes. The melody in his ears, placed there by the mastery of his best friend's bow, drifted down from the highest ridge, beckoning for him to follow. He felt the mist rolling down the cliff, enveloping him until he was but a mere shadow. He breathed in the aroma of a blue-ridged, wet-forest memory, and played. Calling, calling, calling.

Beckoning to those who lost their lives, and to those who might still be alive and drifting, Bannack called with the lost boy's fiddle. The melody spoke of pain, and of promise. Of love, hope, and of grief and despair. Most of all, he spoke to Ryder, the fair-haired smiling boy who would have rode upon the back of a dolphin, had the water not gotten in his way.

CHAPTER 18

# MIND TRICKS AND A FIDDLE

Deprivation—whether it be sleep, food, or water—played hell on a tormented mind. Someone told him that once. Who was it? He couldn't remember. Whoever it was, they were right.

His right ankle throbbed, but he put one foot in front of the other. Again and again. Concentrating on the simple task, he found comfort in the familiar weight of the single spur. The jinglebobs was gone, and he missed the soft tinkling melody when he moved, but at least the spur itself was still intact. Bent and battered, but still there under layers of blood and grime. *Just like me.*

Strange images dogged him. Sometimes he saw his mother, slathering bear grease biscuits onto a platter. Only thing was, she was serving the meal at their table under the sea, with mermaids and mermen as her dinner guests.

Other times he saw Bannack. The first time he saw his hero, he called his name and tried to run to him, but the cowboy turned away and rode straight into the sea. When he blinked, the image disappeared.

He saw Oren Wheeler riding a serpent, speeding straight for him. His father was wielding a broken board, much like the one he beat him with five years ago. Most often he heard Magdalena's call, only to find her drifting under water or clawing at him and sucking him under, her eyes wide and unblinking in the gaze of death.

Nickel shifted the weight of the body over his right shoulder, screaming as another wave of sharp, spasmodic pain radiated through it and down his arm. He had tied it against his body with a length of moldy old sacking to keep it stationary, but it did nothing to keep the pain at bay.

*Don't think about what you're carrying. Think about something else. Anything! My spur. When Bannack comes, maybe I'll get the other.* He latched to that straggling thought, picturing himself riding away on a fine horse, the older man leading him to a brand-new life—one devoid of Davy Jones and a bloodthirsty sea.

His burden, wrapped in the remnants of a ship's sail, grew heavier by the hour. He had to cross creaking piles of debris, step across rivulets carved into the earth, and dodge animal carcasses, furniture, and broken houses. He saw it all through a blurry haze decorated with black floating spots. If he fell, so would she.

"I won't drop you," he promised through clenched teeth. "I'll get you home, I swear to God. I'll get you home."

Nickel's legs weren't so certain. The left one kept buckling, sending him to his knees. A few minutes' rest, and he would regather the body, now stiff and unmanageable, back over his good shoulder and stumble onward, bent on taking her home. Time—hours, minutes, days—they no longer held meaning. Hell was forever, and his alias had run plumb out of nickels.

Nickel stumbled again and fell, reaching at once to collect his load before the body hit the ground. The sharp spasm in his shoulder forced a strangled grunt between parched lips. He floundered, unable to pull himself up, yet unwilling to give in. His vision blurred as he sank, gulping back tears.

Wrapping his good arm around the shroud, he collapsed into the sand and buried his face in the folds of the battered canvas. His burden smelled of death. Soggy, salty death.

He didn't reach her in time . . . his luck did not save her. "I'm sorry," he cried. "Oh, God, I'm so sorry!" Nickel lay down next to her and closed his eyes, wishing he could share her wrap. Maybe he could squeeze in with her so she wouldn't be alone. He would just drift off to sleep—no one would know. *We will be together, Ryder. Forever.*

As his consciousness drained, someone, somewhere, started playing a fiddle. The music was soothing, and soon the beat of his heart slowed to the low, gentle melody of the strings. The world was black, yet something stirred on the wind. A sound, soft notes drifting into his subconscious, tugged at him.

"Ryder. Ryder, Ryyyyderrrr," she called. "Come with me."

"Mags?"

"Get up, my Nickel. It's time to go."

He cracked open one eye. She stood before him, her long dark hair blowing in the wind. A strand of it locked between her lips, and he strained to reach up and brush it back in place. His fingers found nothing but air.

"I'm stayin' with you," he said aloud.

"Get up," she repeated. "He's come for you."

"Who's come for me?"

She smiled at him, beckoning with her fingers.

"I'm so tired, Mags."

She continued to smile, that same beautiful smile that drew him in every time he looked at her. Nickel rolled to his side and sat up, slowly.

"That ain't fair. You know I can't say no to you."

He was coated in the sludge of silt and sand, dirt and blood. It caked his hair and dried, leaving his mane pointing to the four winds. His clothes were like his skin, both covered in the same grime, yet shredded in places from wind and debris.

Nickel looked up at her, his stunning, pale-faced apparition, and held out his hands. Reaching. "I'm comin' with you," he said.

"I love your laughter, Ryder. It's your gift to everyone around you. Don't ever forget how to use it." Her own smile faded. She looked at him one last time, pressed her fingers to her lips, and vanished from his sight.

"Mags!" he yelled. "Magdalena, stay with me! Magdalena!" Scrambling and stumbling to regain his feet, Ryder called her name in every direction. The four winds did not reply, and the sweet, constant melody in his ears stopped. The vision left him to face the reality he had not the strength to meet: Magdalena was gone. Only her body remained at his feet, wrapped in an old fisherman's sail.

He lifted her to his shoulder, biting down on his lip to detract from his agony. Turning, Nickel took one step to the right, in the direction Magdalena had guided him. Left foot. Right foot. Stop. Left foot, right foot. Do it again.

People were talking, but he kept walking, one step at a time. Nickel realized he could trust neither eyes nor ears—nothing good was real anymore.

Cஐ

"Magdalena!" The name filled the air between notes.

Bannack looked up from the fiddle and drew the last note across the strings. As the music faded from his ears, robbed by the frantic calls of a woman's name, he let out a muffled groan. No more running high on the ridge for him.

"Sounds like we've got another one, Marbles," he said. Marbles, still entranced by the music in his ear, merely blinked at him.

"Hear that?"

Marbles turned his head to listen and swore.

"An-nother hole to dig," he said, for the cry was not that of a joyful reunion, but of despair and heartbreak.

Bannack stepped off his platform, ready to hand the fiddle back to its owner. The man, the father of the son he had played for, shook his head.

"Naw, I want you to keep it, Mister."

"I can't take your son's fiddle," Bannack replied, and tried to thrust it back in the man's grasp.

"No! Keep it with you, play it. My son would'a wanted it to be with a man of music. It oughta be played, and I won't be playin' it where I'm goin'."

They watched the man turn and wade knee-deep into the debris-strewn water.

"W-W-W-What are you doing, Mister?" Marbles called, suspicion cutting through the stutter of his speech.

"Hope you won't hold this a'ginst me, Mister." The man turned his gaze skyward and held the revolver to his temple.

Marbles's hand swept to his holster, and his face drained when he discovered it empty.

"No!" both men yelled, rushing into the water. "Don't do it!"

"Shore was some purty fiddle playin'," he replied. "Obliged to you both."

They lunged forward but halted at the deafening report. Neither man would ever forget the splash that followed. The man would never hear a fiddle again. Leastways, not in this life.

Bannack held the fiddle out in front of him and thought about setting it adrift after man and boy, but that wasn't what was asked of him, so he tucked it under his arm and clasped his friend's shoulder.

"I'll see if I can fetch your revolver," he said.

"N-No."

"You sure?"

Marbles just stared at the body in the water, still clutching his hand over the empty holster at his hip.

છ

Shuffling feet and a murmuring voice drew Bannack's attention; he turned from his comrade and stared hard at the grubby figure limping past him. Caked with mud and silt from head to toe, his face was unrecognizable.

In truth, the boy's face held the sallow hue of death. His eyes seemed sightless. Intricate inked designs plastered across his skin peeked through layers of blood and filth. He looked more creature-like than human, like some sort of half-boy, half-water-beast.

*We've been here too long. I'm losin' my head*, Bannack thought.

The young man staggered under the weight of something—or more likely, *someone*—wrapped in canvas.

"Ryder?" Bannack called the name aloud on a whim.

The figure flinched, but his gaze did not veer from his path. Remembering the boy's promise to wear that single spur until he returned, the cowboy's eyes slipped down to the young man's feet. Booted, they were, with just one spur, bent beyond repair. Ryder.

"Dear God, it's Ryder!"

Marbles looked up at Bannack's words. "R-Ryder?"

He started to run. "Ryder!"

છ

As Nickel ventured closer to the edge of the map, two silhouettes rose dark against the sky over the flattened town. They wore the broad-brimmed hats he recognized as the cattleman's hat.

He blinked, shut his eyes, and heaved a deep breath. *They ain't real. They ain't real. Nothin's real.*

Shifting his burden, he looked to see if the monsters were still there. They were men again, and they had spotted him. One man in a large crowned hat turned from his friend and covered the distance, small it was between them. It was Bannack, calling his name.

Nickel's limbs began to shake—he staggered a few more steps, determined to ignore the latest cruel trick of his mind. The make-believe Bannack stepped in his path, leading a horse, but Nickel kept walking. He wasn't real, so it stood to reason he'd walk right through him.

Except he didn't. Instead of passing through the mind-trick Bannack like a fine mist, he plowed straight into him. His hero's voice was in his ear, his hands on his elbows, steadying him. This was the first mind trick that touched him!

Someone he didn't know took the shroud from his arms. Nickel tried to protest, but the cowboy spoke over him, telling him it was okay.

"Bannack?" he said aloud, his voice gruff and halting. "Is . . . are you a monster?"

"Some would say, son. But I'm real. I'm real."

"You ain't a mind trick?"

"I hope not."

"But . . . you came."

"Said I would."

Nickel didn't feel the tears slipping down his cheeks when the cowboy grasped his forearm in an awkward greeting. Neither one spoke; there was nothing to say. Bannack had come for him, just as he promised.

☙

Nickel gave way to the pain racking his body and slumped to the sand. What he saw around him did not register as Indianola. Judging by proximity of the water, he should be near the mainframe of the city. It wasn't there. Where was the soda fountain, where he and Mags shared in ice creams and other delights? The photographer's studio, where his likeness hung for clients to see? The dry goods store, mercantile, even the theater—it was all gone. He closed his eyes, but the sights were lodged in his mind.

"Ryder. Water."

Someone pressed a canteen into his hands. He held it, shaking his head.

"I gotta get her home," he said.

"Rest a minute first."

Rest. How? His head lolled forward on his chest.

"Ryder, drink the water. You hear me? Drink."

Through a haze, he felt the men assessing him, discussing his injuries. He heard them mention something about getting him to a doctor.

"How bad is it?" he asked.

"Your back's tore up pretty bad, son. I can clean it, but you won't like it."

"Is it still there?"

"Your back? It's still there, but you're missin' skin."

"Aww damn! My tattoos. They're still there, ain't they?"

"You read like a newspaper, you're so full of ink."

Ryder held his foot in front of him.

"It hurts awful bad," he said. "Worse'n my back."

The strange cowboy knelt by his boot and nodded a quiet hello.

"That's Marbles," Bannack said, walking over to his horse. "Let him look." He dug around in his saddlebags and pulled something from the flap.

Marbles felt of the leather shaft of Ryder's boot and tugged to pull it off. Nickel screamed. Once, twice more the cowboy pressed and tugged, then shook his head.

"G-Gotta cut it off, B-Bannack," he said.

"You ain't gonna cut off my foot!" Nickel cried.

"The boot, son. He means your boot."

Nickel didn't want his precious boot cut off either, but it was better than his foot.

Marbles worked quickly, but by the time he had finished the job, Nickel was sweating and seeing black orb-like spots in his vision again. He leaned forward, trying to get a look at his ankle when the devil himself bit into the raw flesh of his back. He lurched forward with a shriek, but strong hands held him down. Another round of fire drenched his wounds, and he fell forward in a dead faint.

They didn't let him stay down. Dragging him up, they turned his head back and forth, talking to him until he blinked. He tasted bitter, tepid water on his lips, and accepted a drink.

"Wh-What did . . . you do?" he asked Bannack in a shaky voice.

"I said you wouldn't like it, cleanin' your back. Best you didn't know it was comin'."

Nickel held his hands over his eyes. Bright lights blended with the black orbs; he didn't want to see either one. Didn't want to move, either. Whatever Bannack poured over his back sizzled and burned worse than any beating Oren had ever given him.

"Where were you, Ryder? How long have you been walkin' on that foot?"

He did not know how many miles inland he had been washed, nor did he care to. What did it matter? But Bannack repeated the question.

"A lifetime," he replied, and promptly vomited on the ground at Marbles's feet. Taking advantage of Nickel's insensibility, Bannack retreated to the horses and nodded for Marbles to follow.

"What do you think?" Bannack asked his awkward friend.

"He's alive," Marbles said. "I ain't too s-shore some-somethin' ain't b-broken in that ankle."

"Hard to tell, it's swelled so much."

"He won't be w-w-wearin' b-boots for a w-while," Marbles agreed.

"He must've walked a long damn way, carryin' that body."

"W-Who is it?" Marbles asked, eyeing the makeshift shroud.

"I've got a guess, but I hope to hell I'm wrong."

Bannack glanced at Nickel, who was still stretched out on his stomach, purging a living nightmare from his gut.

Kneeling by the body, he unwrapped a corner of sail and pulled it back over a cold, pallid face. In death, she looked nothing like she did in life. Bannack recognized her all the same. Replacing the corner, Bannack swore low and vicious and rubbed his arm across his eyes.

"Dammittohell," he said. The cuss came out as one jumbled word.

Marbles paled but asked anyway.

"It's his girl, Magdalena Hayworth," Bannack said, keeping his voice low so as not to upset Nickel further.

"They were circlin' each other five years ago when I was here. He was some sweet on her, I reckon. He sent me a tintype of himself with her and Les Harold, and a sailor friend."

Both men turned to stare at the young man lying near their feet. He had been drowned and torn up, bore raw, open wounds, skin missing on his back, and he limped on what was probably a broken foot. Despite all that, Ryder Wheeler had trudged through the destruction of his entire city, carrying the body of his girl just so he could take her to her final resting place. Both men removed their hats, paying silent respect to Magdalena Hayworth and the broken young man who loved her.

# CHAPTER 19

# BIRTH OF A SIREN

There was nothing left. Nothing he recognized. He meant to take her home—where else would she be laid to rest? But the Hayworth house, like all the others, was gone. He didn't even know where her parents were, or if they were alive.

"Son, we need to bury her."

Nickel heard and immediately rejected the idea.

"Ryder." Bannack knelt in front of the boy, removed his hat, and ran his fingers through his hair. His weathered face looked grim. Tired. "She's not there anymore," he began. "You need to—"

"I ain't puttin' Mags in a damned hole."

"We don't have a choice. We can do it here on the beach. Hold a proper funeral. It's a pretty spot, sure enough. We'll bury her right here, where we found you."

Nickel stared at the cowboy, barely blinking.

"She's gonna go to sea."

"Do what?"

Magdalena loved the sea even more than she loved him. She had proven that by her decision to stay, rather than pursue a life with him. It was the wrong decision, for the Mistress betrayed her. Nickel never would, not even in death. She deserved a sea lover's burial.

Besides, there were the stories of sirens, like the one tattooed on Nickel's arm. Joly said they were creatures borne of a violent death at sea. Magdalena loved those stories almost as much as the sea itself. How would Mags turn into a siren and come back to life if they buried her in a dark hole in the ground?

He asked the cowboys how they expected her to come back, and the men exchanged wide-eyed glances. Marbles took a step back, leaving Bannack to deal with the reply.

"I don't follow," he said. "What's a siren?"

Nickel blinked. Clearly he misunderstood the question. Everyone knew what sirens were. Maybe he just hadn't heard the story of their birth.

"Folks," he said, pausing to collect his emotions, "women who drown or are killed by the Mistress, they come back as sirens, but they gotta be returned to the sea. Mags can't come back if she ain't in the water."

"Says who?"

"Everybody knows that." Nickel tried to stand on both legs and wobbled. "Help me or don't," he said, trying to collect the body in his arms, "but she's gonna get a siren's burial."

The cowboys palavered. Something seemed amiss in their understanding, but Nickel's mind was shutting down. Dimly, he watched the men speak in low tones and animated gestures. They were blurring, so he closed his eyes for a few moments. His head pounded in tune with the pulsations of his foot. He was just beginning to slip into the shadows when a voice called him back.

"Your mind ain't right, boy."

Still, they helped him carry her across unsteady, shifting piles of debris under their feet, and laid her down in the sand.

"I wish I had somethin' to remember her by." His voice sounded far away, as though he were speaking through a great distance. Bannack figured he was; for the boy's mind was warring to return, or to leave altogether.

"Pull the cloth back if you want. Cut a lock of her hair. It'll keep," Bannack suggested and handed him a small knife.

Nickel did as bidden, winding the dark tresses around his fingers. It didn't seem right though, to take from her and give nothing of himself. He had nothing to give; then a thought struck him.

"Bannack? Do you have a nickel?"

"Got a dime. Why?"

"No sir. It's gotta be a nickel."

The cowboy whose name Nickel didn't recall fished around in the pocket of his vest and handed him the coin.

Nickel pressed his lips to the metal and held it tight, feeling the coin against the pulsing inside his fist.

Searching for her hand, he forced the nickel between her clenched fingers. For a few minutes, Nickel allowed grief to overcome pride; he sobbed for his love, great racking cries bubbled from deep in his gut to shake his frame as they exploded.

A few minutes, and then he remembered her words.

*"I love your laughter, Ryder. It's your gift to everyone around you. Don't forget how to use it."*

"I swear I won't forget," he told her. "Never." He kissed her hand and those cold, cold blue lips, and covered her up. He cut a hole in the shroud, one large enough for her to rip through when she turned into the beautiful elusive creature of the deep. Now she would not be imprisoned when she turned.

Glancing at Bannack, he nodded, then pushed her shroud into the receding tide. He was afraid she would become snagged on floating timbers, for the water was teeming with them. The other cowboy, Bannack's friend, waded in up to his chest since Nickel could not, steering her out toward open sea.

Aside from the debris, it was a good spot. Nickel couldn't be sure, but he suspected it was near enough to where Joly must have disappeared. His old friend would look out for Mags, no matter whether he was of this world or the next.

The cowboy clambered back to shore, wringing water. Words were said, but he did not know if they came from his mouth or someone else's. Nickel began to sing her favorite song, but his voice broke and he could not continue. Bannack, not knowing the lyrics, picked up the melody and played as best he could, the mournful tune on the fiddle bearing the inscription JAMES, INDIANOLA, TEXAS, 1870 carved in crude letters on the back.

Nickel gathered a handful of soil. Mostly sand, he sifted it through his fingers, memorizing the touch, the feel of each tiny grain. Then, he tore off a patch of his trousers and bundled the sand inside. He tied it tight.

When he rose, prompted by the men, Nickel took one last look at his beautiful Mags, bobbing up and down in a calm, swollen sea, and grinned through his tears.

CB

Day was fading into night. Soon Indianola would be blanketed in darkness, and he no longer had to look at the wreckage. Nickel allowed them to lead him to a supply wagon—not that he had any choice in the matter; Bannack attested to that.

Pulled by a team of bulky horses with feathered feet, the wagon was littered with lanterns. Several of Victoria's citizens were handing out supplies, redressing wounds, and administering care to the injured. Bannack marched Nickel into the thick of the makeshift hospital, bidding he seat himself on the back of the buckboard.

A kind woman tended to him while Bannack's soft-spoken cowboy friend held a lantern for them to see by.

Bannack did not stand idle. Nickel tensed as the man unwound the cloth he had tied around his arm to hold it steady.

"Somethin's busted," Nickel told him. "My shoulder." He jerked when Bannack poked his fingers into his skin, feeling for his bones, he supposed.

Backing off out of the main circle of lamplight, Bannack spoke to his friend, then the nurse.

"Stand up," the cowboy ordered upon his return. Nickel obeyed, finding himself face-to-face with the quiet man. He could not remember his name, and said so.

"Son," Bannack said from somewhere behind him, "this is Marbles. We hired him on at the Middle C. You'll be working with him."

Nickel's vision was swimming in waves. The man didn't hold the lantern still; he kept swinging it back and forth, back and forth. When Marbles dropped it near his feet, instinct drove Nickel forward to catch it. As he lurched to grab the lantern, strong, quick arms grasped his shoulder from behind, wrenching him backward.

"Aahh!"

Another hard wrench, worse than the first, and a sickening pop thundered through his eardrums. The sweet shadow of blackness followed.

CB

Large fireflies glimmered in the dark, some moving, others just floating, hovering on the ground and in midair. Their glow was warm and vibrant, soothing. Nickel basked in their light, wondering why they seemed to fly sideways. One settled near his head, and he reached out to touch it.

A face appeared, illuminated by the glow, and he jumped.

"He's coming around," the face proclaimed. He felt a strong arm under his head.

"Ryder, water," someone said. Nickel blinked. He could identify light and dark but not the shadows in between.

"Fire . . . firefly?" he asked. He hadn't known the bug lights could talk. How'd they know his name?

"I don't think he's quite returned to us yet."

"Let the boy enjoy a minute or two wherever he's at. Ain't no need to rush him back to this hell."

The voices continued, but Nickel concentrated only on the one nearest him—the talking firefly that promised water.

"I'm gonna raise your head, son. Drink."

The arm across his shoulders, cradling his neck, increased pressure. Lifting his head, Nickel tried to gulp the water, but it was snatched from him too quickly.

"Slow, boy."

"Didn't know fireflies were so damn demanding," he muttered. "Bug could get squashed that way. Even if it does talk."

"Is that right?" the voice asked.

"That's right," Nickel repeated. He reached for the water, and this time they allowed him to drain the canteen. The voices continued, speaking over his head.

"We'll have to keep an eye on the shoulder. That ankle too. I don't like the swellin'."

"Are you sure it's not broken?" a woman asked.

"I ain't sure of anything."

Nickel felt someone grasp his foot. He whimpered but did not call out.

"Ryder?"

"That you, firefly?"

The voice sighed. "Ryder, listen to me. I'm gonna give you a bite to eat. Chew it, don't bolt."

"Bossy bugs," the boy muttered but obeyed the demand. The first bite had a wild, savage flavor he could not identify. He detected berries in the meat, and some sort of foreign aroma that lingered on his tongue even after he swallowed. At that moment, Nickel decided the strange jerked meat tasted every bit as good as his momma's biscuits—without the bear grease.

*Wait, Momma!*

"Momma!" The pretty fireflies left, only to be replaced by a dozen lanterns scattered across the dismal beach. Nickel heaved himself up, fighting off hands to gain his own two feet.

"My family! Where's my family?"

Why hadn't he thought of his family first off? Momma and his brothers and sisters. Les and Joly. Where was everyone?

"Easy, son." The voice was back, the one that gave him water. Bannack. Nickel whirled to face him and staggered sideways, but the cowboy caught him before he fell.

"Your momma's alive, son. She's at the courthouse, waiting on you."

"I didn't think about 'em," he cried. "Why didn't I remember to ask?"

"Your mind's just comin' back," Bannack explained. "I don't know what happened out there, Nickel. Whatever it was, you did what you needed to survive. You took care of your girl too. You did good. Better'n most."

"But my momma!" Nickel's body trembled, and his breathing was labored and shallow.

"We sent a runner to the courthouse to tell her we found you alive. Ryder . . ." Bannack paused again, then pressed on. No use hiding the truth any longer. "Some of your kin made it, some didn't."

Les. He hadn't found him before. If something happened to Les Harold too . . . Terror rising in his chest, Nickel clutched the cowboy's shirt.

"Who? Who made it?"

"Posse and Alastor, a younger boy, I never caught his name. Looks like you though. One or two others. I don't know names, son. I'm sorry."

"Th-There's gotta be more'n that!" Nickel peered into the older man's face, but even in lantern light, he didn't like what he saw.

"Les?" Nickel spit the name out. If his best friend was dead, he'd never recover.

"Les Harold is fine," Bannack replied.

Nickel closed his eyes and exhaled. "Say it again."

"He's fine, son. Les has been out there lookin' for you since the water receded. His father's alive too."

"What about his momma?"

"No." The word fell heavy from Bannack's lips.

"Ahh no!" Nickel hid his face in dirty palms and shuddered. He didn't know how much more loss he could take, but he had to know. "What about . . . about my little sister, Hera?" he asked through shaky fingers, tripping over his words.

Silence.

"Hera!" Nickel said, shouting. "Tell me Hera's alive!" He wanted to grab the cowboy by his shirt and shake him—shake him until he confirmed Hera, Mags, and the rest were alive.

"I'm sorry, son. Your momma said she was lost to the floodwaters with the younger children. I'm real sorry." Bannack's words were simple, but his tone reflected the deep understanding within his heart and mirrored in his eyes.

Any other time, the news would have destroyed Nickel. Now he stood on one leg and slumped within himself.

*Beautiful, precious little Hera. She knew. Oh, God, she knew! And the other innocents. Those cherub-faced siblings, too young to die.*

"There's a girl too," Bannack told him. "She's been stickin' like a burr to your family. Don't look like she's got anybody else."

Lucy Parker. He had forgotten about her. In the face of hell, she made him a man, and he forgot about her.

"I gotta go to them, Bannack. Please." Nickel staggered, supported by Bannack and Marbles on either side of him. Neither man offered to carry him, a consideration he appreciated. No one would carry him home like a child. His momma, his kin, his friends—they would see him walking back home.

Various groups of people, illuminated by lantern light, littered the beach. They were more prominent around the courthouse, but the cowboys led him through them, right up to where the steps should have been. They stopped at a group of broken individuals huddled together to wait out the night. He could not see faces, for they shielded their eyes from the world around them.

"Mrs. Wheeler, ma'am," Bannack called. She kept her face tucked away, but they heard her muffled reply.

"You didn't find him, did you?"

"We sent a messenger. Didn't he show? Look up, ma'am. We brought him home."

Molly, Les, Lucy, the siblings. They all moved as one, peering from behind filthy hands, shawls, and blankets pulled from the debris. It was clear they expected to see a lifeless body in the arms of the great cowboy. The bedraggled form standing between them did not look like their Nickel, so reaction was slow.

"Hey, Momma," he called, and hopped forward on one foot. Molly Wheeler screamed, startling other parties resting nearby. She ran to her golden child, but Bannack grabbed her arm to slow her down.

"Easy, ma'am. He's some hurt. Best take it easy and don't knock him about." He let her go and stepped out of the way, watching while Nickel was swallowed up by his hysterical mother and the remnants of his family. All, save for one startled and angry soul.

Alastor Wheeler.

ॐ

Bannack rubbed the back of his neck and cleared his throat. "I'm goin' for a walk," he told Marbles. "Secure a wagon." His voice sounded extra gruff, so Marbles didn't argue. He knew the relief his friend felt; all that time they had searched . . . it terrified him, the thought they'd find his body, yet afraid they wouldn't.

He returned just before daybreak with no transportation other than the two saddle ponies he and Marbles rode in on. At least a few would get to rest their feet.

Marbles saw him coming and met him, out of earshot.

"How's Ryder?" Bannack asked.

"B-Boy ain't s-said a word since you l-l-left. He ain't w-well."

"We'll leave now. Nothin' left to keep 'em here, I reckon."

"Get a wagon?"

"Nope. No empty wagons goin' that way." Bannack explained what he found: most of the buckboards streaming in were staying to help; those leaving with straggling survivors were already loaded beyond capacity. Many people had neither horse nor wagon, so they started out on foot, having given up the search for their loved ones and abandoning their former homes and possessions. The Wheelers would have to follow suit.

"Some of us are gonna have to walk. Might run into somebody on the road to Victoria with a wagon to spare."

Marbles said nothing.

Bannack found Molly Wheeler crooning over her boy. Les and the others gathered around him as though he were some sort of deity. Bannack wondered if he was.

Nickel's reunion was heartening, but the shadow of devastation hung low over the Wheeler clan and their friends.

Bannack noticed two people refrained from basking in Nickel's golden glow of luck.

Alastor Wheeler kept well away from his brother and, in fact, hadn't even welcomed him so far as Bannack knew. That was something to tuck under his hat for later. The lad seemed to alternate between sulks and scowls and envious stares.

The other was the girl, Lucy Parker. She huddled alone a short distance from the Wheelers, not quite a part of their family or anyone else's. Her father was the only kin she had to speak of, but no one seemed to know—or care—where he was. Bannack couldn't quite figure if the girl held to herself for her own personal reasons, or if the Wheelers had pushed her aside. Either way, the girl seemed forgotten in the glory of Ryder's return.

*Nickel*, he thought to himself but shook his head. It would be strange to think of him as anything but the Ryder from five years before.

Another glance answered at least one question: Lucy Parker's gaze never wavered from Nickel, who seemed oblivious of those around him. He was war-torn, an overnight veteran at sixteen, and it showed in the shadows of his face.

Bannack knelt with his knee in the sand and a hand on Nickel's forehead. The boy opened his eyes and whispered his hero's name. "Hey, Bannack."

"Hey, Ryder. It's time to move on, son. We'll get your family settled in Victoria. I couldn't get a wagon, so some of us'll ride, but the rest have to walk."

"I'll walk," the boy said.

"Hell you will. With the size of that ankle? You'll be ridin'."

Nickel tried to sit up but fell back with a groan. Again and again, he tried on his own and finally made it to an upright position with Bannack's arm supporting his back.

"I ain't comin' back, am I?"

"Nothin' to come back to, son."

Nickel stared out at the sea, his kelp-green eyes hallowed and unblinking.

"I hate her," he murmured.

Bannack figured it wasn't the girl he buried in his thoughts at that moment.

Nickel dug his fingers into the sand, extracting a fistful of sand and silt. Reaching for a tattered rag tied about his neck, he loosened it and yanked it free, scooping the sand into the fabric. He tied it back up in a bundle and clutched it in his fist. His knuckles turned white.

"I'm ready to go," he said.

"Anything you need to do first?" Bannack asked.

"No sir. I ain't lookin' back."

As Bannack and Marbles drew the Wheelers together and prepared for the first leg of their journey, it became clear that Nickel meant what he said. While the others huddled together, looking around at the wasteland that was only days ago their home, they dissolved into tears.

Nickel settled into the saddle of Bannack's personal mount and stared straight ahead. He released no tears, nor did he turn his head to look about. When someone handed his remaining little sister, Aphrodite, up to him, he cradled her into the crook of his good arm and said nothing.

Molly refused to ride, opting to walk with the men and carry her youngest remaining child. Zelus held her free hand. Posse and Alastor fell in with Les Harold and his father, each holding a child.

It was Nickel who took the first step, urging Bannack's horse forward. Bannack halted the reins and looked up into the young, deadpan face. The boy stared straight through him, seeing nothing.

"Ryder," he called, tapping him on the leg. "Does the girl go with us to Victoria?" he asked.

"Mags?"

"What's her name? The Parker girl."

Nickel blew a breath of air. "Lucy. Aww, don't tell her I forgot her. My head's awful tired, sir."

"Your mind ain't workin' right just now, but it's all right, son. I've been there before."

Bannack walked back to the girl, still standing by the courthouse, clutching her damp, threadbare skirt in her hands. Tears were streaming down her face.

"Please," she pleaded when he approached. "Please take me with you. I got no one left."

"Reckon you can ride behind Nickel and his sister, so long as you don't jostle his back. If you can't hang on, you'll have to walk."

The girl flew to Nickel's side, lest he change his mind, and Marbles helped her swing a leg over and showed her how to hold on. His instruction wasn't necessary, for she threw her arms around the boy's waist and buried her face against his shoulder. Bannack lifted his arm to signal Marbles, and they were on their way, threading through the remains of a once-glorious city—Indianola.

CB

Progress was painfully slow, though no one noticed. One mile bled into the next. The destruction didn't change; the debris field did not lessen. People they passed all looked the same; one face ran right into the next, though many of them recognized Indianola's luck child and called out his name.

"Nickel!"

"Look! It's Nickel!"

They heard the name called over and over again. A few searchers came forward to touch him, to shake his hand or grasp at his skin, convinced they would find their loved ones alive merely because they had touched the lucky Nickel who had survived the storm.

Nickel acquiesced with the love and patience of a king serving his realm, murmuring a few words of kindness and prayer every time a voice of desperation cried his name.

He touched objects, children, adults, and even a dog someone saved in the wreckage. Bannack noticed he did it without thought, as though he had done it his whole life.

He began to realize the boy meant something special to the whole town. What had he been doing over the years? Whatever it was, folks loved him. That alone confirmed his gut reaction five years back: there was something different about that boy. Something worth saving.

# CHAPTER 20

# THE BURDEN

Traversing the wreck of the prairie, the cowboys had to oversee the fording of swift, dangerous ravines and channels cut through the land, determining the wisest crossing point without losing another soul.

Bannack and Marbles carried the children on horseback, who forged the angry waters, swimming their horses and plunging up on the bank only to deposit their precious cargo on the other side. They turned around for the next person and kept at it until the last person was safe on the far bank.

They gave the horses a respite from passengers, and the group plodded along on foot. Nickel dismounted too, but he could bear no weight on his foot, so Bannack fashioned a crude crutch from a tall, wooden oar lying in the road. The cowboy lent the strength of his arm for the young man to lean on, matching his stride with Nickel's short crow hops.

People—live ones, anyway—became a scarce sight; few wished to brave the waters of the ravines. Bellies were empty, but no one complained, not even the children.

Their silence bore the weight of the group as they dodged the wreckage. Bannack and Marbles saw the outlying damage once already, but for Nickel and his family, it was a new world, a never-ending hell.

Heads turned as they approached a house sitting precariously on its rafters, the roof and much of its siding having been torn away. Les Harold's father, Edmund, placed a hand on Molly Wheeler's shoulder. The woman shuddered and grasped his hand.

Two men sat on a large blue wooden box by the house, watching their approach. They nodded but did not speak when the group passed by.

Bannack passed Nickel off to Marbles and mounted his horse, spinning the animal to keep an eye on his charges and the men. He did not like their looks, nor they him, by the way they kept eyeballing him. He urged his group forward, but Nickel let out a yell and broke from the pack, his oar crutch digging holes in the ground as he hopped toward the men.

"Get the hell off that trunk!"

"What's it to ya, kid? We's just restin'."

"Get off it!" he screamed.

"Hey, we found it first. Drug it a good distance already, so you go find some place else to sit!"

"You did not! It came out of that house behind you!"

One of the men looked behind him and chuckled. "It was a house, I guess," he said. "You can't prove where it came from, kid."

"The hell I can't!" Nickel forgot his injuries. "That's the Hayworth house!"

"Don't see how you can tell, seein' as how it's turned inside out," one of the men argued.

"I *know*." His face contorted into an expression almost animalistic in hate. "The Hayworths had green flowered wallpaper." Nickel pointed through the door, where the priceless paper hung in tatters. Most of it was gone, but a few sections still clung to damaged walls, a reminder of Magdalena's mother and her affinity for green. She had suffered many fights with Mr. Hayworth over the paper, and had won. Not that it mattered now. Those men had gone into their house and had pulled the trunk from the remains of the family home.

*Her trunk.*

Rage settled in the pit of his stomach, and he slunk forward, slightly crouched in a stalk.

"Nickel, no!" Molly Wheeler warned.

"You best listen to your momma, boy."

"Get. Off. The. Damned. Box!" Nickel raised his crutch to strike, and the man on the left jerked as if to grab for a gun.

"Don't you do it!" Bannack yelled.

The man looked up and found himself already in the cowboy's sights. Bannack put pressure on them, riding steadily forward, not blinking. Marbles backed him up, his own saddle gun leveled and ready.

"Suggest you listen to the boy," Bannack said. "Get up. Slow."

The men rose, their palms spread in the air.

"Relax, Mister. He's the one spoilin' for a fight."

"I expect he's got good reason. Get away from the box." Bannack nodded to Marbles, who lifted a knife and two revolvers from the men. Further search turned up a dagger in a boot. The cowboys did not return their weapons, for they knew what they were. The lowest of the low, the scum in the wake of tragedy. Scavengers.

"Empty their pockets," he said.

"Now wait a minute!"

Marbles obliged and jumped back at what he found.

"Bannack, they got fingers in their pockets!"

Brown eyes flashed. Without taking his eyes off the bastards before him, he called over his shoulder.

"Harold, take Molly and the children up the road. Now. Don't let 'em look back, I don't care what you hear."

"You ain't gonna shoot us! We ain't kilt nobody!" The men were edgy. Devoid of weapons, they knew they had no chance of a fight, yet running seemed just as out of reach.

"D-D-Damned v-vultures don't need to k-kill. Job's already b-been done for you."

The larger man lunged for Marbles, but the .44 slugs caught him and his buddy in the chest almost simultaneously, blowing their bodies backward. Bannack glanced around before returning his gun to its holster. He dismounted, only to find Nickel still behind him.

"Dammit! You're supposed to be with the children." Bannack snapped and swept his arm behind them. Though he was not a tall man, the cowboy's wide-legged stance demanded obedience.

Nickel was not swayed. "I ain't leavin' that box." He ambled over to it, rubbing his hand over grime to show the blue top underneath. Someone tampered with the lock but hadn't succeeded in opening it. Yet. "Ain't leavin' it behind," he repeated.

"We're not dragging a big-ass box all the way to Victoria." Bannack crossed his arms over his chest. His brows furrowed over his eyes, emitting a fearsome glare.

"It goes with me to Moral, or I stay here." Nickel raised his voice, trying to match the fierceness of Bannack's stare.

The cowboy ripped his hat off his head and slammed it over his knee. "Dammit, Nickel! Do you see the size of that thing? We don't even have a wagon to haul it in."

"Then I'll carry it."

Bannack opened his mouth to argue, but the youth turned his back and sank to the ground, swiping at the box sides to clear away the sludge.

INDIANOLA, 1874 was painted across the front lid. Bannack frowned and paced the road, waiting for Marbles to return from searching the dead men's belongings. He came up with a sum over five hundred dollars total, no doubt all of it stolen money.

"W-What do we do with it?" Marbles asked. "They got r-rings and ear-earrings, s-some of 'em still got the s-skin attached."

"We'll turn the money and jewelry over to authorities in Victoria. Maybe do a write-up in the paper for the billfolds and jewelry, in case someone comes lookin' for them."

Marbles nodded. "W-What about him?" he asked, gesturing to Nickel and the box.

"He wants to bring it with him."

"To Vic-Victoria? W-What for?"

"Nope. To Moral."

Marbles's eyes widened. "M-Moral? Sh-Shit!" he stuttered. "W-What'd he s-say when you told him n-no?"

"I ain't told him nothin' yet."

"We can't . . . can't lug that thing all the w-way to M-Moral, B-B-Bannack."

The cowboy remained quiet, his eyes on the Indianola boy. He was working furiously to clean the lid where the scavengers had rested, trying to erase their memory from existence much in the way he and Marbles had erased them.

Colors began to appear under the filth: white and blue, red and brown paint. Sails. A big three-mast clipper ship was painted on the front, just like the one grounded on the prairie. The top of the trunk was adorned with a swallow in flight in each corner, and a large red and indigo compass rose painted in the middle. There was something wrong with the compass though—north was pointing west. Bannack cocked his head. It was more than an amateur's mistake, but something told him it was no amateur who painted that trunk. It boasted character—which led Bannack to believe Nickel must have been the artist.

"Sir?" The voice came at his elbow. Les Harold stood before him.

"Mr. Bannack, sir? That was Magdalena's box."

"Magdalena. You mean . . . ?"

"Yessir. Magdalena Virginia Hayworth. Nickel said you helped him bury her. He traded for that ole box to give her, painted it up real pretty with the things she loved. She said it was her dream trunk and kept her treasures inside. He was gonna marry her, you know, bring her north with him."

Bannack exchanged glances with Marbles, trying to decide what to do. A decision had to be made. They had women and children to get to safety, and no wagon to do it in. The trunk was massive! A grown man could curl up inside, and no one would be the wiser. It would take at least two men to carry if it was empty. Victoria was a good ten hours' ride on horseback, but most of them were on foot. They damn well couldn't carry a heavy box that distance, let alone to Moral.

Marbles shook his head and spread his hands, signaling the hopelessness of the situation. They had to leave it, and by the look on Nickel's face, he knew it too.

His shoulders shook, tears streaming down his face as he slid his hand over the rough surface.

"Ryder."

Bannack strode over to the heartbroken boy, examining the trunk lid. He noticed something else in the wood. Tilting his head with a squint, he watched his new apprentice uncover the painted secrets only he knew was there under a layer of silt, mud, and dirt. Bannack swore with a worn-out voice filled with defeat and dread. They would be lugging that damned big-ass box all the way to Moral, Texas.

"Grab a handle," he told Marbles.

CB

Nickel wiped snot on the sleeve of his shirt. It was too big, but it was also Marbles's only spare. Nickel found the extra size worked well, for it didn't rub against his back as much as his own would have. At least what was left of his skin wouldn't burn in the sun.

He clung to the trunk and watched the pair of cowboys approach him, knowing what they would say. He had to leave it behind. Everything he had built for her, everything he had given her. Her life was stored in that trunk, but it would remain on the side of the road for the next pair of scavengers to loot. She had told him she loved his laugh, the sound of his voice, but he didn't think he could bear it.

Scavengers would bust the lock he made for her, rifle through her belongings, casting aside her hopes and dreams in search of something worth selling.

Bannack and Marbles were coming, but he refused to look them in the eye. They would make him leave it behind, and he didn't want to go. He should have just curled up next to Mags, pulled the shroud over his head, and let them bury him with her.

Bannack's strong hand guided him to his feet. The cowboy clutched his good arm.

"Mount my horse and get off that foot," he ordered. Then, as Nickel leaned on the crutch, he and Marbles each grabbed a rope handle and hefted. The weight of the box brought an inward groan from each man. They exchanged tired glances, but Bannack hefted his end, so Marbles did too. Together, as a team, they carried the box past an openmouthed Nickel and walked on down the road, lugging Magdalena's trunk between them.

To their relief, when they tilted the box, water leaked from one corner, draining some weight. Still, dreams were heavy things to carry. Nickel never realized just how brutal they were to bear alone until faced with the responsibility of caring for those of another. He refused to let those grand Middle C men bear the weight of his Magdalena's dreams alone and tried to take the handle from Bannack. The cowboy wouldn't budge, so he fell in behind him, holding onto the handle, straining his good shoulder to relieve some weight from the cowboy in front of him.

Bannack turned dark eyes on him but said nothing as Nickel hopped along on his crutch, trying to keep up the pace. Les Harold's father fell in behind Marbles, and the four men carried the trunk until the fibers of the ropes dug into their hands. They stopped to set it down, adjust their grip, and hefted it again.

They walked on, every step taking them closer to Victoria, and yet getting nowhere. No one, Nickel realized, asked him to search inside, or to lighten the load. He didn't even know what secrets it held, nor did he intend to find out. He put one foot in front of the other. The debris field did not seem to end, and Bannack did not call out how many miles they had walked. Maybe Bannack didn't know, either.

∽

Lucy Parker stuck to Nickel's side even as he struggled to carry his share of another woman's burden.

She murmured soft words of encouragement, but every time he looked at her, pangs of guilt stabbed his chest. He should have marched up to that porch and bloodied Alastor's nose for kissing his Mags. He should have grabbed her up in his arms and made love to her right there, instead of running off to slay his heartache with Lucy Parker. His luck would have saved her. Mags would still be alive, had he been with her instead. It was a bitter truth he could not swallow.

"Ryder?"

The sound of his name on Lucy's lips irked him. Aside from Momma and Bannack, Mags was the only one who still called him Ryder.

"Call me Nickel," he told her.

"Nickel then," she amended. "I-I love you."

More than Nickel's ears met her soft-spoken admission. He glanced at Bannack, who was still in front, gripping the handle of the box, but the cowboy turned his head and pretended not to notice the lovelorn girl's words of affection. She was waiting for a reply, but Nickel had nothing to say.

"Yeah," he mumbled after a slight pause, "I know, Luce." It was weak, but it was the best he could do. She seemed to accept it, for she continued.

"Thank you for staying with me that night. You gave me your luck, and I—I am grateful."

It hurt to look into the adoration in her eyes. *Oh, Lord, she was right!* She was alive because he was there to give her his luck. If he had been with Magdalena, it would have been Lucy Parker they would have buried on the beach instead. Had he chosen one over the other?

He liked Lucy, liked her very much. She was sweet and pretty, and she adored the ground he walked on. Yet, if he had to do it over, Nickel knew he would have sacrificed her life to save his beautiful Magdalena. It was a shameful thought, but it was there, nonetheless.

Curse Nickel's luck! Curse it to hell! His luck had saved a girl's life, but the sacrifice for his decision had been far too great a price. Lucy touched his arm and prattled on. There was a tremor in her voice, and he realized he terrified her.

"I loved it—what we shared that night, Nickel."

He nodded.

"I was thinking, once we get to Victoria, well, I . . ." She paused, trying to take a breath, and he heard a rasp in her lungs. "Would you stand with me before a preacher?"

Nickel tripped over his own feet and dropped the trunk, causing Bannack to stumble. He picked up his end again, but the men set down the box and called a halt to rest. Bannack nodded for them to step away, leaving Nickel to face Lucy Parker alone.

"You wanna get hitched?" he asked, pulling back. He rubbed his eyes and swayed on his feet.

"Yes." Lucy clasped her hands together, wringing them. He didn't want to look at the hope plastered across her face.

"But I'm not stayin'. When Bannack and Marbles head north, I'm goin' with them." It was a sound argument, but he had a feeling it wasn't strong enough. He was right.

"I know. But I want to be a part of you, Nickel," she pleaded. "I'll take anything you give me. I'd go with you—anywhere!" Lucy bit her lip, her round eyes searching his face for signs of consent.

"I don't know if they'd let me bring you with me," he protested.

"Then, if you made me, I'd stay behind and wait for you to send for me, just so long as you make me your wife." Her eyes were pleading. She touched his hands. They were shaking.

"I was gonna marry Mags," he told her. Something thick lodged in his throat, making it hard to swallow. Grief.

"I know, but she—she loved Indianola more than she loved you. She wouldn't have left it." Lucy's tone was harsh, marred by the pitfalls of jealous desperation.

Nickel massaged his neck with his fingers and stared at his feet. He didn't want to look at those pleading eyes anymore. "She would have," he argued, "now that there ain't no Indianola. My luck, I could've saved her."

"But you didn't," she reminded him. "You were with me."

Nickel closed his eyes, too exhausted to argue. Lucy's timing to broach the subject of marriage was awful.

"Your luck couldn't save us both, could it?" she asked.

"Guess not."

"Then I wish you would've saved *her*, Nickel, 'cause life for me isn't worth much without you in it." She was crying. Not great racking sobs, but soft tears slid down her cheeks, nonetheless. "She had her mind made up," she blubbered through her tears, "and it wasn't you. I always loved you!"

The others had all turned away, pointedly ignoring Lucy's tear-stained desperation. He wished he could turn away too, but then the girl really would have nothing. She was too good for that. Lucy was his friend, after all; *somebody* had to look after her.

"It don't matter anymore," Nickel told her. "It's always been her, but she ain't here now. I'll marry you, Luce, if that's what you want." It wasn't a heartfelt proposal, but it was all he had to offer the girl he had saved from the storm.

The girl cried out, throwing her arms around him, and he grimaced at her touch against his bruised and battered skin.

"I'll make you love me, someday," she promised.

Nickel bit his cheek, refraining from comment until he could speak without a harsh remark. When he did reply, it was a half-hearted agreement born from fatigue.

"Sure thing, Luce. Come on, they're waitin' and we've got a long walk to Victoria."

Somewhere between picking up Magdalena's heavy trunk and the whirlwind engagement to Lucy Parker, Nickel's mind went numb. He did not notice the morning had passed into the afternoon, or the group of travelers that passed by, heading into the wreckage of Indianola they were leaving. It was all the same infernal trudging, for the cast was set.

No matter he was now betrothed, both to an Indianola girl and to the apprenticeship of a small, stoic Texas cowpuncher; no matter he had been drowned by the Mistress three times in five years, he had friends to see him through. Bannack and Marbles proved they meant to shoulder his burdens all the way to Moral without complaint, and they would not do it alone.

Nickel took one last look over his shoulder, burning the path he had traversed in his memory. There, far behind him on the beach, kissed by the lapping waves, stood a makeshift cross with a heart carved in the wood. He fished for the little bundle he had tied around his wrist. Inside bore a lock of dark, raven hair. He closed his hand around it, envisioning her standing there at the water's edge, waving goodbye.

Tears dripped, unnoticed, off his nose. Ryder stopped walking, turning his back on his family to say his final farewell to what had been the town of his childhood and the girl he loved.

"I won't let them call me Ryder anymore," he whispered to her. "That name'll always be just for you. I love you, my Indianola girl."

Blinded, Nickel waited until the sob in his throat subsided, shouldered his crutch, and slowly turned toward the road where Bannack, Marbles, and Lucy Parker stood with his family and Les, awaiting a young man with an uncertain future, forever branded by the blessing, and the curse, of Nickel's luck.

# CHAPTER 21

# ROAD TO VICTORIA

Bannack stumbled and righted himself. No one had noticed, except for Marbles, who shook his head. With or without that blasted blue trunk, they would never make it to Victoria. Children and adults alike were spent. Bannack and Marbles themselves hadn't had sustenance in days, and they hadn't experienced what the Wheeler clan had gone through, or what Nickel had faced.

What had the boy suffered? Les Harold said a timber had struck him in the back and he was swept away by a raging prairie sea. Where did he end up? How far had the boy walked on that swollen foot, carrying the body of the girl he loved?

Damn. Nickel wasn't a boy. He was a sixteen-year-old veteran, having seen and suffered more than anyone ever should.

After another mile, he took the child from Marbles's arms, gave her to Molly, and called for another rest. The troupe collapsed where they were. Bannack pulled small passengers off the horses and called to Ryder. The young man slumped in the middle of the road, his face in the dirt.

Bannack knelt before him, placing a hand on his shoulder.

"Ryder."

"Nickel," came the deadpan reply. "Ryder is Magdalena's name for me. It don't belong to nobody else."

"All right then, Nickel." He had never used the nickname before and was surprised how easily it rolled off his tongue. Somehow, it suited him.

"Ain't gonna make it, sir." Nickel's mouth moved, but he did not even raise his head out of the dirt to speak. "Hurtin' too bad."

Bannack lifted the borrowed shirt from his back and swore under his breath. The coloration of his skin was a solid blackish-purple; he saw where the debris had struck, tearing at his flesh. No wonder he hurt.

"How the hell have you been carryin' that trunk?" he asked. Nickel's reply was incorrigible. The cowboy called for Molly Wheeler to sit with her golden child and showed her the regression of the boy's back.

"He needs bed rest. I don't have anything left to rub on those wounds. We've gotta get him to Victoria, ma'am."

"What about Magdalena's box?" Molly asked.

"I can't haul Nickel if I'm carryin' that box. We'll have to leave it."

"No!" Nickel strained to rise, grasping the closest handle, trying to pull himself up. "I'll walk. I'll carry it."

"No, you won't!" Molly chided. "You'll listen to Mr. Bannack."

"It's you or that trunk, Nickel."

The youth was still struggling to gain his feet but could not find his hands and knees.

"Save it, not me," he begged.

"Mr. Bannack?"

He looked up. Posse, the eldest, stood before him.

"I'll carry the trunk for my brother."

Les Harold joined him. "Me too."

Even young Zelus jumped to his feet, offering to help. Bannack considered the offers, and his gaze fell upon Alastor Wheeler. The boy glared at him but made no such offer to aid.

"Fine," he said, still watching the wayward brother. "Nickel, lay down!"

"W-We could b-build a tra-travois," Marbles suggested. "W-Weave our ropes together to m-m-make the bed. It'll h-hold him."

Before Bannack could mull over the suggestion, Posse spoke up. "Don't know what a travois is, but why don't you just buy my brother's luck? If that don't fetch a wagon, nothing will."

"Buy his luck?" Bannack asked.

"Well, shore, they don't call him Nickel for nothin'." Murmurs of agreement echoed through the Wheeler clan. Even Molly was nodding.

"Nobody'd have to haul that box on foot if you bought my boy's luck."

Everyone was looking to Bannack. He took off his hat, ran a hand through his hair, and frowned down at them. They were all touched in the head, every last one, and he was too damned tired to put up with silly superstitions.

"You think he can snap his fingers and make a wagon appear? Maybe you ain't noticed, but life don't hand you luck. You gotta make your own way."

Nickel raised his head and stared at him. A chorus of snorts and hollow chortles surrounded him. The young man's family, even Molly Wheeler, was laughing at him as though he had just told a grand joke.

They wouldn't be laughing when he pulled them all back to their feet. The "nearby" town of Victoria wasn't getting much closer. He watched Nickel struggle to gain his knees, then his feet. Shadows of pain set in the corners of his mouth and pooled in the green depths of his eyes, but Bannack helped him up.

The sand-streaked brown-haired boy did not flinch when he met his gaze.

"If it ain't enough I'm standin' here now, I'll make you believe in luck, sir, if you've a nickel to spend."

Bannack didn't have one, nor did he believe in encouraging dependence on a foolish myth, but Marbles shuffled forward, holding out his hand.

"It's my l-last one," he said. "W-Would it work if I b-b-bought it?"

Nickel took the coin, grasped the awkward cowboy's shoulder as if the deed was already done, and sank back down to the ground next to the blue trunk, his eyes on the road ahead.

"Is th-that it?" Marbles stuttered.

"Yessir, that's it." Nickel kept staring ahead. Waiting. Help would be coming soon now; he was sure of it.

"Hey, Nickel," Posse called, holding up the youngest child. "Any way you can luck us into a wagon with food and water too?" The eldest Wheeler boy held his breath, and then let it out with one whispered word: *Please?*

"Why not?" he replied, waving his hand in the air as though the deed was already done.

"Son, you don't think Marbles givin' you that coin's gonna get us help, do you?"

Nickel didn't turn his gaze from the road.

"Works for ships—why not a wagon?"

Bannack rolled his eyes and groaned. The group refused to rise and continue the march, convinced help was now only moments away.

Infuriated at Marbles for giving in to his superstitious nature, and to the

Wheelers for their naivety, Bannack mounted his horse and rode down the road, venting his angst with words not fit for the ears of a sailor, let alone a woman with a small herd of children.

He scouted a few yards off the road for something to use as a travois to carry Nickel and found a shredded sail tangled up in an uprooted tree. Much of it was shredded and not worth the effort of disentangling, but he found a section large enough to triple-fold and stretch to make up the bed of the travois.

He was standing in the stirrups of his saddle, reaching over his head to saw at the tree roots, slicing the shredded canvas entrails away from what was salvageable with his knife, when he heard an unmistakable sound.

Bannack froze, his blade still embedded in heavy, damp sail, and listened. His horse turned her head to the road and perked her ears. Wheels and trace chains rattled over the uneven prairie road. His head swiveled toward the sound.

A buckboard pulled by a team of big-boned draft horses clattered into view, a man and woman perched on the seat. The team moved slowly toward him, zigzagging the safest course through debris.

Bannack's mouth moved, but nothing came out as they neared. The woman, a sprightly gal under a large bonnet, spied him and pointed. The man reined the team to a halt and set the brake, eyeing the knife in Bannack's hand. He repositioned a shotgun lying in the seat behind them—more so to draw attention to the firearm than to actually move it. It was a smart move, Bannack thought. Showed the man's head was more than a hat stand.

"Mister, you all right?" the man called with a friendly wave.

"No, hold up!" he called. He slashed at the sail, yanked it free, and draped it over his arm, placing his knife back in its sheath. Bannack spurred his mount and loped up to the wagon, keeping his hands within view. He knew what he looked like and probably smelled even worse. It wouldn't do to scare the young couple away before he pleaded his case.

"You lookin' for family?" he asked.

"No sir, nobody in particular. Word's spread. Victoria's been sending wagonloads of supplies. My wife and I had a wagon and team, so we loaded up to help who we could. Is it as bad as they say?"

Bannack shifted in the saddle.

"Hell. Been buryin' the dead for days and lookin' for a friend."

The woman covered her mouth. "Did . . . did you find your friend?" she asked.

"Yes ma'am. Alive, but he's sufferin'. He was swept away in the storm, nearly drowned. His family ain't had food since before the storm hit, I reckon. We got women and kids."

"Where are they?"

"Just behind me, yonder on the road. Be obliged if I could pay their way to ride back to Victoria with you folks."

"No sir!" the man cried. "We won't be takin' pay, but we will tend to your friends, Mister. It seems you're in luck. I'm a doctor. Well, my father is, but I've been his apprentice since I was five. Name's Bram, and this is my wife, Lottie."

Bannack paled at the young doctor's choice of words—luck.

The man reached out to shake the cowboy's hand, and he wrung it, barely able to croak his own name.

"Bannack," he growled, his voice thick with emotion, and tipped his hat to the woman.

"Mr. Bannack, our wagon's yours. You have enough folks to fill it?"

He nodded once, folding the salvaged sail canvas without dismounting, and tossed it in the back of the wagon. He noticed boxes piled high behind the seat, and the man followed his gaze.

"Foodstuffs, and your family's welcome to them. We'll follow you."

Bannack rode back to the Wheeler clan with the young doctor driving behind, but his mind was disheveled and confused. It was too good to be true. Wasn't it? They were on the road, after all. Wagons had been coming in from Victoria as people arrived in search of their loved ones, so it was a mere coincidence, the arrival of the doctor and his wife not fifteen minutes after Marbles bought Nickel's luck.

He was still shaking his head when the celebratory shouts of Nickel's family drowned out his thoughts.

The doctor's wife climbed down and tended to Molly, Lucy, and the children. They passed around canteens of water, and the young doctor grabbed one along with his medical bag. He headed straight for Nickel, who was still stretched out on the road. He appeared to be asleep but opened his eyes when Bram knelt down before him.

Bannack took a few steps back, watching the young doctor examine Nickel's wounds with great care. Marbles shuffled over to him, but he refused to meet his friend's gaze.

"Th-The wagon c-c-came," he said, his stutter unusually thick.

"It did."

"H-How'd he d-do that?"

"We're on a road," Bannack said, a little too loudly. "Wagons use roads."

He saw Nickel turn his head. The boy fixed him with a baleful, all-knowing stare, and for an instant, a smirk tugged at the corners of his mouth. It was there and gone, for Bram pressed into his rib cage, searching for broken bones, but he saw it, nevertheless.

Marbles saw it too.

"B-B-Bannack?"

"Yeah."

"S-Something about that b-boy." He paused, taking his time to search for the right words. "Things is about to ch-change on the r-r-ranch, ain't they?"

Bannack neither accepted nor denied the question. He stood, arms folded across his chest, staring at the golden boy of Indianola. Except for Alastor, Nickel's siblings took their turns thanking their brother for "bringing" the wagon.

The womenfolk petted and kissed him, championing him for his gift. Bannack held back when they loaded the big blue box into the buckboard and looked on as the Wheeler family followed, sinking into soft blankets and quilts spread over the wagon bed. Nickel was moved first and laid on his stomach to ease the bruises on his back. The youngsters followed, the women and men last.

Lottie sat with her passengers, passing out foodstuffs while her husband scrambled back into the driver's seat. He released the brake, and as the wagon lurched forward, Marbles followed behind on horseback.

Bannack mounted his own weary animal and rode a distance ahead, seeking the solitude he needed to gather his fatigued thoughts. Had anyone thought to ask, Bannack would never have admitted the truth: he was spooked.

# CHAPTER 22

# VICTORIA

She was bustling with activity. Supply wagons and searchers were still streaming out, and survivors were still straggling in. Every rooming house was full, so the young doctor and his wife took the remaining Wheelers and their cowboy escorts into their own little home. They spread blankets and bedding across the floor, and Molly and the few remaining children collapsed in a heap, too tired to eat.

Posse, Les, and Alastor followed suit, leaving a frayed Nickel to his own thoughts. Sleep did not come. Every time he closed his eyes, he saw her face. Sallow white, tinged in blue. Lifeless. He tried to focus on the memory of her lips and how they tasted, the sweet purr of her voice, but then he remembered her on the porch in the rain, locked in Alastor's embrace.

Alastor! Magdalena knew the rivalry between them. How could she choose that dimwit over him? Nickel raked his fingers over his eyes and up through his hair, but the memory played on, over and over.

Turning his head to the left, his gaze fell across Alastor's face. His brother opened his eyes and widened when he caught Nickel's dark glare.

"What're you lookin' at?" he whispered.

"I hate you." Nickel mouthed the words, startled by how much he meant them.

Alastor raised his head.

"Hey, Nickel," he said, "figure maybe I oughta tell ya—"

"Go to hell!" he snapped.

"But Magdalena . . ." Alastor tried again, then shrugged and gave up just as easily. "Suit yourself," he said, chuckling.

Nickel rose from his bed with a strangled moan and limped outside. His head spun, and he sank against the support post until the wave of dizziness passed. When he looked around, he saw Lucy Parker huddled in the corner, alone. She donned a thin shawl around her slender shoulders and tearstains on her cheeks.

"Hey, Luce," he whispered.

"Nickel," she said. "You should be asleep."

"Reckon I'll never sleep again." He eased down next to her, leaning forward to prevent trauma to his back. Even the rub of the borrowed shirt against his raw skin set his teeth on edge, but it was better than lying inside fighting off the demons living in his mind.

Lucy rested her head against his shoulder, and he instinctively wrapped his arm around her, but his mind was numb to her nearness. He watched the bustle of town with the farseeing stare of vague recognition.

"I'll never live up to her, will I?" she asked.

Nickel didn't answer, and the knowing didn't do much to ease his strain. They sat together, strangers in thought, watching the town swirl by. It wasn't so long ago their own town was bustling with the hum of daily activity. How could it be gone?

"What do we do now?" Lucy asked him.

"Get hitched, I guess." Nickel knew from experience they would need a witness. Old Joly, captain of the seas, had the power to hitch folks together. His knots never came unraveled, but he always demanded a witness to the proceedings.

Damn. Poor Joly. He hated not knowing what became of the weathered seafarer. Joly did more than teach him the art of ink—he taught him the important things in life, like how to tell a story, how to drink and fight, and how to live by the code of the sea. He also taught him how to tie a taut knot—both in rope, and in man and wife. Once Joly made him official, he stepped back from time to time and let Nickel perform a few marriages of his own.

"You've a great power in you now, boy—the power to bind man and woman together. Tie a solid knot, Nickel, one that won't unravel when pulled," Joly had told him.

That was well and good for other folks, but what of him? He had taken her innocence. Even though she had given it willingly, he owed it to Luce to get hitched, but he didn't know how to tie his own knot. He always figured

Old Joly would be the one to marry him and Mags. Then again, he figured on a lot of things that would never be.

Staggering to his feet, Nickel rubbed red, bleary eyes and sought Bannack. When told about the nuptials and how they needed a witness and a preacher, the cowboy raised an eyebrow but refrained from comment.

"Will you stand with us, Bannack?"

"I reckon so if that's what you want. Let's go find a preacher."

A preacher could not be found to do the job. Nickel supposed too many souls needed prayer or last rites.

Instead of giving up, Bannack suggested they resort to the law office for a quick tie-up. They found a lawman on the street in front of his office, talking to a small huddle of Indianola victims. The badged man nodded at their approach and listened to Nickel's request with an air of surprise.

"Indianola?" he asked, appraising Nickel's ragged appearance.

"Yessir, but if it's all the same to you, I don't wanna talk about it." He glanced at Lucy but could not return the warmth in her smile. "I'm just here to do what needs done."

"You sure, son?" he asked. "Seems a strange time to get hitched unless you have . . . oh." The sheriff looked from the weary groom-to-be to the happy bride, and shrugged.

Nickel bobbed his head. Let the lawman think whatever he wanted, he didn't care. He would do right by giving the girl he bedded his last name. Worthless as it was, she seemed to want it.

"You look like you need a doctor, not a wedding."

"There's plenty need it more'n me," Nickel replied, sharpening his tone.

"Well, I'm no preacher, but I can do the job now, as long as you don't mind it being quick. Town's filled with your brethren, and I've been trying to arrange supplies for as many as I can."

"They come first," Nickel said, "but if you got the time, a quick hitchin' will do us fine."

The lawman dragged his gaze over Bannack, holding his hand out as though to appeal for help.

"Are you their witness?"

"I am." Bannack's statement was calm. He offered no other words of encouragement or otherwise.

The sheriff sighed. "Then step inside, and let's get the deed done."

☙

A cursory glance in the sheriff's little mirror told Nickel he looked as played out as he felt. Bruises, oh, the awful bruises! They would heal. The gashes would too, though not without scars. Maybe in time he would even stop smelling dampness and mold through his nostrils, but the jagged pain searing his insides with every breath—when did that go away?

Lucy Parker didn't seem to notice his bedraggled appearance, or his inner strife. She nestled beside him, her hand in his, and offered a shy smile of appreciation. Nickel tried to return it, but his facial muscles just couldn't contort into the grin he was known for. He was supposed to hitch up to Magdalena and head north to start their lives together. She had said she wouldn't go with him, but that was just fear talking. Mags would've come around if Alastor hadn't gotten in the way.

Damn that Alastor, anyhow! Now Mags would forever belong to the underwater world of the Mistress's abyss.

The thought of water made him cough. His lungs throbbed and his voice rasped like a blacksmith's file when he spoke.

There was no pomp and fluff to the ceremony, no soft words, flowers, or frills. It would have been over in a minute, had Nickel realized the importance of a last name.

The lawman was peering at him, blinking with an impatient air of expectation.

"Well?" he asked.

"Can you say that again?" Nickel mumbled.

The lawman frowned a little, but his gaze flickered to Bannack, who stood by Nickel's right. The cowboy inflicted a slight nod of his head, and the lawman repeated the question.

"I said, do you take Lucy Parker for your wife?"

*Magdalena. I take Magdalena!* Her name lodged in his throat, he wanted to shout it aloud.

"Shore. Guess I do."

The lawman repeated the question to Lucy but stopped at Nickel's name.

"You never told me your name, son."

"Nickel."

"Your name's Nickel? Your *given* name?"

"Ryder's my given name."

It was a bold-faced lie, but Nickel figured no one would strike him down for lying to a lawman, not like they might if he fibbed to a preacher.

"Ryder what?"

"What?"

"What's your last name?"

"I don't got one."

Lucy's smile slipped a little. She knew his real name, first and last. Before she offered it up for everyone to hear, he reiterated.

"I don't got no last name." Nickel's nostrils flared, and his head snapped back, daring anyone to argue.

"Well, son, what name are you going to give your wife if you don't have one?"

Nickel hedged. He hadn't thought of that. Did he need a last name just to marry up with a girl? He tried to think of one, but nothing surfaced worth using. He shifted the weight of his crutch, easing the pain of his bad ankle.

"I don't . . ." he began, but his new boss stepped forward. Gripping Nickel's shoulder, the cowboy spoke in a loud, clear voice.

"Bannack."

"Sir?" the lawman asked.

"His last name's Bannack."

Nickel's jaw dropped. The great cowboy looked Nickel in the eye, his face chiseled with tired pride.

"He's my little brother."

Through war-torn exhaustion, Nickel saw respect and admiration in his hero's eyes. Bannack was claiming him!

His throat closed, and tears gripped him. Lowering his head lest they all see him cry, Nickel repeated the sheriff's oath to Lucy Parker, spoke two little words, and it was done.

Lucy let out a cry and kissed him, right there in front of Bannack and the sheriff. She clung like a serpent to its meal; he had to shake his arm free to make his mark next to hers on a little piece of paper. Bannack signed his name under Nickel's mark, and they stepped out into the bustling street of Victoria.

"We're married, Nickel!" Lucy cried. Her eyes sparkled, and there was a lightness to her voice. "Can you believe it?"

Nickel couldn't. A few little words, a mark on a piece of paper, and he had a wife. A wife, and a new name. Ryder Bannack. Now there was a name to be proud of!

Turning to look at his hero, Nickel summoned the ghost of a smile, but it soon faded. Bannack stalked off under some pretense to find Marbles and take care of travel arrangements. He wished he could follow, but now he had a brand-new bride hanging off his arm.

*What do I do with her?* he thought. He *knew* what he was supposed to do with a new bride, but his wounds were agonizing, and every time he looked at Lucy, guilt over Mags bit another chunk out of his heart. Rest was the most sensible thing he could think of, so he talked her into lying down in his temporary bedroll within Bram and Lottie's home. She clung to him, bidding he rest with her, but even as she drifted off into slumber, Nickel's mind rejected the notion of sleep. He was the only one, for the remaining Wheeler clan lay about the room where they fell, wrapped in quilts provided by Bram and Lottie. Even his mother succumbed to her exhaustion, brought on in part by Bram, who had given her something out of a green glass vial to help her sleep.

Wiggling out of Lucy's grasp, he slipped outside and eased back to the bench of the young doctor's home to wait for the cowboys' return.

While he waited, he retraced his study of Victoria. There was still a sense of urgency hovering about the residents of Indianola's neighbors. Rooming houses were so full that makeshift shelters and hospitals were being set up under nearly every covered roof in town. Everyone, it seemed, was housing homeless Indianolans. They were straggling in, a few at a time. Many were on foot, others brought in by wagon.

Nickel checked every face, searching for someone he recognized. Most looked just like him; faces colorless, devoid of feeling. They were ragged and filthy, some missing clothes, others covered in scraps of cloth or wrapped in bedraggled old blankets. Most of them needed medical attention and nourishment.

Rising on unsteady legs, Nickel limped out to the stragglers on his over-sized oar crutch and hailed them, one by one. Recognition was slow to set in, but as his identity registered, Indianolans surrounded him to share their grief. They called his name over and over, and he reveled in each tearful reunion. All of them asked about loved ones, whether he had seen them, and he in return asked about Joly and his siblings lost to the sea.

No one, not even Nickel, had good news to share. No one had seen Joly, either. Not that it surprised him. When he wasn't at sea, his old friend lived on the edge of the map.

The sailor's shack was probably the first to go, after the wharf itself.

Still, Nickel stood in the middle of the street, searching every face in the heart of Victoria, hoping to see the ever-smiling, craggy Old Joly.

"Nickel?"

The whisper was faint, yet familiar. He looked about, searching for the source, trying to place the little voice. It sounded rather like a mouse, meek and tired. He scanned those around him, but no one appeared to have heard it.

Maybe he was imagining things, hearing voices that weren't there. After all, citizens moved like the tide all around him, rising and falling, dodging wagons and horses, and transporting supplies. A hand grasped his arm, and an old woman he recognized from home drew near. Tears welled in her eyes but did not fall. She clutched his hands, squeezing them. Though he did not recall her name, he leaned in, allowing her to embrace him. She clung to him as though a mother to a long lost son, patted his face, and smiled through a wry, twisted mouth. "Luck child," she whispered, releasing his hand and moving away. He watched her amble down the street, praying she was not alone in her world. `

"Nickel Ryder!"

Nickel's head snapped up. He heard that! Only one person called him Nickel Ryder. One tiny, precious little soul—his little sister Hera.

"Hera? Hera!" He whirled in the street, frantically seeking the little girl lost to the sea. He shouted her name over and over, twisting to listen for the answering call. Nothing.

He stumbled to the other side of the street, cursing the crutch slowing him down. Someone grabbed his shoulder, and he jumped. Les.

"What's wrong?"

"I heard Hera!" he cried.

"Nickel. You need to get some rest."

"She's out here, I swear!" Nickel's voice rose in pitch. "I heard her call my name!" he cried, casting about, searching for the lovely little face among a sea of strangers.

Les shook his head. "You thought you saw Mags too," he reminded him.

"I *did* see her!" He cupped his hand against his ear, hoping to hear the call again.

"Nickel . . ." Les took hold of him, trying to lead him out of the road and toward the doctor's house.

"I heard Hera! You gotta believe me!" Nickel's shouts only seemed to sadden Les. He patted his back, gently.

"She ain't here. None of 'em are—you know that." He was patient but adamant. It wouldn't do for Nickel to lose his mind now.

"I swear it. I heard her, Les. She called for Nickel Ryder. Nobody calls me that but her." He twisted, trying to break free of Les's grip, and called Hera's name.

His best friend merely looked at him. Les thought his mind was slipping, he could tell.

"I ain't crazy," he said, but it was all bluff. He was beginning to feel he was right. Sometimes he would see them, so real he felt he could reach out and touch them. Deep down he knew they were picture memories, but maybe it wasn't normal to see people who weren't really there. Had he been hearing things? Hera hadn't responded when he called. If she was here, she would have answered.

"Come on, Nickel," Les pleaded. "Go lie down."

"No." It wouldn't help. It was worse when he lay down. That was when the darkness crept in.

*What if the monsters catch me when my eyes are closed? No thanks,* he thought, but he let Les steer him out of the street anyway.

They passed a laundress tottering out of her house with a basket of clothes. Setting the burden down, she skimmed a pair of britches off the top and shook them out.

Something fell out of the folds and rolled across the ground, stopping at Nickel's foot. Les bent to reach it and placed it in his hand. The tarnished five-cent piece was warm in his palm.

Heaving a long sigh, Nickel gave it back to the laundress.

"Dropped this, ma'am," he said. "It'll bring you luck."

She looked him up and down, held it a moment, then tucked it back into the palm of his hand and closed his fingers around it.

"If it's to bring luck," she said softly, "you keep it, Indianola." She squeezed his hand, and when Nickel opened his mouth to object, he noticed mist in her eyes.

She turned on her heel, toting the basket of clothes, and left him gaping after her.

"Nobody's ever given my luck back to me before," he murmured aloud.

"Come on, Nickel," Les began, but he didn't finish the sentence. Instead, he grabbed his shoulder, the bad one, and he flinched.

"Don't touch me," he rasped between his teeth.

"Nickel," Les whispered. "Look!" He pointed, and Nickel followed the end of his friend's finger toward a little girl running toward them as fast as she could on short, stubby legs.

"Hera!" He lunged forward on his crutch, but before he could make up the distance between them, a pale-faced woman in shredded clothing scooped up the little girl and took off running in the other direction.

Hera tried to scream and wriggle, but the woman held her hand over her mouth.

Nickel called after her, threw the oar down, and tried to run. He didn't get far before his ankle turned, spilling him onto the street.

Les Harold didn't wait to help him up. Yelling after the little Wheeler girl, he took off in a dead run, racing after the figure threading her way through the busy street.

Nickel and Les were no strangers to dodging citizens on the run. How many times had they raced through the ports during the unloading of ships, dodging sailors, livestock, and cargo? How many times did they play among the netmaker's inventory, pretending the intricate nets were spiderwebs?

But this was no game, and Nickel cursed his injuries. He could not run without collapse, no matter how hard he tried. When he spotted Bannack and Marbles striding toward him from across the road, he screamed their names and headed for them.

"Hera!" he cried before they reached him. "My little sister, she's here! Some woman snatched her up and ran! Les is after her!" Nickel pointed, and the cowboys were gone without a word spoken.

There was no demand to stay behind, and he was glad of it, for he wouldn't have listened anyway. Some crazy woman had his little sister—but now the woman would pay. Retrieving the oar, he followed the chase as best as he could, but by the time he reached the edge of town, the pursuit had come to a head.

Bannack and Marbles were in the thick of some sort of verbal altercation. They had the woman cornered with a wall at her back. She held a squirming Hera tight against her breast and was yelling profanities at the men surrounding her. The sheriff was there too, Nickel noticed, for he held the cowboys at bay.

Les, noticing his friend's arrival, slunk over to him.

"That woman's crazier'n old Whistle ever was," he said. "Bannack and Marbles cornered her, but the sheriff stopped them. She's done told the sheriff Hera's *her* daughter, and we're tryin' to kidnap her. He ain't even takin' Hera into it—look at her fightin' to get away!" Les waved his arm at Hera, who was yelling and clawing at her captor's arms. "That lawman don't know who to believe, so he won't let us take Hera away from her."

"He's damned . . . well . . . gonna," Nickel said, panting. He broke through the oglers, and Hera cried his name.

"That's my little sister, Sheriff!" he cried. He made a rush for Hera, but the lawman blocked his path. "That woman's tryin' to steal my sister, Sheriff! We thought we lost her in Indianola. Don't know how she wound up here, but my momma's been mournin' her and all the others we done lost."

As Nickel spoke, Hera opened her mouth and chomped down on the woman's arm. She howled but did not let go.

"Lies!" the woman spat at him, jerking Hera's head under her arm.

"You hurt my sister, and I'll kill you!" Nickel lunged, ready to clobber Hera's kidnapper, but Bannack cut him off and held him at bay.

"He's tellin' the truth, Sheriff." The bone-weary Indianolans shuffled forward, each of them, to lay claim to their lost Indianolan daughter.

"Hera Wheeler," a man said. "She be the daughter of Molly Wheeler, right enough. That woman shore ain't Molly."

"Nickel's her brother. Known the family all my life," a woman said. Many others piped up in agreement, bringing doom to the spitting child-snatcher.

The sheriff bodily forced the woman to turn her loose, and the woman set up a frantic wail, grabbing for the little girl's legs as she ran. It took the lawman and the cowboys to strong-arm her into submission, and at the sheriff's command, they dragged her off. Nickel hoped it was toward the jail.

Hera flew into Nickel's grasp, and he wrapped his arms around the child, sniffling into her tousled hair.

"It's okay now, Hera," he whispered. "Nickel Ryder's here."

# CHAPTER 23

# THE COLOR OF DECEIT

Marbles leaned against the wall of the front porch, puffing on a smoke someone had pressed into his hand. A gift of gratitude, the Indianolan had told him. Bannack got one too, only he put his in his vest pocket. The man was wound tighter than the springs in a pocket watch. Marbles watched his friend pace back and forth under the overhang, clenching and unclenching bloodstained fists, and shook his head.

"You shore are sl-slow to swallow your f-f-fight," he told him. "Set d-down and have a s-s-moke. You're makin' . . . makin' me nervous."

Bannack stood still for the breath of a minute before he was at it again, back and forth, back and forth, scanning the surrounding town.

Marbles drew in a long puff and exhaled slowly, letting the smoke curl from his lips. It was a damn fine cigar, and he meant to enjoy it no matter how agitated Bannack was.

The man was still bent on a fight; the altercation with Hera's abductor set him off. From what the sheriff told them, the woman lost her whole family in the flood. Instead of grieving, she decided to steal another lineage, one child at a time.

The sheriff offered a modicum of sympathy for the woman's plight. Bannack, on the other hand, proved savage by suggesting a necktie party. Loss or gender was no excuse to separate a child from her family.

Marbles wondered if Bannack's punishment would have borne fruit, had it been his decision.

Marbles closed his own eyes and leaned back, trying not to think about the hell they crawled out of, or the long trek ahead of them. For the moment, he had a good cigar and a little rest due him. No more threat, and the Wheeler clan had even regained a lost gem.

The cowboy thought about little Hera Wheeler. No one knew how she wound up safe in Victoria when everyone thought the storm swept her into the sea. No one asked.

To the Wheelers, it didn't matter. She was back with them, and she was safe. A blessing in the aftermath of tragedy—best take it as such and not dwell on how it happened.

Except for one thing. She came to Nickel. Les Harold told them about how Nickel thought he heard Hera's voice calling him, and he hadn't believed it.

"Thought his mind was gone," Les had said. Marbles listened to the story about passing the laundress, and cold shivers snaked down his spine when Les told about spotting Hera after the woman gave Nickel her dropped coin—a gift of luck.

"S-Somethin' un-unnatural about that b-b-boy," he muttered. He hadn't realized he said it aloud until Bannack stopped pacing.

"What?"

"Nickel."

"What about him?"

"H-He only saw Hera after a l-lady gave him the lucky n-n-nickel."

Here was a fight. Marbles saw it in the set of Bannack's jaw as he spun on him and braced himself for the verbal onslaught.

His friend did not disappoint him. He sat through the curses, smoking on his cigar, waiting for the storm to fizzle.

"You oughta know better!" Bannack yelled. "There ain't no such thing as luck. He don't need you fillin' his head with that rot!"

"I g-g-guess it's harmless, b-believin' in a little l-luck," Marbles said.

"Harmless? The hell it is! What happens when he's backed into a corner? Life or death happens all the time out here. You want him dependin' on somethin' that just ain't there?"

Marbles closed his eyes and took his time answering. Bannack was spoiling for another fight, but he'd settle for an argument if he gave in to one. He never could figure why he was such a hot-blooded warrior. Fighting was sometimes necessary, but it always wore him out afterward.

*Guess my blood just cools a whole lot quicker,* he reasoned.

"Well?"

Marbles almost smiled—almost. He didn't open his eyes, but he could feel the smaller man standing over him, muscles tensed and ready to spring. He knew better than to tell his friend to calm down. Instead, he cleared his throat, took another draw, and exhaled.

"N-Nickel ain't no older'n me w-when I signed on for the P-P-Pony," he said. "He's seen as m-much hell as me too. May-maybe quit w-w-worryin' so much ab-bout his luck, and trust that b-boy's brains."

"He's inexperienced."

"Yep. But he's smart. Just d-don't take away his h-h-hope, Bannack, 'cause to him, that's what l-luck is."

The air beside him was quiet. Without turning his head, Marbles fished inside his vest pocket and offered a lucifer to light Bannack's cigar. Bannack hesitated, then accepted with a grunt.

When Marbles heaved open one eyelid, he found his friend stretched out on the bench, dragging on the cigar.

"You think you're so damn smart," he growled.

Marbles shrugged and closed his eyes again.

"T-T-Tired, d-damned tired."

∾

The Indianola boys stood in a huddle, looking at the barren shelves of the general store, and sighed. It would be grim fare on the trek north, and they all knew it.

Bannack and Marbles were perusing the meager remains, so Nickel did the same. He found a discarded sack of flour and showed it to Bannack. The cowboy shook his head.

"Look inside."

Nickel did and scrunched up his nose. The bag was squiggling with little worms. No wonder they left it behind. He tossed it down in an empty corner and turned to his hero.

"Not much left, is there?"

"We'll be travelin' on half rations for a few days. There's a ranch about four or five days' ride along the way. Stopped there on the way down—they're holdin' horses for us. We can restock foodstuffs there."

"Good, I don't wanna take food away from Indianolans, anyhow."

"Look around. If there's anything left you need, put it on my bill. I'll be back."

Nickel nodded, watching him go. Bannack had an annoying habit of walking off with no explanation to anyone.

Les joined him and commented on his rapid disappearances.

"So? He don't need to answer to nobody. He's the boss."

The friends rifled through the shelves, and Nickel added a few possessions to the bill, careful not to overcharge. A tin cup, a small folding knife, and a comb. Nickel asked the merchant if he had any copies of Mustang Grey, but the man just shook his head.

"Can't hardly keep dime novels in stock. Bought up by boys like you soon as they come in."

Nickel frowned. "Nothin'? Don't have to be Mustang Grey."

"Sorry, son."

Damn. It would have been nice for Les to read aloud while they camped for the night. Otherwise, nights on the trail would not differ from the past few nights in Victoria—haunted and sleepless. Without a good story to cling to, his mind would retreat to the horrors of that memory. Nickel bent forward on his oar crutch a little, trying to ease the painful gashes in his back. They told him not to tense his muscles, but how could he relax? The force of the screaming sea had rolled and beaten his body, yet it was his insides that were broken beyond repair.

He longed for something: a shred of relief, something to focus his mind, even for a little while. What better way to escape than a good story?

Gripping the edges of the counter, Nickel closed his eyes and shook off the stab of disappointment.

"You aren't going to cry, are you?" the merchant asked him.

"He's got a lot to cry about," a voice said behind him. "We all do." Posse laid an awkward hand on Nickel's shoulder. "You and Les done here?"

He nodded, not trusting himself to speak.

"Wrap up those packages, Mister," Posse said. "Our boss'll be back to pick 'em up." He led Nickel outside, where they walked around to the rear of the store to wait for Les.

A collection of crates, barrels, and wooden boxes were piled against the mercantile wall. Nickel thought it wasteful to let them sit there; why not use them for something else?

He and his brothers had built many a chair for Momma out of busted-up shipping crates. Shelves too.

Intending to use one for a bench, he picked up a crate, only to discover they were not all entirely empty. His crate housed three small paper boxes, printed with words he could not read.

Interest piqued, he opened a carton and peered inside. Forgotten treasures! Nickel held up the contents with a slow-forming grin just as Les Harold walked around the corner. His best friend stopped to stare at him, slack-jawed. Posse took one look at the boxes and swore.

"Shit, Nickel, not firecrackers! You know Bannack won't never let you have those!"

"Did I say I was gonna ask him?"

"He won't pay for 'em."

"They was thrown out with the crates. Ain't no sense in payin' for what's been tossed out already."

"What are you gonna do with 'em? Momma said you couldn't have any after last time—"

"Momma ain't ridin' with us." Nickel clutched the little packages against his chest. "Besides, you never know when someone'll need a little spark."

Les and Posse exchanged looks and groaned at the same time.

"Aww, shit."

Nickel's excitement was short-lived as he spotted Alastor striding down the street. His little grin turned into a grimace. He knew exactly what he would like to do with his gained booty: Place those bangers in Alastor's back pocket and light the fuse. He said so aloud, and Posse rolled his eyes.

"Why do you hate him so much? You two never got along, but damn, Nickel, you never threatened to blow him up, either."

"I don't wanna talk about it."

"Do it anyway," Posse urged.

"What's it to you? You can't be peacekeeper all the time! Some things can't never be forgiven."

"Little brother, if you don't tell me what's goin' on between you and Alastor, I'll tell Bannack about those little fire sticks of yours."

"You do, and I'll light one under your saddle." Nickel watched his brother's stern visage turn into a scowl. Oldest son he might be, but Posse never took one of Nickel's threats lightly and they all knew it. Nickel never bluffed, not without purpose.

Still, this time Posse held his ground and Nickel caved. Too weary to fight, he told Posse and Les about Alastor and Mags, and how she had been letting him court her.

"That don't sound like Mags," Les and Posse said in unison. "She hated Alastor."

"That's what I thought," Nickel agreed. "But Lucy said—"

"*Lucy* said?" Posse asked, waving his hands in the air. "You're listenin' to *Lucy Parker* about Magdalena?"

"I saw them together, just before the storm! She . . . they . . . ahh!" Nickel yowled, slamming the heel of his foot into a barrel. It was his bad foot, and the pain shot straight through his body and radiated through his teeth.

Hunching down, he covered his head with his arms to wait out the hurt.

"Hey, Nickel. Maybe you don't know it, but Lucy Parker's lost her head over you," Posse said.

"I know," he rasped in reply.

"I guess you don't. Luce, she's one of those girls . . . she never had much, you know? Never had a momma, and her daddy shore didn't stick to home. Maybe she don't know better, but she's the sort'll do anything to get what she wants. *Anything.*"

Nickel lifted his head, just a little. "What're you sayin'?"

"I'm sayin' Lucy Parker lied to win you over to her side. I don't know what you thought you saw that day, but if Alastor was kissin' her, I'd bet my life she wasn't kissin' him back. She lied, Nickel. Luce lied. It's what she does—all she knows to get by, I guess. She's always been waitin' for her chance to steal you away from Mags. Everybody knew it. I figured you did too."

Posse's words were hard to digest, so Nickel rolled them around in his head, trying to make sense of them. Lucy was kind and sweet; he had never known her to be deceitful. Was she? Was he that blind? He turned to Les for confirmation or denial.

"Tell me I didn't hitch up with a liar," he begged. "Les, tell me I didn't side with Luce when Mags was innocent!"

His friend shifted and stubbed his foot in the dirt. He wouldn't look him in the eye.

"Tell me!"

"I dunno. It wouldn't surprise me if Luce put him up to kissin' her, just to send you runnin'. I wish you hadn't married up with her," he said softly. "We could've told you this before, but you ran off without tellin' nobody."

"Mags . . . was blameless?"

Les nodded.

"And Luce *lied* to me?"

Another nod.

"If I would've stuck with Mags . . ."

Les and Posse both shrugged, neither one willing to address the truth.

*I judged her! If I'd stayed, Magdalena might still be alive.*

Victoria was spinning. People and buildings blended together into a haze of colorful noise. Nickel ambled blindly, oblivious to those in his path. He had to look upon Lucy Parker, to watch her eyes speak. What would they say? Would she deny her role in Magdalena's fate—and his own?

He found her playing with Hera by the gate, waiting on him. Little Hera ran, throwing her pudgy arms around Nickel's legs. He hugged her and sent her inside to his mother. Hera had been through enough; she didn't need to witness an ugly confrontation.

Lucy greeted him with a broad smile as he stalked through the gate, and threaded her arm through his.

"Are we leaving soon?" she asked.

"*I am!*" he snapped back, dislodging her from his arm. He could barely look at her.

"Nickel? You don't look well. Are you all right?" Lucy tilted her head to the side, her large eyes bright and questioning.

"All right?" he parroted. *Does the girl have no shame?* "Girl, I don't guess

I'll ever be all right again." He stumbled closer, poking his crutch into the ground for a leaning post. Lifting his bad ankle off the ground, he fixated on her face, searching for signs of deceit. He wished it had a color, something identifiable that smeared across her pretty lips so that when she lied, he'd know.

"You lied to me, didn't you?"

"What?"

"Alastor and Mags—you lied!"

Lucy's eyes widened. He watched her skin turn pallid all the way down her neck, and his stomach clenched like a hardened fist.

*There it is. I guess deceit's got a color, after all.*

"Alastor didn't . . . he didn't tell you, did he?"

Nickel raised a brow. *Tell me what?*

Out loud, he said, "Say he did."

"Oh! No!" She flew against him, grabbing hold of his arm again and clawing at his sleeve. "You don't understand!" Lucy's breath came out in short, garbled gasps, yet words poured from her lips. "Alastor don't do any favors for free, you know that! He said I had to let him bed me if I wanted his help. It was before you and me though, and it didn't last longer than a minute! He finished so quick, he didn't even . . . he . . . before . . . before . . . you know. I only did it so he would agree to keep Magdalena busy for a little while—I couldn't get close to you with her in the way!" She doubled over, still clinging to him. Trying to embrace him.

A million words crowded his mind all at once, yet not one of them reached his tongue. The depth of her betrayal was like the depths of the sea: unfathomable.

"Nickel, I did it for us, me and you! Don't be mad, please! I love you. I only wanted to be with you!"

Nickel shook off her arms. Was it his imagination, or did his skin burn through his shirt from where she touched it?

"I figured it was the sea monsters I had to fear," he said, speaking in a low, rasping voice. "All this time, it was you!"

"No! You don't understand. I had to do something! I would have lost you if I hadn't."

"You think you'd keep me after this?" His fingers itched. Nickel ached to draw his knuckles into a fist, to hit her. Instead, he denounced his father's blood and merely pushed her away.

"Alastor wasn't supposed to tell!"

Nickel gaped at her. She wasn't even sorry. Sorry she got caught, sure. But she didn't seem to hold much remorse for her actions. How could he ever think she was sweet and pretty?

"He didn't tell," he replied. "You did." He turned away, but she latched onto him, hysteria bubbling out of her mouth. She reminded him of a stewpot left unattended, bubbling over until it frothed and melted down into a hot, blackened mess.

"Don't leave me! I couldn't bear it if you left me now!" Desperation hinged thick in her voice. Snot ran down her nose, but she didn't seem to care. Over and over she cried, telling him she loved him and that he didn't understand. Of that much she was right. How could she let Alastor bed her?

"Alastor!" he screamed at her. "You screwed Alastor!" He didn't care if the world heard his accusation. Lucy was the devil, even worse than the Beisht itself.

"He wouldn't help me unless I did!" Her voice held the frantic sound of the condemned just before death.

"You *killed* Mags!" Nickel was shaking. It started in his legs and traveled up to his teeth, which began to rattle.

"I didn't mean for her to die!"

Again, he shook her off, discarding her on the ground like a limp rag. "I'm goin' north to Moral."

"Please, I'll make it up to you," she begged. "I'm your wife now. You gotta take me with you!"

"You're a murderin' bitch, Lucy Parker. You don't belong in a place called Moral, seein' as how you ain't got none."

&#8531;

Goodbye. It was a word Nickel just didn't know how to say. He ducked his head and stood, facing his family with a great big lump in his throat. Much as he loved the sound of his own voice any other time, now words wouldn't come.

Bannack and Marbles were somewhere behind him, busy tying down Mags's big trunk to the back of the buckboard. Nickel thought they tied it down to stay busy and out of the awkward farewells, not so much because it needed to be.

He held onto Hera and Zelus, his favorites, and tried to reason with the latter's obsessive pleas to go along too.

"Momma needs you to be the man of the family now," he told his younger brother. He understood the desire, the fear of being left behind, and said so.

"You'll be okay," he promised. "In a few years, you can come north with me if you want."

With Hera he could find no sound explanation, weak or otherwise. She clung to his neck with fat little fingers and great salty tears. He held her tight as he dared, snuffling into her hair.

When it came to saying goodbye to his mother, Nickel couldn't do it. Instead, he stood before her, wishing he knew how to thank her for loving him all these years.

"I ain't bringin' Luce," he whispered.

"So I see," she replied, waving a hand at the hysterical girl sitting on the ground at the gate.

"I'll watch out for her. You just take care of yourself, my Ryder."

"Yes ma'am." Nickel swallowed a sob. He had to be strong; they were all looking at him. The young ones looked up to him; he couldn't let them catch him breaking down like a babe.

"Wish I could'a done better raisin' you," she told him. "You deserve more'n I can give."

"You done fine. Ain't nobody got a better momma than me."

"You make that cowboy help you write letters to me, you hear me? Les's daddy'll help me read 'em. Maybe I'll learn to read 'em myself if it ain't too hard."

"Yes ma'am."

Forgetting his injuries, she crushed him in an enormous hug. Nickel didn't care. He returned the favor, wishing he didn't have to let her go. She pawed at his face, cupping his damp cheeks between her palms, kissed him, and shoved him away.

"Go! Clamber up on that horse and find your happiness, my golden child. I don't want you feelin' bad 'bout me. I've got Hera and Zelus. I'll be all right. You go—make your mark, Nickel!"

She pushed him toward Bannack and released him only to grab the startled cowboy's face.

"You take care of my boys."

Bannack dropped his hat.

"Yes ma'am," he muttered. "I'll keep 'em safe."

"See you do! I don't want my Nickel hurtin' long. Help him recover from all this loss, cowboy. He needs a strong man to look up to, so don't you dare disappoint him!"

Before Bannack could reply, Molly Wheeler darted in and kissed him square on the mouth.

"Let me know if you change your mind about that wife of yours," she said with a tearstained smile, patting his cheek.

Nickel did not watch the other farewells. He did not watch Les Harold say goodbye to his father, nor Molly to her other sons. Instead, he climbed the horse Marbles held for him and fell in behind the awkward cowboy.

He heard a young feminine voice scream his name but did not turn around to look. Lucy Parker had no claim on him now.

Indianola was dead, and so was Mags. As far as he was concerned, so was his short-lived marriage.

Nickel focused on the long and wandering trail ahead.

# PART THREE

## ON THE TRAIL

CHAPTER 24

# MUSTANG GREY

Aside from the time he spent apprenticing on the ranch outside of Indianola, Nickel had never been out of earshot of the ocean in his life. Even when the wind was right, he still tasted the salty air and the gulls yapping overhead, signaling the Mistress's nearness.

He was bone-weary, but as he lay on the prairie, looking up at a massive blanket of stars, sleep refused him. Where was the ocean? The Mistress always spoke to him at night, the tide rising and falling in his ears, a constant lullaby.

They had ridden for a few days without the smell of the Mistress in their noses, or the tide in their ears. This—the solitude, the nothingness of the rolling hills and grasslands—was deafening. Nickel tossed in his bedroll, then turned, only to roll back. The rustling of canvas against his clothes was something to focus on. Something, but not much.

After another hour of unbearable silence, playing memories of his beautiful Indianola in his head, he sat up, clasping his hands over his ears. The stars were fading. Soon Bannack would stir if he wasn't up already. A hasty breakfast, and off they would go.

A sniff in the dark turned his head. His brothers were still enveloped, unmoving, in their bedrolls, but Nickel could just make out Les Harold's form in the graying black. He, too, was sitting up, rubbing his eyes. Les sniffed again, and Nickel realized his friend was crying. Shucking his bedroll, he crawled over to sit with Les.

Les swiped at his eyes, ducking his head away. "I don't know how to do this," he admitted. "They're all gone. Everyone we knew." Les sniffed again. "Even the ocean. I didn't think I'd miss her, you know? The Mistress. But now? It's so loud out here! I can't hear nothing."

"I know. Me too."

"I can't hear the water anymore, Nickel."

"I do, in my nightmares."

"But don't you miss it?"

"Can't sleep for thinkin' about it."

Les heaved a great sigh, and his eyes filled all over again.

"Sometimes I think it's all just a dream. We'll wake up back in Indianola, and it'll all be there. My momma'll be alive, and Old Joly and Mags."

"We don't know Joly didn't make it," Nickel said, but his tone was flat. He didn't believe Joly made it, either. The old sailor's shack was probably the first house to go. "He might have gone to the courthouse before it got too bad."

"Nobody saw him," Les replied. "Besides, you know Joly. He wasn't one to run from a storm."

*No,* Nickel mused, *he wasn't.* Storms at sea scared the man as they did every sailor, but they fascinated him too. Rather than run, Joly was a man to stand in the rigging and scream at it, shaming the skies for impeding his journey. He could picture the craggy old man doing just that, standing on the roof of his shack, maybe, shaking his fist at the massive waves as they crashed over him. "*Maybe* he took shelter," he heard Les say.

"Maybe I could've caught that damned dolphin," Nickel said aloud. Wrapping his arms around his knees, he swore under his breath. They would probably never know what happened to their old friend Joly, the sailor who taught them everything.

Les shifted and let out a groan of pain. It was the kind a greenhorn made after spending days in a saddle.

"I'm so tired," he croaked. "Aren't you tired?"

Nickel just stared at his best friend. Of course he was tired. His body was tired—so was his mind. Hell, even his hair was tired. Besides that, he had to rub ointment from a jar Mrs. Mercy had given him on his back whenever the pain sank too deep. He was as weary of that as he was of riding with one boot off to alleviate the swelling of his foot.

"Nickel, your brothers, they came to me. Want me to get you to talk to Bannack."

"About what?" Nickel perked up a little. Anything Alastor asked of, he wouldn't do. But Posse? What did he want?

"He's pushing us too hard. You can talk to him. He likes you. We can't hold this pace, Nickel. We aren't horsemen—none of us." Les rubbed his backside and moaned again.

Nickel lifted his chin. "I am."

"You're not. You're a poor fisherman's son. You got salt and seawater in your blood, just like me."

Nickel jumped to his feet, ignoring the protests of his ankle, and cringing at the intensity of the aches in his joints. "I am *no man's son,* you hear me?" He neglected to lower his voice, and the bundles lying on the other side of their small camp stirred.

"Sorry, Nickel, I didn't mean nothing by it," Les said.

"You wouldn't be sayin' that if Mustang Grey were here."

"Mustang Grey never survived what we just did, neither," Les pointed out.

"Course not. There's no water where he rides. Ain't nothin' to flood."

"Yeah, well, if he had lost his town and everybody in it, he'd be complaining too."

"Mustang Grey ain't never complained a day in his life!"

"How do you know?"

"You read the books. He never complained about nothin'."

A shoe sailed across the cold ash and struck Nickel in the back. He whirled, his fists clenched, as Alastor held the mate high in the air.

"One more word about that stupid pony rider or his 'book,' and I'll throw the other one!"

"Do it," Nickel said through clenched teeth. "I dare you." He crouched, placing one hand near his boot where Joly's blade still lived.

Alastor reared back as if to throw but hesitated.

Animosity oozed from every inch of Nickel's form. He was younger, but he knew how to take a punch. Oren Wheeler had given him enough practice perfecting how to take a blow. Thanks to observing his hero Bannack in action the first time they met, he knew how to throw one too.

The tension between brothers made Les Harold nervous. He staggered to his feet, groaning.

"Come on, ain't you two had enough of this? You ain't gonna kill each other."

"Alastor! I told you to have that cook-fire ready by dawn." Bannack strode into camp and threw a saddle at his angry charge. "Now we eat cold in the saddle. Catch your mounts."

"To hell with that! I ain't goin' nowhere today!"

"Fine," Bannack retorted. "Stay behind and sleep all day. You'll play hell catchin' up to us on foot."

"I got a horse." Alastor faced the cowboy, looking like a wild beast. Nickel figured if he had hackles, he would have raised them.

Bannack crossed his arms over his chest. "The hell you do."

"Hell I don't!"

"You pay for that animal?" Bannack asked, his tone hard but level.

"No, but I'm ridin' it, ain't I?" Alastor tried to cross his arms like Bannack, but instead of looking tough, he looked like an angry child.

"Floppin' like a fish on a horse's back don't mean you're ridin' it. Those horses go with me. As for you, stay or go. I don't give a shit."

"Aaah!" Alastor screamed, winging his remaining shoe at the cold ashes. Bannack ignored him and walked off to dine with Marbles at the wagon. Posse followed, leaving Nickel and Les to tie up their bedrolls and saddle their mounts.

Breakfast, thanks to Alastor's neglect of the cook-fire, resulted in stale biscuits and jerked meat, swallowed down with canned peaches and water. Nickel missed the cowpuncher's coffee the most. Nothing cuffed a man in the gut like that stout, black venom in a cup. It would be another long, dreadful day in the saddle, and the pace Bannack set showed no mercy.

Nickel's mind numbed the pain of long days in the saddle by drifting inward, dreaming of his beautiful Magdalena and the kisses he had stolen in her mother's garden.

She was standing on the pier in her favorite calico dress, a foamy green, like the ocean. Her dark hair was plaited, but the ocean winds whipped it into disarray, leaving those luscious long tresses flying around her face.

She beamed at his approach and laughed in delight over his gift.

"Ryder, Ryder," she giggled. "Did you pluck those flowers from my mother's garden?"

"I never pluck nothin' that don't wanna be plucked," he replied, and darted in for a kiss. Magdalena obliged, humming softly into his mouth. The tiny vibration of sound, paired with the tickle of her hair flying across his face, sent shock waves through his body. He grasped for her hands, deepening the kiss, the stolen flowers cupped between them.

She gave in under his persistent lead, letting her fingers drift down the length of his arm. Her mouth tasted just like the wild honey her mother served her guests at the inn. Nickel caressed her lips with the tip of his tongue and slipped between them.

Magdalena broke away, her face painted with a pretty blush, and placed a yellow blossom behind her ear.

"My mother will have something to say about the theft of her flowers," she said.

"Let her." His voice cracked as he followed her, unable to stay away.

She ran a few short steps, darting into the surf. When he reached for her, she kicked water at him and squealed as he gave chase.

He let her run, enjoying the freedom of the day, laughing when the waves crashed over their knees. Her skirt was heavy and limp with water, but he knew she didn't care about the tongue-lashing her mother would give her for inappropriate behavior.

Mrs. Hayworth tried to maintain ladylike decorum for the sake of her spirited daughter, but she reprimanded with the same brilliant spark glittering in her eye that Magdalena had.

Nickel lengthened his stride, catching her waist, yanking her in to cover her face in stolen kisses. She laughed, holding him at bay the best she could.

"I dreamed last night of cutting my hair, dressing like a boy, and setting sail on a ship," she told him. "As much as I want to be out there," she said, gesturing to the open sea, "I'm glad I'm here, with you."

Memories faded, and Nickel's mind shifted, conjuring up the bitter taste of salt water filling his lungs. The Mistress tossed his body against boards and debris, rolling him over the bodies of men and women who succumbed to the storm.

Torrential waters threw him against the side of a large schooner, and the spur on his boot snagged between boards and caught, jerking his ankle. He grasped blindly for a handhold—something, anything to latch on to. His fingers touched cold, clammy skin, and as the boat shifted in the current, his head surfaced. He opened his eyes, and his waterlogged lungs exploded in a scream.

His shout brought the cowboys scrambling for their guns. They whipped in their saddles, their cow ponies spinning as they searched for danger.

Nickel sat his horse, unable to move. The grass had turned to water. It was all around him, sucking him in. Again and again, it threw him against her body, her pale, lifeless face looming before his eyes.

Shaking his head against the memory, he grasped the saddle horn with both hands and muttered a low scream into the crook of his arm. Great heaving sobs racked his weary frame.

Someone had a hold of him from below, pulling him out of the saddle.

"I know, little brother. Come on, get down."

Posse. His face was pale, and dark circles decorated his brother's eyes, but he stood as tall as a lone tree on a vast plain. People said Posse felt nothing, that he was numb to pain. It was a ridiculous notion. He bled the same as everybody else, only he did it all from the inside so he had room to shoulder everyone else's.

Nickel folded into his big brother's arms.

"She's dead!"

Posse patted his back, closed his eyes, and heaved a sigh. "I know, Nickel. They all are."

Posse's embrace was awkward but heartfelt, for he was mourning too. Mourning the loss of their siblings, of their friends and neighbors, of their world, now wiped off the face of the map.

Les Harold half slid, half fell out of the saddle, limping over to join his friends in mourning. The three boys shared each other's pain without words. Posse grasped Nickel and Les by the backs of their necks, his strong, seafarer's fingers offering the understanding and support he did not know how to say aloud. They sat, crumpled together in the grass, shouldering Nickel's angst and their own.

Only Alastor remained aloof and seemingly unaffected. He stayed well away from the trio and their tears, looking on with his hat in his hands. At length, he eased over to the wagon and sat down in the bed to rest.

It was Bannack's appearance that stemmed Nickel's tears and made him reach for the wild rag tied around his neck. He mopped at his face, shamed by his display of emotion.

"Guess I ain't much of a cowboy," he mumbled by way of apology.

"Aww," Les replied, wiping the ruddy stains from his own face. "I bet even Mustang Grey cries from time to time."

Nickel shot him a red-rimmed glare and sniffed. "You're crazy," he said. "Ain't no way."

"Bet he has too! My momma used to say everyone cries."

"Not Mustang. He's too tough."

"Bet he did when those arrows was shot through his wrist!"

"Yelled, I expect."

"Same thing."

"No, it ain't! Posse, tell him yellin' ain't the same as cryin'."

Posse managed a half-hearted grin and a chuckle. He looked at Bannack. "It's over, sir. We're done. Let the boys ride together, and they'll argue the whole way to the ranch over Mustang Grey."

"Mustang Grey again, huh?" Bannack asked.

"Yessir."

"Seems to me I heard that name mentioned before."

"I just *bet* you have," Nickel said. He noted that Bannack was quick to catch his gaze. There was no hint of a smile on his lips, but something in his eyes told Nickel his suspicion was a sound one. Either Bannack *was* Mustang Grey, or he damn sure knew who was.

"He's all they ever talk about," Posse said. "They read his books over and over—wore 'em out. Mustang Grey was Nickel's hero till you came along."

"Flannel-mouth!" Nickel chided. He stole a glance at his real-life hero, and a shade of embarrassment splashed across his blotchy face. Bannack nodded at him from the saddle.

"Change mounts. We've got ground to cover."

"Some hero," Posse mumbled under his breath. He slapped Nickel's shoulder as he passed and headed back to the driver's seat.

Cautious of the soreness in his ankle, Nickel hopped around on one sock-foot, helping Les catch and saddle a fresh mount from the remuda. His friend grasped the horn but could not pull himself back up into the saddle.

Nickel knew how he felt. His own muscles screamed with every jostle, every movement, and he had spent the past five years training with the ranchers outside of Indianola.

"My legs don't work no more," Les said with a wince. He bent halfway to his knees, rubbing at his inner thighs. "You never told me riding horses hurt this much."

"Come on, Harold," Bannack prodded. "You had five years to learn how to mount a horse."

"I didn't know I was comin'!" the fifteen-year-old snapped back at the brown-eyed wrangler.

"Les, don't!" Nickel whispered, for Bannack's eyes had hardened. He spun his mount and rode up against Les's mount.

"You'll watch your tone with me," he said, pointing a finger in Les's face. "I won't warn you again."

"I meant . . . Well, my momma never meant to let me go, so I never learned the things Nickel did. I only ever rode a couple times, when Nickel asked me to."

"Do you want to be here?" Bannack asked. His tone was sharp. As usual, he came straight to the point, leaving no room for indecision.

"I just wanna be near my best friend. Whatever he wants to do, well, that's all right with me." Les paused, looking about. "I don't like all this grass, though. It's too loud."

"The grass is too *loud?*"

"It makes the wrong sounds," Nickel added. "We ain't none of us been able to sleep. It's so quiet it hurts our ears."

Bannack seemed to mull this strange new observation. Nickel gave Les a push up into the saddle and mounted his own fresh horse. They fell in with Bannack, surprised the cowboy seemed content to let them ride along with him.

To pass the time in the saddle and ease the tension, Nickel started in on Les about Mustang Grey, and the pair passed the afternoon's ride in heated bliss, arguing over whether a man like Mustang Grey was too tough to complain or cry. The argument drew Marbles's attention, for he fell in to ride with them.

"Wh-What's all the squ-squabblin'?" he asked Bannack in his usual halting manner.

"They're bickerin' over Mustang Grey. Seems like their favorite thing to do."

Marbles perked up, grazing both boys with grim amusement. "That a fact? M-M-Mustang Grey, huh?"

"Yep."

"What about him?" Marbles wanted to know. He reined his horse a little closer.

"Nickel told me Les has been readin' 'em books out loud for years." Bannack paused, and a slow grin flitted across his face and disappeared. "You know, them little dime books."

"I know," Marbles said.

"Seems they spend the bulk of their time arguin' over the books."

"B-B-But I thought they w-were b-best friends."

"They are. Can't you tell?"

Marbles took another look at the boys, both gesturing like they meant to sprout wings and fly off. He gave Bannack a puzzled look and shrugged. They rode along in unobtrusive silence, listening to the heated discussion about whether Mustang Grey ever cried.

"What about that time he had to shoot his favorite horse?" Nickel blurted out. Everyone looked at him. "Wouldn't you cry if you had to shoot your best horse?"

"Never had a horse to shoot," Les reasoned.

"Well, if you did."

"I guess, but I ain't Mustang Grey, neither."

"Mr. Marbles, wouldn't you cry if you had to shoot your horse?" Nickel asked, eager for a second opinion.

"Well," Marbles drawled, "not s-sure I'd have the t-t-time if I was left a-afoot with Injuns after me."

"I told you!" Les shouted. Nickel frowned but didn't stay beaten for very long.

"So what? That don't mean Mustang never cried!"

Posse looked up. "Now wait a minute," he intervened. "This afternoon

261

when we was together, you called Les crazy 'cause he said Mustang Grey probably cried too. Now you say he did?"

"I changed my mind," Nickel replied, flinging a biscuit at his brother.

Posse caught it and stuffed it in his mouth but spoke around the mealy dough.

"And you, Les! You change your mind too?"

"You heard Marbles. He was too busy runnin' from Indians to stop and cry."

"Yeah? Well, Mustang Grey never ran from nobody! He fought them devils back head-on."

"That ain't how it happened, and you know it. He was carrying the mail. He couldn't stop to fight—he had to run!"

"It wouldn't have taken him long to shoot down his enemy."

"He had arrows in his wrist, you salt-headed jellyfish!"

"Not the whole time, barnacle-butt!"

Had Nickel and Les been a little more observant in their companions, they might have noticed the amused smirk on Bannack's face as he caught Marbles's eye.

&#x2683;

That evening when Bannack called a halt to camp for the night, the boys fell to their chores, tending to their horses and to the cook-fire, their bodies bent beyond exhaustion, their mouths silenced.

Until midway through dinner. Unable to take the solitude any longer, Nickel blurted out the first argument he could think of.

"Mustang Grey rode one hundred miles in a day, chased by Indians. Bet he never complained once, not even when they shot him through the hand!"

Campfire groans protested the inevitable, but Bannack and Marbles perked up, the latter leaning forward, eager for a little entertainment.

"He did not ride one hundred miles in a day!" Les shouted. "Nobody can ride that long in a day!"

"How the hell do you know?" Nickel retorted. "What do you know 'bout ridin' horses?"

"I know it hurts everything south of your ass." Les grabbed his own rear end and made a wry face.

"That's only 'cause your ass is green." Nickel reclined in the grass, propping himself on his elbow, his plate by his side. Now that he had an argument started, he could get comfortable.

"It ain't green! If anything, it's blistered red from that stupid saddle."

"Shows how much you know."

Les dropped his fork. "What's that supposed to mean?" he asked.

"It means you don't know nothin' 'bout ridin' 'cause your rump roast is greener'n your dog's shit that time he ate all that seaweed." Nickel plucked at a piece of grass tickling his face, and grinned at his friend.

Bannack pulled the brim of his hat down low and turned his head away, but Marbles couldn't resist a snort.

Les retrieved his fork and shook his head. "I'm tellin' you, no man could ride one hundred miles in one day!" he proclaimed.

"Mustang Grey did!"

"He did not! I read you that story. It was forty-five!" Les waved his plate in the air, dangerously close to dumping the contents on the ground.

Nickel sopped up the remains of his own dinner with a biscuit, still grinning. "You read it wrong, then. It was a hundred."

"He couldn't ride that far if his horse sprouted wings, Nickel. It ain't possible."

"I say he did! What do you know? You saddled your horse backward!"

"I never seen a saddle up close till that first day."

Nickel waved an arm in mute dismissal, as though Les's faculties had left him and further argument would be fruitless. "You did it *yesterday.*"

Marbles laughed outright, and Bannack stood up and strode a short distance away, holding his hat over his face.

Les's face reddened. "So what? It was dark."

"Mustang Grey never saddled his horse backward just 'cause it was dark," Nickel pointed out.

"Yeah, and he never rode no hundred miles in a day, neither."

"Oh, yes, he did!"

Les remembered his dinner and stuffed a forkful in his mouth. "Bleeding from his arm?" he asked as he chewed. "One hundred miles?"

"You don't ride with your arm. You ride with your ass."

"That don't enter into it," Les shouted. "All that blood loss, he'd be dead!"

"I reckon he staunched the flow." Nickel watched his best friend frown and chase his food across his plate. He never could figure out how to eat and argue at the same time.

"With what?" Les asked.

"His shirt? I dunno. You read the books."

"Sp-Spiderwebs," Marbles said, his stutter breaking into the argument. Bannack turned back to listen.

"Spiderwebs?" Les asked, setting his plate down.

"S-Sure. P-P-ack 'em in a w-w-wound to staunch b-blood flow."

"Ugh! Whoever heard of that? He wouldn't have had time to stop and look for spiderwebs if he was gallopin' across the prairie chased by Indians."

"M-Maybe he w-wasn't riding as f-f-fast as you think." The boys fell quiet, gnawing on this new idea. A minute dragged into two, then Les spit the notion back out.

"Even if he was riding slow, he couldn't cover a hundred miles in a day. 'Sides, what if he got spider-bit, stealing their webs?"

"B-B-Better than if he was b-bit by Indians."

"Mustang Grey's so tough, he probably would'a just bit that spider right back," Nickel added.

With a yell, Posse rose, dumping his plate in the dishwater pan, and strode off.

"Where you goin'?" Nickel called after his back.

"To find a spider! Maybe it'll bite me and put me out of my misery."

"Don't forget to bite it back!" Les yelled after him.

Nickel lifted his head and looked to the form of Bannack, who was standing with his arms crossed by the fire.

"What do you say, Bannack?" he asked.

"I say you two squabble like a couple'a old hens, the way you bicker from dawn to dusk. Shit, if one of you says the sun's high in the sky, the other'd argue it was the moon."

"What else've we got to do?" Nickel asked.

"Plenty, when you get to the ranch."

"Yeah, but what do you think of Mustang Grey? He could'a rode a hundred miles in a day, right?"

"How far a man rides depends on speed and how often he switches mounts."

"Book said he only had one horse, and he was running full speed," Les said.

"One hundred miles straight in a dead run? On one horse?" Bannack asked.

"Yessir. In one day," Les added.

"He did it!" Nickel argued.

"How?"

"'Cause he's Mustang Grey."

"That ain't a reason!" Les said.

"Is too!"

Bannack snorted. "Don't worry about it, Nickel," he said. "I reckon your Grey stands as much chance ridin' a hundred miles in a day as a ten-year-old boy stands to ride a damned dolphin."

Nickel screwed a grin upon his face and turned to his hero.

"Thanks, Bannack."

## CHAPTER 25

# THE TELLING

The dead of night was as long as a full day in the saddle, Nickel discovered. At least, it was when sleep deserted him. After a few hours of tossing in his bedroll, Nickel had had enough. He dumped his bedding and stumbled out of camp to reply to the call of nature.

Once his bladder was empty, he wandered a little, straying outside of camp. He rubbed his sore shoulder and gazed skyward. The stars were magnificent, even if they weren't stretching out to meet the ocean's horizon, except in memory.

"Still can't sleep?" a voice said. Nickel spun but did not immediately see the voice's owner.

"To your left."

It was Bannack, sitting his mount in the dark.

"What are you doin' up?" Nickel asked.

"I'm always up. Somebody's gotta keep an eye on the remuda, and I don't trust y'all for the job yet."

He shrugged. "I could do it."

"You might fall asleep."

As if on cue, he rubbed his weary eyes. "I ain't slept since we left."

"More the reason why I don't want you nighthawkin'."

"But if you ride all day and up all night . . . ?"

"Marbles switches off with me, two hours at a stretch."

"Aww, I could do it, honest I could," Nickel said. "Ain't fair for you to lose sleep. I wanna do my share."

"Obliged, Nickel, but it ain't safe. Next time we trail a herd, you'll get your chance. Your brothers too. You'll fall sick, you don't sleep at night," he said as he dismounted.

"I'm okay." Nickel felt the cold, penetrating gaze burning through him in the shadows. "Guess I gotta be," he amended.

"Do you remember that talk we had five years back? I asked you about that fork in the road."

"The one leadin' over the mountain, or the one everybody else walks on."

"That's the one. Recall what you told me?"

"Shore! I said I'd rather make my own road, and you told me I was gonna be okay."

"Still want to make your own road?" Bannack glanced sideways at him.

"Don't know any other way, sir."

For a moment, the cowboy was quiet. He removed his hat, ran his fingers through thick, brown hair, and disappeared under his hat again. "How you holdin' up, Nickel?"

"I dunno. Don't know what to do with it all just now," he admitted. "Times I think maybe it's just a bad dream, that it didn't really happen. I'll wake up, and Mags'll be alive and ready to marry me. My brothers and sisters'll be clamberin' over me like a bunch of loud, flappin' chickens instead of washed out to sea. Indianola, she'll still be there, same as she always was."

"I know. Me and Marbles, we know about hell. Tragedy, loss—it don't just leave a man. Something like that, it can poison your mind. Hate to see that happen to you."

Nickel kicked at a rock, picked it up, and slung it into the brush. "How could it all go away?" he asked the cowboy. "Everything, my whole life—it's all scattered across the prairie or floatin' in the ocean. Only reason I'm alive and they're not is 'cause of my luck. But I gave it to the wrong girl, and now Magdalena's dead. Should'a been strong enough to save her, maybe the town too."

"Son, you can't go on believin' you've got power to alter death. No luck charm's ever gonna change mankind or nature. You'll wind up killin' yourself, believin' that strongly in luck. You did the best you could. You battled the elements and somehow, hell if I know how, you survived. What's more, you brought your loved one back with you and laid her to rest. Nobody could've done better."

"You could have."

"I wouldn't bet on it."

"You really don't believe it was my good luck, do you?" Nickel was incredulous. He had never met *anyone* who didn't believe in what was laid out before him. What else could it be? His luck protected him from death, as it protected the fortunes of those immediately around him.

Grown men had been buying luck from him, a nickel at a time, for the last five years. Why would they do that if luck wasn't real?

When he posed the question to Bannack, the stoic man sat down on a large flat rock and commanded Nickel to do the same. He obeyed.

"Unfounded nonsense," the horseman replied. "It was just an excuse for a bunch of grown men to believe in foolish things to explain away what they didn't understand. You can't *buy* luck, Nickel, and you can't save another's life just by believin' you have it."

"Marbles bought it on the road to Victoria," Nickel argued. "What about the wagon?"

"Marbles sets too much stock in foolish notions, I expect. He was tired and desperate."

"And it worked."

Bannack held his hand in the air, then closed it with a shake of his head. "We were on a road. We were bound to run across a wagon sooner or later."

Nickel snorted, unconvinced. "With a doctor and supplies? That wasn't luck to you?"

"Fortunate coincidence, yes. I don't believe Marbles brought the wagon by buyin' your luck."

"I brought the wagon *because* he bought my luck," Nickel corrected.

"Either way, I don't believe it."

"What about the spur?"

"What spur?"

"The one you gave me 'fore you left that day five years back. You gave me the spur off your boot."

"So?"

"That's what saved my life in the storm."

"Wanna tell me about it?"

"Yessir, long as I don't gotta chew it twice." Nickel focused on the stars as he spoke, for they were the only familiarity left in his life.

"I was with Lucy Parker when the storm hit. Water was risin', threatenin' to wash away the docks. I spent the night with her 'cause she was scared of storms. Come mornin', the prairie was gone. The Mistress done ravaged the town and was flowin' ten, maybe fifteen feet over the town. Lucy, her house was back off the beach a'ways, out on the prairie, but it weren't no good. I was afraid the water was gonna pull the house down around our ears." Nickel's voice rose in crescendo and fell with the memory, his emotions riding the waves of the telling.

"Men were stringin' ropes secured between buildings—guidelines, they were—and we sailed toward the courthouse on cotton bales. Sections of bridges were washin' toward us, pullin' houses with 'em. Struck a boat full of people—they didn't surface again. Debris hit us too, but I managed to get Lucy to the courthouse.

"People was crowded in, but Les wasn't there. Neither was Magdalena, so I took the boat and went back out there to look for 'em."

Nickel paused, heaving a deep, shaky breath. "I guess the Mistress wanted me awful bad. I don't know what she threw at my boat, but I fell in the water. Somethin' hit me in the back, and I was swallowed up by the current and washed out into the prairie. I kept reachin' for a board or a rope to hold onto, hopin' I could pull myself out of the water, but dead bodies kept rollin' over and over me and boards kept hittin' me. Don't know how long I was in the water before the waves pushed me into the ship, but that spur caught and held.

"Maybe it was the flesh of the boat, or a net, I don't remember. Guess it don't much matter what it was. It stuck—felt like it was gonna tear my foot right off, pullin' me outta the current the way it did. I grabbed a rope danglin' off the ship's edge and held on. The wind shifted, maybe, I don't know, but the ship rolled, dragging my head and shoulders out into the air. My fingers hit against cold flesh, and I opened my eyes."

Nickel squeezed his palms over his ears and pressed, trying to block the memory of the screams exploding from his lungs. He felt the rough, calloused palm of his hero on his back, just resting there.

"It was your girl, wasn't it, son?"

"She was—she was just . . . aww shit!" Nickel pulled his arms across his stomach and stooped over, rocking back and forth. His bad shoulder throbbed as though it had a pulse of its own, but he didn't care.

"You don't have to tell me any more, Nickel." Bannack's voice sounded thick.

But he did. Just once, he had to tell someone. "She was . . . impaled! It was a metal rod, maybe from the factory, lodged straight through her belly and stuck to the ship wall! I didn't . . . I don't even know if . . . if . . . did she feel that? Was she alive to feel that? Or was she . . . she . . ."

Bannack swore, long and low, and patted his shoulder in a coarse and awkward manner.

"Did you dislodge her yourself?" he asked after Nickel gained control of his emotions enough to speak.

"Yessir. Carried her up the rope to the deck of the ship. We stayed there till the storm passed. I dunno how long it was. I don't remember nothin' else till I woke with her next to me on deck. Guess I got her down and just started walkin'. Knew I had to get her back home."

The cowboy offered no word of consolation. Perhaps he didn't know of anything strong enough to say. Nickel knew he was right. Nothing could heal, no word was going to take away his pain and suffering, or the memory of Mags. He wiped his eyes with his neck rag.

"Thanks, Bannack," he mumbled.

The cowboy scratched his chin as he turned to look at him. "For what?" he asked.

"You came back to get me, just like you said you would. And you stayed to find me."

"I didn't know if we'd find you or not."

"But you stayed."

"Yeah, well, we take care of our own."

"I'm gonna repay it someday, sir, for what you done for me and mine. I swear I will."

"You just listen to what I say and learn, Nickel. Learn what I know so you can work for me. That'll be payment enough."

"It won't never be enough," Nickel mumbled. He glanced at his hero, who was about as lean as the oar of a boat, but larger-than-life in Nickel's book.

"Bannack?" he asked.

"Yeah?"

"Are you—well, I mean, are you Mustang Grey?"

He heard, rather than saw, the man turn to peer at him in the dark.

"You still think I'm Mustang Grey?"

"Yessir, I do."

The reply was so long in coming that Nickel feared the cowboy wouldn't reply. Maybe he had fallen asleep.

"I'm just a man called Bannack," he said slowly, his gaze centered on the darkened horizon before them. "Nothin' more."

"Are you sure?" Nickel asked, and cleared his throat, for disappointment lodged thick in his craw. "I swore you was him."

"Nobody'd wanna read my story," Bannack replied.

"I would. You're better even than Mustang if you really ain't him."

"I ain't Grey, but I reckon I can introduce you to him some time."

Nickel's head snapped up. He swiveled and stopped himself from jumping upright. It wouldn't do to rile the horses. "You *know* him?"

Bannack stifled a yawn and rubbed his palm over his eyes. "Rode with him a time or two."

"You did? *Really?*" Nickel leaned forward, clutching his hands into fists against his chest.

"Shore did," Bannack said. "Well, there's Marbles comin' to spell me. You'd best get back to your bedroll, Nickel."

"But what about Mustang Grey?" Nickel asked. "You can't just—"

"You got two hours 'fore breakfast."

With Bannack's dismissal, the conversation was over, leaving Nickel nothing to do but retreat to his own bedroll, knowing sleep was not to come. Maybe Bannack wasn't Mustang Grey—but he knew him! That meant he was real. Flesh-and-blood real, not just a bunch of made-up stories.

And yet, Nickel wondered if the real man held up to half of the stories he and Les knew so well. What if he wasn't the hero in real life that he was in his books? Nah. Bannack was the real Mustang Grey—he had to be. No one could ever out-cowboy his friend Bannack.

CHAPTER 26

# THE GREEN BOYS

Bannack pushed the Indianola boys to the edge, driving them to pick up their pace, sometimes traveling long after dark. Thighs, buttocks, and legs of the green boys were bruised and blistered, deeming the act of sitting excruciating.

Nickel suffered along with the rest, but he never voiced the complaints of his brothers. The boy had still not slept a full night, evident by the dark circles encasing his eyes until he looked like a raccoon on a ten-day binge. Still he rode, changing mounts without waiting to be told, taking up the camp tasks with respect and admiration for the great cowboys leading the way.

He kept himself awake in the saddle by amusing Les with consistent banter, always about their favorite topic—Mustang Grey.

Marbles expressed his concern one day to Bannack, voicing his opinion that they were pushing the boys too hard, and that Nickel seemed on the verge of breaking down.

Bannack replied by handing his friend the telegram received from the ranch while they were in Victoria, and the matter dropped. They prodded the boys out of their bunks earlier in the morning and dropped off to camp later and later in the evening. Their sense of urgency was not understood, nor explained, but Nickel seemed aware that speed was necessary, for he began rolling out of his bunk when the men rose, poking and threatening his brothers to do the same.

Something was bound to break. Bannack expected it, so he was not surprised when the lost Indianolans imploded. He didn't witness what started it all, but he heard the yell. They all did. It was not one of fear or danger, but something animalistic, borne from a primal rage.

He spun in the saddle in time to see Alastor Wheeler plunge his horse straight into Nickel's mustang, knocking the younger brother out of the saddle. The pair tumbled to the ground amid snorting, rearing horses.

Alastor threw the first punch, catching Nickel in the jaw, spinning him in the dirt. The roar that escaped Nickel's throat brought to mind the horrific Rebel Yell, the battle cry designed to terrify those infernal blue-bellies into flight. He sailed into the attack, and the brawl showed no quarter.

Exhaustion weakened both parties, but they drove on, punching, cuffing, and biting, bent on blood. Words flew; bloodstained fists punctuated name-calling as the brothers pitted their angst and anger on each other. Les, not one to stand idle and let his best friend befall attack, let out a yell and jumped on Alastor, giving Nickel an opportunity to land a heavy blow. The brawl widened as Posse set the brake, barreling out of the wagon to leap into the fray, only to be swallowed up by the fight. Soon all four boys were screaming obscenities in a melee of dust-laden fists, arms, and legs.

"Th-Think they'll t-t-tie themselves up in a knot?" Marbles asked, riding up beside Bannack.

"If they don't, I will," he retorted.

"N-Need help?"

"Nope. Go catch their horses, will you? Look them over. Alastor rode his horse straight into Nickel's mount."

Marbles turned his horse, paying no more heed to the battle than he would a gnat.

Bannack took his time unwinding his rope, for the punishment the boys inflicted on each other would be a lasting lesson, one that would likely ring their ears for days.

Not that it would stop them from fighting again, now that blood was spilled. He understood the nature of brothers, knew it well. Rivalry and jealousy was a hard pill to swallow, and poor attitudes were easily fed. Alastor Wheeler had the makings of an explosive personality, one which could fester and rot, given the wrong nourishment.

He was getting the best of Nickel, despite his friend's help. Les Harold was loyal, but he was no fighter. At best, he slowed Alastor down, swinging his fists like he was romping through a field of butterflies. Apparently, he had not grown up under the violent nature Nickel had, where a boy learned how to brawl and scrap for everything he wanted.

Posse didn't seem to be taking one side or the other; he laid into both brothers equally, but the grudge was not against him.

Alastor waded through the blows and grabbed Nickel by the neck, attempting to ram his fist into the younger boy's stomach. Nickel twisted so the blow landed on his side. Posse partially blocked his retaliation, so Alastor dove on his legs, sat on his chest, and pinned him down.

"I'm gonna . . . teach . . . you," he said, panting.

"You done run out of water to drown me," Nickel yelled as he kicked back, driving his mangled spur into his brother's flesh.

Alastor let out a yell and struck out with both feet, kicking Nickel's bad shoulder with all the force he could muster, spinning his nemesis in the dust.

Nickel screamed, grasping his shoulder as he tried to push himself up. His free hand moved fast. Reaching for his foot, he slicked his blade from his boot and held it, his wrist tucked under, ready to throw.

Alastor froze, his sides heaving.

"Put the blade down, Nickel!" Bannack used the opportunity to ride in on his horse, Tarantula. The animal twisted, spinning straight through the exhausted fighters. The boys broke momentum, and as they scattered, Bannack reached down and grabbed hold of the first collar he could reach.

Alastor Wheeler came up fighting, but Bannack tightened his grip, dragging him alongside his horse with precious little care. He dragged the Wheeler boy over to Marbles and the horses and dropped him on the ground.

Alastor, dripping blood from his nose and a gash near his ear, wheeled and jumped at Bannack, attempting to haul him off the horse.

"Get down . . . off that . . . horse, and I'll teach . . . you too, you crazy sonofa—"

Bannack's boot caught him square in the chest, knocking the wind out of him. He staggered backward, fell, and lay still, gasping for air.

Marbles was examining a cut on the cannon of Nickel's mount.

"Ain't b-b-broke," he told Bannack, "b-but he won't b-be ridden again this trip."

The gelding was indeed favoring his leg, and as Bannack dismounted to run his hand over the animal's injury, his blood raged. Stripping the saddle, he peeled it off and threw it at Alastor. His verbal storm rained down upon the boy's head, and when the curses ran their course, he yanked the boy to his feet.

He swept his arm toward the limping animal. "You're damned lucky we don't have to shoot that horse, or I'd put a bullet through you too!" The veins pulsated in Bannack's neck as he yelled.

"It's just a stupid horse," Alastor wheezed.

Bannack's eyes seemed to snap. He picked up the saddle, dusted off the seat, and thrust it into Alastor's arms.

"Fine. You'll walk the rest of the day, carryin' that saddle. You drop it even once, and I'll tie you to it and leave you where you land."

He turned back to Nickel, still on the ground holding his shoulder. He bared his teeth, and his breath erupted in short, wheezing gasps. Bannack dropped to one knee, feeling of the shoulder, accessing damage.

"Popped out of joint again?" he asked.

Nickel gritted his teeth and nodded.

"Get up. Drop your arm, let it hang, but support it with your good hand." The cowboy spun him around and grabbed him from behind, bearing pressure on his back while rotating the arm until the shoulder found its place.

Nickel screamed when it popped and sank to his knees.

Bannack removed his neck rag and tied it around his arm, fashioning a sling. He was not gentle in doctoring.

"No more brawls," the cowboy ordered. "You're no good to me crippled. Don't use that arm for anything, you hear me?"

"Yessir." Nickel held his shoulder and winced.

"Spell your mount and ride in the buckboard."

Nickel obeyed, though he abhorred the notion of being removed from his horse. How would he ever cowboy like the greats by bouncing around in an infernal buckboard?

Settling in among the bedrolls, he sniffed and wiped his nose on his arm. It came away bloody.

Posse glanced at him as he climbed in the driver's seat and handed him a neck rag. "You and your damn cowboys," he said.

⅋

None of the Indianola boys had ever traveled so far from home. Another three days of riding buckboard landed the sullen lot into the midst of the James Mercy Ranch. It was a small spread nestled against sloping hills and scrub.

Nickel switched from the wagon to a remuda horse. He didn't care if he was bucked off; he would not meet ranch folk riding a wagon like a greener.

As they approached the homestead, riders swung out to meet them. Bannack and Marbles greeted the men, allowing seasoned eyes to weigh and measure their ragged little party.

"Say, there you are!" one called, and reached out to grasp Bannack's hand. He gave it a hearty shake and repeated the greeting with Marbles.

"James Mercy, Mercy Ranch." Bannack's introduction left much to be said.

"We damn near gave up on you boys as lost." James Mercy, a strapping man sporting a five-day shadow, turned to his friend. "Judson, these are the Middle C men I was tellin' you about. They stopped here on the way down to Indianola."

Judson looked like he had been rolling in slop. Covered from head to toe, it was hard to tell where the small man stopped, and the ground began. He nodded, his sharp gaze assessing Nickel, Les, Posse, and Alastor.

"Heard tell storm blew hell outta Indianola," he said. "That true?"

"Indianola's gone," Nickel replied.

The ranchmen looked startled.

"Gone? What do you mean, *gone*?"

"Ain't nothin' left except the courthouse. Mistress swept it all away."

"Ocean rose up and flooded the land, storm blew over six miles inland and twenty miles or so up and down the coast," Bannack explained.

"They said it was bad, but nobody done told us that!" Judson exclaimed. "Houses? Businesses?"

The Indianolans confirmed the loss with a shake of their heads.

"How many lost?" James asked.

"A few hundred, I expect," Bannack said.

The men gaped, slack-jawed, and slowly removed their hats.

"Be damned," Judson muttered.

"Say, I shore hope you found your friend," the other said to Bannack. "The one you was comin' to get?"

"That's Nickel, there." Bannack pointed him out, and Nickel straightened under the scrutiny of these strange range men.

"Well, clamber on down, boys. You're all welcome here. Stay as long as you need. We'll see to it you're fed and comfortable."

"Obliged," Bannack said.

Nickel realized they would not rest until they saw to their own mounts. It was an unspoken rule, and one Bannack and Marbles both lived by, so when a ranch hand offered to take the reins of his weary mount, Nickel refused.

Leading the reins himself, he limped into the stable next to Bannack and Marbles and their mounts, where they stripped saddles. No one spoke as they fed and rubbed down the horses, but he slipped a little extra grain for the red mare who had carried him.

While his brothers unhitched the wagon and turned out the team, Nickel fetched his crutch from the buckboard and ran his fingers over Magdalena's trunk.

*It ain't as blue as it used to be,* he thought. *Leastways, not outwardly.*

He rubbed a patch of silt off the side, revealing the coloration of the painted scene underneath.

"It'll be safe enough here for the night."

Looking around, Nickel watched Bannack lean against the buckboard side. The cowboy swiped his hand over the trunk and rubbed sand off his fingers.

"I'll see to it nobody bothers it," he told Nickel.

"I painted it for her, you know," Nickel said with a swallow, for the lump was growing in his throat again.

"Figured as much."

"Traded for it. She said she was gonna keep the world in that trunk."

"No wonder it's so damn heavy," Bannack grumbled but without malice. "You fixin' to open it?"

"I don't know if I can." He didn't have the key, but that didn't matter. He might pick the lock. Bust it if he had to, but something about rifling through her belongings didn't sit well in his gut. Not so soon.

"Do you think I should?" he asked. "Would you?"

"That's up to you, Nickel. We're haulin' a hell of a heavy trunk for not knowin' what's inside it. I reckon, whatever's in it is wet or ruined. Might salvage somethin' if you air it out."

"Don't think . . . don't think I could stand it—openin' that lid just to see it all ruined. The not knowin', that might be better."

Bannack didn't reply.

"Are you gonna make me leave it behind if I don't open it?" Nickel asked. What if he did? How would he bear riding away, leaving Magdalena's whole world behind?

"I didn't haul that thing this far just to leave it behind now, little brother."

"Why? Why'd you bring it? You could've left it in Indianola. Could've left me there too."

"The hell I could, Ryder," Bannack replied, using Nickel's first chosen name. "The hell I could." He tapped on the compass rose painted on the lid.

"There is one thing I've been meanin' to ask you about this trunk."

"Yeah?"

Bannack gestured, pointing his hand one direction, then another.

"That compass. Why in the hell is north pointed off to the left? You've got east pointed north and west in the south."

"Why does everybody ask me that?" Nickel asked. "That's where north was at when I painted it."

Bannack sighed and rubbed the scruff on his chin.

"Well. I reckon that's as good a reason as any." He threw his saddle blanket over the trunk.

"It's bad luck to . . ." Nickel tried to explain, but Bannack raised his hand and turned his head away.

Bannack was tougher than anyone he had ever met, frosty and chiseled with scorn, but he held true to a code. Nickel hadn't figured out just what that code was yet, but it was one he meant to follow.

"You comin'?" he asked over his shoulder.

"Bannack?" Nickel stood, rolling the brim of his hat in his hands.

Hard brown eyes turned on him.

"What?"

"You're him, ain't you?" Nickel kept his voice calm, level. If he tried hard enough, maybe he'd sound just like Bannack.

"Who?" Bannack raised an eyebrow.

"Mustang Grey."

He took a deep breath and exhaled loudly. "This again?" Bannack asked.

"They wrote dime novels about him, you know. He's a real hero."

"So you've said. Repeatedly."

"He rode for the Pony Express before the war ate him up. Ain't nobody seen or heard of him since, but I reckon he's just layin' low. I know you said no, but . . . ain't nobody cowboys like you! I won't tell anybody if you are."

The frigid light in Bannack's eyes softened just a little.

"Come on, little brother. Let's go buy some horses."

CHAPTER 27

# MERCY

He hadn't answered the question. Why? Nickel studied the great cowboy standing on the corral fence, his boot heels hooked over the rail. The man was lost to the sight of the milling horses. Every so often, he would point out one or two to the rancher, and discussion would ensue.

*Haggling prices, probably.*

Whatever they discussed, Nickel couldn't keep his mind on the task. He kept thinking of his favorite dime novel. No one knew what had become of Mustang Grey. The larger-than-life hero vanished with the war. That he had fought, Nickel had no doubt.

Posse often said Mustang Grey might not have walked out of the war, but Nickel knew better. No war would kill the likes of Mustang Grey; he didn't care how many Yankees shot at him.

Bannack had been in the war too, but that was the extent of his knowledge. He was a man unequaled in horsemanship; men heard his name as far south as the Lynch Ranch in Indianola—what little was left of it.

The cowboys there enjoyed speculating about Bannack. They didn't know much either, other than that he partnered with a man named Creede Cashman on a ranch somewhere around the Blacklands called the Middle C.

Partnered, they said, but refused to work for.

"It's said about Bannack," one of the Lynch hands had told Nickel, "that he don't work for nobody. Figures he's got no equal in his trade, and the cattlemen know it. Everybody who's anybody tried to lure him to their brand at least once. He won't be hired out."

*Mustang Grey would be good at his trade too. Real good. Better than anybody.* Nickel stole another long look at Bannack. He had a few visible scars; one long one on his cheek, another on his hand. How many did the man have tucked away, unseen? Did any of them match the grand stories of Mustang Grey?

Someone brushed against his sleeve, and Nickel snapped out of his reverie with a jolt.

"Ought not let f-folks sneak u-up on you," Marbles scolded. Nickel listened to the slow, faltering words of the awkward cowboy, and agreed.

"I reckon you're right. Livin' with Alastor all these years, I oughta know better. I was just thinkin'."

Marbles climbed to the top rail of the corral and took a seat. He didn't ask, but Nickel saw the opportunity and ran with it.

"Say, Marbles? How long you known Bannack?"

The man paused, and his brow furrowed.

"Why?" he answered.

"I think Bannack ain't really Bannack."

Marbles turned to stare at him, his eyes searching.

"Wh-Who, then?"

"I think he's Mustang Grey."

Slowly, Marbles closed his jaw. He turned, fixing his gaze on Bannack, who had climbed over the fence and was walking among the herd, inspecting forelegs and examining teeth.

"Think about it," Nickel said. "There ain't nobody better'n he is with horses, everybody says so. He was in the war, same as Mustang. He's a hero, way he stayed behind to find me after . . . after . . ."

Nickel spat out the bitter brine he still tasted, lodged in his throat, and under his tongue.

"Is he? Is Bannack Mustang Grey?"

"Y-Y-You ask him?" Marbles inquired. He scraped his boot heel over the lower rail of the fence, so Nickel did the same.

"Yeah, but he just looked at me awful funny. Grinned, but he wouldn't answer."

"He g-grinned, huh?"

"Don't guess I ever seen him do that before. Bannack, he's got scars though. I dunno if they match Mustang's or not."

"L-Lots of men have s-scars," Marbles said. "Some of 'em are locked a-away, some in plain v-v-view. You got your own n-now."

"Yeah, but my scars don't make me Mustang Grey."

"Maybe M-M-Mustang Grey would w-wanna be a little m-more like you. Ever thought of that?"

*Mustang Grey? Wanna be like me?* The notion was so absurd Nickel meant to reject it, only he didn't get the chance.

"Nickel! Come here." Bannack was calling him. Nickel leaned his crutch against the fence, ducked through the rails, and hobbled over to the expectant horseman.

"What do you think of this one?" he asked, indicating a large-boned chestnut with a broad, triangular snip over his nose.

Sweeping his eyes over the animal, Nickel mentally checked off everything from nose to hindquarters. The horse looked sound, but something nagged at him.

"I wouldn't want that old pie-face," he said, finally.

"Why not?" Bannack asked. "Is he sound?"

"Looks sound to me, but I still don't like the looks of him. I guess it's his eyes. That horse looks like he don't have a lick of sense. Like he'd drown in the water trough 'cause he forgot to lift his head after drinkin'. Maybe you oughta buy Pie-Face for Alastor."

Bannack snorted, and as Nickel looked, he noticed the little grin was back. "Pick your horse, Nickel."

Nickel's breath hitched in his throat. "What?" he squeaked.

"I want you well mounted." Bannack anchored a hand on his hip and gestured toward the herd. "Pick your horse."

"You mean it?" Nickel ran his hand across the back of his neck, already inspecting the horses. How to choose?

Bannack crossed his arms and waited. Nickel went over the whole herd, assessing each one with roving eyes and slick fingers, proud of the knowledge that he had pleased his friend.

In the end, Nickel circled back to two horses. They stood together, watching him approach with keen interest.

The mare was a beautiful little blood bay with small pointed ears and bright, intelligent eyes.

The gelding was a flashy paint, larger than the bay, but well-built. He looked to be a fast runner. Nickel circled them, petting and speaking to each

one. The paint watched him with what could only be described as cocky in-
difference until the little mare stepped forward to search his hand for treats.
He had none, so he scratched her forehead instead.

The paint, apparently appalled at being turned down for the bay, stamped
his foot and nosed Nickel's arm, pushing him away from the mare to receive
the full benefit of a good scratch.

"You're a puffed-up critter, ain't you?" Nickel asked the gelding.

"He's an imp," the rancher said as he approached. "Only horse I ever saw
that stares at his own reflection in the water trough. Still, if you're wanting
to decide between the two, you should know that little mare tangles with the
devil every time a man throws a leg over her."

"Yeah?" Nickel asked. He stepped back to study the mare again but saw
no sign of devilment. She stood with her eyes half-closed, swishing her tail.
He shrugged. "She seems pretty tame to me."

"She's full of shit, is what she is. Climb on her back once, and she'll surprise you."

"Can she be ridden?"

"Sure! If you can stay on long enough to work the knots out of her."

"Shoot, I could do it bareback." Grabbing fistfuls of mane, Nickel prepared to swing up on the mare's back, but a sharp call from Bannack checked
him.

"Dammit, Nickel, you stay grounded!"

"Well, I was just—"

"I know what you were 'just' gonna do. You've been playin' tough, haven't
you?"

"I ain't playin', Bannack."

"No? Then tell me your shoulder and ankle ain't botherin' you so much
anymore. How 'bout that back of yours? Won't hurt if you're thrown on it,
will it?"

Nickel hedged. He would not lie. Not to anyone but especially not to
Bannack.

"It's hell," he admitted, "but I aim to pull my weight."

The cowboy heaved a long sigh. When he spoke, his voice was softer,
without the angry lilt.

"I know you do, but you're no good to me busted up. It's bad enough we're gonna have to light out tomorrow. It's still a long ride north to the Middle C, Nickel, and I don't know if you're up for it."

"I am too. I can show you! I can ride. Didn't I just ride here from Victoria?"

"Yes, but it was on a calm mount, and you were in the buckboard much of the way."

"Aww, she ain't so rough, I bet."

Bannack spun him around and lifted up Nickel's shirt. The scrape of fabric against his wounds, of rough, calloused fingers poking his skin, brought an involuntary cry to his lips. Bannack held his hand in front of Nickel's face. His fingertips were stained with blood from where he pressed and poked at him. Nickel paled. He must have scraped his back open again when he ducked through the fence.

"You know what would impress me?" Bannack was yelling again. "Show me you got common sense to go along with your backbone! Hell, I know you're tough. We've all seen it. Now show us you can use your head too."

Nickel sank. Bannack had called his bluff. With nothing left to hide, he let the pain and fatigue show through the mask of his pride.

"It hurts," Nickel admitted through clenched teeth. "Hurts like hellfire! I guess I ain't so tough as I thought."

"Could've fooled me. Might have gotten away with it too if you hadn't scraped open those stitches in your back. Blood trail spottin' your shirt gave you away."

Bannack steered Nickel away from the horses and out of the corral. This time, he limped through the gate instead of climbing through the rails. Bannack shuffled him clear up to Mercy's homestead, where he was pushed into the hands of the missus.

"Be obliged, ma'am, if you'd see clear to tend to my little brother," Bannack said. "He was tore up by the storm in Indianola."

Leaning in, he whispered something low to Mrs. Mercy, something Nickel couldn't quite catch.

"I suspect," he then said aloud, tipping his hat brim toward the flock of young women gathered in the room, "y'all can give him better care than me."

"We'll take good care of him," she promised. Nickel looked after Bannack, who was already walking out the door, and groaned. Much as he enjoyed petting from women, he didn't want to stay behind. He still had a horse to choose.

The cowboys were choosing their new remuda, and he was inside with a bunch of women.

The missus helped him into a bed and gasped when she lifted his shirt to have a look at his wounds.

"What on earth!" she exclaimed.

He didn't know if it was the injuries or the ink across his shoulders causing her alarm. Les had assured him the ink was still there—luckily the debris caught him lower down in the back and hadn't ripped off his tattoos. He had seen some unfortunates whose skin had been ripped to shreds by the waves and hung like tattered old shirts two sizes too big.

He closed his eyes against the memory and cried out as the rancher's wife helped him out of his shirt and bade him lay down on his belly.

The mattress was soft, softer even than the one in Victoria, and he sank into it with a sharp pang of guilt. He shouldn't be enjoying the feel of a feather-down, not with so many lives ruined. His retribution showed through the gentle fingers of Mrs. Mercy, who cleansed and resewed the open stitches. There were patches where the skin was gone, leaving little left to sew.

She told him she did her best and smeared a strange, smelly ointment over those open to the air. He jerked, biting his tongue against the pain, stifling his cries.

When she was through, she gave him a tea concocted of flavors he did not know, sweetened with wild honey and something else—something that bit through the sweetness of bee nectar, stinging his throat with a heat that made him cough. She smiled at him, bidding he drink down every drop.

He obliged, rolling the foreign taste over his tongue. It heated his insides, though it was not wholly unpleasant.

"What is it?" he asked, handing her the empty cup.

"It's a special honey tea," she said, refilling his vessel. "Do you like it?" She placed a hand on his forehead, and he peered up at her. His mind was warm. He could almost see it fuzzing around the edges, like an over-ripened peach.

"I love honey," he said, "but it ain't never made my head hot from the inside before."

Mrs. Mercy chuckled as she watched him down a second cup.

"You can thank your friend Bannack for that."

Nickel closed his eyes for a moment, then snapped them open again. No. The bed was too comfortable. He had to get up. Lifting his head, he looked toward the door and saw a girl about his own age. She stood, hugging the doorway, watching him with bright, starry eyes. A long braid hung over her shoulder. He tilted his head, trying to decide if he remembered seeing her before, but his eyes lost focus, and he rubbed them. There were a few more sips to his tea, and he finished it, which seemed to please his caretaker.

She smiled at him. "Lie back and rest," she said, her voice low and gentle. "The tea will help you sleep well."

"Sleep?" Nickel jerked, struggling to retrieve his wandering mind. "You mean you slipped somethin' to make me tired? No!" he shouted. "I don't wanna sleep!" He bolted upright, holding his head.

"You need rest, child." She grasped his arms, trying to persuade him to lie back down, but he balked.

"I ain't no child. I just can't go to sleep!" Nickel dragged himself out of bed, grimacing at the pull of the fiery stitches in his back.

"Get off that foot and back in bed, young man!" she scolded, but he hobbled past the herd of girls and straight for the door. He made it as far as the front yard before Mrs. Mercy's calls alarmed the men. Posse, Les, and Alastor, who had been washing at the little pond fifty yards off, looked up. So did the men at the corral.

Nickel kept going, propelling himself forward without crutch or caution. He didn't know where he was going, nor did he care.

He had to keep moving. The darkness would set in if he didn't. Davy Jones and the Mistress. The Beisht. They would all be there, waiting.

"He'll open those stitches again!" the woman cried. "Somebody hold him!"

Les and Posse were running in from the pond, wet and shirtless. Bannack and Marbles strode with purpose, their faces set and grim. Nickel whirled, heading the other way, only to find his path blocked by strangers. Ranch hands. He spun, his breath erupting in his throat with explosive breaths.

"I ain't goin' down!" he shouted at them. "You can't make me sleep. I don't need it!"

Memories would flood him in sleep. He would see their faces, relive the last moments of their lives. They would come for him, drag him down with them, and hold him under until his lungs filled with water . . . again. He would belong to the Beisht Kione, marked by the Mistress. Why didn't anyone understand that?

He saw Bannack motion to Les and whirled to face his best friend.

"Back off!" he yelled.

"Hey, Nickel," Les replied. "What's wrong?"

"Make 'em back off, Les. They don't understand."

"Aren't you tired, Nickel?"

"Nope. Not enough to close my eyes, I ain't." He turned again, shifting as the circle of men tightened.

"But you ain't slept! The rest of us rested in Victoria, but you ain't slept since—"

"Don't argue with him and don't nobody grab him. He'll try and fight. Seen behavior like this before." Bannack took a tentative step forward, and Nickel retreated. He wobbled as though casting about for dry land and clawed at his eyes. They were crimson and watery.

"You ain't seen nothin'!" Nickel shouted. He measured the distance between Posse and Les, for they were the weakest point in the human wall. They appeared to be floating in water, and he squinted at the ground, lest the grass turn to an ocean under his feet.

He needed to push past them before it did. He could corral a dolphin and outrun the cowboys—he knew how to ride dolphins and told them so.

"I'm a dolphin rider! Not even Mustang Grey rides dolphins! You ain't gonna catch me on my finback!" He took a few steps and staggered, unable to walk a straight line.

"Okay, Nickel. You're right, I can't ride a dolphin." Bannack held out his hand. "Show me how. Maybe we'll saddle one."

"They'll write books about me too," he told him. "I'll be a dime novel."

"Sure they will. Be a damned good story too. Why don't you come on over here, and we'll talk about it?"

Nickel assessed the distance and shook his head. "Too much water in the way."

"Water's not deep," Bannack said, ignoring the looks of confusion etched in the weathered faces of the cowboys. They started to approach, but Bannack waved them off when Nickel looked away.

"It will be!" the boy promised. "She'll rise over your head and crawl down your throat."

"It won't flood the prairie, Nickel. Not here."

Nickel laughed, but it was a cackle hedging on hysteria. "'When the peacock loudly bawls, soon we'll have both rain and squalls.'"

With the recitation of old Whistle's chant, the Indianola boys recoiled, beating a hasty retreat.

"'If the cock goes crowin' to bed, he'll rise with a watery head.'"

"Shit! He's lost his mind, just like Old Whistle!" Les backed away from his friend, fearful the loss of sanity might spread.

"Stop it, Ryder!" Posse warned, using his little brother's old name. "You curse us, and I'll have to bloody your nose!"

Bannack rolled his eyes and groaned. "Nobody's bloodyin' anybody's nose," he said.

"We'll have to if he curses us. Only way to change bad luck is to draw blood."

"Dammit! I've had enough of your foolish luck nonsense!" Bannack swore again, and Nickel staggered a few steps toward him.

"Somebody make him stop that! He'll bring another storm!"

"Come on, Nickel. It's been hell, and I'm tired."

"No! Don't you know you never curse into the wind? You done called another storm."

The Indianolans murmured in agreement. Bannack looked to Posse for help.

"It ain't done," Posse explained. "Bad luck to cuss into the wind. A man does that, he'll bring a storm. It's the rule of the sea."

"Rules of the sea don't apply here, boys."

"Rules of the wind," Nickel corrected. He wagged his finger at Bannack. "You better buy my luck, or a storm'll come. The water, she's deep enough." He lifted one foot off the ground, peering below him, then the other.

Heaving a sigh, Bannack tried again. "Nickel. Why don't we go back inside and have a drink?"

"I ain't tired."

"Fine, you're not tired. Sit up with me, and I'll play that old Indianola fiddle if you want."

"What if the water rises?"

"It won't t-t-touch your l-luck." It was Marbles who spoke.

Bannack rolled his eyes at the reference, but Nickel nodded as if it made perfect sense.

"Okay," he said, "but you can't make me sleep. I ain't duckin' underwater for the Beisht to grab me up. The Mistress, neither." He staggered on Bannack's heel, lifting each foot high as though wading through knee-deep water.

Marbles and James Mercy, the rancher, followed, but the Indianolans remained rooted to the ground.

"He's gone crazy!" Les cried, snatching at Bannack's arm. "What if he curses us and brings another flood? Maybe he caught what Old Whistle had!"

"You mean that old feathered fool that brained himself tryin' to fly off that house? Nickel's lost reason 'cause he's half-drunk and deprived himself of sleep too long. He'll come back around."

Bannack shook off Les's hold of his arm and gripped Nickel by his shirt collar, steering him through the door.

Nickel dropped in a backless stool and leaned forward, satisfied no one would make him succumb to the watery depths of eternal slumber. The monsters of the deep couldn't reach him—not if he didn't close his eyes.

He watched Bannack mutter something to the rancher and his wife through a blurry haze, and frowned.

"I thought you's gonna plaaay," he called with a slur. Bannack fetched the Indianola fiddle from his war bag and sat down to test the strings.

"They didn't write no book about Mustang Grey's fiddle," Nickel said as Marbles pulled up a seat next to him. "How come that wasn't in his book?"

"Guess Mustang didn't have time to play, runnin' from Indians all day and night."

Marbles took a pull from Mercy's jug and passed it to Nickel. The fire within made him cough, but the men just grinned at him. Bannack took the jug, enjoyed a long drink, and offered it back. Nickel made a wry face.

"Don't tell me you're done already?" Bannack jabbed. "Ain't much of a cowboy if he can't hold nectar sweet as this."

They bit back a grin as Nickel grabbed the jug and turned it up, taking a long, burning swallow. Tears spilled over his cheeks, but a few more rounds passing the jug and the burn moved to his extremities, warming him from the inside out. Just like Mrs. Mercy's honey tea.

People drew in as Bannack began to play, eager to listen to the melody of the strings, but Nickel frowned. Pretty as they were, Bannack's choice of song did little to lighten the weight of his eyelids.

The strings of that old Indianola fiddle sang under Bannack's bow. He played soft and low, remembrances to the hundreds lost in the storm, and of comfort to the families tormented by grief.

For well over an hour, Bannack played, coaxing peace from the sacred strings. Indianola played sweeter than ever, wrapping her blanket of serenity over the shoulders of all who listened.

Mercy and his family, the hands, Marbles, and the Indianola boys—none were unaffected by the music. Bannack's song choices were threefold, however, and with each song's end, he cast a glance at Nickel, still fighting his own battle.

The youth's face was gray except around his eyes, which were ringed in black circles and red from excessive rubbing.

Every time his eyes began to close, he caught himself, jerking awake, rubbing his eyes and shaking his head. They had poured enough moonshine down his gullet to fell a bull, yet the sixteen-year-old warrior remained upright, refusing to succumb to the inevitable.

Bannack shifted in his chair, running the gamut of songs in his brain, extracting slow love songs of the mountain and children's lullabies alike.

Nickel's brothers dropped out of the game early, Les without even tasting a drop of cowboy nectar.

The luck charm himself, drunk as he was, refused to close his eyes. His head swayed to the music, his eyes so bloodshot and bleary it hurt to look at them. Mrs. Mercy took up humming along with the music, a subtle force that weakened Nickel's armor. Stifling a yawn, he tried to stand, but the vile drink had stolen his ability to put one foot in front of another. He reeled, tried to right himself, and fell over the rung of his own chair. Bannack watched him fall and played on. When Nickel didn't rise, Marbles leaned forward and rolled his eyes up in his head.

"B-Bannack, you sh-shore felled him like a t-t-tree," he said. Bannack finished the song and put down the fiddle. Taking one more drink, he handed the empty jug to Judson and bent over Nickel. There was no stir, no movement of the eyelids, no sign of slumber. He was knocked cold.

James Mercy poked at him with the toe of his boot and shook his head.

"Say, I know you boys are eager to leave on the morrow, but I don't think you'll be going anywhere unless you mean to leave him behind with us."

Bannack rolled his eyes as he and Marbles hefted the unconscious boy to his knees and dragged him into the bed. It didn't need to be mentioned: The great Indianolan Nickel might not be as shiny as he once was, but they would not leave him behind.

# CHAPTER 28

# JOSEPHINE

"He's awake, and boy oh boy is he mad." Les's warning did not affect the cowboys crouched over the washbasin on the back porch, though Bannack's reply was immediate.

"We leave before dawn tomorrow."

Les grumbled something unintelligible and sulked off in search of the middle daughter.

"He's been m-makin' progress too," Marbles said, watching him go.

"Then he better make it faster," Bannack said.

Now that Nickel was awake, Les's task proved almost impossible. Nickel was a natural draw to women, but he suspected Les Harold already knew that.

Nickel limped out, leaning on his oar. They were going to need to make him a much smaller crutch. He was shirtless and barefoot, his hair standing in all directions.

Judging by the scowl on his face, he was on the prod and boiling for a fight. Even the tattoos wrapped around his arm and snaking around his side and up to his shoulders looked extra cagey.

"Mornin'," Bannack said with a nod.

Nickel impaled him with a hard glare, but the cowboy shook it off and stepped aside, toweling his face with a little cotton flour sack. He offered it to Nickel, who snatched it up and threw it down.

He bent low to wash his face, letting the water run in rivulets down his cheeks, dripping off his nose and chin.

"F-F-Frothy today, ain't it?" Marbles asked Bannack.

"Sure is."

Nickel didn't bite, though only because intervention stepped onto the porch and curbed his tongue.

She was carrying a plate of food in one hand, a mug of hot coffee in the other, and a shirt tucked under one arm. Large brown eyes met his, and a rosy blush piqued his interest. As he scrubbed his face, he watched her from the corner of his eye. She seemed to forget herself, openly gaping at his arms and bare chest, or rather, at the tattoos adorning him. Her eyes were wide, her lips parted in a perfect "O." The plate in her hand dipped, a fat slice of ham in danger of sliding off to be eaten by the owl-eyed dogs at her feet.

"Don't drop your breakfast, darlin'," he said with a wink. She jerked, righting the plate and shifting her gaze. She scolded the dogs, but he noticed her ears were red. Nickel dried his face, grinning into his towel.

"I don't think she's interested in breakfast, son," Bannack said.

Marbles snorted, and Nickel shot a dark look at the grinning cowboys before turning to the girl.

"Is that for me?" he asked.

"Momma said not to make you wait to eat with everyone else," she said, handing him a freshly laundered shirt. "Clear the basin and you can use the table."

He slipped the clean shirt over his head and did as asked, clearing a spot for his breakfast. His having a shirt on seemed to ease her embarrassment, and she gained a bright smile.

"May I sit?" she asked. "I'd like to talk to you." She clasped her hands together, intertwining her fingers, only to pull them apart and twist at her wrists. She glanced into Nickel's eyes, then quickly looked away.

"If you want." Nickel watched Bannack jab Marbles in the side to get his attention, and nodded toward the house. His bristles faded as the men went inside to their own meal, and the girl pulled up a chair on the other side of the small table.

"Which one are you?" he asked.

"Josephine," she replied. "Some call me Josie, or just Jo. I wanted to tell you how much I loved your town."

Nickel paused, a wad of fresh-baked bread stuffed in his cheek. He took time enough to swallow before responding. "You been to Indianola?"

"Many times. My father let me trail along sometimes when he and the men drove cattle to the shipyards."

Nickel raised an eyebrow. "He let you ride the trail?"

"It's not *that* far," she countered. "Besides, we don't have boys in the family, only us girls. So Daddy taught us to rope and ride and shoot too. We pull our weight as well as any boy." She let out a little huff at the end of her speech, as though daring him to speak ill of her ability to rope and ride.

"I bet you do." Nickel smiled as he appraised her, but of sincerity. She looked lithe and strong.

She cleared her throat under his appreciative gaze and touched her face. "You have a large family, don't you?" she asked.

Nickel shook his head with a grimace. "Not anymore."

"Oh? Oh. I'm so sorry. I shouldn't be bothering you. I'm sure you don't want to talk about it."

He shrugged and speared a baked apple slice on his plate. "Ain't no use pretendin' it didn't happen."

Josephine chewed her lip and twisted loose strands of hair around her braid. "I know you don't remember me, Nickel," she said after a pause, "but we met before."

Nickel abandoned his fork. "We did? When?"

"In the dry goods store in Indianola. They were still calling you Ryder then."

"You remember my old name?"

"Yes. You made an impression on me. I remember looking at all those beautiful dress goods unloaded from the ships. They had purple and pink silks, fancy hats, and funny-smelling spices. I was wearing a dusty old split skirt and boots, and my father's old cattleman's hat. It was far too big, so I had to tie it on my head to keep out the sun and weather. I felt so small and ugly next to those beautiful silks, and a group of local boys were teasing me, saying I looked like a boy with braids but stunk like a cow. Then you came running in with your friends and overheard the conversation.

"I remember you looked me up and down and remarked how they were blinded by the salt in the air. You called me pretty, right there in front of the girl standing with you. I never forgot that."

Nickel's jaw slackened, though he found his tongue. "I remember now! That was you tucked under that big awful hat?" He laughed at the memory.

"It was."

Nickel, having polished clean his plate in record time, set it aside and leaned across the table.

"Well, I swear," he said.

"Nickel? I couldn't believe it when you rode in. You don't know how many times I begged my father to go back to Indianola, so he took me along on the next drive. I remembered your name and asked around for you. They pointed me to the beach, and I saw you with that same dark-haired girl. You were running in the surf, laughing."

*Mags. Dear God, she was talking about Mags.* The memory stabbed like the blade of a knife, and he didn't quite clear the tears from his throat as he replied.

"All that way, and you didn't come over to say hello?"

She shrugged. "I was too late. I sat down on the sand and watched you and her. You snatched her up and kissed her, and I wished . . ." She glanced at him, then looked down. He watched the color of embarrassment stain her cheeks and leak down her neck, but she stood by her confession.

"You don't wanna be her," Nickel murmured. "Not now."

"Where is she?"

Nickel spread his hands wide, staring into them. He saw nothing. "I sent her off to sea."

"Sea?" Josephine frowned and shook her head. "What?"

"Buried her . . . at sea." He ran his hands over his face, dragging his fingers downward. They were treading on dangerous territory—too much talk.

"Oh! No!" she cried, throwing her hands over her mouth.

Nickel rose a little too rapidly, almost upending the table. "Wanna go for a walk?" he asked. "I never was one for sittin' still too long."

Josephine called to her mother, and they walked along in companionable silence for a few minutes, with nowhere particular to go.

When he recovered from the memory of his Mags drifting out to sea, he tilted his head to look at Josephine. Even in profile, she was pretty. Prettier than he remembered, and he told her so.

She rewarded him with a bright smile, though veiled with sorrow.

"I'm so sorry," she began.

"I know. You don't have to be. I don't care much for sympathy. Ain't figured out yet how I'm supposed to feel about people feelin' sorry for me. Ain't figured out how to get through the day yet, either."

"It was all so grand," she said. "The town. So bright and bustling, and the flower gardens! So many wonderful things carried off those ships. The people were grand too, weren't they?"

"Most of 'em."

She sighed. "I wish I had the courage to speak to you that day. Maybe we could have been friends. Maybe you might have kissed me one day, just like you kissed her."

"You thought of me like that?"

A little smile played upon her lips. "You don't understand what it's like for a young girl the first time a handsome boy tells her she's pretty. I was feeling my worst, and you walked in and washed it all away. I think about you often. More than I care to admit. The younger of my father's hands, several try to court me, but none of them compare to the memory I have of you in that Indianola dry goods store."

She stopped, for they had reached a little grove of trees out by the pond. Stepping into their shade, she sat down in the grass and wrapped her arms around her knees. Nickel sat down beside her, wondering if she would rather have her arms wrapped around him.

"Nickel?" she asked.

"Yeah?"

"That day on the beach, if I had said hello, do you think we would have kissed?"

"I might'a thought about it but wouldn't never've done it. Mags, she was my girl."

"Then she was very lucky to have you."

"You ever been kissed?" he asked.

"No. Not that the hands haven't tried, but I know how to handle those silly cowboys."

"Good for you." Nickel screwed up his face and offered a half-hearted smirk. "I'm one of them silly cowboys too, you know."

She giggled. It was a delightful sound. He had not heard much in the way of honest laughter since before the storm hit. "A cowboy maybe, but not a silly one," she told him. "They were telling your story while you were asleep. I never heard of such bravery before. Is it all true?"

"Depends on who did the tellin'," he replied.

"The quiet one, Bannack."

"Then it's all true, whatever he said."

"Your friend Les told some stories on you too."

"Okay, *mostly* true."

She giggled. "I'm glad you're here, Nickel. Funny, I always thought of you as Ryder. Calling you Nickel now after all these years seems strange to me."

"Sometimes one name just ain't enough, I guess." He glanced at her, for she was resting against him. The wide, searching eyes told him what was on her mind.

"I'd kiss you if you want," he told her, "but you oughta know I'm hitched."

"Hitched?" She sat up. "Hitched as in . . . married?"

"I guess."

"How? I thought . . . I mean, you said that dark-haired girl was your girl?"

"Her name's Lucy Parker. She always wanted more from me, but I was awful stuck on Mags. After the storm, she had nothin'. Lost her home and her daddy to the storm. She didn't have anyone else, and I lost my Mags. Luce asked if we could get hitched in Victoria."

"Lucy asked *you?*"

"I obliged."

Josephine chewed on the information presented her and spat it back out. "Why isn't she with you now?"

"I left her in Victoria with my mother and my family. What's left of 'em, anyway. Meant to bring her north with me, but . . ." Nickel spread his hands wide. "I can't abide betrayers and liars. Knew someone like that once. He was a bad man. Luce . . . I found out she lied to me, and it cost me my Mags."

Snagging a long blade of grass, he tied it in a knot and threw it aside to grab another. Lucy made him question Mags's loyalty. She and Alastor. The thought made his stomach lurch.

Nickel told her everything, the whole horrific story. Josephine was easy to talk to, easier than Lucy, who said she loved him. Josephine didn't interrupt or judge. She just listened.

Snuggling in against his arm, she fixed her gaze to his face.

"I understand her reasoning, but Lucy Parker was wrong," she said gently.

"You understand her reasoning for what she did? Maybe you can explain it to me," he said with a sniff.

"She adored you. She loved you and didn't want to lose you. I wouldn't either if you were mine. But I don't agree with what she did. If she cared, she should have known you belonged to your Mags. I saw you together on that beach and knew it was useless to interfere. That awful lie she told gained and lost you all at once."

"I thought of Mags the whole time I was with her," Nickel admitted.

"Are you thinking of Mags now while you're here with me?"

"Does it bother you?"

"Of course not," she said. "She was yours. Lucy Parker shouldn't never have asked you to marry her."

"I wouldn't have done it if only I knew of her lie."

"Will you send for her?"

"No!" But Nickel shrugged. "Ain't sure," he admitted with a sniff. "She wants me to forgive her, but I ain't shore I can. Be a long time away if I do. Don't have the stomach for it just now. Keep thinkin' how Mags might be alive if it wasn't for her and Alastor."

They were quiet for a time, sitting side by side, lost to their own thoughts. Across the pasture, they could see the men in the corral. They were looking over horses again. Bannack was with the horses, going over his final picks for the trip. *A man obsessed with horseflesh.*

Nickel looked at Josephine and thought about his future. He had a bride in Victoria, where she would stay. Never would he get over Lucy's deceit, or her role in Magdalena's death. Would he ever send for her? It'd be a lonely day in hell if he did.

Maybe there were better girls ahead. Nice girls, like Josephine. But they didn't understand him the way Josephine seemed to. After all, she had thought of him over the years. Dreamed of him. Often. He didn't know her well enough to think about loving her, but they'd be leaving soon; there was no time. Nickel admired what he knew of her so far. Maybe that was enough to build on.

*Besides, she shore is pretty,* he thought. She watched him silently, refraining from questions, and he appreciated that too.

"I like you, Josephine," Nickel blurted.

"I like you too," she returned. "More than I ever did before."

"I can't . . . I wanna be fair. Things are so twisted up. I don't know what to do."

Josephine touched his hand. "You'll be fine, Ryder. Can I call you that?"

Nickel hedged. Magdalena's name for him. Still, it might be nice to hear it once in a while. "I'll think about it," he said.

"I won't ask anything from you," she whispered. "You still belong to your girl, and I *don't* mean that awful Lucy Parker. I want you to find happiness, no matter what it takes."

"How have you been here all this time, thinkin' of me, and I never knew it?"

"Somehow it was enough to know you were out there. You looked happy. I never thought you'd ride in on Daddy's ranch one day, and I'd be here sitting so close to you."

"You still wanna kiss me?"

She jumped a little, her eyes wide, and she flushed a pretty scarlet hue.

"Yes." Josephine leaned into him, and he slipped his hand down to cup her jaw. Tilting his head low, he pressed his lips to hers, chaste and gentle until she overcame her nerves and kissed him back.

He moved in, sliding the tip of his tongue across virgin lips until she shuddered against his mouth, opening her own. When he drew away, she threw her arms around his neck, knocking him backward with her embrace. Her lips sought his again and again, and he obliged.

Nickel retreated, heaving giant gulps of air. Much as he tried, he couldn't contain the grief. It bubbled over at will, much like a forgotten coffeepot still on the boil. Still, he would not cry. Not anymore. Tears did little to ease the loss of Indianola—the pain was just too deep.

"It's not you," he rasped, "it's not you."

"I know," she said. "I wish I knew what to say."

Digging his palms into his eyes, Nickel shook his head. He wished he could erase the pictures in his mind. There was nothing to say. Nothing could change the new reality of his life. His past was wiped out. Gone! Josephine couldn't change it, not with words. Not with kissing either, no matter how good it was.

"She said she loved my laugh," he said. "Said it's my gift, but how the hell am I s'posed to do that when she's gone? They're all gone!"

She held his hand, squeezing as tight as she dared.

"They were talking about you while you were asleep. The grown-ups, that is. My parents and your cowboy friends. They said you're broken inside, that you've seen things . . . that you have fear and bitterness in your heart. They're worried you won't come out of it. I don't understand it, because I can't imagine losing someone I loved that much, let alone facing the fall of an entire town. It doesn't seem real, beautiful Indianola not being there anymore. I don't know what you've seen."

Nickel sat in a slump, wishing he could wipe away the images burned in his mind. "There ain't no words for the things I seen."

Josephine clutched his hand even tighter and brought it to her lips. "I don't suppose anyone could walk away from all that and be the same person they were before."

"I don't know myself anymore. Am I s'posed to be Ryder, or Nickel? Maybe I ain't even s'posed to be either one." He kicked at the grass with his foot, just to listen to his spur jingle.

"Can't you be both?"

"I ain't sure I'm much of either anymore," he said, watching as Josephine drew tiny designs across the back of his hand with her fingertips.

"Deep down, I think you are. You're just trying too hard, too fast. I don't want you to fall," she admitted. "The way you were the other night, when your friend Bannack lulled you to sleep, frightened me because I didn't see the boy I remembered."

"The other night?"

"You slept for two days, Nickel."

"*I did?*"

"Bannack and Marbles agreed to stay put as long as you were down."

"They waited that long? Bannack didn't wanna stay more than a night!"

"Well, he did," she said, and dismissed further questions on the subject.

301

"But back to that boy I remember from the dry goods store. I fantasized over him, that handsome Ryder. Now, I will forever remember the kiss of an Indianola cowboy named Nickel. You're still you, no matter what people call you."

"What good's being me when I couldn't even save the people I loved? Not Mags, not my family."

"Your friend Les told us how you were lost, going back out on that boat to find him, and Magdalena too. You tried! There's nothing more you could have done, is there?"

"I should have been with her. If I was there, I could have saved her."

"Or you might have been lost with her."

"Nope. My luck protects me. Wish I never listened to Lucy."

Josephine leaned her head against Nickel's shoulder and sighed. "I hate that Lucy Parker for her deceit! Now you're not free to marry another."

"I ain't plannin' on sendin' for Lucy any time soon, or marryin' nobody else, neither."

"Will you do me a favor, Nickel?"

"Shore, if I can."

"If the time comes when you're ready to take another bride, will you think of me first?"

He grinned, just a little. "Like that kiss, did you?"

"I fear I'm lost, Nickel."

He kissed her again, slow and easy. She had a taste to her, something sweet, and he wondered if she tasted that way all over.

"If my head was right," he said, "I'd drag you north with me now."

"And I would go without a fight," she replied, "but you need to figure out who you are, and what you want now. You need time, and I won't be any man's mistake."

"Shore wish you would'a said hello that day in Indianola. Maybe I would've been stuck on you, at that."

Dipping her chin, Josephine crossed her arms and traced her forearm with a thumb. She swallowed, ended with a sigh, and smiled. Nickel pondered over her subtle strength. It seemed to radiate from within. Where Lucy was pale and feminine, Josephine was rosy and confident. She had the air of someone who knew cowboys and how to handle them. The girl was also a good rider. She had to be, or her father would not let her on the cattle drives to Indianola.

Lucy Parker sure didn't have *any* of that. She was filled with fright, maybe from being alone so often. It couldn't have been easy, living alone much of the time while her daddy was away, wherever he went. Sometimes he sailed or fished, but there had always been rumors—rumors of another woman in another town.

Still, Lucy harbored no qualms about deceiving him for her own gain, rather than think about his happiness and welfare. And she expected him to believe she loved him? Josephine was far more worthy of his trust.

"If I ever decide I wanna get hitched again, you'll be the first to know, but I ain't so shore I'll want to. Don't guess it'll matter by then. You'll already be hitched up to some lucky puncher, ropin' a passel of young'uns."

She screwed up her face in mock disgust. "Ugh! No thank you!" she cried. "I'll be happy enough here on my father's ranch, waiting for you."

"Might be a long wait. You shore you won't take a fancy to some stranger passin' by?"

"I haven't so far. Although if your friend Bannack comes back this way, you send him to me," she teased.

CHAPTER 29

# THE FIGUREHEAD

He stayed near Josephine for the rest of the day, calmed and content by her nearness. Her family threw a grand dinner in honor of their guests, but Nickel ate without his typical gusto. His mind still drifted. At times, the dark images would settle like a fisherman's net around his brain, and he would stop eating mid-chew, only to gaze toward the barn, where Magdalena's trunk still rested, waiting.

Waiting . . . for what? Dare he open it? He wasn't certain he had the strength, and yet Bannack's words plagued him. Water had filled the trunk; he saw it drain when the cowboys picked it up on the road out of Indianola. Her things, whatever she kept inside, would mold and ruin.

A lock of hair, a trunk with his misguided compass rose painted on the lid, and molding secrets locked inside—that was all that remained of Magdalena Hayworth.

He couldn't take the low voices, the sympathetic tears, the worried glances cast his way. They were treating him as though he would break with the slightest jostle. *So this was pity.*

Nickel's lips twisted, his eyes closed but remained dry. His fork clattered to the porcelain plate below, and he rose from the table and stormed through the door.

ॐ

No one came after him, a gesture he appreciated. It was bad enough being alone in a roomful of people, but he couldn't take the empathy shining from the eyes of the women, or the uncomfortable silences of the men who had nothing to say in the face of sorrow. He grieved without tears, his hands on the trunk, over one of the few words he knew how to read: Indianola. The date was 1874, the year he had surprised Mags with the painted chest of dreams.

"What do I do, Mags?" he asked in a rasping voice. He waited, but the box did not reply. He reached for the lock, fingering it with trembling hands. The key was long gone, but the lock was firm. He would have to break it if he wanted to open it.

"Enough's been broken," he said aloud.

"Know a thing or t-t-two about b-broken."

Nickel turned his head at the sound of the voice, and creases furrowed across his brow. Marbles? They sent *Marbles?*

The man strode forward with the gait of a true horseman, though he did not have Bannack's swagger. He leaned against the buckboard, eyeing the monstrous blue beast.

"Would you open it if you was me?" Nickel asked.

Marbles mulled the question over for a few minutes before answering. For a man of few stuttered words, he told a remarkable tale.

"L-Lost people too," he said. "My m-m-momma, my b-best friend, and a g-girl. Momma took sick."

"What about your friend?" Nickel prodded when he fell quiet.

"I was g-grounded on the field, took a b-bullet. He stood over me, fightin' to protect me. Saw him sh-shot, then struck d-d-down by an en-enemy sword. My uniform still c-c-carries his b-blood. Mine too."

Nickel swallowed hard. He knew so little of Marbles. The fact that he had a difficult past seemed surprising, somehow. "What was his name?" he asked.

"Al-Alexander L-Loring."

"And the girl? Was she *your* girl?" Nickel tried to picture what the awkward cowboy's sweetheart might have looked like. Judging by the grim lines etched in the older man's face, she must have been something special.

Marbles shook his head, then shrugged. "W-Wanted her to b-be. Never t-told her."

"Aww, why not?"

Using his sleeve, Marbles wiped at the lid of the trunk and scowled at the offending grime caked over it. "Not so g-good at talkin'. Time I wor-worked up courage, I found her b-body. B-B-Bastards mutilated her."

Nickel's mouth fell open. "No!" he cried. "*People* did that? *To a girl?*"

Marbles folded his arms across his chest and nodded.

"The sea," the boy offered, "the Mistress, she done mutilated my Mags. All the others too."

"I know." The cowboy glanced at the trunk. "You got m-memories to see you through. Your g-girl knew you loved her. I b-b-barely spoke to mine. I g-guess if I had a trunk with her things, I'd take c-c-care of 'em."

"Bannack says everything's wet inside and might ruin."

Another nod.

"The key's gone," Nickel said.

Marbles seemed to have talked himself out, for he did not reply. Instead, he pulled a small metal shard, filed down from a blacksmith's rasp, from inside his vest pocket and dug the tip into the lock. Deft fingers twisted and poked at the mechanism until the lock fell away in his hand. He put the tiny tool away and tapped on the trunk. Easy.

It was now up to Nickel. Slowly, he thumbed back the latch. His fingers trembled, his eyes leaked, and a great lump of bitter sorrow threatened to suffocate him. Still, he lifted the lid. The air inside was soggy, and the rot of stale Indianolan salt water seared his nostrils and burned down the back of his throat. He cried out.

Slamming the lid shut, he fell off the wagon bed, landing on his back. Another hoarse yell, and he was on his knees, coughing violently. He gripped his head, trying to squeeze the flood of memories out of his mind. He recalled the Mistress climbing into his mouth, waterlogging his screams as she drove him into debris, carrying him out into the prairie. He tumbled under water, lost in the raging torrent as it shredded his clothes.

He remembered her, pinned to the ship's side, and then he was on the beach, slogging across miles of debris, carrying her body.

She smelled like the trunk—of saltwater rot. He retched until vomit came out his nostrils and his mouth.

Knee-length black boots with brown cuffs appeared in his line of vision. He wavered, still coughing. A neck rag fluttered down to him, and he snatched it, coughing into the fabric. Marbles wouldn't want that back.

"L-Let me tend to the ch-ch-chest. I'll see it's r-r-respected. It'll be ready to go by m-m-mornin'."

Nickel hacked up a reply and waved a hand in confirmation. He heard the scrape of the box against the wagon and bit his tongue. Marbles grunted as he lifted the thing by himself, staggering under the immense weight as he turtle-waddled it inside the house.

Before he caught his breath, the door popped open and Josephine Mercy ran to collect him. She braced him under mute protest and hauled him to his feet.

His lungs shook, his stomach threatening another revolt, but Josephine kept walking him. It became clear she had been instructed to walk him away from the house—away from all traces of the odor.

She took him back to the grove, a small, wooded oasis in the middle of the range, and they plopped down where the only smell wafting under his nose was scraggly old cedars and warm Texas air—air devoid of salt and seagulls. He sucked it down in large gulps until the sputtering subsided, and at length, he began breathing through his nose again.

Nickel laid down on the ground and closed his eyes. For a few minutes, the slumber of exhaustion overtook him. When he came to, he found Josephine had pulled his head in her lap and was gently stroking his hair.

He looked up at her, but she said nothing of his outburst, nor did she seem to care to bring it up.

"You leave in the morning," she told him.

"Yes," he rasped.

"It will hurt, watching you go," she said, pinching the fabric of the blouse at her throat.

"Don't much like it either, but I swore I'd work for Bannack and that's what I intend to do."

"I like him, that quiet cowboy."

"Yeah?" he asked, a little suspicious.

"Bannack's smart," Josephine said. "I can tell. He moves with purpose, and he's always thinking about his next action. He's an attractive man too." She giggled a little. "I might be hiding under the trees with him by now if you weren't here," she teased.

Nickel chuckled at the idea of Bannack hiding out in the trees with a girl.

"Well, lemme go get him if that's who you want," he said with a good-natured laugh.

She smiled a little and clutched his hands with a sigh. "Will you write to me?"

Their little joke was over, leaving him to face yet another goodbye.

"I shore would, but I don't know how. Can't read, neither." It wasn't an easy confession to make aloud, but it didn't sway her determination to write.

"Oh," Josephine said, tapping her fingernail against her bottom lip. "Well, what about Bannack? Would he read my letters to you?"

Nickel stretched his legs and shifted; there was a rock digging into his back, and he dug it out and gave it a toss. "I guess he would. Might write what I gotta say for me too if that's okay with you."

"I don't care who writes it—any word from you will be a blessing."

"Then send me letters," he said, gazing up at her. The sunlight filtering through the trees overhead gave the girl an angelic glow, though he decided Josephine was a bit too impish to sprout wings. "Middle C Ranch," he reminded her. "Don't forget."

"I'll remember." She leaned over him and rolled up his sleeve to look at the tattoo on his arm. "Can I see it?" she asked.

"How much you wanna see?" Nickel asked. A little spark of mischief hitched at the corner of his mouth.

"How much is there?" she asked, her eyes widening.

Nickel snorted at her play of innocence. "Didn't you count them when you were starin' at me earlier?" He sat up and removed his shirt to let her examine Old Joly's fine work.

"Oh! They really are all over you." She traced one of the sparrows and read the words on his knuckles.

"I shore hope so. Took me long enough to get 'em."

Her face flushed as she brushed her finger over the mermaid perched atop the Beisht's head, sword raised, ready to plunge into the brain of the beast.

"She's bare-chested," she whispered. "Just like the lady carvings on the ships. Why are they always . . . bare?"

"You mean besides the fact that men love a topless woman?"

Her blush deepened.

"Ship figureheads and tattoos, they mean the same thing. A bare woman's good luck. She calms the sea, shamin' nature into behavin' so the journey ahead's calm and clear."

"Does it work?"

"How many ships've you seen docked in Indianola with those lady-figureheads?"

"Almost all of them."

Nickel nodded. "What's that tell you?"

"I always thought it meant sailors liked unclad women."

"Well, they do, but it means every sailor wants the Mistress on his side. It don't matter how tough he is."

"Do you think it would work for cowboys too?"

"I guess," he said with a laugh, "but I don't know where we'd put a figure-head on our horses."

Her lips quivered. Glancing over her left shoulder, then her right, Josephine heaved a deep breath and began to open the buttons of her blouse.

Nickel's breath caught in his throat. Riveted, he watched her small, slender fingers tremble as she wrestled button after button to her navel. Shedding the blouse, she untied her camisole and pushed the neckline down, revealing breasts so fine he felt the siren tattooed on his skin cringe from green-eyed jealousy.

"I wish for you a safe journey," Josephine whispered, drawing closer. "One free of attack and foul weather."

Nickel's only response was a low growl.

"May the winds be pleasant, and your path easy."

"Mmm-hmm, pleasant," he murmured with a little choke. This was some kind of girl standing in front of him, bearing her breasts. Was it to wish him a safe journey? Or did she want more?

His fingers twitched. He wanted to hold them, feel the weight of them in his hands, but if he touched her now, he might lose his mind and spoil her.

"I ask nothing more than for you to write to me," she whispered. Grasping his hands, she led them to her breasts and heaved a shattered sigh when he latched on, cupping them, stroking her soft skin with his fingers.

Burying her face in the crook of his neck, she touched his bare chest, timidly, then with bravado, trailing little pathways down his stomach, and paused at the band of his britches.

"Jo," he began, for he meant to tell her the truth. He didn't know if he could offer her what she wanted from him. His world was cold and raw, and he was still drowning, only this time in a hellish nightmare he would never awaken from.

"Jo? I can't—"

"I know," she broke in, "no promises. I know I'll likely never see you again, but I pray we will. Either way, I want you to remember me, because I'll never, ever forget you."

⋄

Daybreak found the trunk had been aired out; the belongings had been cleansed by the Mercy women and replaced without Nickel even peeking inside. That suited him fine. So long as other women had touched her things instead of rough, ignorant men, it was not a degradation and he had not raided her privacy.

His throat still itched from the memory of that musty, damp odor, but he shoved it down and made ready to leave.

Marbles had saddled Imp, the cocky painted gelding. They decorated him just like a real cow horse, complete with new saddlebags, rope, bedroll, and gear. He even had a rifle slung into a scabbard, something Nickel never owned in his life.

"Whose rifle?" he asked Bannack, who told him to mount up.

"It's a Winchester, and it's yours," came the gruff reply.

"What? But I . . ." He paused, for the little bay mare was being herded into the remuda of horses Bannack had purchased.

"She's yours too," the cowboy said. "Say goodbye and mount up. We're gonna swallow miles today."

Nickel marveled at the expense of Bannack's gifts. Two new horses all his own, and a fine rifle! Les and his brothers, he noticed, were not armed with new weapons, although he figured Posse was the only one who might handle one if he needed to.

Nickel said his farewells to the rancher and his family, thanking them for taking him in and providing care. The missus gave him a warm hug, and her eyes were misting as she let him go.

"You take care of yourself, Nickel," she said. "Don't be a stranger to us. You are always welcome here."

James Mercy agreed, clapping his shoulder. "I said it before, son, and I can't help but throw the offer down again: you'd make a fine hand right here. Lord knows I need a few more good men riding for me. You sure you don't want to stay on here with us?"

"For God's sake, Ryder, take it!" Alastor yelled. "We'd all be happier stayin' here. Take it!"

"Please, Nickel," Les agreed. "We all like it here." He cast a long look at the middle daughter, whose name Nickel couldn't recall. Nickel glanced at Posse, who shrugged.

Searching out Josephine, his eyes lingered on hers. She didn't say a word, just stood with her hands clasped together, awaiting his decision. In her haste to dress before he left, she had neglected the top button of her blouse, leaving a little gap revealing her throat.

Damn. He could ride for Mercy, and he'd be with Jo every day. It'd be so easy. It was a budding family ranch with plenty of room to grow. Maybe, soon enough, he'd have himself a *real* wife.

Like Lucy, Jo wasn't Mags. Not even close, but she was sweet and pretty, and what's more, a girl who wouldn't deceive him.

Wavering, he looked up at Bannack and Marbles. The latter was already mounted, but Bannack stood grounded, his arms crossed over his chest.

"Looks like you hit that first fork in the road," he said. "Give him your answer."

*My answer?* he thought to himself. *There ain't but one to give. Too bad they ain't gonna like it.*

"Mr. Mercy, sir," Nickel said, careful not to look at Jo and her open button, "I'm shore obliged for the offer. It's a real temptin' job and any other time I might'a taken it, but the truth of it is I ride for Bannack and nobody else."

Mercy threw his hands in the air with a forlorn smile. "Ahh, well, I had to try. I respect your loyalties, son. Bannack will teach you well, but a man can't teach loyalty. Some things just have to be given."

Amid a chorus of farewells and grumbling from his brothers, Nickel mounted the handsome paint and fell in between Bannack and Marbles. Jo cried out for them to wait, just one minute, and flew into the house. Bannack's jaw tightened at the delay, but to his credit, he held his mount, Tarantula, in check. Jo came flying out of the house just as the cowboy gave up waiting and stuffed a parcel in Nickel's hands.

"For you," she said. "Open it on the trail when no one is looking."

He offered a quizzical look, hoping she would elaborate, but she gripped his hand. The girl was trying hard not to cry.

Feeling he needed to return the token of remembrance, Nickel cast about his person, searching for something of worth. He had nothing, so he pulled the wild rag from his head and handed it to her with an apology.

"Wish I had more to give."

"Someday, maybe," she said.

"Maybe so." He squeezed her hand, leaned down, and, in front of her parents and sisters, the ranch hands and cowboys, swept his lips across her cheek.

"You can call me Ryder," he told her. Sitting up, he turned Imp's head north and swung out in line behind Bannack.

"No use lookin' back," he told himself. His past was gone, erased by wind and water. Now, his proverbial mountain lay ahead, and it was time to traverse it.

# CHAPTER 30

# THE CROSSING

A few days later, Nickel decided his brother Posse wasn't so far off the mark, after all. His hero was crazy.

"Damn," he muttered, glaring down at the murky water before them. Another crossing. He hated the crossings.

No matter whether they were great gaping expanses of water or feeble little ribbons cut through the land, the water mocked him. He didn't know the names of the rivers—didn't care. What was wrong with him? He lived by the ocean all his life and had conquered her three times. What did he have to fear from a silly little river?

Bannack called to them, and Marbles set across with the remuda. For a man as awkward as Marbles, he sure could cowboy. Back and forth, back and forth he rode, singing aloud to the horses as he pointed them to the chosen spot on the far bank. His movements were effortless, as though he and his horse were one great beast instead of two.

What surprised Nickel more than anything, though, was the man's singing voice. When he spoke, Marbles stuttered, tripped over his words, and fell flat on his tongue. He would stop mid-word only to pause, then start over. It was a slow, painful speech, but all that changed when he sang. Where was the hitch in his voice? No clumsy starts and stops, no partially repeated words, not even the smallest stutter. His voice wasn't a great gift to the eardrums, but it wasn't awful, either. The horses seemed to like it well enough, for they crossed without a snag.

Even Imp pawed the water, impatient to catch up with the little blood-bay mare.

Les crossed in front of the wagon with Bannack, who was busy shouting orders at Posse. Nickel noticed his eldest brother drove the team with a white-knuckled grip as the water lapped against the sides of the buckboard.

Maybe he wasn't the only one struggling with the sight of water.

Nickel couldn't wait any longer. Imp danced, indignant at being left behind, so the horse surged into the river with a jump that nearly unseated his rider.

Nickel had no choice but to ride through it, wondering if sea monsters ever made it as far inland as a Texas river. Not the big ones, of course, but maybe the tiny ones washed up through the inlets and ate their way up the river basins. He'd have to ask Posse about that once they were back on dry land.

"Nickel! Pay attention!"

Bannack's call jerked him away from thought of monsters only to realize he had let Imp stray farther downstream. The paint didn't like the crossing, easy as it seemed, and was angling toward a steeper point in the bank. Nickel turned his head and the paint spun, spraying water and fighting for his head.

"Come on, Imp!" he shouted, steering the paint back toward Bannack, who was splashing through the shallows on the blue roan, watching for signs of disaster.

"Bring him in!" he shouted.

Nickel sawed on the reins, and he felt the cocky paint would have listened, had a little furry monster not chosen that moment to round the bend, pushed by the current. It was a ball of dark matted fur, and it was heading straight for Imp's legs. The paint squealed and reared, spinning on his hind legs. Nickel grasped for the horn, but Imp lunged and bucked, throwing him into the river. His head went under, but he bobbed to the surface, sputtering.

Imp lit a shuck for the bank without him, but he could see the blue roan mare flying through the shallows, breaking into the deep. Nickel swam out to meet him, grabbed Bannack's offered hand, and clambered up behind him.

"Hang on!" he yelled, but instead of heading for shore, the cowboy urged the mare to follow the furry pint-size monster sweeping downstream. It caught up on a snag, and Bannack reached out and plucked it from the depths by the scruff of the neck.

Bannack's mare, Tarantula, needed no urging. She headed for the bank and climbed out of the river, slapping Bannack with a wet mane as she shook herself off. He handed off the furry ball—a pup—to Marbles and motioned for Nickel to dismount.

He knew he was expected to slide off the horse, but he couldn't move. Now that he was safely across, tremors started down in his toes and worked upward until his teeth rattled in his head. When Bannack reached around to encourage him to dismount, Nickel latched onto his arm with the grip of death.

"Damn, let go!" Bannack started to jerk his arm free, but one look at Nickel's stark face checked violent movement. Instead, he looked back over the river they crossed.

"It's like that first day, isn't it?" he asked.

Nickel nodded, teeth chattering.

"All right then," Bannack said. With a yell, he whipped Tarantula's head toward the water and laid heel to flank. The blue roan leaped into the water and raced across, spraying water over both riders. Again, Bannack turned the roan's head into the middle of the river. Water lapped over the tops of Nickel's boots, and he tried to scramble higher, but an iron hand reached around and held him down in the saddle.

Tarantula struck a deep spot, and when water surged over his lap, the screams broke through the bubble in Nickel's throat.

He screamed and yelled, grasping at Bannack's back and kicking water. He could feel watery fingers sliding up his legs, clutching his waist. She would drag him downward and hold him there until his lungs exploded from the pressure. His eyes, burned from the depths, would cease to see, and he would float to oblivion, slaking the eternal hunger of the she-beast who stalked him.

Bannack was yelling at him, but he couldn't understand what he was saying over the sound of Indianola's screams burned into his brain. He could hear them, and her—all of them. The citizens screaming as the water flooded in, ripping through homes, tearing apart entire families.

Nickel clasped his hands over his ears and closed his eyes, but the darkness only brought back the visions of the dead and dying and those grieving, searching in vain for the ones who would never be found—or worse, never identified.

Out of the ruins and over the sound of the water, a familiar sound tugged at his eardrums. Soft at first, it grew in intensity, and he turned his head to listen. A chant?

"Nickel's luck, Nickel's luck! A nickel for your luck, boy! A nickel for your luck!"

They were yelling from the riverbank, Les and Posse. Marbles rode in leading Imp, and in the middle of the stream, Nickel was wrestled to the back of his own mount. He sat, hauling down on the reins, petrified by the lapping water. They were leaving him!—except they weren't. The cowboys rode, one on either side of him, coaxing him onward.

"Easy on the reins," Bannack told him. "Remember when you rode with me before?"

Nickel remembered. Bannack had forced him to face his fear then as he was now. There would be no getting out of the river until he could face it alone. Only now there were two of them at his side.

"This ain't no damn ocean," he muttered.

"Nope, it's not."

Nickel urged Imp forward. The horse took a few steps before he reined him in again, but the water wasn't getting any higher, and nothing appeared to be reaching for him from under the depths. Bannack and Marbles each held out a hand in case they needed to grab hold of him, but Nickel rode on his own.

Back to the far bank, then the near. Back and forth he rode, screaming his defiance at the river below with each pass. He rode until the cowboys dropped back to watch, confident he no longer needed their assistance. A few more passes, and as he rode up the bank, he dismounted and collapsed to embrace the dry land.

"Nickel's luck, ha!" Alastor toed his arm with a muddy boot. "Ain't no wonder they treat you different from us. You're broken inside, you crazy bastard."

"A-Any man been through In-Indianola what ain't b-b-broken, ain't a man I'd trust." Marbles glared at Alastor until he backed down and stalked off, grumbling.

Nickel looked up when Bannack rode by and stopped to peer down at him.

"I-I'm sorry," Nickel offered up to his quiet leader.

"We'll throw camp in the grove, yonder," Bannack said.

As he rode away, a squiggling little ball of fluff wriggled out of Les's arms and staggered after the horseman on short, dark legs.

Nickel had forgotten about the animal Bannack had pulled from the river. It looked to be a young dog under all that wet, matted fur. It ran for all its worth, trailing behind the blue roan. One sharp bark turned the cowboy's head. He reined in again, observing the whelp. The dog ambled up to the horse without fear, sat down, and beat the grass with a friendly tail thump.

Bannack bent low, scooped the pup off the ground by the scruff of its neck, and plopped it in his lap. To Nickel's surprise, the pup curled up in the crook of the cowboy's arm and closed its eyes. Bannack, it appeared, now had another mouth to feed.

# CHAPTER 31

# THE TELLING OF SCARS

After pulling his chores bare-assed, Nickel wrapped himself in a blanket by the fire and watched his clothes dry. He didn't feel much like conversation, not even to argue with Les Harold over his favorite topic—Mustang Grey. After a few failed attempts, his best friend gave up. His brothers turned in early, even though the sun hadn't even set yet, leaving him and Les with two unobtrusive cowboys, a wild little dog, and dark, lingering thoughts.

Marbles put on another pot of coffee, and they watched it boil. Nothing was said, though he had a feeling the men were carrying an entire conversation without a spoken word. *How did they do that?*

It was dull without conversation. Maybe too dull. Even the pup seemed to agree. She wriggled out of Bannack's lap, fell over her feet, and righted herself. Nickel watched her amble over to his saddlebags. She pounced on the bag, sank her needled puppy teeth into tough leather, and began to chew.

"Hey! None of that, pup." He whisked her up and held her aloft. She snapped at his fingers and pawed at him in protest. Reaching around, Nickel grabbed a nearby stick and offered it to her. The pup accepted the consolation prize and settled in to a good chew.

"Good thing she's cute," he said, accessing the teeth marks in his saddlebag with a frown. He shook it at her and told her no, but she didn't look up from her stick. He opened the flap to look for his folding knife and discovered the newspaper package Josephine had gifted him before he left. In their haste to depart, he had forgotten to open it.

Pulling it out, he weighed it in his hands and frowned. What on earth could the girl have given him? Certainly nothing better than what she gifted him back in the copse of trees.

"What is it?" Les asked.

"A present, I guess," he said, poking at it with a finger. It was hard—a book, no doubt.

"From who?"

"Josephine Mercy. She gave it to me just before we left her daddy's ranch. Guess I forgot about it."

"You forgot? Shoot, Nickel, if a girl like Josephine Mercy gave me a present, I'd remember to open it."

"Too much on my mind, I guess."

"Well? Open it now!"

Nickel glanced at Bannack, who shrugged and tossed a few more sticks on their fire.

"Save that newspaper. Wouldn't mind something to read," Bannack suggested.

Nickel obeyed, carefully cutting the string so as not to damage the cowboy's new reading material.

Inside was a book. Nickel didn't have to read the title to know which book it was. He let out a whoop.

"Whooeee! Les, look! It's Mustang Grey!"

Everyone but the pup looked up at the cover he brandished about. A piece of paper fell out, dangerously close to the fire, and Bannack snatched it up before the sparks set it aflame. As he lifted it, he glanced at the page and froze.

"Well, shit, Nickel! What the hell'd you *do* to that girl?" He handed the page over, and Nickel's eyes nearly popped out of his head. Josephine, that dear, sweet girl, had drawn a rapid picture of herself, and him, bare-chested.

"Nothin' she didn't want." He grinned in spite of himself. "I guess you weren't s'posed to see that."

"I guess not," Bannack agreed with a chuckle.

"I ain't so good at readin'," Nickel said, offering it back. "Since you saw it anyway, maybe you could read it to me?"

"If you want." He took the paper, still chuckling at the drawing, and read.

*Ryder:*

*This is my favorite book—I want you to have it. Don't forget to ask that handsome Bannack to help you write me. I know chances are against*

*me. You'll forget or find another. It happens. I'll write so long as you do.*
*If you ever want another wife, I'd make a good one. Meantime, carry*
*me with you for safe travels.*

*— Josephine*

Bannack handed the note back, studying his young protégé.

"You keep it up, and you'll break every gal in Texas." Amusement lined the contours of his eyes.

"Yeah, well, she told me she'd've been after you if she hadn't met me," Nickel said, rolling his eyes.

"Is that so?" Bannack's grin broadened as he cocked his hat up and back on his head like a crown.

"She thought you were strikin', whatever the hell that means." Nickel made a display of gagging noises.

"Means she's a damn smart girl. I like her."

"She likes you too, dammit. Said she might've tried to lure you out into the trees if she hadn't met me."

"Hmm, judgin' by that picture, it's too bad you're along, then."

They all laughed. Les tried to grab the picture, but Nickel folded it up and placed it back in the book. It was one thing for Bannack to see it accidentally, but he wasn't about to go waving it around for everyone else—not even Les.

Coffee was poured, but Nickel set his aside, staring at the familiar cover. "Can't believe Mustang Grey's her favorite too. Damn, maybe I should've taken her with me."

"What would Lucy Parker say about that?" Les asked.

"What would Josephine's *father* say about that?" Bannack retorted.

"I bet Mustang Grey's got more women after him than I do, even," Nickel announced.

Bannack, who had picked up his coffee mug, snorted into it with a loud chuff. "Bet he don't."

"Well, Josephine likes him, so why wouldn't every other female?"

"Don't know many grown women what cotton much to those dime novels."

"But he's a hero! Women love that stuff."

"How do you know what women love?" Les asked.

"I know a lot more about it than you do."

"What *did* you do with Josephine Mercy?" his friend asked, but Nickel bit back a grin and sipped his coffee instead.

The cowboys chuckled at his wry face. He couldn't get used to cowboy coffee. Seemed any minute it would stand up and walk off on its own. Still, he drank it for no other reason than Bannack and Marbles did. It was the thing to do.

"Finally met a girl who likes Mustang Grey, and you go and leave her behind," Les grumbled. "What if ole Mustang shows up at her daddy's ranch? He'll be the one under the trees doin' who knows what with your girl."

Nickel waved him off. "No, he won't."

He scrunched his eyebows. "How do you know?"

*'Cause he's ridin' with us,* Nickel thought, slaying his hero with an all-knowing stare. "She already had a taste of me," he said aloud.

Marbles rolled his eyes with a snort. "M-Maybe they *should* write one'o them d-dime novels about you, N-Nickel."

"Maybe so," Bannack agreed. "You could be as infamous as Mustang Grey." The cowboy's eyes, usually frosty and cold, were alight with strange amusement.

"I already started on it," Les said.

"Started what?" Nickel couldn't believe his friend was serious. *Les Harold? Write a book?*

"Don't look at me like that. Came to the idea after you lost your mind at the Mercy ranch. You said you wanted to be a dime novel. Thought it was a good idea. Nobody knows you better'n your best friend, right? Hell, your story's just as good as Mustang's, anyway."

"Well, shore, but what do you know about scribblin' books?" Nickel wanted to know.

"Don't seem so hard to me. All you gotta do's write one word, then another and another, till the story's told."

Nickel mulled the idea around and around. Les Harold wanted to write his story. *Was* writing his story. Maybe it was worth telling, but he wasn't sure it would be one anybody would want to read. Les? Write a dime novel? It was almost funny. Almost.

"Will you write about Mags?" he asked, unconvinced.

Les nodded. "Mags and Old Joly, me and everybody else in Indianola if you want." For being the levelheaded one, Les's voice was rising. *Who's getting excited over a funny notion, now?* Nickel thought to himself.

"So it'd be their story too?" he asked aloud.

"Through your eyes, but yeah, I guess so."

A story of Indianola. Maybe the idea had merit, after all!

"Okay," Nickel said, "but you gotta put Bannack in it too."

"Since when am I in this book of yours? I ain't an Indianolan," Bannack mused.

Nickel jumped on his friend's grand idea and ran with it. "You gotta be in it! You been the one stepped in and changed my life. You kept us from starvin' all those years."

"Hold on now," Bannack said, holding his hands in the air, palms out. "You put me in it, then you'd better put Mustang Grey in the book too, Les."

"But you ain't Mustang Grey," Les said. His protest fell on deaf ears.

Bannack bit back a grin. "Nope. I ain't."

"The hell you ain't!" Nickel cried. "Tell the truth. We've been ridin' with Mustang!"

Les's eyes widened, and his gaze snapped to Bannack's face.

"Are you? Are *you* Mustang Grey?" he asked, leaning forward.

"Aww, shit." Bannack glared across the fire at Nickel as he spoke. "You're just not gonna let this go, are you?"

"You know I ain't," Nickel replied. He curled his lips in a half-sneer. He all but had Bannack's confession this time, he was sure of it.

"For the last time, boy, I'm *not* Grey. But I told you I'd introduce you to him some time." He rose, stretched, and headed for his bedroll.

"When?" Nickel and Les cried in unison. "When will you do that?"

Bannack stopped in front of Marbles and clapped him on the shoulder.

"Boys, meet Alexander Grey Saville III, retired Pony Express rider and dime-novel hero." He waved his hand with an air of exaggerated boredom.

Marbles jumped to his feet, nearly spilling his coffee cup.

"D-Damn you, B-Bannack! What'd you do that for?"

"So they'll finally leave me the hell alone. G'night, Grey."

Marbles cursed at Bannack's retreating back.

"No cursin' into the wind. It's bad luck," Bannack sung out. He was still chuckling when he slipped into his bedroll.

☙

Bannack's reveal chased Marbles away from camp, dragging his bedroll behind him. It also sent the boys, the whole lot of them, into an argument lasting long into the night. Even Alastor joined in, berating the awkward horseman, laughing at the absurdity of the idea.

By morning, Nickel still didn't know what to make of Marbles's identity. Nowhere in the books was Mustang Grey portrayed as a stuttering cowboy who was afraid of women.

"Joke's on you two shitheads if it is true," Alastor said. "Ridin' all this way with your dumb hero Mustang Grey, and you didn't even know it."

"It ain't true," Posse said. "Bannack and Marbles, they're just funnin' you."

Nickel wasn't so convinced. If it were untrue, why did Marbles get mad when Bannack introduced him? Had he and Les argued clear across the prairie about Mustang, only to have him hear every word?

Crawling to the water's edge, Nickel cupped his hands and splashed his face. He could feel his muscles tighten. There was a chill in the air, but it wasn't the cold that bothered him. Sight of water still made him want to run. Where, he didn't know, but it was a ridiculous notion. A man couldn't run from water all his life, not if he wanted others around him, anyway.

So, he scrubbed at his face and neck and washed his arms. It wasn't quite a bath, but it was enough to chase away a few of the dreary-eyed monsters he battled at night when he was supposed to be sleeping.

A noise to his left alerted him to the presence of another, and he looked up.

Marbles nodded a quiet greeting and squatted down on his heels to wash. Nickel concentrated on trying not to stare. He gulped a few times, fixating on the pebbles below his feet, but his eyes kept skidding upward.

"Y-You want p-p-proof, don't you?"

"My brothers don't believe you're him."

"Do you?" Marbles asked, splashing river water on his face.

"You ain't like the books, but I don't figure Bannack would lie, would he?"

"B-Bannack hates a lie." He gestured to Nickel's bar of soap. "You d-done with that?"

Nickel offered his lye.

As he reached for the bar, Marbles eyed the letters tattooed on his knuckles and frowned a little.

"Hold f-fast?"

It wasn't the first time Nickel had to explain the depth behind those two little words, but it was the first time he truly understood them.

"It ain't just the riggin' those words help a man hold onto," he said. "It's life. I don't guess I ever understood that, not till now." Nickel paused, warily watching the gurgling water under his feet. His throat was closing up again, and he cleared it.

"Persevere? Is that the right word?"

Marbles nodded. "It's a d-damn good wo-word." The cowboy washed his face and scratched at his chin. He didn't seem to like the stubble growing there, for his scowl deepened as he clawed at it.

"There's t-times I could've used a re-reminder like that m-m-myself." Marbles hesitated, then tugged at the homemade leather gauntlet that never left his wrist. "My hold f-fast," he said, and removed the gauntlet.

Nickel saw the man's wrist was mangled and scarred. Two great holes had been sewn shut, but it didn't hide his disfigurement.

"Somebody shoot you?" Nickel asked.

Marbles glanced at him and nodded.

Nickel shivered a little, trying to imagine what it must have felt like.

"Bullets?"

"Ar-arrows," Marbles replied.

Arrows in the wrist. "Mustang was shot in the wrist with arrows," Nickel said slowly.

"I know." Marbles continued to wash, unaffected by the sudden shift in Nickel's suspicious young mind.

"He was shot in the shoulder too. Twice."

"Wh-Which shoulder?" Marbles asked.

"The right. I remember 'cause it was far from his heart."

"S-Still hurt like h-hell." Marbles removed his shirt and turned his back.

Nickel's jaw fell open. The great rider didn't need to say another word. His scars told the stories for him.

# CHAPTER 32

# BANNACK'S HOMECOMING

*I*t's a strange thing, discovering who your hero is. You expect them to be larger-than-life, but they live their days just like everybody else. At least, Marbles did. The man rode through each day like he wasn't a champion but a regular, ordinary man. Why?

"If I was him, I'd want everybody to know my name. Why hide the truth?" Nickel reined in next to Posse, who drove the wagon.

"He's not like you," Posse replied. "He's actually *quiet* and wants to live in peace without a bunch of loco, starry-eyed kids pesterin' him." Posse snorted as they watched Les trying to keep up with the hero. He fired one question after another without taking a breath in between.

"I see Grey's point. Nickel, look at him, riding all stiff-backed in the saddle. He don't like the attention. If you respect the man, don't crowd him. I expect you'll learn more from him by watchin', and not runnin' your mouth so much."

Marbles, or Mustang Grey, did look uncomfortable. He shook his head a few times and waved his arm. Les did not relent his interrogation.

Finally, he pointed to the wagon, barked an order, and sent the boy scampering back to the rear of their little outfit.

Nickel decided Posse was right. He wanted to show his respect, so he hung back, even though he itched to ride up to him and ask the questions flooding his tongue.

*Pretend he's just Marbles,* he thought, and hoped he would be granted the opportunity to learn the *real* story of Mustang Grey one day.

ೞ

Still forbidden from riding the blood bay, Nickel rode Imp as much as he dared, his arm still tightly bound within a sling at Bannack's insistence.

"You can't do somethin' stupid if you can't move that arm," he reasoned.

Nickel looked forward to removing that nuisance almost as much as he looked forward to seeing his new home.

They had been on Middle C Ranch land for a whole day, so said Bannack, and still no sign of the ranch itself. Was it as grand as the Mercy spread had been? How the hell did people tell where one ranch stopped and the other began, anyway? The land all looked the same; a sea of rolling grasslands and vegetation wholly alien to him.

Bannack led them through thickets of trees, which confused him.

"I ain't never seen so many trees, 'less you count the ones made into boats," he said.

"Post oak," Bannack replied when he inquired what they were. "Cashman chose his land well. We've got the river here for water, oaks and scrub pine for buildin', and the best damn grassland in the state. Cattle are fat and happy."

"I figured most ranches were bowls of dust," Nickel admitted.

Bannack glanced at him and chuckled. "Been on some that were," he said. "We eat our share of dust—we just don't wallow in it. It'll be a different life, Nickel. I hope you're up for it."

He and Marbles pushed forward, and the boys followed, cutting away from the river through oak-dotted grasslands.

Longhorns raised their heads to stare as they passed by, slobbery bands of green drool dripping from big pink tongues. The weary group rode on, following the switchbacks of the river. They traversed the rocky bed, and Nickel laughed aloud.

"Don't this trickle go dry?" he asked.

Bannack glanced at him. "Guess it would seem like a trickle to you, but this river sustains us."

The water Bannack called a river looked more like a little creek to him, a footbath for a baby bird. Still, if the cowboy wanted to call the little trickle a river, who was he to correct him? He reined in next to Les.

"You see Bannack's river?" he asked, even though they were riding through the middle of it.

"It ain't a river," Les whispered.

"I've swallowed more water'n this," Nickel agreed. "Hell, I've pissed more water'n this river."

"Well, if you'd stop swallowin' so much water all the time, you'd quit pissin' rivers."

Nickel snorted, amused by his best friend's comment. He might have laughed aloud, had he any energy to do so. Bannack and Marbles turned their horses and halted, their heads tilted toward the breeze.

"Anybody smell that?" Bannack asked, sniffing the air like a bloodhound.

The other riders inhaled, so Nickel did too.

"You think someone's got a big cook-fire goin'?" he asked. The men exchanged dark glances and kicked their horses into a fast lope, leaving the boys no choice but to follow.

On the other side of the river, the trees thinned, surrendering to prairie grasses. Some were almost as tall as a man.

"Nickel, look!" Les shouted. A big black cloud of smoke hung heavy in the air, fed from an unseen source.

"What is it, Bannack?"

Tarantula pranced and spun under the agitated rider. Riding tight circles back and forth as he assessed the smoke, Bannack let out a yell.

"It's the homestead! Ranch's on fire!" The trenchant alarm sent ripples of panic through the exhausted Indianolans. Had they ridden from one catastrophe only to land in another?

"Alastor! Drive the wagon down there—they may need the team!"

"What about the remuda?"

"Let 'em go!"

Spurring their exhausted mounts, Bannack and Marbles plunged into a dead run, eating up ground at a dizzying pace. Wind whipped at Nickel's face as he rode, stinging his eyes, but he kept up, riding abreast with the men, Les and Posse following close behind.

They crested a rise, and the Middle C Ranch lay before them, a picturesque cog of barns, corrals, and outbuildings dotting rolling hills.

Nickel had imagined a wasteland of dust and limp, brown land devoid of movement. This—this was green! But for how long? The smoke was so thick that they pulled their neck rags up over their noses as they rode past the main house.

The front door swung open and a handsome woman ran outside, struggling to carry a basin of water toward them. They halted.

"Bannack? Oh, Bannack, is that you?" she cried, abandoning the basin to grasp the cowboy by the arms. "Thank God you're safe. We were so worried!"

"Catherine!" Bannack shouted. White-knuckled, he gripped her by the waist. "What's goin' on?"

"Your house is burning!" She pointed and doubled over, hacking over the smoke. "The fire is headed straight for us!"

Bannack clung to her as a lifeline, searching her face for the news he didn't want to hear. "Aurelie! Catherine, where's Aurelie?"

The woman held a wet cloth over her face and suppressed a deep, throaty cough.

"Catherine, *where's Aurelie?*"

"We don't know, Bannack." She pulled the cloth from her mouth. It was tinged in red. "No one has seen her. Your house . . . Creede says it's gone. Print is inside. He tried to save it, but he's badly burned!"

Bannack released her. "You stay here! If the fire gets too close, you grab the nearest horse and ride down the road to safety, you hear me?" He didn't wait for her reply.

Bannack and Marbles ripped the neck rags from their faces, dunking them in the basin she held out for them, and retied them over the bridges of their noses. Nickel gave his new rag from Victoria a good soaking and stole a bold look at the attractive brown-haired woman called Catherine as she urged them to be careful.

He heard Les and his brothers trailing behind but did not slow for them to catch up. Over a large swale, and through a grove of trees, chaos ensued.

Men, hidden under neck rags and painted with black grime and soot, were running for the water wagons, beating out flames with drenched shirts, blankets, buckets, and shovels.

They jumped from their horses and fell to the task, lining up with the retreating ranch hands and cattle punchers.

"Keep your clothes wet! Know where the water wagons are!" Bannack yelled at them. The addition of men aided in beating the line of flames back, but the winds were picking up strength, scattering sparks on the wind. They were losing time, and ground.

Nickel no longer recognized who he was fighting alongside, or where Bannack was, but he saw the remains of what must have been the great cowboy's home. He did not stop to offer condolences or contemplate what the loss of the house meant for his own future; he saw only that if the fire broke over the swale, they would lose the entire Middle C.

He didn't know how long they beat at those flames, but they did not seem to gain much ground. Les stumbled into him, and they retreated a few steps to gauge the shift of the wind. Smoke billowed above them, floating into a form so sinister, Nickel almost lost his stomach.

The blanket someone had given him to beat out the flames dropped from his hand. He wanted to turn tail and run. Run! Far away, some place where the black-headed monster would never find him.

"Les?" he asked.

"Yeah?"

"You see what I see?"

"Don't say it, Nickel!" They stared at the creation of the wind as it billowed the smoke formation into an enormous gray beast. A long, snaking neck curved straight up in the air, looming over them with its great black head, gaping mouth, and narrowed eyes. Its serpentine body twisted with the air as though wrapping its coils around its hapless prey: the ranch. Great tongues of fire licked the air all around it. It was a sea of fire, and the great cloud-Beisht was swimming straight through it.

"I think it's followin' me!" Nickel's eyes bulged as he gaped at the hellish creature.

"I—uhh, it's just a cloud of smoke."

"It's not. It's the Beisht Kione."

"Stop sayin' its name! What if it hears you?"

"Don't matter. It knows where I'm at. I gotta kill it, Les! I gotta kill it."

Nickel ripped the shirt from his back, drenching it in a barrel dangerously low on water, and screamed the Beisht's name, attacking the fiery tongues of the devil at his feet.

"You want me?" he screamed at the great black cloud. "Come get me, you sonofabitch! Just leave them alone!"

His lungs hurt, and his arms burned. Sweat and smoke seared his eyes, rendering him nearly blind, but he fought the monster, whipping it into submission with every stroke of his arms.

Someone grabbed him from behind and yanked him backward, thrusting a wet cloth over his eyes.

"Back up!" the man yelled. Nickel didn't recognize the voice as Bannack or Marbles, but the tone held just as much authority.

"You're dryin' out, and those flames are flankin' you, boy!" The speaker pushed him back to a water wagon, out of the line of fighters, and a wet cloth soothed his scorched, peeling skin.

"Stay back, kid."

"I ain't a kid," he panted, "and I'll pull my weight!"

"N-Nickel!" Marbles, who had run in for the wagon, grasped his shoulders. "C-Can your luck b-bring us r-r-rain?"

"What? No, I don't think so. I mean, I don't know."

Marbles clasped the tall man who had pulled him from the fire and shook him. "A nickel! You got a nickel?"

"Are you loco? We're losin' ground!"

"A n-n-nickel!" Marbles shouted.

"It don't always work like that!" Nickel yelled at him, but the stuttering cowboy continued to shake the taller man.

"G-Give the b-boy a-a nickel!"

"We don't have time for this!"

"Now!"

The tall man shook his head, reached inside the wagon under the seat, and pulled out a hastily discarded vest. He searched inside the pockets and slammed two coins inside Nickel's hand.

"Satisfied?" he yelled at Marbles. The cowboy grabbed Nickel's hand and looked down at the pair of shiny nickels resting in his palm. He closed his fingers around them.

"N-Not your f-fault if it don't w-work, but I had to try."

Before the boy said a word, Marbles was gone, running off to join the other men. Nickel moved to follow, but the tall man pushed him back again.

"*You* stay at the rear."

Nickel fought the urge to throw his middle finger in the air at the retreating man. Who was he to tell him to stay behind?

"I ain't no boy," he said aloud, though no one was paying any attention.

Out of the corner of his eye, he spotted two men making a break through the flames, chasing down a third man. He was screaming something, Nickel couldn't quite make it out, but the pair had to muscle him down to drag him back to safety.

The struggling trio swerved away from the flames, and he realized Bannack was the one they were fighting to retrieve.

"Aurelie!" He screamed the name over and over, trying to dart past the fires to reach his house. The scene tore at Nickel's chest. It was looking like his frantic hero was about to break, and he didn't want to watch the destruction.

He didn't want to turn his back on his friend, either, so he shot a prayer skyward, hoping it would penetrate the thick smoke hovering over them.

When he turned back, he glimpsed Alastor, standing with his arms crossed, watching Bannack with an oily grin plastered over his face.

Nickel's fists clenched at his sides. His brother caught his murderous gaze, the smile faded to a sneer, and he walked away from the inferno, stamping at a small blaze at his feet.

Nickel ignored the screaming of his muscles and picked up a discarded shovel to beat out at the fire, when something wet plunked on his nose and tickled his lips.

Another hit him in the cheek, and when he reached up to scrape it away, a few water droplets hit his hand. He jerked his head skyward and let out a whoop when a few hard drops struck him in the face.

"Come on!" Throwing his hands high over his head, Nickel bargained with the clouds. "I figure you owe me, so bring 'em rain!"

He never thought he'd be asking for rain again, not in this lifetime, and yet here he was, scarcely a month after the drowning of Indianola, praying for a rainstorm.

The tall man's nickels worked. The heavens opened up, driving hard, pelting rain upon the hell down below.

Weary men turned their gazes skyward, and shouts went up across the burning battlefield. Rain fell in torrential sheets, dousing the inferno. Amid the coughing of the men, the yells grew. They were beating down the fire!

The men worked in the rain, heedless of time, beating out stubborn, strangling flames. They took no chances, slinging shovels and pitchforks full of mud over glowing coals.

When the fires were all but snuffed out, the men, hacking on smoke, dropped their tools to celebrate as the rains washed away the scorching burn of Purgatory.

Nickel and his brothers did not take part in the cowboys' joy. For the Indianola boys, a new problem arose out of the ranch's salvation. Water.

"You done called another flood!" Les cried. "*What'd you do?*"

Nickel spat out a mouthful of rainwater, slicked back his drenched hair, and held out his hand, showing the two coins.

"Marbles asked if I'd make it rain. Made that tall bloke over there give 'em to me."

"And now we got another flood!"

Nickel leaned on his friend, coughing, too spent to care. They staggered away from the smoke and spitting fire, crested the hill where the grass was still fresh and unscathed, and collapsed together.

Rolling over, Nickel lay facedown in the grass and nibbled on the wet blades to ease his parched tongue as the rain soothed tiny burn spots from flying sparks on his hot, peeling skin.

They huddled together, lost in a strange and foreign place. What if it didn't stop raining? The wind was blowing steady, slanting raindrops sideways into their faces.

Prairies could flood; Nickel experienced that firsthand. What if the trickle of Bannack's river turned into an ocean?

Les shifted from one foot to the other, and Posse scanned the horizons as though certain he would see monstrous waves reaching for them at any moment. They retreated to the high ground, the hill separating the main house from Bannack's burned-up home, but Nickel could not keep still. He paced atop the hill, back and forth, back and forth, glaring skyward.

"I control you now," he muttered. "You won't never own me, Mistress! You hear me?" His voice grew. "I own you!"

He heard a rumble from the clouds and shook his fist at the falling water.

"I'm not afraid of you—I hold fast!" he screamed. The first part was a lie, but so long as he stood his ground and kept yelling, Nickel figured the water would believe him and let them be.

"Keep tellin' yourself that," someone spoke at his left ear. Nickel turned and clenched his fists. Damn Alastor and his greasy habit of slipping off to disappear, only to reappear later—and always behind his mark.

"Look at the way they're all lookin' at you."

Despite himself, Nickel looked. Down the hill, dirty, straggling men—unidentifiable under broad, soggy hats and wild rags—gathered in a group to peer up at him.

"Don't cowboys hang boys what go crazy in the head?"

"If they do, your neck's as good as stretched."

Alastor snorted. "Ryder Wheeler, golden boy of Indianola," he sneered.

"Don't call me that! I ain't no damned Wheeler!"

"That's what Father says too—that you ain't a Wheeler."

"*Says?*" Nickel asked. "What do you mean, *says?*"

The smirk faded. "Said," he blurted. Alastor paused, wiping rain out of his eyes, and Nickel scowled. "You're just a throwback from some dumb sailor what made it with a mermaid or somethin'. Probably why the Mistress keeps tryin' to claim you."

"I remember a time she had help," Nickel said with a snarl. "Besides, better a dumb sailor's bastard than Oren Wheeler's son—or brother to a worthless barnacle like you."

Alastor rolled his eyes. "I guess you'd rather be that dumb cowboy's little brother, huh?"

"Yep."

"Saw him down there, you know."

"Bannack?"

"Didn't look much like a hero to me, scramblin' around like a dog, lookin' for his woman in hot ash. He ain't never gonna find her."

Nickel reared back and caught his brother square in the eye. The punch caught Alastor off guard. He stumbled backward, fell, and rolled end over end down the hill.

Nickel stifled a yell of his own, holding his knuckles in the palm of his hand. His skin was mottled with tiny burns from flying sparks, but they didn't matter. Neither did his useless brother.

Thanks to his lucky rains, there was no longer a threat to ranch and life, but, like Nickel, Bannack's world was gone, and he meant to see to it his friend did not face it alone.

# CHAPTER 33

# CONSEQUENCES OF FRIENDSHIP

*Primal fear is an empty hole devoid of conscious thought, of touch or sound. Voices do not reach you, fire does not sway you, flood does not move you. Your breath grows ragged; your heart pulsates in your chest in an attempt to flee. Veins run cold, the tongue dries, and panic leeches through your skin, looking for residency.*

Bannack was on a first-name basis with primal fear and its lech of a companion, panic. He learned of them both throughout his life, throughout the war, and throughout the search for Ryder those days in Indianola. They had found him again, rendering him incapable of logic or thought.

Aurelie was home during the fire, she had to be. No one else had seen her. Why didn't she run to the main house for shelter with Catherine?

Men tried to pull him back, to strong-arm him, but he fought them off, bloodying noses and cracking jaws.

Now that the fires were doused, no man, and no amount of heat, would stop him from searching for his wife. If Aurelie was anywhere amid the cinders of their home, he would find her.

Donning gloves he had taken off one man he punched, Bannack fell to his search, sifting through still-glowing ash with a half-burned beam.

Rain cascaded off his hat, skewing his vision as though looking through a waterfall, but he did not feel the wet, sopping clothes sucking at his skin.

"Dammit, Aurelie!" He tasted her name on his tongue, the sweet fire of the woman he craved.

"Where are you?"

☙

An aggravated cough near his left shoulder alerted him to someone's presence. He thought he made it clear for them to leave him the hell alone. Some fool wasn't listening. He whirled, fists at the ready, to glare into young Nickel's face.

The lad was tying a rag over his nose, hacking up water and smoke, but he stepped beside him and laid a hand on Bannack's shoulder.

"They done told me to stay away, but I told 'em to go to hell."

Bannack studied his young protégé. The lad's eyes were black with fatigue and strain. He had ridden well for one having never journeyed beyond the outskirts of Indianola before, but he was hurting and favoring both his ankle and his lame shoulder.

The boy was spent, yet he had thrown his weight into fighting fire. Now here he was, naked from the waist up and ignoring his own discomfort, already betraying orders to back a friend.

"Watch your step," he ordered, pointing to the precarious network of black beams hanging above their heads.

Neither spoke as they searched, tossing aside anything worth salvaging to deal with later. They weren't at it long when the tall horseman came riding in on a dead man's run, jumping off before his horse stopped.

"Bannack!"

The cowboy, who had been holding a washbasin in his hand, tossed it in the save pile and looked up.

"She ain't there!"

"She's alive? Cashman, tell me she's alive!"

"Aurelie's alive, sure enough, though you'll wish her dead." He held out a letter that he kept covered by a piece of oilskin cloth. Bannack shuffled through the ash and debris at his feet to accept the letter, though one glance at his face revealed the dread coursing through the cowboy's veins—he did not want it.

"Catherine found it stuck to the back door of the main house. She read it—I didn't," Cashman warned, "but for what it's worth, I'm sorry."

Nickel watched the letter crumple in Bannack's fingers. His shoulders slumped, and he grasped at his throat. His head recoiled from the letter, and he dropped it at his feet. The cowboy closed his eyes, but when he made a move to speak to his friend, his words dried out and fell like dust.

"Bannack?" the tall man asked. "What is it?"

The cowboy swayed on his feet and swallowed a few times, as though gathering the tools needed to speak.

"She ran off with . . . someone. Shot my horse," he said. "Shot it, robbed me, and fired the ranch."

"Your *wife* did this? But that can't be!" Nickel exclaimed. He started for Bannack, but the tall man blocked his path and pushed him back.

"This ain't your affair, boy. Best take your friends and go on up to the main house."

"But I—"

"Now." He began pushing Nickel along as though he were little more than a nuisance child who needed a good shooing. "Run along."

Nickel scowled. Who was this bossy fellow, anyhow? No one spoke to him that way before, and the big man's attitude was rubbing him raw.

"I ain't a child," he shot at the man, but his words were ignored.

"Garrett! Take the Indianola boys to the main house. Don't let Catherine tend to 'em alone."

A cowboy with a crooked nose approached to herd the boys back to the house. Screaming behind them turned Nickel, but the cowboy kept a firm hand on his shoulder, marching him forward with little regress. He spun his head and craned his neck, catching glimpses of Bannack bellowing his wife's name.

He slandered her with curses so severe Nickel felt sure the repercussions of such language in the face of a storm would bring a host of bad luck upon his shoulders—he already told Bannack it was bad luck to yell obscenities into the wind. Maybe it wasn't the same on land as it was on sea. Rules seemed to be different somehow, way out here in the hills and grasslands.

Another yell turned Nickel's head—Bannack had grabbed hold of a board and was beating the tar out of a burned-up ridge beam. The tall man was trying to talk to him, though he kept well out of reach.

"Lemme stay with him," Nickel pleaded. "Bannack's my friend."

"Bannack ain't nobody's friend," Garrett said.

"He's *my* friend."

The cowpuncher snorted. "Best stick your nose in your own affairs, kid, 'fore you get it wiped off your face."

"What's that s'posed to mean?"

"It means a man don't befriend a lobo wolf and not expect to get bit."

"Is that what happened to your twisted ole beak?" Nickel muttered under his breath.

03

"It's gone," Catherine Cashman was telling someone. "Everything he worked so hard for, it's all gone!"

Nickel didn't hear the reply, but he heard the pretty woman well enough. She was clutching her hands together, crying for Bannack.

"How could she run off and burn him down? She stole his money, his titles, everything! The note says she even shot his best stallion! He meant to sire a new bloodline with that animal. Bannack is such a good man, and she left him with nothing!"

"You'd best try to calm yourself, Mrs. Cashman," the voice said. "You know you ain't s'posed to get worked up, or you'll start coughin'."

"But why? I don't understand!"

"Bannack married poorly, shore 'nuff. I reckon he knew it, but he loved her anyhow. Nobody expected this, not even from her, but shoot, ma'am, I done seen how she was. Jealous of that Wheeler family down Galveston way—where was it they gone? Indianola? She shore hated his sendin' money to that poor Wheeler woman with all them kids. Couldn't understand why he'd taken that fisherman's son under his own roof. Travelin' all that way to fetch him did her in, I expect. She was some riled last I seen of her."

"Yes, I recall she was, but to burn him out! She nearly burned the whole ranch!"

"Yes ma'am, nearly did. Never would've thought it, but there's a woman needs her neck stretched. Guess Bannack's gonna have to ride after her and see that it's done."

"It'll destroy him!"

"Expect it already has, ma'am."

She cried out and began to cough. The man crossed the room but stopped short when he saw Nickel standing in the doorway. His blood ran cold.

"Mrs. Bannack done all that on account of me?" Nickel asked, and his voice cracked over the name.

"Who're you?" the ranch hand asked cautiously.

"Ryder. I'm the one Bannack brought back from Indianola."

"Aww, hell! You're *him*?" The man brought his palm to his temple and held it there, taking a small step backward. "What'd you just hear?"

"She burned Bannack's home on account of me."

The man shifted his feet and pawed at the back of his neck. He looked mighty uncomfortable caught amid the ugly truth.

Nickel turned and ran outside, only to plow straight into Bannack himself. His friend took no notice of him, however, but stormed past him.

Marbles and two other men were on his heels, but it was Bannack who barked orders. He began throwing random gear into his war bag with rapid abandon.

"I'll replace what I take with me, Cashman." His voice was dark and gruff.

"I'll ride with you." The reply was immediate, and Nickel assessed the man who spoke as Cashman with a start. The tall fellow—the one Marbles forced to buy his luck to make it rain—was none other than Creede Cashman, owner of the Middle C Ranch.

"No time," Bannack said, raiding the pantry. "You got Catherine to think of. I ain't got nobody." He twisted a sack in his grip and turned around. "Gonna borrow a horse," he said. "If I don't come back, you know where to find it."

"Bannack!" Creede's protest went unheeded.

"I'm coming along," a man with sandy-blond hair, streaked with soot, said. This time Bannack didn't respond.

"I'll r-ride too," Marbles said, but Bannack bucked at that with a vehemence that startled them all.

"The hell you will! Somebody's gotta stay with the Indianolans."

"Not me!" Nickel cried out. "I'm ridin' with you!"

Bannack didn't even glance at him as he plowed through supplies he might need.

"You hear me, Bannack? I'm goin' too!"

"Better stay here, boy," the sandy-haired fellow said.

"No! He ain't left me behind. I ain't leavin' him."

Bannack looked at him then.

"It's Oren Wheeler, Nickel. He's the one who run off with my wife. You don't need to be around when I catch up with them."

"O-Oren?" Nickel spat the word. "*Oren?* It can't be!"

"I'm gonna kill him, Nickel." Bannack rushed out the door, scattering men in every direction. Marbles followed on the run, but Nickel grabbed Les's arm and the boys caught up with their awkward hero.

"You know I ain't stayin' put," he told Marbles. "If you leave me here, I'll just saddle up and ride your trail. It's Oren."

"*Oren Wheeler?*" Les had to run to keep up.

A thousand questions crowded Nickel's tongue, but there was no time for explanations.

Marbles seemed to understand Nickel's determination, for he offered a pair of fresh saddle horses bearing the Middle C brand.

He saddled his mount next to the legendary rider, and Les followed suit. Nickel had the forethought to grab his saddlebags and sling them over his saddle. By the time they mounted, Bannack and the Middle C man were specks on the horizon. Marbles called to them to ride swift.

Spurs touched flank, and Nickel and Les were streaking across the prairie on fleet horses, racing to catch the Pony Express rider come to life through their childhood storybooks.

Given any other circumstance, he would have whooped aloud for the sheer joy. He was riding his dream—why the hell did Oren Wheeler have to go and ruin it?

Les, faithful friend he was, neither asked questions nor complained; he just rode Nickel's shadow. When the trio caught up with Bannack and the other cowboy, Bannack yelled out at them.

"Soon as you lag behind, we're leavin' you!"

Nickel didn't intend to lag anywhere. Despite his riding companion, sickening thoughts swirled around in the pit of his belly. He wanted to purge himself, but the truth wouldn't leave him. It was his fault. He'd never make it up to his friend.

After everything he'd done for him, for his family, and now in this horrid twist of fate, his wife had burned him to the ground and run off with Oren Wheeler, Nickel's own father.

Nickel rode hard, but in truth, he didn't dare to peer at Bannack without bile rising in his throat. He would likely never forgive Nickel for the role he played in his destruction. How could he?

☙

He did not think to question how Bannack knew where they were going. Maybe it had something to do with the deeds stolen from his safe, or maybe he just knew his wife. Whatever the reason, the chase led them northwest to the outskirts of a tiny town called Coldwater Station.

It was a full two days' ride, but the cowboy who rode with them said they made record time in reaching the town, for they didn't stop except to rest the horses.

The first night was short, and Bannack camped alone, his back to his friends. He did not lay out a bedroll, nor did he eat or sleep. He just sat by his horse and waited for the first star to disappear in the sky so they could mount up and ride on.

The sandy-haired man spoke to Nickel and Les in low, hushed tones. "Never introduced myself," he said. "JC Sterling, foreman of the Middle C." He sighed. "Thanks to your help, I still have a ranch to manage."

"What's gonna happen when he finds his wife?" Les asked.

"Gunplay, more than likely, and that's why I'm along. Bannack doesn't pull the weight I do with lawmen and judges. If he gets himself in trouble, he'll need a friend he can trust."

"Then he's got three more," Les said.

Nickel agreed but could not speak around the glob of guilt stuck in his craw. As had become routine, he did not sleep that night. They were supposed to be tucked into their new bunkhouse, slumbering away the drudgery of the journey, dreaming of their new life on the ranch.

Instead, here he was in the middle of a dark prairie without town or family, reeling from his own losses and left to suffer watching his hero battle the consequences of their friendship.

# CHAPTER 34

# ONE VERMIN DOWN

The slumped shoulders of Bannack did not alter when they mounted a few hours later. Pursuit continued with not a word spoken, not until they reached the tiny town of Coldwater Station. If they were there, it wouldn't take long to find them, Nickel decided.

Coldwater was about as big as a minute, having sprung up around a well with exceptionally cold water, hence the name.

They partook of the namesake and watered the horses. As the horses drank, the cowboys held a rapid-fire discussion. They reached a decision, for Sterling held his finger in Bannack's face.

"You'd do well to let me do the talking."

Tightlipped, Bannack gave the foreman a look of death and shoved his finger aside.

Bannack, Sterling, and Marbles led their mounts to a crooked building across the street and half-hitched the reins around a post.

"What is that place?" Nickel whispered to Les.

"Shingle says LAND OFFICE."

That a town as piddly as Coldwater Station even had a land office surprised Nickel, yet there it was, complete with its crooked shingle hanging from one nail.

Bannack stormed inside despite JC Sterling's repeated warnings to keep a civil tongue. The boys followed on his heel. Nickel hoped they looked tough and forbidding, but the man behind the desk didn't look scared. He just looked offended.

Crinkling his nose, the middle-aged fellow glared at them from over the top of his wire-rimmed glasses. He wore a crisp, starched collared shirt and an expression that looked to be preserved in the brine of a pickle barrel. Clearly, the man knew little of hard labor, riding around in his upholstered desk chair all day.

"I hope you're not dragging your filth across my floor."

Bannack slammed his palms on the desk. Dust and black grime fell from his clothes, showering the man's paperwork.

"Hey!" he shouted.

"What I drag in here depends on you, Mister," Bannack snarled. "A woman named Aurelie Bannack, was she in here? Probably with a big barreled oaf named Oren Wheeler."

"People come and go," the man shot back, shuffling his papers to shake the offending dirt from their pages.

Bannack dug in his vest pocket, pulled out a tintype, and tossed it on the desk. "That's her."

"You know, a pig farmer waddled in the other day. Even he was cleaner'n you boys, and I doubt he'd seen a bath in a year."

With snakelike precision, Bannack pulled his revolver and grabbed the man by the back of the neck, pulling him across his own desk.

"Look at the damn likeness!" he ordered. The clerk sputtered, and his eyes glazed over.

"Easy," JC warned his friend. The foreman remained calm and spoke in a cool, friendly tone that belied the heady situation. "We're lookin' for the woman in the picture," he explained. "We'd be obliged if you'd have a look and tell us if she's been in here with deeds to a parcel of land."

"Tell him to take that gun out of my ear!" Beads of sweat formed above his lip.

"Look at the picture, and then we'll talk about the gun."

The man picked up the tintype with quivering fingers. Nickel feared he might drop it, and then Bannack probably would shoot him.

"She . . . she was here earlier. You missed her by a few hours. Sold me a nice parcel. Paid a premium for it too."

"Uh-huh. And what was the name on the deed?"

"Her husband's name, of course."

"What was the damn name?" Bannack shouted.

"I don't remember!" He flinched. "How do you expect a man to think straight with a gun pointed at his head?"

"You won't remember nothin' ever again, you don't start talkin'."

"Gentlemen," JC said. "Now, Mister, you work with a lot of deeds, so I'll give you the benefit of the doubt. However, it being a sale so valuable, and so new, surely you recall the name?"

The man gulped, his eyes bulging like a frog in a frying pan.

"Now, this is Mr. Charlie Bannack. It's his wife we're chasing. She stole the deed and used that other bloke to fool you into buying that parcel. The land wasn't hers to sell, sir. We need to know where she went, and we need that deed back."

The man behind the desk stared at the gun, then at Bannack.

"Your wife, huh? You say she ran off with that other feller?"

"She did."

"Huh. And I wonder why!" the clerk said, narrowing his eyes at Bannack.

"Don't shoot him. Not yet." JC rolled up his sleeves. "Now see? That's the kind of talk that's gonna give you a headache."

He stepped forward, and before Nickel could blink, the foreman grabbed the man by the hair and slammed his head against the edge of the desk. The clerk crumbled in a heap, and JC stepped around him, rifling through drawers.

In short order, he found what he was looking for and handed the deed to Bannack.

"Here's the bill of sale too. Might wanna be careful it don't get torn or burned up," he suggested.

Putting his revolver away, Bannack snatched the paper, crumbled it in his hand, and tossed it into the little cook stove. The flames flared up, engulfing the paper before their eyes, and, having little else to burn, died back down.

"Got enough papers to warm the coffee?" Bannack asked.

"Aww, too bad we can't stay for a cup," JC replied. He wrote a note, laid it on the desk in front of the bloodied desk rider, and grinned at his friend.

"One vermin down," he said. Bannack stalked outside to where Marbles was waiting and bumped his head on the swinging shingle. With a curse that would put the best Indianola sailors to shame, he grabbed the sign, ripped it off its hinge, and threw it in the dirt as he mounted.

Nickel and Les stood on the steps, blinking. They shuffled aside as JC sauntered past and mounted his own horse.

"Well? You boys coming or not?"

Glancing at his best friend, Nickel shrugged.

"Come on, Les. I don't wanna fall behind."

"I sure don't wanna make Mr. Sterling mad," Les said, "but I wish we'd stayed at the Mercy ranch."

&#x2183;

JC Sterling nosed around and learned a man and woman fitting Oren's and Aurelie's descriptions had just holed up outside of town. They had taken refuge in a little cabin, built and abandoned by a family who could not make a go of farming the land or battling the elements.

With the death of the wife, the man wandered off and no one ever heard from him again, leaving the cabin open to road-weary travelers.

They eased down the road, yet much too quickly for Nickel's stomach. He was about to come face-to-face with Oren Wheeler. Last time he had, Nickel had pulled the trigger on him. Oh, why had he missed? He could not afford the luxury of missing again—Oren would not think twice about killing his own son.

# CHAPTER 35

# AURELIE

Winded and exhausted, Nickel struggled to see through a burning haze. Soot and heat from the fire seared his eyes, and he ached for relief. He wanted to tear up and relieve the burn, but there was nothing left. No tears, no moisture. Only pain, and an unbearable desire to lie down and sleep.

He'd sleep for a whole month if he could. Maybe he would, after Bannack's affairs were settled. Then, too, he had his own demon to deal with.

It was no ordinary man they were chasing. Oh, no, it was Oren Wheeler. How the sea had not purged him from her breast, Nickel couldn't figure, but if she wouldn't do it, he'd do the job himself.

"Should'a killed him the first time," Nickel muttered. He hadn't realized he had spoken aloud until he felt the eyes of his companions on him.

"Killing isn't an easy thing," JC Sterling said. "Hardens a man. Look at Bannack."

"Even if it's deserved?"

The foreman nodded, but Nickel wasn't ready to accept such sage advice. Not from a man he didn't even know—cowboy or not.

"Well, wished I would've kilt him anyhow. I mean to do it when we catch up with him."

This time, it was Bannack who snapped. Drawing rein, the cowboy spun in his saddle. "No." His gruff voice startled Nickel, for the man had barely uttered a word since they left on this crazy wife hunt.

"You've seen enough. Be damned if I let you take a chance on Wheeler. You might falter. He won't. Better you know now, he's gonna die today, son. By my hand. Maybe you ain't thought it through, what that means to you. Maybe you have. Either way, Wheeler's seen his last sunrise."

Bannack loped onward, for the little cabin built into a hill loomed ahead. Nickel followed, chewing on the meaning Bannack planted for him.

"He's gonna kill him," Les said as he rode alongside. "Oren's still your Pa—"

"No, he ain't either! I ain't a Wheeler, you hear me? I'm a Bannack. He said so."

The boys looked to the cowboy disappearing over a hill.

"He might think he's gonna kill him," he muttered under his breath.

"Nickel, no! What're you gonna do?" Les reached over to pluck at Nickel's sleeve. He shook him off.

*Damn Les and his good hearing!* Les Harold could hear a mouse sneeze in a haystack.

"I dunno, but if I get the chance, I'm takin' it." Nickel sat straighter in the saddle, holding his chin high, preparing for the inevitable argument to follow.

"Don't. Don't do nothin' dumb. Bannack's right, don't you know that? He'll kill you."

Leaning to the side of the saddle, Nickel spat on the ground. "I guess I ain't survived drownin' three times just to be wiped out by the likes of Oren Wheeler. He ain't got my luck."

"Maybe your luck's run out, Nickel. Ain't you ever thought of that?" Les clenched his jaw and scowled at his best friend.

"You sound like *her.*"

"Maybe she was right! You sold it off all these years, and the town got wiped off the map. What if she was right? What if you sold it all away?"

Nickel shrugged, his eyes searching the little town, already looking for his nemesis. He had supposed him dead. Otherwise, Oren would have come back before now to seek revenge for shooting him.

Why now, after all these years? And of all the places he could land, of all the women he could run off with, how in the bloody hell had he tangled up with Bannack's wife?

"Nickel?" Les was staring at him, an expression of worry and doubt smeared across his face.

"You worry too much," Nickel told his friend. It was their age-old argument, so he knew what the reply would be before the words left Les's lips.

"You don't, so somebody's got to!"

"Maybe my luck's gone sour," he mused, "but I'm bettin' it ain't."

"It's an awful heavy bet," Les argued.

Nickel's mind snapped back to the dime novel, and their favorite line supposedly uttered from the mouth of Mustang Grey himself.

"Maybe I'll die today, maybe I won't. No use waitin' 'round to find out."

Spurring his mount on the path of Bannack's trail to seal Oren's fate, he heard Les yelling after him, scrambling to catch up.

"Luck or no, you ain't Mustang Grey, Nickel! You hear me? You ain't Mustang Grey!"

Bannack and Sterling reined in under the protection of a little copse of trees and bid Nickel and Les do the same.

As they did, they ventured to the edge of the clearing on foot and peered out. Smoke hung like a cloud in the air from the stone chimney. Someone clutched his shirt, and he looked down at an ashen-hued hand. Les.

"You look awful," Les said.

"You just now figured that out?" His best friend was still covered in soot, dried sweat, and grime—in two days, they hadn't done more than grind the mess into their skin with grubby hands and arms. They looked—and smelled—like a little group of forest trolls that hadn't been introduced to a bar of lye soap. Small wonder their presence offended the land office man.

෨

It took Bannack and Marbles only a few minutes to find the best vantage point overlooking the dug-out cabin. Easing to the edge of the hill and crawling into a little swale, they positioned themselves as close as they could, with the sun at their backs. If anybody meant to shoot at them, they'd have to burn their eyeballs to do it.

"What do we do now?" Les asked nobody in particular.

"We w-wait," Marbles replied.

"Wait for what?"

Bannack shook his head. "No good. We wait too long, the sun'll set behind us, and we'll be silhouetted against the sky."

Nickel was beyond waiting. Oren Wheeler escaped death once before . . .

he might do it again. As the men talked among themselves, he saw the cabin door open. They froze, watching their prey walk out to a stack of firewood.

"Th-That him?" Marbles asked, lowering his voice.

"That's the bastard," Bannack whispered back.

Marbles nodded, his keen eyes watching Oren's every move as he collected a few sticks of fuel. "You th-think it's j-just the t-t-two of them?" he asked.

Bannack gripped his rifle, slowly bringing it into place. "I reckon they're alone," he said. "I figure we'll—"

A shot interrupted Bannack's plan. He ducked low, then rolled to face the sound.

"Goddammit, nobody was watchin' Nickel!" he yelled at Marbles.

"M-M-Missed," the cowboy stuttered, pointing. Nickel's shot had struck a split Oren was carrying. Firewood flew as he ran, hell-bent, to the dug-out and disappeared inside.

"You couldn't have waited?" Bannack asked, flinging a slew of hardened words upon Nickel's head. "Sonofabitch! We could've lured 'em both out! Now they'll hole up and we'll never get 'em out!" He punched at the ground in front of them.

"You said it wasn't no good to wait!" Nickel protested. "I ain't takin' chances on missin' him again!"

"You just did miss, boy, and now we've lost our edge." JC observed Nickel with a frown and a shake of his head. "I thought you said he wasn't a hot-head?" he asked Bannack.

"No, I said he wasn't loco," came the retort.

The report of a shotgun split the air, and a hunk of sod flew up down below and way off to the right. They ducked down again, for Oren had chosen to shoot rather than hide.

"Well, from the look of that shot, he don't know where we are." Bannack seemed relieved.

To his left, Marbles flattened out, gripping his revolver, and waiting for direction. Not that he needed any. Marbles knew what needed doing. The only question left to answer was how to do it.

"Hey, cowboy! You hear me out there?" Oren Wheeler's voice carried across the yard to grate on their ears.

Bannack turned his head toward Nickel, positioned on his belly to his right. The boy's visage darkened, and he scrambled to jump to his feet.

With a quick grab, Bannack yanked him back and pinned him to the ground. "You stay down!"

"Been screwin' your wife, cowboy!" Oren yelled from the safety of the front porch. "She's a damned fine lay, but you ain't gonna want her back, you hear me? She's done had a better man between her legs now. She don't want you!" Oren went on, yelling all the vulgar details of his trysts with Aurelie.

Bannack squirmed, trying in vain to drown out the voice, but it was Marbles who grabbed the back of his neck and held him facedown in the bank, much like he was doing to Nickel.

"B-Baitin' you, Bannack. R-Raise your head and he-he'll blow it off," the cowboy warned with a low growl. "He d-don't know who we g-got with us, so let's use him."

"Ain't usin' Nickel as bait!" Bannack shot back.

"Nope, but no-nobody knows Oren Wheeler b-better'n Nickel. Don't pay mind to that f-f-foulmouthed b-bastard. Listen to Nickel."

The boy wriggled free and rolled to his side.

"What do I do?"

"Is he a good shot?" Bannack asked Nickel.

"Dunno. He ain't had much use for guns before now. I don't guess he's ever used one till the day I shot him. He ain't smart like you, Bannack, but that don't mean he can't hit us, neither."

"Even if he ain't a g-g-good sh-shot, Aurelie is, ain't s-she?" Marbles asked.

"She oughta be—I taught her."

The bitter irony was not lost on Marbles, nor was it lost on the Indianola boys.

"What kind of woman did you hitch up with, anyhow?"

Bannack glanced at his young protégé, then peered over the swale. Oren was standing on the porch, his rifle ready, but it was the figure in the cabin window that sickened him. There she was, her long tresses askew as usual, pointing a double barrel out the window.

"The damned devil, boy." He gritted his teeth. "I married the damned devil."

"Oren Wheeler's a sonofabitch," Les said. "Maybe he kidnapped her."

Bannack shook his head. "Ain't no kidnappin' about it."

A quick peek over the swale revealed Oren going inside. He slammed the door as though to announce his disappearance, and the men frowned. He wasn't giving up. What was he up to?

"We'll split up," JC suggested. He, too, was stretched on his belly, taking refuge behind the swale.

"I can work around to the back of the house—" Bannack started to say, but JC shook his head.

"They'll expect it."

"Well, I don't see as we have much choice," Bannack replied. "They can hole up for days."

"Not if something drives them out," Nickel interrupted.

"Like what?" JC Sterling asked. His voice was thick with sarcasm. "We get close, and they'll shoot us down, kid."

"Not if they don't see us," Nickel replied, eyeing the foreman with disgust.

JC rolled his eyes skyward and swore. "I swear, Bannack. Couldn't you find a boy gifted with smarts? This one's real good at pointing out the obvious."

"Shut your damn mouth, Sterling!" Bannack said with a snarl. Tilting his head toward Nickel, he asked in a softer tone, "Whatcha got?"

"If I can reach my saddlebags and get to that roof, I can make 'em forget all about us."

"To the roof?" Bannack studied the cabin nestled in the side of the hill.

"Yep. They got a fire goin' in there."

"So?"

"So, I got a little present we could give 'em." Nickel grinned at his hero.

"What?" Bannack asked, narrowing his eyes.

"Bangers," Nickel said with pride.

"Bangers? What are bangers?" JC asked.

Nickel screwed up his face and sniffed back a nostril full of soot.

"Bangers, fire sticks, those ones what whistle and explode."

"*Dammit Nickel!* You've been carryin' dynamite in your saddlebags?" Bannack reached out and slapped the side of his head.

"Ain't like dynamite sticks or nothin'. They're just the kind you celebrate with."

"Where in the fiery hell did you get—never mind." Bannack rubbed his forehead. "I don't wanna know."

"Mr. Bannack, sir?" Les interrupted. "Nickel, he dropped a handful of bangers into someone's chimney once and cleared the place out quick."

The cowboys—Bannack, Marbles, and JC Sterling—all lay in a row gaping at him.

"What?" Nickel asked, shrugging. "It was an accident."

"I'll bet," Bannack muttered.

Marbles snorted. "You're all r-right, kid."

They turned their sights to the grove of trees behind them. Inside, the horses were tied up and waiting. They were on a bit of a hill, enough to warrant cover so long as they kept low.

Bannack mulled the notion over, measuring the distance between themselves and the cabin. He studied the roof and glanced at Nickel's leg.

"How's that ankle?"

"Fine," Nickel said.

"Can you run on it?"

"Nothin' to it."

"Don't you lie to me."

"I can do it, Bannack."

Without warning, the cowboy reached out, grabbed hold of his ankle, and gave it a good yank. Nickel came off the ground and swallowed a yelp.

"Uh-huh," Bannack growled. "Here's how it's gonna go. We'll use your distraction, Nickel, but you ain't climbin' no roof. You can't get outta there fast enough. You retreat to the horses and stay there."

Nickel started to raise a fuss, but Bannack's visage left no room for argument.

"Horses! Somebody needs to guard them. You leave those beasts, and I'll lay the tar to you myself!"

He turned to Les.

"Harold, I'll get you cleared to circle behind. The cabin's dug into that nice hill, so you should be able to walk that grassy roof without them hearin', long as you walk soft. See how that hill slopes down in the back? Easy enough for retreat. Once you drop those firecrackers, I want you runnin'. You run off that dug-out, straight for the trees, and stick with the horses. Sterling, he'll have your back. Don't you slow down. I don't care what you hear behind you. Get up there, light 'em up, and get down—quick. Can you do that?"

Les's face turned three shades of green, but he scrubbed his hands on his shirt and then clenched them into fists. "How do I light them, sir?"

"You don't need to. I reckon once those firecrackers hit that fire, they'll blow."

"Yessir," he said. "Marbles, you stick between Nickel and the cabin. Nobody goes inside but me. Chances are the smoke'll keep me from seein' clear, and I don't want to shoot one of you instead. If anyone sees my wife or Wheeler run out, cut 'em down."

"I can't shoot at a woman!" Nickel protested.

"You'll be with the horses, dammit! You won't be shootin'."

"But if . . . if somethin' goes wrong . . ." Les said, tripping over his fear.

"Then use your head, boys. If I fall, she'll kill you both, and Marbles too, given the chance. It's your lives or hers. She ain't worth it. You boys are." He gave Les Harold his last instructions.

"No noise," he whispered. "Don't let them hear you till you throw those firecrackers, then you run like hell off that hill. Nickel will be waitin' in the trees."

"Anything else, sir?"

A dark grin formed. "Don't blow yourself up."

Les Harold's eyes widened, and Bannack's stomach clenched. Les Harold was not built like his best friend. He was too fearful to be a risk-taker. Maybe he should have let Nickel prove his skill regardless of a bad ankle. He was crazy enough to pull it off. But Les? They were doomed.

The great cowboy turned to Marbles.

"Grey? If they kill me, they'll cut him down if they can," he said, gesturing to Nickel.

"I'll take c-care of it, B-Bannack," Marbles promised.

They transferred his bangers to Les's trembling fingers, and Marbles forced him to crawl to the rear of the group.

"Y-You get to the h-horses," he ordered.

"No. It's my business much as it's his."

Marbles grabbed his arm. Laid flat on their bellies like worms, he still posed an intimidating threat. "You b-been told who I am. I p-proved it, didn't I?"

"Yessir, but—" Nickel started to argue, but Marbles cut him off with a rough hand clapped over his mouth.

"Figure y-y-you owe me—M-Mustang Grey—a f-favor," he said, and released him.

"Aww! That ain't fair." His complaint was shooed away with a firm hand gesture.

"N-Nickel, you st-stick to those h-horses today. I'll teach you ev-everything I know."

Nickel gritted his teeth. There was only one thing he wanted more than killing Oren Wheeler with his bare hands, and Mustang Grey himself had just named it.

He wiggled his way toward the tree line and slipped into the woods, where their horses were waiting.

From his rear vantage point, he saw Marbles ahead. He had watched until he was certain Nickel was safe, then his gaze swiveled forward, where Bannack was preparing Les for his run.

"That oughta be me," Nickel said with a growl. "Les don't like takin' risks."

Imp stood tethered nearby, dozing, and flicked an ear at him. He watched, helpless, as his best friend made a wide, rounded circle. He came almost as far as the tree line, and Nickel had to plant his feet to keep from running out to try to switch places.

Les moved away, angling for the hill that made up the cabin's back wall. Reaching what should be the roof, he dropped to his hands and knees and inched slowly toward the chimney. Nickel swore he could hear Les's heart pounding.

He made it to the roof and dropped to his hands and knees. Here he inched toward the chimney.

Nickel had lost sight of Bannack, but then the cowboy popped up under the porch roof, adjusting his neck rag over his nose. He'd need it if their plan worked.

Tilting his head upward, he gripped the revolver in his hand, knelt by the door, and waited.

03

Bannack watched the young Indianolan duck under Nickel's haversack and face his task with trembling hands.

The cowboy pulled his neck rag over his nose and mouth and positioned himself by the door, revolver ready. Waiting.

He could no longer see Les or the roof. Where was the explosion? Moments were ticking by. What the hell was going on up there? He could just see Sterling peeking out over the top of a discarded whiskey barrel, watching the roofline over his head.

Sterling nodded at the roof, and Les Harold let go. At first, nothing happened. Just as Bannack began to worry Nickel's bangers were duds, he heard his wife's voice cry of alarm from inside the dug-out.

"What's *that*?"

The tiny shelter erupted in chaos. Pops, whistles, cracks, and screams accompanied the detonations. Bannack heard Aurelie shrieking over the din. Hundreds of little fireballs bounced around inside the dug-out and shot out the front windows. Soot and smoke puffed out of every crack in the cabin wall.

Not expecting such a spectacle, Bannack hesitated before breaking inside, hiding in plain sight against the wall.

Nickel's firecrackers did their job well, blowing the hot coals in the fireplace out into the room where small flames were leaping to life, fueled by dried-out walls and floorboards. He could not see his enemy, but they were too busy coughing and hacking to notice him, either.

Aurelie was still screaming. "My dress is on fire! Help me!"

He caught sight of her then, twisting to beat at the flames licking up her voluminous skirts. With her preoccupied, he shot toward the sound of Oren Wheeler's cough, ducked, and moved.

Wheeler, still blinded by smoke, returned random fire.

"Stop shooting! Stop, you'll hit me!" she cried.

Bannack fired again, and the howl Oren Wheeler set up told him he hit his mark.

Aurelie rushed for the open door, but Bannack caught her by the waist, threw her down, and stamped out the fire consuming her skirts.

"You go outside, and the boys'll cut you down," he told her.

"Bannack? Bannack? Is that you?" All at once her voice was soft and searching. She struggled to rise, her nose pointed toward fresh air in the open doorway.

"My darlin' Aurelie," Bannack crooned, his voice dripping with sarcasm. "I should've let you burn."

"Bannack! Oh, but I've missed you. He kidnapped me, love. He took me, made me do it all! I didn't want to leave you!"

"Shut up, you lying bitch!" Oren yelled from inside the wall of sulfurous smoke and flame. His cough rattled his throat. He was hard hit; Bannack could hear it in his voice.

"It's true, Bannack. You know I love you! He took me, ravaged me! Kill him, and let's go home, my husband."

Aurelie regained her feet, coughing into a hidden hand. As she turned, a glint of metal caught a ray of sunlight. Her eyes flashed as she struck him. Bannack let out a yell and crumpled to the floor, but he twisted to fire into the shadow of the hulking man somewhere behind him.

Bannack's .44 slug found its mark, slamming through the chest of Oren Wheeler. He swiveled, ready to fire again, but Aurelie had the upper hand. Her shadow loomed over him, her blade poised to strike again. Despite the smoke-filled room, this time, she would not miss.

Bannack fingered the trigger but did not pull.

"Aurelie," he pleaded, "have you no love in your blood? I'm your husband."

She laughed at him. "You're as loyal as a dog," she cried. "I hate dogs!" She let out a shriek, and the knife in her fingers gleamed.

Clutching his side, Bannack felt blood ooze between his fingertips. He mashed down on the trigger, but the knife had already dropped from her hand. He heard it clatter to the floor.

Aurelie sank, a dagger stuck to the hilt in her chest. A second stain grew from his bullet, which had lodged in her belly. But where had the dagger come from?

Aurelie's breathing was labored, but her gaze remained riveted upon the open doorway. He looked up and sickened at the sight.

A silhouette hovered in the doorway, bracing himself on one foot, brandishing an unfired Winchester saddle gun. The Indianolans said Nickel could sink a blade in the flesh of a gnat with a flick of the wrist. Bannack had supposed it to be exaggeration. Until now.

"Is Oren dead?" the young man asked.

Bannack blinked at the question, his mind still reeling from the reality of the situation.

Nickel walked into the room, bypassing Aurelie to get to his father. He stood over him, glaring down, and prodded the body with his rifle. Satisfied there was no life left, he turned and limped away back out into the sunshine. Nickel did not look back.

Bannack rose on his own, lifting his unresisting wife in his arms, and the Indianolan limped a few paces away.

He carried her into the daylight. She turned her head and gurgled when he laid her in the grass and knelt over her.

"Should've known my lovely wife carries a blade," he said, poking his fingers in the hole she had opened in his side. Bannack swore at her.

"The blade," she murmured.

Her fingers, slick with blood, tried to grasp it.

Spots of his blood dripped, mingling with hers.

"Someone . . . stabbed me. Was it you?"

"You just got done tellin' me you loved me, then you cut me," Bannack replied. "You fired our home! The ranch! Why?" He shook his head. "I don't understand, woman. Tell me why."

Aurelie raised her head and spat a wad of bloody froth in his face.

"I despise you! I hate . . . you."

"Dammit, Aurelie," he said, reaching to stroke her cheek.

"Don't you dare touch me! I'd rather be eaten by vultures than be buried by the likes of you."

She tried to shove him away, to fight him from her, but succeeded only in clawing at his face.

Bannack rocked back on his heels and watched the life drain from his wife's perfect, porcelain face. Her fingers fell free, still clenched in a clawed fist, her eyes sightlessly staring into the depths of chestnut-green flecked eyes she would never see again.

CHAPTER 36

# THE ANGEL AND THE DEMON

Nickel stood next to his horse, watching Bannack kneel, hatless, over his wife's body. Behind him, the dug-out cabin was burning. No one seemed to notice, or maybe it was just that nobody cared. Oren Wheeler's body was still in there. He knew that's where it would remain. The men would not pull him from the flames, nor would he. It was bad enough they had one hole to dig, but nobody cared to waste a droplet of sweat over Oren. Besides, Bannack would not want him buried anywhere near his wife, no matter what awful things she'd done.

Les walked up to him and grasped his forearm. Together, the boys watched the little cabin in the hill burn. How was a boy supposed to feel, standing over his sire's death? For that was all Oren was—a sire. Not a father, not a role model. Not even a friend. No sorrow for his killing: no one would ever shed a tear over his passing, nor would anyone miss him. Nickel hated his father for the things he had done. To him, and to his siblings. To his mother, and to Bannack. Oren Wheeler deserved to be buried in the ground—deeper than most, in the lonesome prairie soil. There would be no sea where Oren could rest in death, accompanied by the only female he ever loved—the Mistress.

The cowboy had won his battle, but the cost was too great. A few haggard steps, and he turned from the body of Aurelie Bannack and walked away. His horse followed. Old Joly's dagger was gone—someone had removed it from her chest.

Nickel didn't know her. Didn't understand her. Hell, he had barely seen her, except in death.

*Damn, she was beautiful.* Aurelie Bannack was probably the finest woman Nickel had ever seen, but the devil lived within her. A woman as fickle as the Mistress, and just as dangerous, for deceit and betrayal laced her heart. A woman like that would not go where his Magdalena went.

Magdalena had another chance at life—as a siren, perhaps, swimming the seas she longed to sail in life. He hoped, wherever she might be, that she remembered him. Thought of him—perhaps even longed for him as much as he ached for her. This woman, Aurelie, a beautiful name for a beastly female. He didn't know *what* she deserved.

"Nickel." Bannack's voice rasped like a blacksmith's file. The cowboy had doubled back, having spotted him. He offered Joly's dagger, handle first.

Nickel hesitated.

"Cleaned it up some. You hang onto that blade, son."

He stepped up beside him and stared down at his wife.

"You didn't listen worth a damn, but you still followed my order." He paused, rubbing a bloodstained palm across his face. "She would have killed me, Nickel. No one else knows what happened inside that door. Anyone asks, I shot and killed 'em both. It *stays* that way. I never want to hear this day mentioned again."

"Yessir," Nickel agreed. "Suits me fine." Without another word spoken, he watched his hero retreat, grief etched in every line of his face, and the slump of his shoulders.

CS

Nickel stood over Aurelie's grave, trying to think of something to say. Someone ought to say something, but JC Sterling and Marbles just stood there, heads down, gripping the ends of the spades they found behind the barn.

A strange sound coming from the burning cabin drew the attention of the small burial party, and they looked up. The fire had consumed the wooden structure while they dug the grave, and now the sod over the roof caved in, creating a landslide into the smoldering chasm below. Marbles flicked his gaze to Nickel, and he nodded at him.

Yes, he understood what that meant. Oren Wheeler had been buried, after all.

"I guess that'll be enough dirt to cover *him*," Nickel muttered.

Looking past Marbles's shoulder, he saw Bannack and his horse standing on the little hill, illuminated by the sinking sun. Ribbons of yellow, red, and gold streaked across the sky as though a painter spilled his pigments and swirled them around.

"It's a pretty evening," Nickel whispered.

JC looked up, glancing from him to the sky.

"Pretty evening to go to hell," he said, and dug the blade deep into the freshly turned earth. Nickel winced at the sound of the first shovelful of dirt as it rained down upon the body below. They didn't have time to secure a pine box. It didn't matter anyway, he supposed. Marbles picked up his spade and started shoveling.

Les Harold followed suit, but Nickel kept his eyes trained on the lone figure on the hill. He followed his wife's last request: not to be present at her burial. What sort of woman hates her husband that much?

Later, as they waited for Marbles to sew up Bannack's wound so they could leave, Nickel voiced his question to the Middle C Ranch foreman, JC Sterling.

"Aurelie. I don't understand her. What kind of woman stabs her own husband?"

"The same kind who burns his ranch to the ground and runs off with some low-life seafaring cur," Sterling replied.

Nickel stiffened and puffed his chest.

"Low-life seafarin' cur," he repeated, tasting the words as he spat them out.

"You were supposed to stay with the horses," the foreman said, changing the subject.

Nickel licked his lips. *Ahh, the making of a fine argument.*

"Yeah, and if I listened, we would've been buryin' Bannack," Nickel said, cross over the sea-faring cur remark. "So you ain't gonna lecture me none, you fluffed-up, speechifyin' prairie-dweller."

The ranch foreman jerked his head back, and Nickel inwardly chuckled at the startled expression in the man's green eyes. Outwardly, he prepared for battle.

Sterling folded his arms across his chest. When he spoke, his tone seemed guarded, as though holding back.

"You ever talk to Bannack like that, kid?"

"I ain't scared of him anymore'n you," Nickel said. "I'm just drawin' the lines."

"Keep it up, and you will draw yourself out of a job."

Nickel grinned at the Middle C foreman with the strange, formal way of talking.

"I ride for Bannack. I'll work *with* just about anybody, but I only ride for Bannack."

The foreman rested a hand on his waist and stared at him as though trying to decide how best to handle the sharp tongue of the young Indianolan.

"L-Let it ride, S-Sterlin'," Marbles called. "He's right. L-Let's just go home."

Before they left, they piled more rocks on Aurelie's grave but left no marker. The lonesome silhouette turned and mounted. Slowly, he rode down off the hill, heading south. The others followed, leaving one lonely grave and a scarred, burned cabin in their wake.

Nickel did not look back at Oren Wheeler's resting place, though his father would never rest. Nickel had his final say, waged his last war against Oren, and came out on top. He did not think twice about throwing that blade, though he thought plenty about who he hit. If he hadn't slipped off and disobeyed the cowboy's orders, Bannack might have been buried next to his awful, beautiful wife.

It was a long, silent return to the ranch. No longer encumbered by rapid chase, they took their time, giving Bannack the lead. The man slumped in the saddle, his head down, looking neither right nor left.

For the two-day journey home, he stopped only to rest his horse. He did not eat, just rode. As they neared the ranch well after dark, Marbles trotted ahead, drawing in to ride by Bannack's side.

Nickel spurred his mount, eager to show his hero he would not be alone.

*Something's wrong.*

Smoke from the fire was still heavy in the air, but no, that did not bother him. No one was where they were supposed to be. Nickel could taste it, the odor of devastation. It had a raw, heady scent, and he knew it well.

The hair prickled on the back of his neck, and he looked to the shadows of the men riding beside him.

Marbles and JC had perked up, casting about in the dark. They found no one in the barn—not so unusual, for at this time of night they should have been nestled in their bunks.

Bannack, too, seemed to pick up on the sense of impending doom, for he jerked his horse in motion and lit a shuck to the main house. The others followed. By the time they reached the Cashman Homestead, they saw multitudes of shadows lingering on the front porch. The ranch hands and wranglers were hatless, and their bare heads hung low. Nickel thought they looked like a pack of dejected dogs, chastised for bad behavior.

They parted for Bannack, for JC and Marbles, even for Nickel and Les. Lanterns and oil lamps had been lit inside the ranch.

*Too quiet.*

The house had the stink of death, and it turned his stomach. Les bumped into his back. He smelled it too, for his hand was clamped over his nose. They followed the flickering lights into the master bedroom where they found Creede Cashman.

The rancher sat, his arms and upper body draped over a shrouded figure in the bed. Catherine Cashman lay in perfect pose, dressed in white, her feet bare, her hair cascading across her shoulders as though in sleep. Her right hand still rested in Creede's own, and he gripped it as though he would never let go.

He turned his head, glancing up at them, and Nickel looked away from the agony of the man's beseeching stare. He had been wrong. Aurelie Bannack was hideous compared to Catherine Cashman. She looked so angelic, she might as well sprout wings and fly into the heavens.

Tears gripped him. Before he could step forward, Bannack knelt by the bedside. He held his hat against his chest and lowered his head to pray, much as he did for Magdalena back in Indianola. When Bannack raised his head, Nickel spotted tracks of salt water leaking down his cheeks.

"She's not ill anymore," he whispered.

Creede started to reply, but his voice broke and the two men gripped each other's shoulders in soundless grief. Both men lost their wives, but only one was worth the price of tears.

Bannack rose and tore from the room, his boots pounding down the hall to disappear into the night.

Nickel started to follow, but Marbles yanked him back with a shake of his head. Great fat tears slid down the cowboy's nose, and he stepped forward, kneeling before Creede and the bed. His shoulders shook, and the awkward hero hid his face in his hands.

Nickel could not move forward, nor could he find his feet to turn around. The purity of Catherine's rest mesmerized him. Did she feel no pain? Was that what Magdalena looked like now? An angel, shielding him from danger? Maybe Catherine would be Creede's luck now, just as he knew Magdalena was his.

He felt a tap on his shoulder and retreated from the room, past the porch full of mourning cowboys, and out into the night.

Indianola images crept into his mind, and Nickel ran from the house, unable to watch yet another senseless loss. He searched for Bannack but did not know his way around the ranch in the dark.

Instead, he walked. For an hour, maybe two, he limped, forgoing his oar and using a large stick as a cane.

Nickel walked on foot, ignoring the protest of his ankle. He circled the perimeter of the ranch corrals until his feet grew weary and he collapsed in a heap in the grass where he screamed and raged at the blackness of night. Nickel screamed at God for taking away so many people. Indianola. Magdalena and his siblings. Old Joly, wherever he had gone. Friends. Relatives. Strangers.

He felt little remorse for Oren Wheeler but bled for Bannack's pain regarding his wife, and the part he played in her demise.

And Catherine Cashman. Oh, bloody hell, what was happening? The world seemed to be ending.

"Why can't I protect them?" he shouted at the stars. "You can't keep givin' me luck if I can't protect them!"

Nickel tore at his pockets, searching for something to throw. He wanted to hit something, to cause pain. Something physical, something to take away all the loss and misery. His fingers closed around something within the lining of his coat pocket, and he pulled it out and made ready to throw. It seemed warm and familiar in his hand, and he felt of it in his palm.

The laundress back in Victoria. She had given him the dropped nickel.

"Damn lot of good it did me!" he shouted and reared his hand back to throw. The grass rustled beside him, and something soft scratched at his leg. He let out a yelp, reining in his fist. Two yellow eyes peered at him in the dark, and the thing clambered up on his chest and licked his face.

He lifted it in the air, squinting, and blew a sigh of relief.

"You," he told Bannack's little pup, "scared the shit out of me, you wild little furball."

The wolf-dog snapped its jaws at him as though in play and wriggled out of his grasp. Pulling on his pant leg, it sank needled teeth into his flesh.

"Ouch! Quit that!" He reached for her, but she bounded a few steps away, then turned and ran back, latching onto his leg again. She pulled and tugged, dodging him when he tried to grab her, always to bound off and come right back.

Curious, Nickel stood up, pocketing his nickel, and followed. The dog snapped her jaw at him again and bounced through the grass. She became easier to follow as they crossed over into the burned-out fields encompassing Bannack's land. With no vegetation to lose such a little animal, he sped up.

The little wolf seemed bent on a mission, so he followed her. She stopped, snapping her jaws, and Nickel looked. There was Bannack, staggering around the shell of his former home. He held a bottle in one hand and appeared to be searching for something. He tripped and fell to his knees and sat where he fell, burying his face in his hands. Nickel watched his friend but made no move to venture closer. Grief was too deep, too personal; it didn't seem right to rob him of doing it alone.

"Come on, pup," he whispered. "Let's go back." The pup raised her hackles and snapped at the air.

"What is that? Why don't you make any noise?" he asked her. She worked the air, sniffing for something, and it wasn't Bannack. Her head turned to the right, and Nickel's gaze followed.

At first, he saw nothing. Then, movement along the copse of trees near

Bannack's burned-out cabin. Nickel thought it might be a trick of the mind, but then something emerged into the open.

Hovering in a crouch, the thing watched the unsuspecting cowboy. It took a few steps and froze, watching its prey: Bannack.

Nickel squinted, trying to sense what it was—a coyote? But no, it moved too awkward, and in another moment, it snuck out into the pale moonlight over open ground. He realized it was no animal at all. It was a man.

The figure knelt, squatting in the burned-out ground, watching for signs of movement on Bannack's part. The cowboy never would have let anyone get so close to him sober, but that bottle looked empty, and his grief had overwhelmed his senses.

*Dammit! Who is that? Why's he look so familiar?* It gnawed at the edges of his brain. The man turned, only slightly, but that three-quarter view was more than enough.

Nickel pulled his dagger. He did not have a sound body, but Alastor did. He saw the blade clutched in his hand, and he knew the intent. Murder.

"Another Wheeler's gonna die today," he whispered into the wind, and started down the hill. He uttered not a single sound.

Alastor, intent on his oblivious prey, did not see Nickel until he barreled right into him, knocking him off his feet. He sliced at his foe, but his brother's hand caught his wrist and flung the weapon from his grip.

Nickel let out a warning yell but had no time to look for Bannack. Alastor was bigger, stronger, and he knew all of Nickel's weak points. Angry over losing the opportunity to plunge his blade into Bannack's throat, Alastor Wheeler took his rage out on his little brother, fighting, kicking, biting, and clawing. He plunged his fists into Nickel's raw back and kicked at his shoulder, trying to jerk it back out of place.

He rolled and fought but could not gain enough strength to do much damage. Alastor threw him to the ground, rolled, and snatched Nickel's dagger. "I'm gonna kill you with your own blade," he snarled, and jumped on Nickel's chest, spitting rage.

Nickel caught his brother's hands and yelled. His muscles throbbed and trembled as he tried to overpower those hands, but he was losing ground. Joly's blade moved closer and closer to his throat.

He thought again of Magdalena and wondered what it would be like to join her.

Before he could find out, he heard something streak through the air above him. It hit Alastor in the face, and he screamed. Nickel rolled as the knife dropped, but it did not hit him.

When he opened his eyes, he saw Bannack's form in the dark, running after Alastor. They disappeared into the trees, leaving Nickel struggling to sit up and catch his breath. He was spent. Done in. Losing Indianola, traveling while wounded and sleepless, fighting fire and men, gaining and losing women—it proved too great a toll.

Nickel floundered, unable to find his feet. If Alastor came back instead of Bannack, his brother would finish the job, but he knew it wouldn't come to fruition. Alastor would never get a second chance at Bannack.

As though proving his point, the cowboy reappeared carrying Joly's blade . . . with Alastor in tow.

# CHAPTER 37

# PATH OF THE DEVIL'S FRUIT

Bannack shoved the boy to the ground and loomed over him. Nickel thought the man looked rather like a rattlesnake: poised and ready to strike upon the slightest movement. Alastor seemed to think so too, for he did not get up.

Nickel reached for Bannack's hand, and he yanked him to his feet.

"If you're gonna kill me, I wish you'd just do it," Alastor said. His nostrils flared, and his breath was labored.

"I reckon it ain't my decision." Bannack called to Nickel, "Your kin, your judgment."

Alastor swore.

"I wanna talk to him first," Nickel said, biting the inside of his cheek. He raked his hand through his hair and swallowed a sigh. *It's come down to this . . .*

"Fine." Bannack jerked Alastor to his feet, marched him to a tree, and tied him to it. Pulling a lucifer from his vest pocket, he lit a lantern lying to the side of the burned cabin and rolled a log up to Nickel's feet.

"Sit," he instructed Nickel. "Talk."

"You gonna let him kill me?" Alastor asked, baring his teeth.

"Why shouldn't I?" Nickel asked. "You meant to kill him."

"You should be dead by now," Alastor growled.

"Should be, but I ain't. Bothers you, don't it?"

"You'll never get what you want. Never get it, 'cause the one you wanted is dead. Not even your stupid golden luck'll bring her back. Never get to work on your hero's ranch, neither, 'cause that's gone too." Alastor laughed. "Sure was easy, destroyin' one man's kingdom. So much for Nickel's luck."

"You had something to do with this? What'd you do, Al?"

Alastor crossed his legs and leaned back, enjoying his last bout of power.

"You and your damned cowboys. Indianola wasn't good enough for you.

Your own family wasn't good enough for you, either," Alastor said, spitting at his little brother, "so I ain't tellin' you shit!"

Nickel started to argue, but Bannack silenced him.

"Don't waste your breath. If he don't wanna talk, that's all right. We'll burn it out of him."

"We'll *what?*"

Bannack put on a show of gathering half-burned wood, bits of dry grass, and twigs to start a fire.

"You don't scare me none," Alastor said with a sneer.

"That's good," Bannack replied. "'Cause I don't wanna hear your caterwaulin' about this burnin'."

"Bullshit. You ain't gonna burn me," Alastor told him.

Bannack just stoked the fire higher and held up Joly's dagger. Examining the edges, he grunted in approval.

"You're bluffin'!" Alastor yelled at him. "You wouldn't knife a boy."

"You're man enough to try to take a life, you're man enough to face what's comin'."

Bound tight to the tree, Alastor showed his lack of fear by spitting on the ground at their feet. "I ain't talkin'."

"That's up to you." Bannack raised the knife. "Nickel, go get a brandin' iron. Check Cashman's barn first, but if the boys put 'em away, you'll find one in the milk and meat house. It's that half-stone outbuilding on the way to the river, by the spring."

Nickel left, taking the lantern with him. The candlelight only illuminated the shadows of night. On unfamiliar grassland, it created spooks that seemed to hover nearby, dodging his meager source of light. He shivered.

"I ain't afraid of the damned dark," he told the night. The trill of a night bird called, and he walked a little faster.

Cashman's barn housed horses he'd give his left arm to own, not to mention an array of saddles and other prized equipment. The man was a king! A king who had just lost his queen.

Nickel sighed, wishing he had known Mrs. Cashman. She seemed like the sort of person he would have liked immensely.

*Back to the task,* he thought. *If I were an iron, where would I be?*

He searched by the saddles and equipment, hoping to find one—he didn't care for the idea of trudging near the river at night, even if it was a trickle. Raising his lantern, he searched a dark corner and nearly whooped for joy— someone had left an iron propped up in the corner, disregarded. He mentally thanked the previous user for their slobbish ways and skittered back across the dark expanse of scorched ground to the scene of his brother's torture. The sound of Alastor's scream doubled his pace.

When he arrived, their prisoner was tugging at the bonds. A fruitless effort, for Bannack's knots were as permanent as a pine box.

"He's cuttin' on me!" Alastor wailed when he spotted his brother. "Help me, Ryder!"

"*You* don't get to call me by that name." Nickel's nostrils flared. "You laid a trap for me and Mags, you and Luce."

"Ain't my fault you fell in it, you dumb shit."

"You bedded her!"

"I would'a bedded Mags too, only she wouldn't have me."

Nickel ripped his blade from Bannack's hand and slashed at his brother. Alastor screamed again as a dark ribbon formed across his neck.

Nickel, blinded by the rage Joly predicted years before, remembered Alastor, standing out there in the rain, crushing Magdalena Hayworth against him, accosting her beautiful lips with his own ugly maw. They made him betray her, thinking for so long it was Mags who had done the betraying. He should have known better!

Nickel sliced again with a primal yell and moved in for the kill. Bannack grabbed him, wrenched the blade from his hand, and drove him backward.

"She'd still be alive!" Nickel cried. "They drove us apart. If I'd been with her, she'd still be alive!"

"Easy, Nickel. If you're gonna lose your head, I'll have to send you to the bunkhouse. We don't kill him." He narrowed his eyes, studying Alastor. "Yet."

Turning his back, Bannack shoved the iron into the hot fire and watched for it to glow.

"Ever seen a cow branded?" he asked Alastor.

The young man cried out, unsure whether to keep his eyes on the violent cowboy, or his own deranged brother, bent on revenge.

"You said it was easy, destroyin' a man's kingdom. I wanna know what you meant by that."

Nickel lunged at him again, this time with nothing but his fists. With calm demeanor, Bannack grabbed a fistful of Nickel's shirt and held him at bay.

Nickel screamed a combination of slurs and incoherent garbles, fighting against Bannack, lunging repeatedly at his brother with the ferocity of a hydrophobied dog. Bannack had to grab him by the neck and strongarm him in a headlock to subdue him.

"I can't hear you, Alastor," Bannack taunted, "and I'm about to run out of patience." He wielded the glowing iron with the other hand. "You don't answer me, and I'll give Nickel the weapon of his choice and let him go."

"No!" Their victim's pleas bounced off their ears and echoed into the night. "Don't, don't let him at me again, please!"

Alastor's appeal was mottled with the snuffling of a young man in tears. "I'm bleeding. Please don't hurt me anymore!"

Bannack waved the iron, and Alastor winced.

"Nickel?" he began. "I'll tell you what I done if you'll both swear off carvin' me up and burnin' me."

No one promised anything, but Alastor caved anyway. "I figured you already knew," he said. "Where do you think I went all those times I left home?"

"You said you was buildin' boats." Nickel's voice was a growl.

"I was, with Pa. Told him all about you over the years. Pa knew when you got letters. Saw your wife that time too, Bannack, five years back."

Bannack tightened his grip on the handle of the iron but didn't answer.

"When you chased them to Indianola, her and the man you said wasn't a real doctor? She didn't stick with him. Took up with Oren. I done seen 'em together. She said you'd be comin' after her, so she run back home. But Pa figured out real quick she was your wife. You beatin' him up was just by chance. So he bided his time and everything I told him played right into his hand. And Pa, he knew where to go when that letter came, tellin' Nickel you was on the way. He told me to slow you down on the trail back. But the storm ended up doin' that better'n I ever could."

"That's why you came along?" Nickel was nearly shouting. "You knew what he was doing?"

"Course I did! I wanted to see Bannack's face when he found his wife gone again."

The cowboy snatched a handful of Alastor's hair and whipped his head back. The iron seared through his shirt, biting deep into the flesh of his shoulder. Alastor's cries did little to soothe his incensed victims.

"Do it," he begged, "kill me, I don't care! Just do it already! You hear me? I don't care! Do it! Do IT!" The weight of his confession seemed to lift off Alastor and his expression went blank.

And that's when it hit Nickel. His brother really *didn't* care. His rage shifted, like a storm cloud passing over.

"Bannack! Wait!" He stumbled forward, one hand grasping at the cowboy's sleeve. "He don't care. Nobody ever taught him how."

"It ain't a matter of teachin'," he said, drawing the iron away from Alastor's skin.

For as long as he remembered, Alastor had been sullen and miserable. He rarely laughed unless Oren expected him to. Their father would beat him if he didn't. Alastor didn't know how to play with the children, and their mother's affection was lost on him. He had looked all his life for his own hero—Oren—to guide him to a source of happiness.

All those years, he had stalked Nickel, trying to find an easy moment to kill him. Now, he stood tethered to a tree in the midst of a burned-out homestead, crying like a babe. He was a miserable wretch.

"You looked up to the wrong hero," Nickel told him. "You thought Oren would help you, but he never did. Just used you. Never did anything for you, did he?"

Alastor's face fell in a moment of realization. "What the hell do you know about it? You lived a perfect life!"

"Perfect? Watching your back every day because your own brother wants to kill you? You think that's a perfect life? You done tried to kill me more'n the Mistress ever did. Your hero let you down, so you didn't want me to have one, either, is that it?"

Alastor lowered his head and sniffed. In the light of the fire, Nickel saw great tears dripping off his cheeks, and blood from his neck. His shoulder hung low, the burn of the iron evident upon his skin.

"Bannack?" Nickel asked. "I got an idea if you'll fetch me some needles and a bottle of ink."

Alastor's eyes snapped open.

☙

Before daybreak, Alastor Wheeler left, subdued and broken, and fearful of the image carved into his neck. A permanent reminder, Nickel had told him, of the *devil fruit* he had become.

Nickel watched him strike out on his own, still riding the pie-faced nag. He didn't hurry, but he didn't look back, either. Were they right to let him go? He didn't deserve another chance. What if he returned? *Then he'll die,* Nickel thought.

Somehow, it just didn't seem likely. Alastor had exacted his revenge, although he lost his wayward champion. With Oren gone, his brother might stand a chance on his own.

*No,* Nickel thought, *that ain't hardly likely, neither.*

"It's over, son."

Nickel didn't ask what Bannack meant. A lot of things were over, he mused, lives included.

Propelled by Bannack's grip, Nickel limped toward the lanterns lighting the grief-stricken ranch house. His hero's silence was heavy, sodden.

He glanced over his shoulder, back toward the road. Alastor Wheeler, now broken, had reached his own fork in the road. Whether he rose above his wayward teachings . . . well, that was up to him.

Bannack led Nickel to Marbles and spat an order. "Take care of him, Grey."

Something nibbled at Nickel's mind, but he couldn't quite grasp what it was. His eyelids were growing heavier, and he sagged on his feet. Someone grasped his shoulder and said his name, and he turned his head and blinked.

# CHAPTER 38

# SWAYING A SKEPTIC

Rolling over, he stretched, scratched his balls, and yawned.

"Dammit, Nickel, nobody wants to see that! Put your pennies away."

He swiveled in the cot, peeping with red, bleary eyes at Posse, who sat in a bunk across the room, leafing through a mail-order catalog.

"They ain't pennies," he said. "They're silver dollars."

His older brother snorted. "Awful short stick next to them dollars."

"Hell, I can't hardly walk for hittin' my ankles with my dangler when I move."

Posse grinned. "Welcome back, little brother."

"What is this, a bunkhouse?" he asked, looking around. "I don't remember walkin' in here."

"You didn't walk in. You hit the ground three nights ago, and they had to carry you in. Slept for nearly four days, Nickel."

His mouth fell open. "I what? That ain't possible!"

"Didn't think so either, till I saw you do it. You got up a few times, but you weren't awake. Pissed in my damn ear, you little bilge rat!"

Nickel couldn't resist a laugh. "You're lyin'."

"Hell I am! You just got up, stumbled across the room, yanked out your prod, and pissed all over me. Crawled back in bed and didn't even hear me yell. I smelled so bad the cowboys picked me up, bedroll and all, and dumped me in the river."

"I did that?" Nickel grinned. "Your ear, really?"

"You got good aim, you little shit. I'm just glad you didn't think I was a girl." Posse made a face and shuddered. "Somebody needs to dump you in the river. You look like somethin' that just crawled out of a bedpan, and you smell worse."

Nickel used his favorite gesture, reserved for his brothers. Posse responded by pointing to a little shaving mirror hung on the wall. One look confirmed his brother's observation. He looked like shit. He was naked except for dirt and sweat-stained britches rolled up to his knees, his hair stood in masses all over his head, and his body was so coated in sweat, grime, burns, and blood-stains, he could barely see his beloved tattoos. He swore, and Posse nodded.

"You're goin' to the river. Now." He picked up a bar of lye, a clean shirt, and britches and piled them on top of Nickel's boots. "I'll walk you down. We gotta talk."

Wrapped in the soiled sheets, Nickel stumbled after his brother. When they hit the water's edge, he shook off his hesitation and kept walking until fully submerged, bedding and all. The cold water stole his breath, and the sheets clung to his wet skin like a shroud. Like Mags.

The cough started, rattling deep in his chest, and he floundered to fight himself free of the clinging bedsheets, lest they become his shroud.

Posse waded into the water and pulled them free.

Nickel snatched the sheets, balled them up, and threw them into the current with a strangled yell that ended in a coughing fit.

"You're a mess, little brother. Now what're you gonna sleep on?" He offered a bar of soap and Nickel took it, hacking to clear his throat. He sat on a rock and scrubbed his body until his skin turned red. Next came the tangled mass of hair. He lathered and rinsed and hopped around on one foot, waving his hand in the air for balance as he stepped into clean britches with damp, clammy skin.

"Old Joly did a fine job on your ink," Posse said, gesturing to Nickel's arm.

Nickel paused and looked down at the serpent wrapped around his arm.

"All I got left of that old sailor," he said. Nickel slipped the clean shirt over his head and pulled it down across his chest. He dreaded the walk back to the ranch—not because his ankle still plagued him, but because of the grim expression in his brother's eyes. They fell into a slow meander back toward the Middle C, and Posse gave him a little push.

"I'm sorry, Nickel. For everything. But this . . ." He waved his arm, gesturing toward the great span of ranch in front of them. "It's over. Creede Cashman, he's so bad off the cowboys take turns sittin' with him so he won't put a gun to his head. There ain't a woman in sight on this ranch now, not a single one, did you know that?"

Nickel shook his head. Of course he didn't know that.

"Bannack, he's gonna kill himself too, or somebody else, soon enough," Posse said, his tone solemn. "Nobody can get close to him. He's done drunk himself into the ground. Been sittin' for days in that ugly ole pile of ash. He don't eat, don't sleep. Sometimes he gets up and digs around, like he's lookin' for something. Mostly though, he does nothin', unless somebody gets too close. He's beaten the shit out of three or four fellows that tried to get close enough to talk to him. Couple of them up and quit the Middle C. Said there's no point in ridin' for a brand where there ain't no women to look at, and a crazy sonofabitch threatenin' to kill them just for talkin'."

Nickel's body jerked, and he clenched his fists and raised them, ready to fight his brother if need be. "He's not crazy!"

"He murdered his own wife, Ryder!" Posse slapped his fists down. "And where's Alastor? Nobody's seen him since the night you two fought, except Bannack. What happened?"

"Nothin', Posse. Not a damn thing."

"I know that look! You're lyin' again."

That was true enough, but he wasn't about to replay Alastor's last night on the Middle C, not even to Posse. So Nickel just dug in his heel and clamped his mouth shut.

The physical wounds from Indianola proved stubborn; his ankle would not strengthen and took to swelling again when he tried to walk on it. He still had stitches in his back, closing the skin over gashes from debris. They were tight and itchy, and his muscles throbbed from overuse. He was ordered to rest with his foot elevated, and bootless. He lasted a few days before boredom set in. What did he know about being still, anyway?

Nickel was ready to explore. He searched first for Bannack and caught sight of the man slipping off with another bottle in his hand. More whiskey. He really was trying to drink himself to death.

*Why wasn't anyone stopping him?* Nickel wondered, but then answered his own question. *They weren't stupid. No one wanted to get punched in the jaw for trying.* He glanced around, but Les Harold was scribbling in his book, and

Posse hadn't spoken more than a half dozen words since the walk back from the river. No one else was around, leaving Nickel ample opportunity to slip off after his grieving friend.

Tarantula was impossible to catch, so he followed at a distance, content to keep the dark horse and his rider in sight. They rode over a rise dotted by groves of trees and into the swath of freshly scorched ground. Nickel marveled once more at how close the fire had come to overtaking the swale and swallowing the main house and its outbuildings whole.

They passed a small stone outbuilding, largely untouched by the fire, though the walls were blackened.

Beyond the stone building, a smokehouse or storage house, Nickel reasoned, lay the waste of what had been Bannack's home. What sort of woman could do something so terrible? He had never heard of a wife setting fire to her own house and running off, but the deed had been done with absolute success. Only a few timbers remained standing upright, though they leaned to one side.

The house, whatever it looked like before, was reduced to a big pile of charred wood and ash. Bannack dismounted, leaving Tarantula's reins dangling. He seemed obsessed over finding something. In the last few days, he and Bannack became equals.

Well, almost. He figured he understood the depth of Bannack's pain, and now Bannack knew his. The man had saved him, funded his family, and brought food to Molly Wheeler's table. They would have starved years ago if not for him. What's more, he had spent days and nights sifting through the remains of Indianola searching for him. Bannack would not have quit on him, so Nickel wasn't about to turn his back now.

Bannack must have heard his approach, for he pointed in the direction he had come.

"Get the hell away from me," he said, emphasizing his demand.

Nickel hesitated, but the cowboy's vernacular left little wiggle room, so he retreated to the top of the hill and sat down cross-legged, where he could watch over his friend from a safer distance. He was a little fearful of the look in the man's eye.

Nickel recalled his initial thoughts as he struggled to grasp the reality of

Magdalena's death. He hadn't wanted to survive that storm, not without her, yet he had. The thought of giving up, of lying down next to her and letting the Mistress wash them both away together nearly crushed him.

He was glad now he hadn't succumbed—no matter what, life was something worth living for. Giving up would've dishonored Magdalena and her memory and betrayed the people who loved him. Not to mention, it would've robbed himself of the little moments that made living what it was: miraculous.

As young Nickel watched over his hero, he brooded over the meaning of his own life. He would likely never again run through the gardens of Indianola, leaping over crates, barrels, and nets to run along the water's edge, or stand in the salty spray with the love of his life entwined in his arms, but did that mean he couldn't learn to enjoy a sunset somewhere else?

In time, maybe he'd find himself wrapped in the arms of another woman. Hell, maybe more than one. Who was he to spurn the life he had been gifted?

Nickel figured he owed it to Mags, to Old Joly, to his siblings lost to the sea, and to every Indianolan, alive or dead, to live his life the best way he knew how. He'd do it for them, but he'd do it for himself too.

He saw Bannack moving about below, kicking at a fallen beam. It shifted and crumbled under his boot, and he picked something up. What it was, Nickel couldn't tell, but it brought the cowboy to his knees. He sat in a heap on the charred ground, holding his head in his hands, and when he moved, it was to draw his pistol from its holster.

Nickel recognized the motion and was on his feet. His horse had strayed, trying to graze on unburned grass, and the boy wasted no time trying to catch the animal.

He barreled straight down the hill, screaming Bannack's name, and plowed right into the startled cowboy, knocking him off his feet. Nickel grabbed for the firearm as he went down, catching Bannack in the face with his knee. The cowboy grunted and struck at him, but Nickel fought to keep his advantage and relieve his incensed friend of his firearm.

"Get off me, you—"

"No! Gimme the gun, Bannack!" He jammed his knees into Bannack's stomach, grasping for the gun. "You ain't gonna do it to me!" he roared, aware that he was no match in strength for the iron-willed cowboy. The man's sinewy strength baffled Nickel, for Bannack was a man of small stature.

"Crazy sonofa—" Bannack cursed. "Shoot the damn thing!"

"The hell I will! Gimme the gun!"

"Snake, dammit! Snake!" Bannack spat and sputtered, fighting the younger boy off him. He grabbed Nickel by the neck, pinned him down, and rolled them both over and over. On the last turn, the pistol landed near Nickel's face, and he snatched it up.

"Shoot!" Bannack screamed at him. Nickel opened his mouth to reply when a buzzing sounded in his ears. He froze as the magnitude of his error washed the color from his face. He stared into the angular noggin of an agitated viper, coiled and ready to strike.

The snake was thicker than his forearm, biggest he had ever seen, and it seemed to know it had the upper hand, pinning both men to the ground.

"Ahh! Dammit, Ryder!"

"Roll!" Nickel ordered, thumbing back the hammer. As he did so, both Bannack and the snake moved at the same time.

"Aaarrghhh!" Nickel screamed, firing at the serpent until the chamber clicked on empty. The head of the beast lay against the heel of Bannack's boot, and he kicked it away. The pair of them lay on their backs, sucking in air and staring up at the sky.

"You bit?"

Nickel blinked at the question. What did it feel like to be snakebit? Did it hurt? How could he tell, since his whole body was one massive ache? Bannack pushed himself up on his elbows with a groan. Blood was dripping from his nostril and trickling from his lip, though he didn't seem to notice. His cold brown eyes accosted Nickel.

"Answer me! You bit?"

"I dunno, sir. Felt somethin' scrape my boot." Bannack looked down, and in the breath of a moment, the cowboy's face showed fear. It was there and gone, but Bannack's sense of urgency was not.

"Lie still!" he ordered, examining Nickel's boot. "You know much about snake bites?"

"No sir."

"Always check for fangs, make sure they ain't embedded. If I was to pull your boot off with one stuck inside, you'd be as good as bit."

Nickel was sweating by the time Bannack removed his boot and peeled off his smelly old sock. He inspected every inch of his foot, every toe, and moved up his leg before starting on the other. He kept coming back to the right foot, shaking his head.

"Shirt off," he ordered.

Nickel obliged, but a cursory examination revealed nothing. He sat up, reaching for his boots. Bannack held up the right one, and the boy's eyes widened. Two long slashes had been carved through the top layer of his boot, but they had not penetrated through the leather.

"You know how damn close you came?" Bannack yelled, slinging the boots away from him. "What if that snake bit down? Rattler that size would'a killed you! What the hell were you thinking?"

"I was just—"

"Shut up! You could've got us both killed! Shit, Nickel, you're a damned lucky—" The word died on his lips as he realized what he was about to say. The great Charlie Bannack didn't believe in luck. "Aahhhhh!" he roared, kicking a section of snake away from him.

"I was tryin' to save you!"

"Damn funny way of showin' it, plowin' me into the ground like you done. You don't wrestle a man's gun away from him like that!" Bannack yelled.

"I thought you were gonna use it . . ." But Nickel's sentence choked on the foul air of Bannack's wrath. The cowboy paced back and forth like a caged panther, his lean form rigid and set to spring. He didn't seem to notice, nor care, about the gathering audience around them.

The ranch hands, alarmed by the shots, had assessed the situation evident by the bits of rattler on the ground. Finding no immediate danger, they fell back to observe the show instead.

Nickel felt the eyes of scrutiny upon him, ranchers and cowboys alike gravitated to the art on his bare body. A few were pointing at the Beisht Kione and the long-haired, big-breasted siren riding upon the sea monster's head, forever emblazoned upon his arm.

Any other time, Nickel would have glorified in the attention. Any other time, but now he knew only that his hero was infuriated with him, and he had to make it better.

"Sir," he offered, "I know you don't believe in my luck, but—"

"Why would I believe in your luck?" Bannack asked. "You claim a man can buy your luck, but I've invested in you for five years. Don't that count for somethin'? Look at me, Ryder! Do I look like a man who's invested in good luck?" He gestured to the pile of ash behind him. "Ever think maybe it ain't luck you're blessed with?"

"Well, then, what do you call it?" he shot back.

"A bloody curse!" Bannack turned his back, shoving through the small gathering of men and scattering them like quail. He shouted again, shoving at a beam, and when it didn't fall, he lit into it, focusing his anger on the scorched wood.

Nickel followed, though only for a few steps.

"Posse says he's leavin'," he called, flinging his words at Bannack's retreating form. "He says I gotta choose who my brothers are."

"Then go, Ryder. Go with him." The voice was flat, devoid of feeling.

"He says the dream is dead," Nickel pressed. "Is it? Is it dead?" He wanted to grab the cowboy by the shoulders and shake him awake.

"Dead and gone to hell," Bannack said. He did not turn to face him, or even look over his shoulder.

"I don't believe you! Dammit, Bannack, I didn't come all this way to be sent back now!"

Bannack spat on the ground. "Get out of here, Ryder. Go get Josephine Mercy."

Nickel paused, digging his bare toe into the blackened soil.

"Maybe you're right, Bannack. Maybe it is a curse. But you know something? It ain't mine. I don't carry curses in my pocket, but I think you do. All those bad things, they happened to you. Me? I lost my Mags. My friends, all of 'em. Most of my brothers and sisters. I don't guess you can just walk away from that. Never. But I ain't cursed, sir. Maybe you're the one who brings bad things, who makes them happen. Maybe it ain't your fault, but you came back to Indianola, and it washed off the map. Your wife left you—stole everything you had. You might be the one still breathin', but she's won because you're lettin' her destroy you, and that makes you a selfish sonofabitch!"

Men backed away at the slur, but when Bannack faced him, Nickel stood his ground. He would be heard, even if it was the last thing he would ever say.

"You heard me!" he yelled at the purple-faced horseman. "You're no hero. Mustang Grey's a better man than you! You're just scared! What kind of twisted bastard would I be if I didn't live for the ones I loved? For the ones who can't? I ain't wastin' my life on a bloody curse. No sir! I believe in my luck, and I think you do too. That's what scares you, ain't it? If you believe in me, you gotta believe you've been the one cursed."

"Get. The. Hell. Outta. Here!"

Nickel started to obey, but as he did, his bare foot struck something in the dirt. It clattered, and he stooped to pick it up. A long, flattened tin. The lid had been mangled shut, and the metal scorched black. Someone had carved the initials "C.B." into the lid.

"Bannack?" he called. "Is this what you've been lookin' for?" He held the tin up.

Bannack's face blanched. Slowly, he stalked forward, taking the tin in hand.

"It is," he whispered.

"Must be somethin' awful important inside. I shore hope it ain't burned."

Bannack glared at him, then tried the lid. It was stuck, but he worked at it, prying worn, calloused fingers under the smashed rim. It gave way, a little at a time, and he wrenched it open. Bannack sucked a lungful of air, then pawed through the contents.

He stared, opened his mouth to say something, then changed his mind. Snapping his jaw shut, he handed the box to Nickel, turned, and walked away from his burned-out homestead.

Tarantula lifted his head at his master's approach and nickered. The little black jaw-snapping furball ran from the field, bouncing after the retreating cowboy. Bannack bent low, picked up the pup, and mounted.

"Bannack!" Without looking inside the tin, Nickel ran a few steps and the cowboy reined in, though he did not face him.

"I don't know where you're goin', but I want you to picture a forked road. You're standin' in the middle of it. Road to the left's worn smooth, a man your age could travel it without tiring. The other cuts right, and it's full of rocks and brush leadin' up to a mountain."

Holding his breath, Nickel stood on one foot and waited. Would he remember? Would he answer?

Bannack grasped the saddle horn and shook it a little, just to hear the satisfying creak of saddle leather.

"What's on the other side of the mountain?" he asked.

Nickel grinned. "Don't know without climbin' it, do we?"

"Mmm. That one sounds scary."

"Maybe. Which road do you pick, Bannack?"

The cowboy turned his head and fixed Nickel with a long, level stare. His face was a mask, carefully constructed to reveal . . . nothing. No pain, no emotion, no gratitude.

"Which road?" Nickel asked again.

"I can pick whatever road I want?"

He shrugged. "No one's stoppin' you."

Tarantula was dancing under him, shifting from side to side, jerking his head toward the horizon. The cowboy nodded at him, just once, shifted the pup in his lap, and pointed to the box in Nickel's hand.

"Your luck," he said, and dug in a single gal-leg spur.

Nickel heard the melody of the jinglebobs long after Bannack disappeared over the swale, out into the unknown.

"What if I don't want neither one?" Nickel asked the horizon. "The first one, that's too easy. I guess if it's that smooth, too many people already been there, and that ain't much fun. I don't mind not knowin' what's ahead or nothin', but what if I want to go straight on instead of turnin' one way or the other?"

Footfalls sounded behind him, and he heard Marbles's voice.

"You m-mean make y-your own r-r-road?" he asked.

"Yessir. Can I do that instead?" Nickel turned his head, watching the corner of Marbles's lip curl into a fleeting grin. It was gone as quickly as it appeared, but he saw it just the same.

"N-Nickel," he said, clapping the boy on the shoulder, "you're gonna turn out just fine. Now why don't you see what's in that box."

# CHAPTER 39

# NAMING THE DIME NOVEL

Holding the blackened tin, Nickel obeyed Mustang Grey, never expecting the full weight of what had driven Bannack away.

It should have burned in the fire. There was no sensible explanation. No logical one, anyway.

Nickel lifted a small stack of letters, written in Les's hand, signed with his own shaky "R" for Ryder. They smelled smoky, but they were intact. Underneath the letters, he saw her face peering up at him.

Dropping the box, he clutched the tintype. Nickel stared at himself, standing outside of the Indianola photography studio, his arm wrapped around Magdalena Hayworth. Les and Old Joly stood on either side.

He dropped to his knees, rubbing his thumb across her face.

"It should've burned," he cried. "Grey? Why didn't it burn with everything else?"

Marbles took a small step backward, his gaze following Bannack's departure. "I g-g-guess we all kn-know the answer to that."

☙

Bannack was gone, although Marbles assured him he would not go far, nor for more than a day or two. He might not have a home anymore—or a wife—but he still had a sense of loyalty and duty to his friends. Creede Cashman, he explained, would not get through his wife's loss without their help.

His brother and Les were another matter. The black cloud of grief hovering over the Middle C was too great; they were packing to leave.

"Everybody I know's leavin' or done left me," Nickel said, watching Posse and Les struggle to saddle ranch horses. His brother was leaving for the Mercy Ranch, and Les Harold with him.

Nickel knew what they figured—since Bannack no longer had a job to offer, he would ride off with them, and double back for Josephine and the ranch of girls.

They figured wrong. Marbles assured him Bannack would not go far. He'd return in a day or two after a brief period of grieving. He might not have a home anymore, or a wife, but Bannack was a man born of loyalty and duty to his friends. Creede Cashman would not get through his wife's loss without help.

No, Bannack wouldn't stay away. And even if he did, the trip here had cost Nickel a lifetime. No one needed his luck more than the grieving men of the Middle C Ranch. He found a new place and meant to make it his home.

JC Sterling gifted a horse to each of them, but that did little to smooth over Posse's dissent.

"Bannack killed our Pa," Posse said. "No matter what he done, he was still our father. You're choosin' his murderer over your own brother, and he ain't even here! He's not comin' back, Nickel."

"Mustang Grey says he is, but it ain't about him no more. It's about me."

Posse snorted in disgust. "Fine. Let's talk about you, *L Bee*. You're betrayin' your own family, stayin' here now. Your own brothers!"

Nickel ignored Posse's anger, as well as his irritating use of his baby name. "You'll always be kin, Posse, but Grey and Bannack, they're my brothers too now."

"You don't ride out with us, then I guess you done made your choice." Posse glanced at him sideways and heaved a tired sigh.

Nickel neither confirmed nor denied the truth of what happened inside that smoke-filled cabin. He didn't need to. His oldest brother took one more look at him and offered his hand.

Nickel grasped it. The two brothers held on, their grip firm. The younger remembered a lifetime growing up in Posse's shadow. Posse the Peacemaker, an advocate of harmony and goodwill. "I'll tell Momma you made it where you wanna be." The older brother released his hand, mounted, and addressed Les.

"Catch up quick if you're comin'."

Wheeling his horse, Posse rode south, back to the ranch of women. Maybe he would venture on to Victoria and Momma and the children.

Nickel closed his eyes, letting memories of his childhood run away with him. Memories of all the children together, of Posse rounding up the herd as best he could, and Alastor back when he knew how to laugh and joke.

"Damn," he whispered, swiping at his eyes. He turned and nearly ran into Les, who stood by, reins in hand. His eyes were red, and he couldn't look him in the face.

"I wish you wouldn't go," Nickel offered.

"Please come with me, Nickel. We can ride back together. That Josephine, she'd be an awful good wife."

"She would, but I already got one of those, and I don't even want her."

"I . . . I don't know how to say goodbye," Les said. Tears welled in Nickel's eyes, and he turned his head away.

"Then don't," he muttered.

"You won't come?" Les looked like he might break down. Even though he asked the question, he knew the truth: Nickel had found his new home.

"Nope. I'll ride with the Middle C until Bannack rebuilds."

"I won't know what to do without you," Les said.

Nickel managed a wry smile. "Write my damn book. I wanna read it."

"You'll have to tell me how it ends," Les retorted.

"I guess it don't." He shrugged. "It just keeps tellin', over and over. Every day's a new chapter, ain't it?"

"In your life?" Les laughed. "Every hour."

"Then I guess you'll just have to keep writin' about me. You come up with a name for it yet?"

"I was thinking about *Indianola's Golden Son*, but I don't know yet. It's true, but it don't sound right."

Nickel swallowed around the lump in his throat, but it kept growing.

Les, unable to bear prolonged goodbyes, made a valiant leap for his horse. He grabbed for his best friend's hand but could not see for the salt water leaking down his face.

He let go and gave the horse its head, loping after Posse lest he have to make the journey alone. Nickel watched his best friend go, wishing he had thought to tell him he was like a brother to him too. The best one he'd ever had.

Choking and swearing, he wiped at his eyes and turned from the horizon. Too many people were going away, and he couldn't look at it anymore.

"He'll be back, y-you know." Marbles leaned against the corral fence, his arms crossed over his chest.

"Don't look like it to me," Nickel replied, glancing over his shoulder at the empty prairie.

"C-Can't write a d-damn dime novel w-without the he-hero." Marbles looked serious, but there was laughter in his voice.

"You're laughing at me."

The amusement faded. "I'd n-never l-laugh at you."

Nickel studied the man again. The stance, the fact that he always rode gray horses, the scars on his wrist. Why hadn't he noticed it all before? But there was that awkward stutter and the man's odd fear of women.

Nickel strode up to Marbles and stuck out his hand.

"I been ridin' dolphins and chasin' dreams all my life," he said. "Figure I done just about all of it, save for one: ain't never introduced myself to Mustang Grey proper-like."

Nickel's stomach lurched when Marbles pushed his hat back on his head, cocking it jauntily to one side. A grin painted his features, and the steel-gray eyes lightened.

The cowboy reached out and grasped Nickel's hand with a bone-crushing shake.

"D-Damn fine to m-meet you, Nickel Ry-Ryder," he said, and pointed behind Nickel's shoulder with a great, bellowing laugh.

There, on the horizon where Posse and Les had disappeared, a lone rider emerged. Even from a distance, Nickel knew better than to call him a horse-man. All those miles they had traveled together, and he still held to the reins too tight, bouncing around with the fast trot.

He drew closer, and Nickel let out a whoop.

"Stop floppin' around like a fish on the back of that horse! Mustang Grey's watchin' you, and he says you ride better with your saddle backward!"

ↂ

It was as Marbles predicted: Bannack returned in a few days' time, though catching up to him was another matter. The man was everywhere, yet nowhere all at once. He made it clear he wanted to be left alone, so Nickel respected his privacy. After all, he had Les back, and Mustang to teach them both the inner workings of the ranch.

Nickel fell into the Middle C, quickly climbing ranks. The other hands bet which was better at horsemanship: their new shiny Nickel or Marbles. One month followed another, and Marbles complained daily of his shadows.

It was fun to watch Les follow him around like a lost dog, still stricken by the gravity of Marbles's true identity.

When he wasn't dodging after storybook heroes or scribbling in his book, Les picked up the sport of card-playing. Nickel thought it a nasty habit that cut into their squabbles, but it seemed harmless enough, so long as he didn't start betting wages.

Creede Cashman was a ghost, rarely seen, slipping from job to job like an ethereal haint. He was still guarded, but Nickel chanced to speak with the rancher from time to time, telling him bits of his own story. The man seemed grateful for the understanding, but it saddened him too, and he began retreating from Nickel.

Marbles said he needed more time, but for Nickel, time meant nothing. The hurt would always be there, but so would the memories. Nickel turned to the Indianola tintype, now sitting on the big blue trunk by his bed, every time he needed the reminder to smile, to laugh, to carry forward. She was always there, wrapped in his arms, gazing into the depths of his eyes with promise.

*With promise.*

One day, he sat on his cot, staring at Magdalena's face, and her chest of hopes and dreams, and opened the trunk. Letters, dresses, drawings, remnants of dried flowers, everything he had ever given her lay inside. The water had done a great deal of damage, but the Mercy Ranch women had done well, cleaning and drying what they might. The books were another matter.

They had been too wet for too long and had mildewed shut, many of them turned into a paste.

Still, the women had dried the books as best they could, wrapping each one in a piece of fabric to keep the mildew-book-paste from rubbing off on everything else.

He opened a small door hidden inside the lid and discovered a small black box, scratched with his name. He knew it was his name, for Magdalena had taught him how to read it. Ryder. He grinned at her refusal to call him anything else.

The box appeared to be a gift, for him. He held it, unsure of what to do. Did he open it? Whatever was inside was the most precious treasure he had, for she had chosen it for him. He reached inside a leather pouch he wore around his neck and fingered the lock of hair.

*"Open it, you silly boy!"* he heard her voice say.

It was a brass medallion, the kind used to decorate the harness of a horse. Inside the circle of the medallion was a boat filled with sailors. The men were at the mercy of the sea, yet protected by the wings of a giant swan. Every seafaring citizen knew the swan was a symbol of grace and protection, and of change. She was guarding him with her life. With her love. Dear God, Magdalena Virginia Hayworth was protecting him with her luck!

He dropped his head, holding it within his hand, feeling the odd warmth of the metal. It should be cold, but it wasn't. Unable to bear another moment of her secrets, he shut the trunk and ran outside, clasping the medallion in his hand. He ran to the river, where he could be closer to her memory.

"I love you too, Mags," he told the water, and strung the medallion around his leather pouch containing the lock of her hair. Something stirred behind him, and he looked up. A twig snapped, and he took a step back.

"Someone there?"

No one answered, but he could feel eyes upon him. The birds in the trees fell silent, and Nickel retreated another step.

"Come out, I know you're there!"

A black streak tore from the vegetation, moving so fast he could not discern what it was, only that it headed straight for him. A bear? He let out a yell and fell backward into the water.

The animal pounced on his chest and snapped its jaws at his face.

"Gaaah!" he garbled, flinging water from the shallows in his haste to get up. A familiar wolf-pup stared at him and cocked her head.

A voice called his name, and he froze. Was he hearing things? He opened his eyes and looked up, spitting water.

"Dammit, Nickel, are you drownin' *again*?"

"If I do, it's your dog's fault."

Bannack peered down at him, then at the tiny pup with the tilted head.

"I can see why you'd jump in the water and drown yourself. She's a man-eater."

Nickel offered the cowboy his favorite obscene gesture.

Bannack chuckled. "I got a name for your dime novel," he said.

"Oh, yeah?" Nickel replied with a broad grin.

"Yep. It's been staring us in the face for years."

"What is it?"

Still grinning, the cowboy tossed a small object through the air. A coin. Nickel caught it and laughed out loud.

"*Nickel's Luck.*"

THE END

# AFTERWORD

While the characters of *Nickel's Luck* are fictional, the town of Indianola and its disastrous history are quite real. Indianola, Texas was a bustling port town. Nicknamed the "Dream City of the Gulf," it rivaled neighboring Galveston. As with any seaport, it was full of sailors and fishermen, but also traders, travelers, trains, and all the livestock and commodities necessary for a growing country. It truly was a town of dreams. Until it wasn't.

In September 1875, people flocked from nearby towns to the beautiful Indianola, eager to witness the trial of a man named Bill Taylor. Taylor had been charged with two murders in the aftermath of a feud. Inns and hotels were overflowing—the town was full.

Unknown to the eager citizens awaiting the trial, a massive hurricane was approaching from the Gulf of Mexico. It directly struck unlucky Indianola on the early morning of September 15. Driven by 150-mile-per-hour winds, the storm raged for three days, tearing apart homes and businesses, turning the prairie inland of the port city into a violent sea. When the hurricane's eye reached the terrified city, many believed the worst was over. It was not to be. The angry ocean, now flooded fifteen feet over town and prairie, turned on the town once again.

Screams could be heard over the wind and waves as the storm changed direction, pushing floodwaters and massive islands of debris back through the weakened town. The buildings still standing were ripped apart, casting homes and humans, animals and debris back out to sea. Massive ships were found six, seven miles inland. The railroad and telegraph office were gone. Over three hundred people perished in the storm. Indianola was destroyed. In fact, only one building remained standing: the courthouse where survivors sought refuge alongside the notorious Billy Taylor. Following the aftermath, citizens searched, many in vain, for their loved ones. Burial parties abounded. Between the devastation and the large crowd of visitors, a clear count of deceased could not be determined. The misery and sorrow of those poor souls—the survivors—were complete. Still, they were a brave and determined lot, and Indianola was rebuilt.

Sadly, in 1886, an even larger storm struck Indianola again. Like the first, there was nothing left. The survivors decided they'd had enough and moved away. Today, the original town site is underwater, but a monument stands on the beach in memory of a once-beautiful city, and of the strong, vibrant people who helped shape not just Texas, but our nation.

I dedicate *Nickel's Luck* to the courageous Indianolans—to those who survived, and to those whose luck ran out.

May your dreams live on. May you never be forgotten.

—S. L. Matthews

# ACKNOWLEDGMENTS

For Dave: My love, my editor-in-chief. The one man who believes in me more than I dare to believe in myself. Thank you for enduring so many years of "the voices" in my head. I couldn't have done it without you.

For Zane: My beloved son. May all your dreams come true. I love you.

For Pops: The man who gave me my first Zane Grey novel and my first wooden nickel. Thanks for all the "Hillside Gouger" hunt teachings.

And for my "big brother" Matt, who brings "Bannack" to life. Thank you.

# ABOUT THE AUTHOR

**S. L. MATTHEWS** is an 18th & 19th century living history reenactor, hobbyist photographer, and avid writer of the Victorian Era and the Old West.

She grew up in the past, weaving on a loom and producing period rifle and accoutrement straps for reenactors, museums, movies, and television worldwide. She bought a quarter horse in high school with her earnings. Now she weaves three-dimensional characters through unusual plots and focuses on stories largely untold through history.

When she's not dressed in Victorian Era and Old West attire, you can find her outside photographing landscapes, nature, or living history, tackling her garden, scouting shops for old books and historical treasures, or playing with her Welsh Corgis.

S. L. Matthews is the author of *Nickel's Luck*, "Ravens in the Graveyard" (in the Untamed West Anthology), "Lest We Forget" (in *Bourbon and a Good Cigar: 52 Western Short Stories* by Scott Harris), and "The Hourglass" (in *Time to Myself: 52 Western Short Stories* by Scott Harris). She lives in Sparta, Tennessee with her family.

## Connect with the Author

slmatthewsauthor.com
facebook.com/SLMatthewsAuthor
instagram.com/slmatthewsauthor

## Leave a Review

If you enjoyed this book, will you please consider writing a review on Amazon and Goodreads? Reviews help self-published authors make their books more visible to new readers.

Made in the USA
Lexington, KY
14 November 2019